JILL LAURI...

Dinosaur Days

PENGUIN BOOKS

PENGUIN BOOKS

Published by the Penguin Group
Penguin Books Ltd, 27 Wrights Lane, London w8 5TZ, England
Penguin Putnam Inc., 375 Hudson Street, New York, New York 10014, USA
Penguin Books Australia Ltd, Ringwood, Victoria, Australia
Penguin Books Canada Ltd, 10 Alcorn Avenue, Toronto, Ontario, Canada M4V 3B2
Penguin Books (NZ) Ltd, Private Bag 102902, NSMC, Auckland, New Zealand

Penguin Books Ltd, Registered Offices: Harmondsworth, Middlesex, England

First published 1999
1 3 5 7 9 10 8 6 4 2

Set in 11/14 pt Monotype Sabon
Phototypeset by Intype London Ltd
Printed in England by
Clays Ltd, St Ives plc

For Sophie and Dido

With thanks to Louise Moore at Penguin; Annabel Hardman and Peters Fraser & Dunlop; and my husband, Jon, for his love and support, particularly through recent grisly happenings

Prologue

It's 1987 – just past the turn of the year – and in dank gloom, near a fold of the land where Constable's meets Gainsborough's Country, yet another piece of stucco gives up the effort of clinging to the timber frame of Little Watling Hall and plops into the moat.

A troubled, gut-sinking night and here is Fliss Harley-Wright lying awake – again – staring up at that crack across the ceiling in the shape of Italy. For years it had only the contours of Calabria, but recently it's taken off and moved alarmingly towards the outer wall, so that now it's got the look of more or less the whole boot. Next to her in their big sagging bed, Ivor is at last sleeping, but she still feels alert and swamped in anxiety. Outside the duvet, the lofty bedroom is morgue-cold. The ancient house creaks and groans, its timber frame moving in the damp air and settling a few millimetres further down, sinking its soleplate deeper towards the stagnant water.

Downstairs in the kitchen, one of the only two warm rooms in the whole house, the dresser is laden with brown envelopes and invoices printed in red. Each is pregnant with threats – telephones and water to be cut off, fuel to be denied, court orders, bailiffs – pay me, pay me – each oozing an invisible poison of fear and failure.

*

Along the upstairs corridor, turn right, down the longer passage of the early Tudor 'E' and turn right again to the northern wing, there is another bedroom – this one steaming in a thick fug of electric heat. Martita Harley-Wright, Ivor's mother, lies on her back beneath an eiderdown of leek-green satin, gently snoring in a rhythmic whicker. Under and over the quilt lie scattered her darling Boysies – four smelly Yorkshire terriers with topknots tied in ribbons who snore along in gentle sympathy with their mistress. Martita's meagre hair, released from its rigid daytime structure, is fluffed out over the pillow, and she dreams peacefully of past glories: of picnics, of dinners, of jazz bands and swimming parties – all in veritable cascades tinted leek-green and scented with Chanel No. 5.

At exactly the same time that Fliss decides exhaustedly to get up and face what already reeks of a bad day, it is 2 a.m. in Upper Westchester, New York, and Constantine Ziminovski is taking a lone breakfast in the smaller dining room. A pretty tented pavilion of grey silk, it sits half-way between the gleaming stainless-steel and granite kitchen and the Adam neo-classical full dining room which can seat sixty-three in comfort and an extra hundred at a pinch.

Constantine Ziminovski is eating oat-bran muesli for his heart, cranberry bran muffins for his bowels and sipping lime mint tea to help the whole process along a bit. Upstairs, amidst the hushed, densely carpeted corridors, his third wife, Katrina, slumbers, but Mr Z ('Zee' – this is, after all, America) long ago mastered the subtle art of sleep rationing. Three hours plus a catnap are quite enough for him, and as he likes to be at the computer consoles on the top floor of his Water Street building more or less as the London markets open, he has to leave no later than 2.30 a.m.

Jeremiah, his butler, hasn't been to bed yet, for it is he who warms the muffins and infuses the tea. But then Jeremiah is a pragmatic man – one who can bend when the wind takes him. He seeks a peaceful life and knows which side his bread (or even muffin) is buttered. He is quite well paid and has a pleasant cottage near the gates to the estate, so in return he has had to learn to adapt to his master's exacting timetable. However, once Mr Z has left for the city, Jeremiah can go to bed and usually sleep in late, for daytime catering is the province of Mrs Slattery, and any special dinners will be done by Antoine de Chaumery. On the whole it's worth the strain of keeping up with Mr Z's schedule for the peace of the later mornings, waking to the sound of bluejays rather than the roar of South Bronx traffic.

This is a special time every day for Mr Z – a half-hour of quiet, occasional contemplation and a chance to catch up on recreational reading. Every night Mrs Bierce, his personal assistant in the house office, leaves out a small collection of the latest magazines, suitably annotated. Today it is *Town and Country* (of no interest unless he's in it, that's for Katrina later in the day), *Architectural Digest*, *Gourmet* and *Art and Antiques*. Flicking through the classifieds in *Art and Antiques*, a small boxed advertisement catches his eye. He reads it twice, then marks it with a green highlighter and goes on to an article Mrs Bierce has in turn marked out for him. The subject is Fragonard and he reads it with lively interest. He is sitting beneath a ravishing Fragonard at this very moment – of an eighteenth-century enchantress in a bower of Rosas Complicata and mundi.

Outside, hidden in the black night, the house is a pretty

stone palace in honey tones. Its overall structure is based on Lord Burlington's Chiswick House in London, but isn't there just a hint of the Petit Trianon round at the back, and surely a smidgen of the Amalienburg to the side? Just enough of an architectural macédoine to make a purist wince perhaps, but in fact, in actuality (if you weren't a snob about these things), really very lovely. Beyond is a stone balustraded terrace reaching out over the first of a succession of rolling, luscious hills, ending in an ocean of deciduous treetops which turns in autumn from green undulation to a dense carpet of vibrant colour.

Mostly on this Westchester hilltop, the air has a slightly misty quality even on the hottest days, and only the lush rural idyll is apparent from the palace balustrade. Occasionally though, when the light clarifies, especially in brilliant winter frosts, the towers of commerce loom up beyond the tree line – probably only those of White Plains, but they are vanguard symbols of the packed megalopolis beyond – the soaring pinnacles and temples to trade of which the Constance Corporation has one of the most spectacular. It's an iced dry night, but Constantine is oblivious to the weather. From the heat of the house, he settles into the already heated back of a deeply luxurious, but utterly unremarkable, Mercedes and is whisked down the sweep of the long drive towards his Mecca.

I

'Who was the man with the big red Vulva?'
Martita Harley-Wright comes beetling across the
yard towards her son, Ivor, who is trying to clear a drain.
She never walks – she always beetles or bowls or scuttles –
often looking like a beetle quite literally, in her customary
black leggings topped by some bulbous covering like an
insect's carapace. Today it is a waxed dark-green cape
against the horizontal February rain and her black stick legs
whirl across the cobbles interspersed with the four tiny
yapping Yorkies hoping for an early supper.

'VOLVO, Mother,' yells Ivor. A pale, sandy man, he is
currently up to his elbows in drain rods and sludge, and his
mother is (selectively) stone deaf.

'Such a big red Vulva,' says Martita, who perfectly well
knows her Vulva from her Volvo, but likes to annoy. She
sniffs the fetid drain air and wrinkles up her little arched
beak of a nose. 'Almost a hearse.'

Ivor offers no answer and only wriggles the rod more
fiercely, but there's something rock solid down there which
refuses to budge.

'It could take a coffin – possibly two.' Martita waits for
a reaction. While she stands still, the dogs stand still too,
their little heads all cocked on one side, gazing up at her,

waiting for the slightest forward motion to set up their yapping and dancing again – willing her towards the kitchen. 'Not that I'll need anything like that. A minivan will do for me, won't it, darlings? An itsy-bitsy little minivan to carry me away to the Chapel of Rest.' She tries a winsome sigh. 'I'm only a little bag of bones.'

Ivor, who has heard it all before, continues rodding, steadily impelling any pent-up irritation down the drain towards the blockage, where it may be of some use. Martita would probably like to continue keeping the dogs in suspense and Ivor's temper in thrall, but the rain is spiking its way sideways through the thick material of the leggings and is seeping down the neck of the cape. It might be better to continue this gibing inquisition later, in the warm. She goes for a quick parting thrust.

'So who was he?'

'Who was who?' She'd heard that all right, even though he'd only muttered.

'You know who. Who was he? The man in the big red Vulva down the drive this afternoon?'

'Oh, that man. Barnaby Fitzgerald.'

'Who?'

'BARNABY FITZGERALD,' yells Ivor, giving an almighty push and feeling something start to move. 'ANTIQUE CHAPPY,' he bellows, as the blockage shifts suddenly and he is hurled forward, chest in the mire, nose down the hole.

'What? What did you say?'

'From Long Pecklam. Antique chappy from Long Pecklam.' He heaves himself up on his haunches, streaked with sludge.

Martita moves one step forward and gives him a very

hard look, but it's enough to set the dogs off. 'Be QUIET,' she rasps with surprising force. The dogs freeze in shock. She thinks better of escaping to the warm kitchen – this perhaps is something requiring instant attention.

'*Why* were you seeing an antique chappy from Long Pecklam down the drive in secret?'

'It wasn't in secret. He was on his way up.' Ivor enunciates very loudly, very slowly. 'I'D TELEPHONED HIM.'

'I'm not selling, you know.'

'Oh, Mother – '

'You needn't think I am.'

'It was only a discussion. Very vague. Just to give us some idea.'

'Just to give us what idea?'

'We've got to see the bank tomorrow. I need some ammunition.'

'I'll never sell.'

'It isn't yours *to* sell.'

'What?'

'The Collection. It's mine.'

'With conditions. You'll never meet them.'

'Barney thinks we might. He thinks he's found the chap.'

'What chap?'

'A buyer. From America.'

'Never. I never will.'

'He thinks he's found the chap who can do it. Who wants to do it.'

'I'll never sell.'

'It isn't yours to sell, Mother. It's mine.'

'I'll turf you out.'

'Here we go again.'

'I'll turf you out and that will be that.' Martita at last

moves off from her starting-block position and the dogs come springing back to life. 'Come along, Boysies – come along, my darlings – sup-sup calls,' and off she beetles towards the scullery door.

Ivor watches her for a moment, trying to wipe some of the slime off his nose with an even slimier hand, and tries to banish uncharitable thoughts.

In the kitchen, Fliss is forcing a gallon of Jerusalem artichoke soup through the Mouli. It's hard work but it makes her feel slightly better. They grew these artichokes themselves: fed some to the goats, sold a few and netted the rest in the cellar for their own eating. There's something about their knobbly solidity which makes her feel homespun and thrifty – and, oh God, do they need to be thrifty. If only there could be more of these areas in their lives. So many things seem impossibly out of their financial control – a stream of inescapable necessities: rates, insurances, petrol, car parts and taxes, coal, animal feed, children's clothes, electricity – the list is endless. She has a flashing vision – all four Boysies locked in a turbine, desperately scrabbling round and round like hamsters to generate power. If only. Then, in her real life, the door crashes open and the little monsters come dashing in, yipping and leaping, their wet fur clinging to their legs, ponging of drain dregs.

'I won't have it,' says Martita, standing in the doorway and shaking the rain off her cape and all over the floor.

'What is it, Titty?' Fliss has from long experience learned to develop a stolid surface calm when necessary.

'Ivor's been seeing people behind my back.'

'No, he hasn't – not "people".'

'What?'

Oh, Fliss thinks, it's one of *those* days, and shouts, 'NOT PEOPLE.'

'Antique chappy.'

'That's Barnaby Fitzgerald and we both called him in.'

'I should have known *you'd* be behind it.'

'Barney knows about our problem and thinks he may be able to help out.'

'What?'

'Our PROBLEM – he knows.'

'We have no problem,' says Martita in a small but haughty voice. She straightens out her spine as far as it will go and tosses back the structure of her hair. This is a dangerous movement, like the displacement activities of wild beasts, and signifies the storm to come.

Once, when Martita was very young and very beautiful (so she says), and still called Maud and was working in the post office in Croydon, she was taken to the Gargoyle Club in Soho by a grateful and randy customer called Sydney, who hoped to get his leg over once he'd got her good and pissed. There she had been spotted by Augustus John, who (so she says) was so taken with the auburn glory of her hair that he had kissed her on the nape, called her his Titian Rose, and ordered her a bottle of Pol Roger '21. It so happened that for that very occasion, or 'outing' as she then termed the venture, she had experimented with her hair – had pinned it up all the way around in a fat pleat from ear to ear and had piled the rest up into a smooth, glossy tower. It was only because of this experiment that the great Augustus had been able to view her nape, and that viewing, plus the effects of the Pol Roger, spelt, in one way or another, the end of the post office, Croydon, Sydney and indeed 'Maud' as she then knew herself. From that day on, the Titian Rose faithfully stuck to the style of her hair. Through decades of changing fashion, through the loss of colour and gloss, with the aid of Autumn Chestnut dyes and potions, which always now left a rim of grisly grey along the skull, with backcombing of the remaining fluff over sausages of horsehair to give it substance, Martita stuck to the precious, lucky structure.

Now she tosses it back so the weight of the horsehair supports pulls her own hair back taut from her forehead and Fliss can see the paper thinness of her white brow. Martita does this only when she's very angry indeed, for it takes time to construct the edifice every morning and wispy flyaway hairs ruin the effect of fierce symmetry.

'What is all this talk of problems? I loathe talk of problems – it's all so petty and defeatist,' she hisses.

'We have to try to face FACTS, Titty,' Fliss yells.

'And Harry loathed them too – so suburban and déclassé – we never had them in Harry's day.'

'We had masses of problems in Harry's day. If we'd only faced them then, we might not be in such a mess and muddle now.'

'I simply won't have it. It's all so pathetic and gutless. We should simply face things with abandon – take a stand.'

'That's what we're trying to do – right NOW.'

'But properly – with verve. We're not – absolutely not – the sort of people who give in.' She looks wildly round the admittedly very large, but definitely scabby kitchen. 'Look at what we *have*!'

'Yes, Titty – *do* look – have a good look – either collapsed or collapsing. We're overdrafted up to our eyeballs – we've got to get hold of some capital or they'll HAVE us.'

Bugger. She's broken Rule Number One and let naked

desperation pop out into the open. Always a mistake. Apart from anything else, she has a suspicion that Martita finds all outbursts obscurely satisfying – a type of brain food.

'Oh, Felicity, Felissssity,' she mutters now, investing the name with enough scorn to turn it into an insult. '*Such* a misnomer – hardly felicitous in nature – should have been christened Cassandra – much more appropriate – our very own little prophetess of doom. I'm sure you were a very gloomy baby – straight from the womb.' She shifts her gaze down to the Boysies and addresses them directly. 'Perhaps her mother's was a gloomy womb.'

The dogs, delighted to be noticed again, immediately renew their chorus and start dancing around her feet, scrabbling at her Hush Puppies. Her scowl transposes into a beaming smile.

'Oo's an Ozzie? Ooo's an Ozzie baby? Oo's a clever Boysie then?' She bends to scoop up one straggled creature. 'I think he may have caught a rat – there's blood on his jaws.' She kisses the topknot.

'I really wouldn't do that, Titty. What about Weil's disease? Though I don't think he could have had a rat – he's hardly big enough.'

'But he has guts, you see – unlike others we could mention – guts and bravado.' She gathers up the tiny, filthy little animal and shakes it lovingly. 'Weil's disease – problems – ' She spits the words out with contempt and kisses the dog on the nose with a resounding smack. 'We're supposed to be above such things.'

'Titty, money is haemorrhaging out of this household – we can't seem to stem the flow and we have virtually nothing coming in. It's essential to sell the Collection if we possibly can and Barney thinks he has a lead.'

'You,' says Titty with finality, 'would sell your souls for a mess of pottage.'

With a considerable flounce, she turns her back on Fliss and stalks out of the kitchen. The Boysies are caught on the hop. This wasn't the plan. The saucepan of boiled lights and heart – *their* saucepan – remains on the edge of the range hotplate, *unserved*. The door has banged in their faces and they can hear the sound of their mistress's footsteps climbing the stairs. Fluttering with puzzled disappointment, they subside in a heap gently on to the hearth.

2

It's another ghastly night filled with phantoms and chimera. THE VISIT TO THE BANK flaunts itself in capital letters, forcing itself into every miserable attempt at sleep. By morning, Fliss and Ivor feel hollow with exhaustion.

Ivor goes to let out the chickens and geese and feed the other livestock, while Fliss tries to administer breakfast to the children – mostly an unrewarding task. Emma is buried in 'A' level revision, while simultaneously removing purple nail varnish from her toes. Daisy, who is secretly on yet another diet, hasn't come down but will grab the inevitable mug of black coffee as she swings out of the house at the last possible moment. Only Henry, at eleven still blissfully uncomplicated and round of face, is cheerfully munching toast and Marmite.

It seems essential to Fliss to maintain an atmosphere of normality for the children; or as much of a normality as is normal for them. They are of course well used to an atmosphere of financial uncertainty, but there's a deep chasm between a daily, almost jaunty sense of being on your beam-ends and a real, immediate crisis, and they've yet to cross it. Fliss is ashamed of her own sense of engulfing panic and struggles to delay its overspill.

Martita has long been up and is bustling around as usual, currently brewing some foul, meaty concoction for the Boysies out in the scullery.

'It stinks in here.' Daisy slinks in. She's wearing a tight navy-blue T-shirt which rides up to reveal an inch of flat stomach.

'Is that what you're wearing?' says Fliss – daft – just asking for it.

'*School* colour,' snaps Daisy defiantly. 'Dress code.' She dares contradiction.

'But, darling, it's freezing outside.'

'It stinks in here,' says Daisy flatly.

'You'll catch your death,' says Fliss with no conviction.

'What's Titty up to?' Daisy shouts through to the scullery. 'It stinks in here, Titty.'

Martita pokes her head round the door. 'It's a good honest smell – free of chemical additives.'

Daisy grabs her coffee. 'You can't breathe in here.' She perches her tiny bottom on the edge of the dresser and shudders delicately.

'You see – you're shivering already,' says Fliss.

Daisy offers up a baleful glare. As the clock hands hit 8.20, all three children seize their various bags and crash out of the kitchen. The bus will pick them up at the bottom of the drive. Daisy takes her mug with her – she'll leave it, empty, in the hedge and pick it up in the evening.

'Ghastly child,' says Martita. 'It's that school, of course. Why on earth you wouldn't educate them properly I'll never understand.'

'They're being very properly educated,' says Fliss stiffly.

'Henry should be going to Immingham,' says Martita. 'Harley-Wrights always go to Immingham.'

'Ivor hated Immingham.'

'He only *says* that. He loved it really. At least he was taught some manners. You should talk to that bank – make sure they cover the fees. It's scandalous if they don't. That boy ought to be going to his father's school. To his grandfather's school. To his great-grandfather's school.'

'Don't be ridiculous, Titty. The fees are over three thousand pounds a term. He won't even be taking Common Entrance.'

'And whose fault is that? Just you see to it.' Martita raises her eyebrows and deposits one of her looks on Fliss, something like a curse.

Fliss feels herself shrivel under it and is more exhausted than ever. By the time she and Ivor are ready to leave for the bank, they hardly have the energy to speak.

They drive into town in one of their several elderly Peugeot 504s. They can only ever afford cars of the banger variety – the sort which just scrape through their MOTs. Many years ago, Ivor took to his habit of plumping for a particular, preferably extinct, model of motor and buying up for a song any old clapped-out, pockmarked example he could find. Then he would cobble them together, swapping bits of one to another as the need arose, to give them one, or sometimes even two, viable if bastardized wagons.

He'd started with Citroën 2CVs, the mere idea of which Fliss had always loved because you could take the seats out for picnics (how typically, wonderfully *French*, she'd always thought), but in real life there was never any time for these imaginary picnics, and they'd come to need larger, more workhorse vehicles for transporting all manner of lumpy mess – everything from hay to sacks of clay – in order to service their various enterprises. So they'd worked up through various phases of Fords and Vauxhalls to the current run of decrepit Peugeots. The cars Ivor put together were often decked in motley colours with odd doors and tailgates, but each was almost comfortingly identical in being rimmed with splodges of rust in exactly the same places, like a baby's nappy rash.

In their silence, Ivor can hear an unwelcome knocking in the engine. Time to attempt another form of doctoring again – winkle out the crankshaft, change the shells. For an unmechanical man, Ivor seems to have spent an inordinate amount of his life lying on his back staring up into automobile underbellies.

At the bank, they are shown into a windowless cell tricked out entirely in shades of oatmeal. Every surface seems either the colour or texture of porridge, from the Berber carpet to the walls panelled in pinhead vinyl to the plasticated desk with hideously coordinated blotter. Mr Dixon, the Under Manager, is the only non-beige *objet* and he is dressed entirely in shiny grey which looks too thin for the time of year, but obviously suffices in the bank's hothouse air.

He invites them to sit facing him in two low-slung oatmeal chairs which leave them gazing up at him in his own swivel, high-backed tweedy number as if he is a Holy Icon. In a way of course he is, considering he holds their immediate fate in his youthful hands. For alas, looming across at them with the tips of his fingers pressed together over the spiral-bound copies of their wholly inadequate accounts, he looks to be about eighteen and a half.

After the scufflings of settling down and some rather stiff pleasantries about the vile weather, there is an embarrassed pause. Fliss keeps her eyes fixed on the enemy across the desk, but Ivor remains in her field of vision, as a blurred image of defeat to her right, slung into the low chair so that his cleaner, better Barbour, worn especially to make him seem a solid citizen, is draped on the floor, and his 'best' corduroys have slithered up to reveal large expanses of pale, sandy-haired leg.

'Well,' says the Under Manager nasally. He breathes in sharply and forces the air out again between clenched teeth. He looks down at his hands and then up again with a clear, candid, youthful brow – and still nothing is said. It can only have been about thirty seconds, but already Fliss longs for instant death and burial in oatmeal. 'Mr Willis and I have now had a chance to examine your figures – '

'Mr Willis?' Ivor leaps on the new name with earnest gratitude.

'Our Chief Loans Officer.'

'Ah, yes – not the manager.'

'Mr *Jameson* is the manager.'

'Of course. We always dealt with his predecessor, Mr Evans – for many years.'

'Mr Jameson has asked me to deal with your case.'

'Right.'

'Mr Jameson is very busy at the moment.'

'Right.'

'Mr Willis and I have considered your accounts most carefully – and your projections of course – '

'Oh, yes.'

'If you can call them projections.'

'Yes. Well, it is difficult . . .'

'With our sort of work,' Fliss leaps in. 'Mr Evans always seemed to understand.'

'Well, things were a little different in Mr Evans's day. We've now got a direct line of communication through to head office.'

'It's very hard to be precise about demand.'

'Precision doesn't seem to enter the picture at all, Mrs Harley-Wright, if I may say so.'

'I thought I'd explained about our work in my letter.'

'Ah, yes – your letter.' The Under Manager flicks open the first of their accountant's beautifully presented cream and sepia folders (as yet unpaid for – the bill lies unopened on the kitchen dresser) and Fliss catches sight of her own handwriting on the top. 'Yes – more of a novel than a letter, if I may say so. This thing you do . . .'

'Ceramics,' says Fliss stiffly, inwardly seething at his implication that her carefully garnered facts, figures and explanations are a figment of her imagination. 'I make pots.'

'Yes. Much of a market for these pots, is there?'

'It all depends. I make domestic ware – cups, plates and things, a few candlesticks and mirror frames.'

'You get a very nice cup and saucer at Habitat nowadays, I've noticed.'

'Well, yes, of course – but there'll always be people who want something handmade and virtually unique.'

'But not *enough* people, it seems.'

'Well, it's certainly a bit – erratic.'

'And you, Mr Harley-Wright?'

'Yes?'

'Yes. "Publishing"?'

'That was always my field when we still lived in London. I started with Faber, had a stint at Penguin – '

'Oh?' The Under Manager's eyebrows shoot up with the

first glimmerings of approval and interest. 'And when would this be?'

'Mr Evans knew all about me – well, about both of us of course.'

'Yes?' That obviously will not do – the UM wants the whole story.

'In the 1970s. After Penguin, I started up my own business in north London – Islington – training manuals – quite a thriving little operation – not far off fifteen thousand feet of plant – but we got hammered by the unions – had a shut-down – then there was the three-day week – did a sort of buy-out with the staff, but it never really worked – basically got driven out in 1975.'

'Right.' The UM blows himself up for another teeth-rasp and looks down at his fingers.

Fliss does a quick calculation and works out that he would have been about nine in 1975. They might as well be describing a scene from Caesar's Gallic Wars for all their tale impinges on his experience.

'So there you were. . . .'

'That's when we came to Suffolk. My parents already had the house of course – I was brought up there – and the estate, quite a bit of land. It was all getting a bit much for them – my father was already in his eighties.'

'This is the Hall, yes?'

'Little Watling.'

'I'm new to the area. Head office moved me up from Chelmsford.'

'It's just down the hill from Great Watling.'

'I can't say I know either.'

'Not to be confused with East Watling, which is just on the other side of the river.'

'No – '

'Or indeed West Watling, which is in a completely different area on the other side of Woodbridge.'

'And this land?' says the Under Manager briskly, relentlessly sticking to his point.

'My father sold most of it to an Arab consortium back in the oil-glut days. I think it's owned by a Sheikh Al-Faht.'

'Um.' Not a flicker on the UM's face.

'Contract-farmed of course – we're surrounded – a few acres left. We're really quite self-sufficient in many ways – a few sheep, goats, veg, that sort of thing . . .'

'And the proceeds? Of the land sale?'

'Well, my father – Harry Harley-Wright – well, he wasn't any sort of businessman – he'd never had to be, I suppose – but he was very sociable – clubbable really – open to suggestions I'm afraid. He went in for all sorts of enterprises. There was a sort of motorized wheelchair thingy with a sidecar, and a special lap-table so you could eat in front of the television without danger of spills – cast in polypropylene – hideous thing really – cost a bomb to develop. He'd met the designer chap in a pub and just fallen for it. And then of course the horses – '

'A betting man?'

'Worse really – breeding. He kept getting into syndicates up at Newmarket – well, anyway, that's where it all went – and then of course he was very friendly with Mr Evans – took a lot of his advice – so when he died there was really rather a pickle left to sort out.'

'A pickle,' says the UM dully. A little muscle spasm streaks down his cheek, but he seems to regather strength for the attack. 'And this current enterprise – "Publishing"?'

'Oh, yes – my *Cornucopiae*. Yes, well, I bought this old

letterpress with woodblocks and I print up books of proverbs and recipes. You know the sort of thing – *A Christmas Cornucopia* – full of bits about Wassail and Mead and Dingly Dell. Sell them to gift shops and tourist places.'

'I see. That's "Publishing". And "Candles"?'

'Well, that's another thing. We've got this set-up in the old apple store. We hand-dip candles – again for local shops – in fifteen shades, everything from peach to pistachio, and a lot of white of course. . . .' Ivor's voice trails away.

The UM is looking weary. 'And the "Smallholding"?'

'Very small – yes.' Ivor laughs. Fliss wants to kick him.

'A certain amount of produce sold, according to the accounts.'

'In a way.'

'Not very consistent.'

'That does seem to be our problem . . .'

'We have such odd things to sell really,' Fliss interrupts, trying to sound bright. 'Cobnuts and bullaces – very good Jerusalem artichokes – '

'Not a lot of call, I'd imagine.'

'We had a go at conventional things like tomatoes, but there are such efficient organizations around us. The whole area seems awash with tomatoes.'

'So as I see it,' says young Mr Dixon, suddenly flicking his fingers through all the accounts as if shuffling a pack of cards, 'what we have here is a total of four businesses.'

'Five, if you count the dried flowers.'

The Under Manager gives Fliss a beady look. '*Five* businesses – *none* of which is trading in profit – all of which are technically insolvent.'

Chilling word 'Insolvent', especially in a bank; it hangs in the air like a bad smell.

'Well, I don't know about that,' says Ivor, 'not exactly.'

'And what would you call it "exactly"?'

'It's not as if there are no assets.'

'The house – yes – the Hall. Well, with the way property prices are zooming up, that's probably your best bet.'

'What?'

'Sell the Hall – as soon as you can. That will have to be the bank's advice. Quite a desirable property, I'd imagine.'

'It's not actually ours. It's in my mother's name.'

'But the overdrafts and loans are in yours.'

Ivor gives a little half-shrug. 'Mr Evans was a very good friend of my father's . . .'

For a second time, the muscle spasm flashes down the UM's cheek and he looks as if he might choke. 'It's not a situation we can allow to continue.'

'No.'

'And you are actually asking for an increase in your overdraft.'

'To meet immediate bills – yes.'

'I hope we're not having a little joke here, Mr Harley-Wright.'

'Certainly not, Mr Dixon.'

'We're not a charitable institution, Mr Harley-Wright.'

'Of course not, Mr Dixon.'

'We'll have to have those deeds – or some sort of surety from your mother.'

'My mother is very – well, she's not the easiest – '

'To put it baldly, Mr Harley-Wright, it's a question of her deeds or your bankruptcy.'

For one so young, he packs a hideously mature punch. It is clearly time for the last-ditch stand, and Ivor nervously produces his only remaining weapon.

'There is the Collection.'

'Yes, you mentioned that at the end of your letter. A collection of pottery, is it?' He says the word as distastefully as if it were a synonym for 'turd'.

'Commemorative drinking vessels from the early seventeenth century to more or less the present – well practically – my father's passion until the day he died. That's ours.'

'Hardly likely to save *this* sinking vessel, is it?' There's the slightest flicker of a grin, then, quick as a lick, 'Any idea of its value?'

'That's tricky – but on the open market . . . well, we've had an approximate valuation from Barnaby Fitzgerald – he's highly respected.'

The UM is looking sceptical. Fliss leaps to the rescue.

'He did a stint on *The Antiques Roadshow* – man with a monocle?'

'Oh? *Him?*'

The UM's interest has been recaptured. Ivor has by now wrestled with his briefcase and whips out the sheet of Barney's white laid Smythson's writing paper – the lone *pièce de résistance*. He hands it over. The Under Manager reads it and breathes out more sharply than ever.

'Well, that would be very satisfactory indeed.' He looks up, the tiniest glimmer of greed streaking back into his black plastic button eyes. 'That would leave you with a very satisfactory lump sum once the loans are cleared.'

'Yes.'

'We now have a very good investment service, you know – customer-oriented – user-friendly. Unit trusts and so on. A little life insurance is called for now, you know, you're very undergeared.'

'Yes,' says Fliss, getting the picture and going with it,

even though indignation is oozing through every capillary, 'that would be a good idea. We need – well, something – I can see that.'

'Just in your own best interests.'

'Absolutely,' says Ivor.

They all stare at the blotter for a moment. An unbearable pressure builds in Fliss's head, waiting for Ivor to ask the next vital question – and at last he says, rather too quietly, 'Meanwhile – for our immediate problems?'

The UM clears his throat. Fliss can see there's an internal battle going on in there, but in the end, thankfully, greed wins.

'I think we can see our way to allowing the increase – for the moment. We'll need a copy of this valuation and a formal statement from you about how and when this, er . . . collection will be disposed of. And then of course some sort of formal undertaking from your solicitor that the proceeds will be deposited with us to clear the debt.'

'Right.' Fliss's brain half groans at the thought of clocking up yet another invoice – and a legal one to boot – and half cheers at the prospect of escaping this vile room with the immediate means of paying the electricity bill suddenly at their disposal.

The Under Manager gets up abruptly and holds out his hand, standing over them as they scramble to their feet – and that is that.

Only of course it isn't. There is a little detail about the Collection that somehow hasn't needed to be mentioned, although now it lurks scratchily at the back of both their minds.

*

Outside the bank, almost surprisingly, it is still market day. They feel strangely unreal, with the same sensation as coming out of a cinema in the afternoon and finding that it's still daylight. After so much tension, not yet truly resolved, they both feel a strong need to behave as normally as possible. The market traders are lined up under their awnings, wrapped against the penetrating damp, serving vegetables with grimed hands in fingerless gloves. Early as it is, some are beginning to give up on a bad day, and are starting to pack away their stock. Fliss buys a huge box of mushrooms knocked down to a pound and wonders what she is going to do with them. Soup? They'd soon be swimming in bloody soup. She leaves Ivor poking about on a stall devoted to third-hand ironmongery and crosses over to Boots.

Chemist's shopping is something she particularly dreads when broke. Relentlessly expensive but relentlessly necessary, it's probably not an issue which people with regular incomes ever consider. Maybe in some Sudanese desert or Chinese village, you could expect to do without, even if you didn't want to; but how, she muses, in normal contemporary English life, bringing up a family, could you really manage without tampons, toothpaste, aspirin, loo rolls, antiseptic, plasters, indigestion tablets, eyedrops, deodorants, razors, batteries – let alone anything so decadent as a lipstick? She goes in and spends a giddy twenty minutes disposing of £28.53 of their newly extended overdraft. She looks at the basket resignedly and wishes she had shares in Boots plc.

Back outside, she makes her way past eighteenth-century houses whose ground floors have been sacrificed to the plate glass of twentieth-century commerce – so much for conservation areas and strict planning laws. Wading through market debris and empty hamburger cartons, she passes McDonald's and Burger King, grinning at each other on either side of the square. Both are crammed – mostly with young women and pushchairs, escaping the cold and sucking their cheeks inside out on thick shakes.

She meets Ivor back at the car park. He is loading a huge, rusted spring and a footpump into the back of the Peugeot. Their vehicle is the lone disgrace in a whole rack of gleaming motors. On one side sits a cheeky, glamorous little Peugeot 205 shining in navy blue; on the other, a complacent BMW in waxed maroon. Mrs Thatcher's Britain is fatly displayed in this handsome town. To those that have, a lot is being given. The property-owning, share-owning democracy is bulging with new technology in black plastic casings – CDs, videos, cordless phones and answering machines – almost all of them made abroad. And there are even people who seem genuinely interested in the label on their clothes, seek out bags, T-shirts and even earrings and shoes that advertise themselves – puzzling for a generation brought up to think that any sort of brand display was 'common'.

But on the town hall steps and round the side of the park and down the picturesque alleyways, a little band of sad, cold, wan, dirty-looking, hungry-looking people is steadily growing. There is a technique to deal with them of course: you try not to catch their eyes, try to hurry past; stay uninvolved. But Fliss can see herself there with them; looks at the little old woman who searches through the discarded fish and chip papers to see what's left, and knows in her bones what it must feel like, as she herself scrabbles at her purse to find some change, diffident and embarrassed – to give.

Now she doesn't bother to ask Ivor why he has bought the enormous spring, nor how much it cost. It's bound to be salted away in one of the barns against some future, as yet unknown, scheme; some Heath-Robinsonesque contraption aimed at yet again saving them from perdition.

'I suppose we'd better go and see Barney,' she says.

'Yup,' says Ivor.

'Well done, by the way – with the bank.'

'Well done you too.'

The little detail though, they leave unresolved, still lurking in the air.

3

Barney's shop takes pole position in the centre of Long Pecklam. In a street stuffed with antique dealers, Barney's is the handsome star: six bays wide and decked out in dark pine green with gold-leaf lettering, Fitzgerald & Calder. Nobody is quite sure about Calder; nobody knows him. Rumour even suggests he doesn't exist.

Barney's speciality is sixteenth- and seventeenth-century oak – 'stuff for the big boys', he calls it – and business is booming. Dutch, German and American dealers arrive regularly at one end of Long Pecklam and work their way up the entire street expressly to stuff whole shipping containers with all manner of English antiques – much of it decorative rubbish by Barney's standards. On the quiet though, he deigns to deal in such things a little bit – more or less as a sideline to keep business ticking over, while his main field is more rarefied. Good authenticated pieces are increasingly hard to find, but he has a wide range of contacts and a nose for discovery. That is how he found them of course – coming up the drive one day on the off chance in search of settles and court cupboards, and discovering, to his scandalized delight, the Collection.

Now he sits in the middle of the showroom at a huge refectory table which serves as his desk. The room is painted deep terracotta and on the hearth of a vast brick inglenook smoulders what seems to be half a tree. Barney's current favoured look is all big-boned and dramatic, in stark contrast to the prevailing mood washing over the nation by Laura Ashley out of Colefax and Fowler, or what Barney refers to as 'Swag 'n' Drag'.

He's on the telephone when they arrive. His fax machine at the end of the table is also steadily spewing out a convoluted conversation. Fliss looks at the well-waxed oak beneath the machine, with its complex patina of three hundred years, and marvels at its ability to support change. Gratifyingly, Barney slams down the receiver as he sees them. It's a relief to feel significant after being reduced to the status of a tapeworm by the UM.

'Duckies, I was trying to get you. I think we're on. It's all a little mysterious – we're still only talking agents so far, but I can smell a Mr Big. Denmans in New York have been on to me and they've obviously got somebody lined up – somebody pretty juicy.'

'Have you said anything to them about the conditions?'

'It's not the right moment. First bait your hook – that's the advertisement. Then cast your line. We're on the slowly, slowly, catchee fishee bit. Once we've got negotiations going we can let them know the full implications. We don't want to put people off before they're even interested.'

They fill him in about the meeting with the Under Manager.

'Greedy little bugger.' Barney smacks his lips. 'Still, I'm glad my little piece of paper did the trick.'

'There is the point . . .' says Fliss. 'Well, we didn't go into any details . . . just gave him the valuation.'

'And that did it – as I say, greedy little bugger. They've got no resistance to figures like that.'

'But of course it leaves out the conditions of Harry's will – he thinks it can go through as a normal sale on the open market.'

'Well, to an extent it can – *technically* – and in the strictest sense it will be. We've advertised it openly. We're doing it in good faith. It's not our fault the old fellow's provisos would stop any major auction house touching it with a bargepole. All right, so it's a little bit iffy – having to go to a single buyer as a single unit. *Well . . .*' Barney gives a helpless sort of shrug.

'And the bit about the twenty-five years – having to maintain it as a single collection. I suppose if the bank knew – I mean, your valuation isn't really based on that, is it?'

'Well, not perhaps in the strictest sense. It's all as long as a piece of string. All right, my figures were sort of based on individual prices for specific pieces, but if there's a buyer out there who'll have the lot – I mean, it's entirely unique – if such a buyer exists well, you see what I mean – that valuation isn't strictly inaccurate, not strictly speaking. In the end, it's worth what someone will pay for it. All right, so we can't split it up and sell the tastiest pieces individually, say to museums. No museum here is going to spend that kind of money on the whole collection and find themselves contracted to display mugs celebrating fifty years of the incorporation of Weston-super-Mare along with all the good stuff – but old Harry didn't have it quite as sewn up as he thought.'

'No?'

'I've been thinking about it a lot. For a start, he didn't stipulate that it has to remain in this country. Now we advertised in America principally because we were thinking that's where the money is and they're more likely to be interested in the twentieth-century stuff. But there's another point. Whatever a buyer signs to here – well, once it's out of the country, it would be very difficult to make anything stick. And who's going to notice if they put the best bits in the drawing room and stash the rest in the attic? And then, with all due respect, we're not talking the Elgin Marbles here – who's going to sue them? Not your father.'

'My mother'll have a damn good go.'

'No, I don't think we'll have much of a problem as long as we find the *right* buyer. Not a nervous type who runs away at the first sign of complications. It won't be easy, but he's out there – and we may have hooked him already.'

'Do we know anything about this mysterious inquirer?'

'Only that it's a "he" and he spotted the ad in *Art and Antiques* – and he's using Denmans to make the initial contact. That's not unexpected really. The sort of money we're talking about usually likes to hide behind an inter-mediary – and to an extent you can too, you're hiding behind me. But there's going to come a moment – I'm going to need to fill them in with the story. Americans like the story. They don't just buy the things as *things*, you know. They're buying a little piece of you really – a little bit of experience to embroider their own lives, and if it's got a tasty little bit of history and heritage to it, well, so much the better.'

'But there isn't a lot of history and heritage to the Collec-tion – not as a whole, there isn't,' says Ivor.

'That's where you're wrong. There's your father for a start, now *there's* a character.'

'It's hard to think of your own father as a "character" like that.'

'It's just a question of disassociating yourselves – see the whole thing objectively. He started it as a child, didn't he?'

'Bits of it he inherited. The Adam and Eve loving cups came from his grandmother – and then when he bought the Hall – '

'He *bought* the Hall? Oh. I thought he'd inherited it.'

'Oh, no. His family were solicitors in Ludlow. He got a bit from them, but then with his demob gratuity after the First World War he had some fantastic lucky coup on a triple accumulator at Epsom – stuck the proceeds into something like copper futures, I think it was – made an absolute bomb – and whipped straight round to Knight, Frank and Rutley – bought the Hall, sight unseen, for cash – just like that. He had this thing about expansiveness and always found life at home narrow and constrained, I suppose. I think he almost enjoyed the war – at least it got him away from home . . . Anyway, there he was, all alone at the beginning of the Jazz Age – only he didn't know that then – in this bloody great house – and there seemed to be money around, lots of it swilling about until the thirties. And he had all these arty friends coming down for weekends – only he didn't really have anything arty to offer back, if you see what I mean. I mean, he hadn't – he hadn't any specific talent, except for giving other people a good time – and the Collection sort of came out of that, I think. A mildly interesting and fun thing which he could share with the others. And then of course everyone always knew after that what they could buy him as bread-and-butter presents and it just sort of went on from there. I suppose it's the only thing he really cared about – apart from my mother of course. The other crazy things – all the different inventions and things – well, they were supposed to supply the money to keep the rest going.'

'Well, there you are,' says Barney briskly. 'You just edit it down a bit. I don't think we need to know your father bought the Hall via his turf accountant. Just the *fact* of the Hall will do. The rest of it's rather romantic really – lots of appeal. The lost, lonely man buying his friendships through his passion.'

'I wouldn't put it like that.'

'You have to be simple and straightforward with these things, dears. We'll just keep it to Hall – Heritage – Passion – Conviction. They'll love it.'

Ivor's face is a study in distaste.

'Now, I'll need to consolidate the full catalogue. So far we've just got a detailed list of the tasty bits and I've only roughed out the rest. It's well over four thousand pieces, you know.'

'Well, yes, I *do* know,' says Fliss drily. 'Someone's had to clean them once a year.'

'Now, that's what I'm getting on to, dear. They ought to have a going-over – a little titivation before anybody comes. We don't want dust, do we?'

'I thought that could all be done here,' says Ivor, 'when we move them.'

'Oh, we won't be moving them.'

'What?'

'They must stay *in situ* – just the way they are. That's what I mean – *that's* the story.'

'You can't be serious.'

'Oh, yes – it's part of the whole unique quality of the

thing. They've got to fall in love with England, with Suffolk, with Little Watling Hall and most of all with *you*.'

They drive back in silence. Neither is by nature a dissembler and Fliss in particular likes things out in the open. She hasn't really got the energy to plot and plan – and could Barney's ideas verge on the dishonest? Somehow they've got to put all this up to the bank and their solicitor in a way which tells the truth, but succinctly enough to help them get by. Then there is Martita, who loves a good plot but despises their predicament – even though it's truly her predicament as well. And then also, deep down in Ivor's soul, there lies The Guilt. The creeping, uncomfortable knowledge that he is trying to flog off something central to his father's life, and almost certainly in a way which expressly goes against his dying wishes.

From the distant prospect at the bottom of the drive, the house looks romantic enough. The central part was built in about 1480, around the core of an even older house. Its massive oak frame was originally a single hall with buttery, screens passage and an open hole in the roof for the smoke to escape, like dozens of other 'hall houses' dotted about this landscape. Those late Plantagenets certainly knew how to build: perhaps the earliest form of prefab known to man, and so many of them still standing, giving shelter, while younger buildings around them crumble to dust. Of course they are demanding charges to live with (charges being the operative word here), and survive not simply because of the quality of their original construction but in large measure because their harassed, though enraptured, owners

34

put themselves in thrall to an unending stream of maintenance and repair.

In Little Watling Hall's case, the original construction
was altered, extended and generally tinkered about with for
the next two hundred and fifty years or so. The first floor,
made of huge oak planks, was added in about 1530. Some
twenty years later were built the massive chimneys tapering
up to tall, twisted stacks, like sticks of brick barley sugar.
Round about 1580 the clumsy rough-hewn staircase was
replaced by an altogether more graceful creation with
twisted oak balusters and more shallow steps. The projecting wings went on a little later and each gable was given
an elaborately carved bargeboard.

Round about the turn of the century, the seventeenth
century that is, someone decided to add the deep encrust-
ations of pargeting to the top of each gable. These plaster
reliefs, each in a cartouche of grape vines, tell on the left
side of the fall of Adam and on the right of Samson,
with both Eve and Delilah depicted as grovelling carpet-
substitutes beneath the solid feet of their wronged men. All
the plaster walls have been repeatedly limewashed over the
centuries that particularly old Suffolk colour – a sort of
rusty, red ochre made up of tallow, ground-up bricks and
originally bulls' blood – the sort of colour associated with
Siena or Florence, but in fact perfectly usual in these greyer,
damper climes.

The windows are mostly the original mullions with later
leaded lights, although some time in the eighteenth century
a previous owner had a bash at tarting the old girl up by
popping sash windows into the side elevations, and these
now have the gratifying effect of at least providing a few
rooms into which sunlight can penetrate. The whole back

of the house is Jacobean, almost new by the standards of the rest, and is built on brick foundations which go straight down, a sheer drop into the moat. This, although impressive as a decorative feature, is a trap for the unwary. Those who leave things on the back sills with the windows open in a draught rarely see them again. The bottom of the moat must be a treasure chest of goodies dropped over the centuries, the most recent being endless cans of the girls' hairspray and sodden copies of *Cosmopolitan*.

There is a long, straight drive bordered on either side by an avenue of cedar trees. These must have been planted at about the same time the sash windows went in. The owner of that period must have cursed his unfashionably aged and asymmetrical possession, and longed for the modern delights of Palladianism and regularity being built by his grandest neighbours. The planting of the cedar avenue must have seemed a daring compromise by a very patient man, encouraging Mother Nature to add a rigid architectural feature to what was until then a rough, winding track. Perhaps it's unfortunate, but only the trees at either end of the avenue have been able to develop their full quota of graceful, horizontal branches. The others are too closely planted and have grown tall, thin trunks whose side shoots have intertwined with each other to form a dark-green tunnel. On the left, the very last cedar nearest the house, the only one with a perfect shape, came down in a freak gale in 1976 and has never been cleared away. Such a huge tree turned out to be held in the ground by short little sprouts of root, which now stick forlornly in the air. The whole trunk lies on its side, as if tossed there by an enormous dinosaur carelessly weeding.

The house stands on a small island in its moat and the

drive leads straight to a wooden bridge, the only access. Until recently there was a drawbridge here, which collapsed under a joint attack from wet rot and beetle, and this replacement was built by Ivor from old railway sleepers. At the front, contained within the two projecting wings, is a gravelled court and the drive swings round sharp right to a flagged yard with various small outbuildings. The large old barns and stores, many of them now clad in rattling corrugated iron, are divorced from the house – stranded back on the mainland.

So far, so romantic – at a distance. It is only as the buildings are approached more closely that the vision of eccentric beauty fades into crusty reality. The drive itself is a mass of huge potholes now filled with bits of broken brick, so that Ivor, with a sense of total familiarity, weaves the car from side to side to avoid the worst. The house probably started to list to starboard many years ago, but now the process is accelerating. Certainly something major has shifted and the intricate chimneypots are no longer strictly at right angles to the roof. The limewash is by now patched and faded. In the areas where water has been absorbed, the plaster has fallen off to reveal the inner core of laths and even earlier wattle and daub. In hot summers, the window frames shrink away from the walls, and in winters they expand again and burst out, exuding fungi. In spring, the whole household can hear the mechanical clicking of death-watch beetles signalling for their mates through the thick timbers. Weeds of all species sprout between flagstones, through gravel and down walls, blocking gutters and down-pipes. A constant daily battle is fought to maintain even a semblance of order, within the more pressing need for earning money and just surviving.

Now as they cross the bridge and park in the front court, Fliss catches sight of Martita's face peering down at them from behind the curtains in her bedroom window, her nose twitching with curiosity like a ferret's. And this is the vision of loveliness with which Barney wants them to seduce the mysterious Americans.

4

On the Hutchinson River Parkway, Thomas Klaus III is trying to reacclimatize himself to the life and mentality of a daily commuter. He thought he'd given all this up fourteen years ago, when he'd first moved to the city and subsequently bought the apartment on East 67th Street, married Paula and had the children. He was supposed to be Metropolitan Man; God had surely meant him for that.

A childhood in the Connecticut suburbs, not too far up the New Haven line so his father could make his own daily commute, hadn't given him any taste at all for the bucolic life. He regularly got hayfever, hives and hideous poison-ivy rash. He disliked sailing and horses. As he grew up, weekend parties in Westport seemed to revolve around Bloody Marys and barbecues, and the conversation too often veered away from theatre, music, baseball and the markets towards Japanese beetle and the decimation of rosebeds – not his thing at all.

When, after college and law school, he eventually made it into the city – New York City of course, the *only* city – he'd silently vowed never to leave. And if it hadn't been for that goddamn bitch, he wouldn't be stuck on this parkway now, at some unearthly hour, trying to cheat the worst of the rush-hour traffic so that he can be looking alert and put together for Mr Z.

Paula had decided, after twelve years of marriage and two beautiful children – *their* beautiful children – that she needed to find herself. 'Find herself', for God's sake. Anyone would think that it was still the sixties – not the settled, zappy, powerful eighties. People 'found themselves' in the age of flower power – tuned in, turned on and all that stuff. Tom, who'd been born in 1950, had, as it happened, done his own little bit of finding – but only a *little* bit. Grown a Zapata moustache, smoked a little weed, fucked around – just a little bit – well, people did. But that was then.

For most of the freewheeling seventies, when supposedly men had been growing hair, women had been burning their bras and stamping around in dungarees, and both had been indulging in the one and only mass mega-orgy in history (the one which wasn't meant to have unpleasant consequences), Tom had been safely married to the lustrous Paula. She'd been so cute then. Just eighteen with those huge green eyes, blonde hair kind of curved around her jawline, tiny little retroussé nose: the perfect secretary on her first ever job straight out of school – and indeed *his* first secretary ever, making him feel so important, so grown up at the ripe old age of twenty-four.

Of course they fell in love. They were perfect for each other. His parents said so. Her parents said so. His dark, macho chunky looks, coupled with her golden glow: they'd make beautiful babies – they *did* make beautiful babies, for God's sake. Two beautiful babies in quick succession, Jody and Erica, the lights of his life – and where are they now?

They'd grown up in that beautiful apartment – almost a duplex if you counted the little guest suite up the spiral stairs – and in a great part of the city. He'd let Paula decorate, for God's sake, and God had she decorated. On his salary he'd let her put them through tartan, moiré silk and lapis – and lapis didn't come cheap. None of it came cheap, come to that. Neither did private schools for the kids and weekends on the slopes (he didn't mind the country under snow – it was cleaner somehow).

All that precious earned income pouring into this life for the four of them, with Tom working every possible hour of the day, and she'd upped and left. Gone to the desert in search of something, she said. In search of *what*, for God's sake? Murmuring things about the Hopi Indians; talked of living on a mesa – wanted a job. What job? They need secretaries who can decorate on a mesa? And she'd taken the kids with her. And somehow, amazingly, the law, *his* law (because, after all, he was still a lawyer and had always kept the faith), had *let* her do it, and not just do it but take half of his painfully earned income with her, and then some, *while* she did it. The mere thought of it is enough to make him crash the gears of his beloved Porsche as he bounces over the Triborough Bridge (well, he has to have something left to bolster his poor ego and the Porsche is it). Jeezus – it all stinks.

And otherwise this should've been a great time. He'd been head-hunted out of Maxim Smith Newburg and into the Constance Corporation as their specialist in labour relations. Trade unions were his thing. He could feel his way around a dispute. He had a knack with people. They liked him; he was a likeable guy. And he could sniff out the angles and pounce when no one was looking. And Mr Z liked him – or he was pretty sure he did. You couldn't be absolutely certain with Mr Z – he had a way of looking at you with his eyelids half closed and you couldn't necessarily work out what was going on in there. But OK, maybe you couldn't expect to see into the head of a guy who was right up there at the top of the Forbes 400, one of the richest guys in America, which made him one of the richest guys in the world.

There was something extraordinarily flattering in being courted by a man like Constantine Ziminovski. The spotlight of his interest and approval was something almost tangible – you could feel the heat of it as a physical presence. But Tom isn't entirely a new boy in this game of dealing with powerful men and he's only too aware that the loss of this attention and approbation, should it ever come, will feel like his own personal Ice Age.

You have to respect a brain like Mr Z's, thinks Tom. It has to be brilliant to have made all that money, hasn't it? Seen the opportunities, bridged the gaps which no one else even knew were there, created profits where only losses existed before, fulfilled the dreams of thousands of stockholders. OK, maybe a few industries have gone down the tubes – a band of Americans are now on Welfare who maybe don't feel all that wonderful about their absorption into the great family of the Constance Corp. Inc., but they would have gone down the tubes anyway. Taiwan, Malaysia and South Korea are just sitting there stuffed with guys prepared to work for peanuts, there is nothing you can do about it.

Meanwhile, in certain ways, the great man is like a little boy and has sometimes to be nurtured as such. He has a touching faith in new ideas if they don't clash with any of his own perceptions. He likes youth – almost for youth's sake – seems almost to have a superstition about it, as if by surrounding himself with much younger employees whom he has promoted to positions of authority, he can feed his own energies just by looking at them. One of the penalties is that he also expects youth to have more energy – bags of it; much more energy than he himself possesses. And it's not that easy to compete with a man twenty years older who needs only three hours' sleep a night. Mr Z may take daily catnaps, locked away in his black-glass eyrie at the top of the building, but heaven help anyone else caught sleeping on the job at three o'clock in the afternoon.

And now, adding to all the subtle pressures of working for Mr Z, Tom is having to commute in daily from up near Pound Ridge. It's temporary – he always quickly reassures himself of that fact whenever he thinks of his current situation, lest too many nasty thoughts creep in and leach out his self-confidence. His mother and he agree it's only a temporary arrangement – just in order to help him out at this very tricky time, when the apartment is being sold up and Paula is trying to soak him for every cent with the aid of her fearsome West Coast lawyers, for whom *he* seems to be paying.

It was his mother who suggested that he move in with them – but she probably knew he'd be too proud to suggest it himself. His parents had moved from the Sound about five years earlier to cash in on the value of their waterfront property. They'd built a beautiful home, smaller of course, but this time contemporary, clinging to the edge of an escarpment with decks cantilevered out over the rocks; his mother's dream. She'd gotten so tired of keeping the old place up. It had been built way back in the thirties and really needed entire remodelling – the kitchen cabinets made her skin crawl. However, into the new house had poured all the

43

old furniture and every knick-knack she'd ever gathered around her. Even his old room in Connecticut was re-created, down to the same college flags pinned to the walls beside his posters of the Grateful Dead. She thought he loved it. In fact it gave him the creeping habdabs – made him feel nervously as if he might somehow be magicked back to a pimply adolescence while he slept.

A year ago, his father had had a slight stroke. Nothing too serious, it hadn't affected his speech or even his mobility all that much. But he couldn't drive and he couldn't climb all over the steep property as he'd loved to, just generally seeing to things – and thus Tom's pride was sort of saved. He hadn't been forced out of his beloved city by that bitch Paula; he was just giving his ageing parents a little time and attention when they suddenly needed it. That's what he'd told Mr Z anyway. You didn't want to give out too many negative vibes with him around; that was just the kind of thing which turned him off – and Powerful, Exciting People are *not* dumped by their wives.

The traffic at last eases and for once he has a good run down FDR Drive. The moment he is safely in the Constance Corporation building, metropolitan electricity begins to run through his nervous system and he feels his zest for the fight – any fight – renewed. Just as well, for only ten minutes after getting in, while he's still munching through his usual breakfast of cinnamon cheese Danish and cappuccino with Sweet 'n' Lo, the direct line from Mr Z's office starts beeping.

'Tom?' It's Mr Z himself, not an intervening secretary.

'Yes, sir,' says Tom, gulping down a huge bit of pastry in one lump.

'Something's come up. I think you're my man.'

'OK, sir.'

'Come on up. Now. I'll fill you in.'

Mr Z's office takes up the whole of the top floor of the building. From without, it's impenetrable in its obscuring veil of black, bevelled glass; but within, it has a fantastic view – on one side over the East River with South Street Seaport and the Brooklyn Bridge, and on all the other three sides over, and somehow *into*, hundreds of other buildings, bristling with ant-like creatures all hard at work keeping the wheels of commerce going. As it is virtually all glass, there is very little wall space for Art, but Mr Z is known to keep his Art at home – all of his homes – and so here there is just one picture, a huge Picasso drawing of mythical nymphs and satyrs dancing on some Côte d'Azur beach. With its simple black lines on a white ground, it echoes the overall theme of black-glass walls and creamy marble floor.

In the middle of the floor, with its back to the river, is Mr Z's desk, the size of a pool table in acid-etched, thick grey glass. Immediately behind, so that he can get to it simply by swivelling around, is his bank of computer monitors, all cased in a mounting of the same grey glass: winking, blinking – some lurid green as if from outer space; others flashing up their new tricksy full-colour icons, nearly all of them relentlessly ticking out essential market information. The one at the end is permanently tuned to the weather channel, so within the beam of one eye Mr Z can always, at a second's notice, see where any hurricane – either literal or metaphorical – is about to strike.

When Tom walks in, Mr Z is sitting with his back to the door. He swivels round, but otherwise remains perfectly still in the high-backed, charcoal-leather chair.

'Sit down, Tom.'

Tom sits.

'How're you doing?'

'Fine, sir. I'm doing just great.' Tom knows better than to say anything else.

'That's good.'

Mr Z's eyelids come down for the 'stare' and Tom tries to emanate easygoing confidence back across the huge desk.

'How's Pound Ridge?'

'It's great, sir. Beautiful. Beautiful country round there.'

'Isn't it just? I love it. Wouldn't miss it for the world. Worth every second of the journey.'

'Absolutely.'

'We're not so far from you.'

'I guess that's true, sir.'

'It certainly is. You must come over some time – meet Katrina.'

'I'd love that, sir.'

'Yeah, come up. I'll get Mrs Bierce to arrange something. She can contact your secretary.'

'I'd be thrilled, sir.'

'It's just beautiful where we are.'

'I've heard, sir. It must be.'

'Come this weekend. I want to give you a feeling of the place.'

'OK, sir, that's fine by me,' says Tom, mentally cancelling all the plans he'd already made with his parents.

'Because then I want you to do a little something for me. I want you to take a little trip.'

'Sure. Anything, of course.'

'Of course,' says Mr Z. He lifts his gaze up to the ceiling for a moment and then back to Tom. 'I've got a little fun thing on the go – just a little thing, but it needs kind of personal handling.'

'Absolutely.' What's this going to be – a lady in the case?

'I want you to go to England. There's something I may want to buy.'

Tom waits for the name of the company: that's normally what Mr Z wants to buy, though Tom isn't usually asked to handle initial investigations.

'Sir?'

'It's a collection.'

'Uh-huh.'

'A collection of pottery.'

'Right, sir,' Tom gulps. Mr Z's antennae are out for a reaction here and Tom is struggling to keep his signals positive – but *pottery*? 'I'm delighted of course, sir, to help in any way I can, but – well, pottery isn't exactly my, er . . . Wouldn't you rather send an expert?'

'I don't want your opinion of the pottery. I've got Denmans handling that side of it.'

'Right.' Phew.

'I kind of – well, I kind of want the whole picture. Just sort of sniff around – tell me what you feel – give me a sense of the thing.'

'Right. OK. No problem.'

'It's a collection of "Drinking Vessels".' Mr Z looks down at a bound folder in front of him and flicks it open.

Tom goes into sage head-nodding mode. 'Right. OK. That's OK.'

'Literally. Cups. Mugs and things.'

'Uh-huh.'

'It kind of intrigues me.'

'Sure.'

47

'It's where I come from.'

'Excuse me?'

Mr Z puts down the folder and picks up a sheet of Constance Corporation Inc. heavily embossed stationery. 'Have you ever thought about our company logo?'

'I – well, er – I just, it was – I just always thought it was very nice. Very elegant.'

'What *is* it, do you think?'

'Sir?'

'What is the image made of?'

Mr Z pushes the paper over to Tom. Desperation.

Tom stares hard. He's never been a very visual person, but inspiration strikes.

'Well, it's kind of a stylized "CZ", sir – for obvious reasons.'

'Well, it is,' says Mr Z, 'a flattened kind of elliptical "C" with the "Z" coming out of it like a sort of streak of lightning.'

'That's it, sir. Dynamic.'

'Only I didn't invent it.'

'No?' A pause. 'J. Walter Thompson?'

'My dad.'

'No kidding.'

'It used to have a sort of semicircle thing under the "C" bit – like that.' Mr Z leans over and draws on the logo. 'Then it had another squiggle like that on the side. You get it?'

'It's a cup, sir. A cup and saucer.'

'A *steaming* cup, Tom – the "Z" is the steam – a steaming cup of coffee – and that's how we got started – with Ziminovski's Deli and Coffee House back in Brooklyn in the thirties.'

'I didn't know that, sir.'

'*Nobody* knows that, Tom,' snaps Mr Z.

'OK – right, sir.'

'You're being very privileged here.'

'Yes, sir.'

'Now, this collection is a collection of cups – you get it, Tom?' He goes back to the folder and reads out in a different, altogether more pompous, measured tone, '"A Collection of Commemorative Drinking Vessels from 1612 to the Present Day".' He looks up at Tom. 'Can you imagine it – 1612? Who knows where my family were in 1612? Maybe digging turnips on the edge of the Carpathians – they should be so lucky. And this is a family that built its wealth on a cup of coffee. See what I mean?'

'It's kind of nice, sir. Neat – but in the literal meaning of the word.'

Mr Z's impassive face suddenly cracks into a broad smile, showing a handsome range of white picket-fence teeth.

'Go sniff it out, Tom. Go sniff it out.'

5

Fliss picks up the telephone. It's Barney.

'He's coming on Tuesday.'

'WHAT?'

'Tuesday. Next Tuesday – you've got a whole week.'

'You MUST be joking!'

'I did warn you, dear. I said we'd have to present them with the story.'

'Not so soon. Next WEEK? It's impossible.'

'Nonsense. You'll manage. The Collection isn't all that dusty, is it? We more or less sorted it out when we catalogued.'

'It's not the Collection. It's everything else. Everything. There's not an inch that's – Barney, *please* – you *must* be joking.'

'Come along, ducky, I don't play games – not where biz is concerned, anyway. Let's brace up and get on with it.'

'But *now*, Barney – when things couldn't look worse. I thought when you said "in the spring" you meant sort of the end of April, beginning of May.'

'The sooner the better from a monetary point of view, I would have thought.'

'But everything looks terrible.'

'I can't see what a few extra weeks are going to do.'

'Leaves, Barney, for a start – greenery – bluebells, clematis, the odd bit of wisteria – it all helps. *You're* the one who says we've got to present them with this sort of pastoral romantic vision.'

'"Him" not "them" – it's only one chap. Just do your best – jolly it all up a bit – get a few fires going and things. Does your central heating actually work?'

'We put it on twice a year – Christmas and New Year's Day – just to keep the system functioning.'

'Well, sacrifice, dear. Get it going and warm the place up a bit. Make sure his room's got flowers in it. Buy some if necessary – that'll do. You know the sort of thing, I'm sure.'

'His room? What room?'

'Where he's going to stay.'

'You never said he was coming to stay.'

'Well, what else would he do?'

'I don't know. An hotel, I suppose. What about the Swan at Lavenham? Americans love the Swan at Lavenham.'

'I'm sure, darling, but it's not the same thing at all. He has to have a taste of a private home – he can't be stranded at some hostelry.'

'Well, can't he stay with you?'

'Definitely not – wouldn't do at all. He's coming to see *you*. You're the ones with the Collection, not me – I'm just the agent – tainted, if you like, with filthy lucre.'

'I don't see that matters. It is business, after all, as you say. You're going to get your cut. I don't see why you shouldn't. You've got a lovely flat over the shop, Barney – couldn't you possibly?'

'Absolutely not, ducky – you're completely missing the point, and I don't think you should be rubbing my nose into my measly little percentage. It's not going to be that much to write home about when I think of all the angst the whole thing's going to put me through.'

'YOUR angst!'

'Now, watch it, darling. Don't get bitter – it doesn't suit you. Let's be sensible. I did warn you. I said we'd have to show them the "story" – and this is the way to do it. It's not as if we don't all know the problems – the conditions of old Harry's will et cetera. It *is* a little tricky.'

'You said they didn't really matter.'

'Weeeelll . . . and I was right – in a way. I think if push comes to shove, it would be very difficult to make them stick – especially in another country – but they *are* a complication, we can't deny that – and rare though this collection is, it's not that easily placed – not for a decent return, it isn't – and we certainly shouldn't assume that buyers will ignore any possible consequences. Whoever it is has to sort of fall in love with it – fall in love with the whole *idea* of it. Right?'

'I suppose so.'

'So get your boiler going and let's get stuck in.'

Fliss puts the receiver down, sick in her stomach, numb in her legs, and looks around the kitchen. It's particularly vile this morning, although even on good days it's no exemplar of culinary delight. One of the high-ceilinged Jacobean bits, tacked on to the back of the house, it had been thoroughly 'done' by Marita back in 1934, when she was Harry Harley-Wright's new child bride. Not having the greatest sense of design, and also not, at that stage, having entirely shaken off the influences of Croydon and the post office, she'd chosen what was then the latest thing in *Ideal Home* magazine and had the room entirely tiled from top to bottom in a shade of bilious green.

On one side stands the range. Of course it couldn't be an Aga – that would have far too simple and convenient, although the Aga salesman did call sometime around 1935 – came charging up the drive full of bouncy confidence one boiling summer's afternoon, only to be sent on his way with a flea in his ear. No, Agas at that time came only in cream, so instead they got landed with the Véronique – an obscure range from Belgium which came, alas, in Martita's favourite shade of verdigris to tone with the walls.

A lugubrious young man from Brussels turned up on a bicycle one morning and had the good fortune of having not only the right colour of range at his disposal, but also a miserable day in early November on which to call. On such a day, the thought of a constantly warm presence in the kitchen was like the promise of a wondrous new friendship. Only the Véronique turned out to be a sad specimen. With its three doors arranged in a triangle, it always looked a bit glum, as if its mouth turned down at the corners. And then the company which made it went understandably out of business when the Nazis overran Belgium, so thereafter the parts were never available and any servicing was of the dodgy DIY variety, involving a lot of energy from Ivor with his oxyacetylene and a hammer.

Far from being the gleaming, primary-coloured, vastly expensive creature now featured on the front of every one of these new magazines devoted to the rural idyll, this range is the bane of Fliss's life. Its green enamel is by now very chipped. Its great hotplate lids are rimmed with a mixture of rust and burnt bits which will no longer come off. Some sort of salts have eaten into the chromed tops and left pockmarks. It is coal-fired and needs constant attendance, particularly on rainy days. It has to be coaxed into action ('Got Up' is the terminology) for anything like a roast or a cake and frantically 'Let Down' for casseroles – all the time quietly belching out a microscopic layer of soot which overlays the entire room.

Dangling from the ceiling is one of those wooden clothes-airers – currently entirely decked with Martita's greyish long johns – all six pairs, because she's been turning out her drawers and has decided to give everything a good going-over. The wide, tall dresser – in its bones rather a splendid piece of furniture, but sadly overpainted bilious green to match – is a study in chaos. The shelves basically display various bits of china – some of it quite good blue and white, and even some Clarice Cliff bought as Martita's breakfast set in the thirties with big splashes of matching lurid green. But in between, over and through, is every sort of bit and bob imaginable.

Screwdrivers; rubber bands; pipe cleaners; old nuts and bolts; foreign coins in tiny denominations; ancient invitations stiff with dust, tucked at the back or dropped behind plates; films long waiting to be developed; drawing pins; picture hooks; two clock pendulums; a plimsoll waiting to have its sole stuck back on (waiting for three years and thus inevitably outgrown by now); dog collars; broken pencils; dried-out felt-tip pens; various pairs of reading glasses; the arms of sunglasses; fronts of sunglasses missing a lens; buckles without belts and belts without buckles; tubes of Araldite; reels of Sellotape; letters awaiting replies; a file marked 'Urgent' with notes in it from 1979; books of course; maps; lots of newspapers; and above all bills – bills tucked behind eggcups and teacups and toast racks in various stages of demand from early politesse to apoplectic rage. Where on earth to begin?

Fliss starts to pull out some of the bills. They ought to be hidden from prying eyes in any case. She'll need a file for them. She goes into Ivor's study – freezing cold and looking as if it's recently been ransacked by the Visigoths. She starts to go through his desk drawers to find one. There are piles of files: 'Accountant', 'Inland Revenue', 'Blacksmith', 'Silage' and on and on, all stuffed full. She starts to empty one marked 'Swimming Pool' on the basis that the pool hasn't functioned for at least two decades, but then decides that emptying out one lot of papers just to tidy up another lot whiffs a bit of robbing Peter to pay Paul. So she goes back into the kitchen and decides instead to gather up all the bits of hardware; these at least could go outside into one of the barns. She is collecting several spanners and bolts when Ivor comes in.

'What are you doing? Don't do that.'

'I'm tidying.'

'Don't do that. I need them. They're the thingies I do the thingy with.'

'What thingy?'

'You know – that thingy – in the larder.'

'No, I don't. What thingy?'

'The stopcock. The stopcock thingy without a cock – you know – it lost its top.'

'Oh, that.'

'Well, don't take them away. We'll need them if there's a big freeze-up. They're the only way to *stop* the cock.'

Fliss puts them back and sighs. 'Barney phoned. There's an American coming – next week.'

'God.'

'I know. And it's worse – it gets worse and worse. He's going to stay.'

'God. Where?'

'Here. Barney insists.'

'God. *When* did you say?'

'Next week. Tuesday.'

'But we were going to redecorate – we were going to paint things up a bit.'

'I know.'

'We can't do it by Tuesday.'

'No.'

'Well, we could do a bit, I suppose.'

'Drop in the ocean.'

'Yup.' Ivor flops down at the kitchen table, considering. 'Which room were you thinking of?'

'I hadn't. I don't know. Martita's is the best of course.'

'Not a hope. We'll practically have to drug her to keep her down as it is. Does she know yet?'

'No. You'll just have to try to explain all over again. She's got to be made to realize how important this is – for *her* as well. He'll have to have the Chinese Room, won't he?'

'Bloody cold.'

'That's another thing. Barney says we've got to run the central heating.'

'We haven't any oil.'

'We'll have to order some.'

'I don't know that we can. We still owe them for some of the last lot – last year. And the minimum order's something like a hundred quid's worth. There isn't all that much of the extra overdraft left.'

'I've got those pots to finish for Mrs Cavendish. She usually pays on the nail – that's nearly two hundred pounds.'

'Not for next Tuesday. We'll have to get the system up and running before then.'

'Could we try another supplier?'

'I suppose so. I'll have a go.'

'I've suddenly thought – *sheets*. What'll we do? All ours are side-to-middled.'

'Doesn't matter, does it?'

'I don't think Americans are used to side-to-middles.'

'I don't suppose many Brits are either, come to that – not any more. I don't suppose you have to side-to-middle polyester, or whatever it's called.'

'Shall I buy some? Sheets?'

'Things are *very* tight, Fliss. Couldn't you borrow?'

'I don't know. I could ask Helena. Oh, God – and we'll probably need pillows and things – ours are all lumpy – unless we could use some of Martita's. And I'll have to try and get everything cleaned up – everything. And I've got to try to get the second glaze-firing done on Mrs Cavendish's stuff – she'll start phoning me soon. I mustn't let her down or she won't order again. And there are all those bowls to finish for the craft market. And then there's *food* . . . Oh, no – he'll have to eat here of course. What on earth'll we give him?'

'How long's he going to be here?'

'I don't know. I forgot to ask. I think the idea is we give him a good time and he falls in love with the whole place – with the whole, you know, whatever – and it should take as long as it takes kind of thing – '

'Well, do that nice chickeny thing you do – that thing with the lemon slices – '

'*And* the olive oil *and* the capers *and* the anchovies *and* the double cream. It's all going to cost a fortune. And there'll have to be puddings – and *booze*. We'll have to have wine – and it shouldn't be El Plonko, should it? We'll have to have proper decent wine.'

'And lambing may start next week. I haven't even put the pens up. I'd better get on with that.'

'Oh, bugger.'

'It is a bit.'

6

Helena comes roaring up the drive in her Range Rover and screeches to a halt within inches of the front steps. Before she can get out, her two black Labrador bitches bound over on to the front seats, across her lap and streak out like electricity. Once free, they start racing round and round the courtyard, barking furiously at each other. Helena doesn't take the slightest notice. She is a small, perfectly formed individual, with an expertly cut bell of shiny red hair around a tiny freckled face. Dressed in her country uniform of stylish, full tweed skirt and leather waistcoat, she decamps elegantly from the tall car, shouting over the racket with practised calm.

'Morning! Sheets ahoy!'

At Martita's upstairs bedroom window, the Boysies are incandescent with shrill-barking excitement, racing from side to side on her sill, desperate to join the fray. A moment later, Martita's face appears behind them, quivering with its ferrety curiosity.

'I've brought a full set,' says Helena, 'including pillows. And I thought you might like a quilt too. I've brought the embroidered Victorian one from our Red Room – too pretty – awash with auriculas. I thought it might bring a little spot of *joie de vivre* to the situation.'

She flings open the tailgate of the car and grasps an armful of linen. 'Oh, fuck – the girls have sat on it. Never mind – it's only a bit of mud – it'll brush off when it's dry.'

She suddenly notices that the dogs aren't with her and shouts piercingly, 'Girls! Girls!' – but the Labs are gone. There is a splash. They've bellyflopped into the moat. Swathed in linen, she rushes to the bridge.

'Oh, God. Teddy will go simply ape-shit if he finds out I've let them run wild. I'm supposed to maintain strict discipline while he's in London during the week. Nanny isn't the word for it – it's *too* depressing. Girls! GIRLS!' But the Labradors, still barking, are now swimming steadily anticlockwise through the stagnant water. 'Oh, well. *Tant pis*. You'll have to lend me a towel.'

'Let me help,' says Fliss, trying to relieve her of some of the burden – but already one of the sheets is dragging on the ground.

'Oh, fuck – it's simply not my day,' says Helena. '*Do* let's go and have a gander at the proposed scene of the crime. It can't possibly be as bad as you say. And I could murder a cup of something.'

She sweeps into the house with Fliss tagging behind.

They stand in the doorway of the grandly titled Chinese Room and absorb the scene.

'Oh, Lord. I do rather see. Apart from anything else, it's so exactly *comme un frigidaire*. Can't you do anything?'

'There's some oil coming, probably tomorrow. Once we've got the boiler going, it'll take the worst of it off.'

'I've got one of those old electric convector things – do you want me to bring it over?'

'Well, Martita's got several electric fires – it's a question of prising one out of her grasp. She isn't very keen on any of this. She isn't being exactly what you'd call unobstructive.'

'Darling old bat – you should put *me* on to her.'

'I think we'll manage,' says Fliss quickly, knowing that Helena, while possessing a heart of gold, can sometimes approximate Titty in the tact department – and Titty has about as much as a train crash.

'Otherwise,' says Helena, now going into the room and having a good look round, 'I do rather see what you mean. It's sort of got rather ghastly, hasn't it?'

'Yes,' says Fliss, now really depressed. She'd begun to hope that perhaps she'd been exaggerating the bedroom's shortcomings.

'The Chinese wallpaper must have been lovely once though. It's just gone a bit blotchy, hasn't it? Whatever are all those stains?'

'I don't know. Damp, I think – or salts or something. The whole house keeps sprouting salts for some reason.'

'The pagoda cupboards are lovely.'

'Yes,' says Fliss, cheering slightly, 'they're all right, aren't they? Harry had his Chinese thing in the twenties – it was all the rage and he had a lot of stuff sent over from Shanghai, I think. There used to be a wonderful screen and some red lacquered tables and things, most of it sold off of course. Titty's still got some nice bits in her room.'

Helena holds out one faded silk curtain washed in shades of puce and purple. Its linings have now disintegrated into shreds.

'Do you know what I think? We should go over the whole house and gather up anything that's the least bit decent and put it all together in here. That way there'll be one reasonably put-together room. You'll just have to stop him examining the other bits too carefully.'

'Well . . .' Fliss is doubtful. 'The nice bits are all Titty's.'

'She'd surely lend – just for a few days.'

'Well . . .'

So they spend the next couple of hours moving heavy furniture up and down the corridors; various pieces from the landings, a chest of drawers from Fliss and Ivor's room, an armchair from Emma's and so on. Fliss tries to solicit Martita's approval for this enterprise, but despite repeated knockings her door stays resolutely shut for the whole time they struggle past it. The finished effect, crowned with the auricula-embroidered quilt, isn't too bad at all, though it no longer really merits its Chinese title.

'You'll have to rechristen it. What about "Mixed Blessings"?' says Helena.

The rest of the house though – minus the bits they've pillaged – looks, if possible, even worse.

'Where's his bathroom?' asks Helena.

'There really is only one – I mean, for us. And Martita's of course, but she'll never share. He'll have his own loo though – down the end of the corridor.'

They go and look at the loo. It is windowless and Helena tugs the string light-pull to reveal a high-cisterned, porcelain throne, transfer-printed with an elaborate design, 'The Neptune', beneath its wooden seat.

'Gosh. Yes,' is all she says.

I'm really not feeling any better about this, thinks Fliss as they go back downstairs.

In the hall it is clear that the moat-soaked Labradors have managed to get in and leave slalom trails of wet, mud-streaked paw prints everywhere. Both now sit by the

Véronique with their tongues hanging out, blithely panting. It is obvious from the blanket covering of splatters from floor to ceiling that they have also recently shaken themselves.

Helena is mortified. 'I'm so sorry.'

'Don't worry at all,' says Fliss, inwardly quailing at all the extra mess. 'It's not as if it didn't need doing anyway.'

'No, it's really too awful. I shall lend you April for the day.'

'Honestly, no – it's terribly sweet of you, but I don't see why you should deprive yourself. And I have got the children – I'm sure they'll rally round.'

'So I should hope,' says Helena briskly, whose own daughters are currently on the slopes of Val d'Isère and have never in their lives had to look a Hoover bag squarely in the face. 'But seriously, *do* have April. She's terribly good and frightfully cheap.'

For a ludicrous moment, Fliss has thought the services of April were being offered as a gift.

'No, I couldn't possibly – ' this now more in the sense of 'I couldn't possibly afford her.'

'I insist. I'll send her over this afternoon.'

Once Helena has left, in a whirl of churned gravel, dogs barking, arms waving, goodbyes shouting, Martita comes down. She's holding two of the Boysies in her arms, and the other two are glued to her heels as she edges warily across the hall, making exaggerated attempts to avoid the mess made by the Labs.

'That woman,' she says. 'Those dogs. They want shooting. I cannot understand people like that. Why does she have animals if she can't keep them under control? Such a mess – it's simply not on.'

This smacks so very much of the pot calling the kettle black that Fliss decides to keep her mouth clamped shut. Now is surely not the best moment for insulting truths to escape her lips.

'And kindly return my house to the state it was in before she came,' Martita continues. 'I cannot understand people today – I simply cannot. Is it the done thing nowadays to move people's furniture about – without permission – when the people in question aren't looking?'

'I tried to ask you – I wanted to consult you, but you wouldn't come out of your room.'

'Cannot a person in her seventy-sixth year take a much-needed rest in the middle of the morning, when she'd been feeling a little unsteady on her pins, in her *own* house, and not wake up to find that house rearranged beyond recognition, without her permission?'

'Oh, Titty – hardly beyond recognition.'

'No, I mean *really.* I mean it. Do answer the question. Because it's something which is beginning to disturb me. I need to know. Have standards slipped so very far in these benighted horrible times?'

'It's only for a few days.'

'And the Boysies have been so upset. They could see and hear what was going on. They've been in a muck sweat. *Look.*' She holds out the two in her arms. They do look a bit sticky.

'I knocked on your door – '

'What?'

Oh, no, here we go again. 'KNOCKED. ON YOUR DOOR.'

'Couldn't hear a thing. The Boysies were kicking up such a racket. I could murder that woman – really I could.'

The telephone rings. It's Mrs Cavendish.

'Just wanted to check on my order.'

'It's fine,' says Fliss, sort of lying.

'Oh, good. I've got to pop up to Bury today, so if it's ready I'll call in.'

'It isn't *exactly* ready – little bit of finishing to do,' says Fliss, remembering that in all the Helena kerfuffle she hasn't turned the kiln up to full power yet.

'Right. Oh. So not this afternoon?'

'Not.'

'Tomorrow?' Tomorrow the pots will still be red hot.

'Could I phone you? When they're ready?'

'Only we've got people for the weekend.'

'Right.'

'It would be *so* nice . . .'

'I did say *next* week if you remember.'

'I know. But I thought they *might* have been ready.'

'Not quite.'

'Oh, well. It's such a pretty green glaze, that – I can't wait to see them.'

'Green? I thought we'd decided on the blue.'

'No – we *started* with the blue if you remember – then I thought – well, then we went with the green.'

Fliss, who'd had to get a rush order of cobalt oxide sent specially from Stoke-on-Trent, *knows* they plumped for the blue. 'Perhaps you thought it was a sort of greeny-blue?' she tries, though she knows it's a full-blooded blue that's currently waiting in the kiln to be taken up to $1,040°$ centigrade.

'More of a green.'

'Right.' Oh, no. Oh, world. Oh, buggeration.

'You've done them in blue?'

'Well – ' Fliss skips a beat, but then inspired memory strikes. 'The green wouldn't be safe – I thought I'd made that clear – not with anything acidic. The copper leaches out the low-level lead, if you remember – especially with something like rhubarb.'

'I don't really go in for rhubarb,' says Mrs Cavendish.

'Or tomatoes – in a vinaigrette.'

'Oh. I *do* go in for tomatoes. Oh, well.'

'That's what I said. That's why I've done them in the blue.'

'Oh, well, what a shame. I'm sure they'll be lovely.'

'I'll phone you as soon as they're ready.'

'Oh, no hurry now. I thought when they were in the green – with these people coming – well, it would have been lovely in the dining room. But in the blue . . . I must've forgotten – had my mind set on the green, I suppose. I'll phone you when we get back from holiday.'

'When is that?' says Fliss quickly, seeing the precious two hundred pounds slip out of her grasp.

'Oh, about a month. We're off to the Seychelles.'

'How lovely.' Vomit. Vomit.

'My poor darling Piers is simply exhausted. The City's like a madhouse at the moment with all this Big Bang stuff – he's wilting. I felt I simply had to get him away or he'd drop.'

'They'll be ready for the day after tomorrow,' says Fliss, now desperate for the disappearing two hundred pounds. 'I can deliver them.'

'Not to worry. It's of no consequence. I'll get in touch some time once I'm back.'

And that is that. Goodbye temporarily to two hundred pounds – and the bill for the materials yet to pay. She puts

66

the phone down with a bang. Nevertheless, she'd better go straight out to the kiln now to turn it up – get that wretched glaze up to temperature – and then try not to forget it. If she does, the whole lot will overfire and have to be entirely remade if the elusive two hundred smackers are ever to be hers.

Martita is still standing there. 'I could, you know. I could murder that woman.'

'So could I,' says Fliss, but it's a different woman.

Helena's April arrives in a very nifty Mini Cooper and hops out clad in tight black cords. Fliss doesn't recognize her for a moment, having only seen her at Helena's in a blue nylon overall, silently dusting corners in the background. Now she gets a good look, she sees a very different, sparky sort of person – not the background type at all. Fliss is drowning in embarrassment. Having spotted her from the house, she rushes out to abort entry.

'I'm so sorry. Helena shouldn't have sent you.'

'She said it was pretty urgent,' says April.

'There's been some sort of mistake. I did explain to her – I said you shouldn't come – but Helena's sort of – sometimes – well, you know – '

'Unstoppable,' says April and laughs.

'Yes. Unstoppable is more or less it.'

'She particularly mentioned a kitchen.'

'Yes – well, *none* of it's exactly – but, well, we had a bit of extra trouble this morning.'

'Those bloody dogs. She said.'

'That's it.'

'Let's have a look.'

'No, honestly – I don't want to waste your time. She

67

shouldn't have sent you – I thought I'd made it clear to her. I can't, I'm afraid, possibly afford to pay you.'

'She said it might be a bit iffy. Mrs Mortimer. She said that. Let's just have a look.'

'No – *really* – '

'Look, she suggested – well, you do those nice vases, don't you? She's got one in her bedroom – the one with all the trailing ivy on it.'

'Yes.'

'Well, why don't we do a swap?'

'What?'

'I'll come for a bit – just over the next couple of days while you're in a spot – muck you out – sort of keep it down – you know what I mean.'

'Oh, God, yes – exactly. "Keep it down" describes my need exactly.'

'We'll get you started – and you can pay me with a vase. I've always liked hers. All right?'

'Sort of bartering?'

'And you can throw in some of those nice dried flowers of yours – when you've got them available – no hurry. I've always fancied a nice arrangement of dried delphiniums – you don't often see them in the shops – they'd look lovely in one of those vases.'

Fliss pauses for a moment. Is this a fair arrangement – on both sides? She attempts a quick calculation of the relative hours and work involved, but gives up. 'All right. If you're sure. All right. It's a deal.'

However, she starts worrying about April's side of the bargain once she's shown her round. April doesn't say a lot, but the phrase 'muck you out' will keep resurfacing, and Fliss quails. The ensuing guilt threatens to wash away any sensation of relief and Fliss waves her goodbye, already weighted with the prospect of needing several ivy-covered vases to provide adequate compensation.

Gloomily she turns to look back at the house. There couldn't be a worse time of the year – just before the buds start swelling, when all deciduous trees and plants are at their most naked. All vestiges of last year's leaves now mostly lie as a thick slimy mulch on the ground. There's not a scrap of camouflage – every crack, stain and patch on the walls is starkly evident; every sheet of Ivor's collection of rusty corrugated iron lies exposed, instead of veiled within summer's softening clumps of nettles and wild garlic. The most she can do, as April says, is 'keep it down' and hope for the best.

Coming back into the hall, she finds Martita staring down the drive.

'Was that a domestic?'

'No, Titty. A friend. April. She's going to come and give me a hand.'

'In my day, that woman would have been on a bicycle *if* she was lucky – in a nice serviceable gabardine – and grateful for it. Not spinning around in scarlet motors.'

'Well, it seems we have something to be thankful for, then, in these difficult, modern, scandalous times,' says Fliss, surprised at her own venom.

'We used to have six of course.'

'Six what?'

'Domestics. Indoors – and on top of that the gardeners. There was Cook of course, and her scullery maid. Then we had Doris the parlour maid and the tweeny – how many's that? Four. Oh, yes, and the dailies – two women from the village. And they really were dailies *then* – not these once-a-week jobbies. And certainly not the sort of people who turn up in little scarlet motors. That wouldn't have done at all.'

'Six indoor staff – *plus* the gardeners,' says Fliss. 'I always forget that. I should write it up on a big sign in the kitchen and read it out loud whenever I feel I can't cope. Six. It's no wonder really, is it? All this. No wonder at all,' and she dashes out to check on the kiln.

'He's going to make his own way from the airport.' Barney is on the telephone yet again. 'He'll take the train from Liverpool Street and he'll have to be collected from Colchester. I know Ipswich is probably nearer for you, but there are more trains to Colchester.'

'Could you collect him?'

'I won't actually be here on Tuesday. I've got that thing up in Harrogate and I don't think I can get back till the evening.'

'You won't be here to help? Honestly, Barney, this is ridiculous. What on earth are we going to say to him? We don't know any of the business stuff or anything.'

'I keep telling you. This bit isn't business – this bit's "ambience". You'll find the whole thing will just happen – organically. Don't worry. I'll be back to help you out on Wednesday.'

'Do you know which train he'll get?'

'I've told him to phone from Liverpool Street. Well, I've only spoken to his secretary, but she'll pass the message on.'

'Right. Well, it'll have to do, won't it? One of us will be there to meet him.'

'There is a *slight* question mark. About the car.'

'What car?'

'The one you'll be picking him up in.'

'Our car. What about it?'

'It's more a case of *which* car.'

'One of the usual of course – we've got two on the go at the moment.'

'That's a little what I feared.'

'What?'

'Darling, I know they're very serviceable, but they are just the teensiest bit – well, *shabby*.'

'I know that, Barney. I'm not blind. The whole world seems to be whirling around in glittering cars at the moment. I don't know how some people do it.'

'Darling, *most* people do it. You're the oddities here.'

'Well, what about our car? It doesn't matter, does it? I thought you were selling us as English eccentrics anyway.'

'Eccentricity doesn't cover cars, dear – not unless they're classics. If they're not classics, they just count as *old* – and old in this context equals unsafe – and Americans are very big on *safe* – safety's a big issue. Do you know, they've even got these airbag things now which sort of bounce you into a cocoon if you have an accident.'

'I don't see that I can do anything about the car, Barney. I'm sorry.'

'You are a little dense sometimes, Flissie. I *wish* you'd pick up my signals. This isn't an "if" – it's a necessity. You *have* to put on a good show.'

'And that's what I'm trying to do – if you'd only let me get on with it.'

'But the show most definitely includes the car. You can't drive him around the countryside in *those* things – you just can't. They reek of failure – and remember, failure is contagious. The rich are always terrified of contamination. You'll have to hire one. A new one.'

'But that'll cost a fortune.'

'Only for the duration. Speculate to accumulate and all that. I've priced it for you – that place in Bury will do it for £19.80 per day, mileage extra – and you can put it on your credit card, so it won't even hurt now.'

'I don't think I can.'

'Of course you can. In fact you have to. They won't do it without a credit card. It's like a sort of extra insurance for them.'

'Mine's full.'

'What?'

'Full. No credit left.'

'I *don't* believe it. And Ivor's?'

'Don't be silly, Barney.'

There is an exasperated pause at the other end of the line. 'You really are the most hopeless pair. If I'd had a clue you were *quite* so – ' He stops; another sigh comes down the line.

'We've always been honest with you, Barney. We told you we were broke.'

'Yes, yes, yes. But there's broke and broke – and glory be, you really are *broke*.'

'I know,' says Fliss humbly. There doesn't seem any point in debating this issue.

Barney sighs again. 'Well, hang on here – let's have a think. There must be something. I know – *I'll* have to hire a car for Harrogate and you'll have to use my Volvo.'

'Really?'

72

'I can't see any other way. I'll get you put on my insurance. You can pay me back for everything once the deal's gone through – *if* the deal goes through.' Another pause. 'My goodness and it better bloody had.'

7

Tom Klaus is feeling slightly pissed. American pissed – not in the British sense of drunk, but in the British sense of pissed off. He is pissed with the Constance Corporation Inc. What kind of a cheapskate outfit is it, for crying out loud? This mighty organization, flooded with money, suddenly went all miserly on him and nixed the more luxurious of his travel plans. There'd even been a hint that they'd make him fly Coach – but at the very last minute, when he'd flapped his *own* frequent-flyer mileage at them and it became clear they wouldn't have to come up with the whole cost of the ticket, they'd bumped him up to Business.

Unbelievable. Here he was on a personal mission for Mr Z himself, and the bastards expected him to fly on the Red Eye, stuck at the rear of the plane alongside all the backpackers, with his knees poked somewhere up by his chin. Frankly he expected Concorde at the very least. Mr Z himself of course only ever flies in his own plane – this not being any teeny-weeny Piper Comanche or even a Lear, but a full-size 737, beautifully fitted with bedrooms no less, and a saloon panelled in exquisitely grained padauk wood – or so rumour has it.

For a moment, Tom had thought of complaining to Mr Z himself. Surely he couldn't know what a travesty was being perpetrated in his name. But then again, perhaps he could. Perhaps that is precisely how you became one of the richest men in America – just by allowing these penny-pinching episodes to occur kind of at arm's length, so they didn't touch you directly with their tackiness. Come to think of it, the Constance Corporation Inc. *is* kind of a cheap operation. For example, it's really harsh on the use of phones for private calls by anyone below upper management. There are public payphones in the marble and granite lobbies, and most people are expected to use these, making illicit love affairs and job hunting extremely difficult. But now he comes to consider a little more, maybe he's not so keen on complaining directly to the Big Man and voluntarily putting himself at the mercy of 'that' stare. Maybe it isn't worth it; he'll put up with the arrangements as made.

So altogether Tom's feeling pretty miffed by the time he almost stumbles out of the plane at Heathrow and joins an endless, reptilian line in Immigration – so long that it winds right out of the hall and into the transit concourse. It is not yet 6 a.m. and the entire rest of the world, probably the universe, has decided to fly into London, all at the same time.

He stands in the midst of a vast polyglot, multicoloured mass of exhausted people, all trying to behave beautifully. They shuffle slowly forward, kicking their carry-on luggage in front of them, until at last they are seen by what appear to be only four rather bad-tempered-looking officials at various desks. To Tom's particular fury, several more desks stand empty, unmanned. He seethes as he eases his own Mark Cross attaché case forward with his toes.

It's not as if it had been a good flight anyway. The plane was a senior citizen of a 747 – definitely seen better days –

well, rumour is more than strong that Pan Am is a little shaky – and the flight attendants seemed positively antediluvian. Where were the luscious stewardesses of yesteryear – the ones in every hot-blooded male's fantasies – the ones Mr Z seems to make a habit of marrying? His third, the latest, Katrina, is still vividly in Tom's mind at this very moment. He met her up at the house last weekend, and a more perfect physical specimen it would be hard to imagine.

The ones Tom now got were bullet-faced and irritable. There wasn't a red-taloned, long-fingered, big-breasted, soothingly voiced nymphet among them to inspire a few horny dreams over the Atlantic. Just brisk, rather angry efficiency as 'champagne' was poured (and who were they kidding? He could swear it was domestic – the label was covered by a napkin, but he could tell) and smoked mackerel was served instead of the expected smoked salmon (Jeez – smoked *mackerel*?). By the time he'd at last managed to drop off to sleep, the plane was beginning its descent and he was rudely awoken by the abrupt, graceless arrival of a cup of coffee and a cold croissant.

In the Immigration line he feels increasingly angry. All the Brits and EEC citizens rush jauntily by, flapping their passports casually at a lone official. The rest of them – the real foreigners – are still grimly shuffling forwards; shades of Ellis Island. Women in saris clutch sleeping babies to their shoulders. They look drained with fatigue and desperate to sit down. Next to them, anxious husbands in turbans re-examine their landing cards and flick through their passports for the umpteenth time.

The older children rush forward to the barrier and rush back again, trying to make a game out of it, fishing moments of fun out of the most unpropitious circumstances and collapsing in giggles. The same with the African families in brilliantly coloured robes, which had already started to look highly unsuitable from the moment the grim, grey sky was glimpsed on landing. The Japanese families maintain small, sleek groups in tight circles, their heads bent over as they work out some currency or linguistic puzzle, their necks all weighted with gleaming cameras and lens cases. The Americans, of both sexes, fit into two clear categories – either sneakered, jeaned, GAP T-shirted and baseball-capped, or Louis Vuittoned up to their eyebrows. While neither variety is particularly anxious (their entry into Her Majesty's kingdom being more or less a foregone conclusion), they are all furious.

Tom fits into the second category. Well, not Vuitton literally of course, for in fact apart from the attaché case, he is so exclusively dressed by clothing establishments within a stone's throw of Buckingham Palace that he doesn't know why the officials don't rush forward and bow him through there and then. Beneath his Burberry trench coat with matching lining and scarf, he wears his Gieves and Hawkes suit, his Turnbull and Asser shirt, his Dunhill tie and socks and his Lobb shoes – what other credentials do these cruds need, for Pete's sake?

When at last he reaches one of the little desks, uncomfortably aware that several of the Indian families in front of him have been placed to one side on a row of chairs and are obviously awaiting some further investigation, he is greeted by a sour-faced little woman with three earrings in her lobe.

'What is the nature of your business?'

'I'm a lawyer. Negotiations.'

'Welcome to Britain, Mr Klaus, and have a nice day.' She

smiles suddenly. Have a nice day? Said here? What the heck is this place coming to?

At least in the baggage hall there are plenty of carts and all free – none of those God-awful machines at Kennedy which have to be force-fed with crumpled dollar bills before they will release their shin-scraping wagons. The one he chooses now, however, turns out to have wonky wheels and as he tries to stride purposefully through the Green Nothing to Declare channel, it keeps slewing sharply to the left and straight towards the waiting Customs men. With horrible inevitability, having come too directly into their line of vision, he finds himself stopped and his cases thoroughly searched, even down to his talcum powder and deodorant, while other much more likely, hippie, hairy people are allowed by unhindered – there's no justice. Oh, beautiful – this is already just a *beautiful* day, he thinks grimly, as at last he emerges into the gunmetal early morning light and bitter cold, to look for a cab – every moment cursing that no car and driver have been provided for his use.

He goes straight to the Constance Corporation Inc.'s London office. Originally he had assumed that an hotel room would be booked for his use in London, to act as a base and allow him to recover from the journey. But the surly woman in the New York office had stated that this would not be necessary. Mr and Mrs Harley-Wright were expecting him as soon as possible on Tuesday. He could freshen up at the London office and travel on to Suffolk as soon as was feasible. Feasible? In his view 'feasible' meant the next day, after a comfortable stay at the Grosvenor House and dinner at Le Gavroche. He just cannot *believe* this cheap bullshit he's been fed.

The Constance Corporation's London building is in

Knightsbridge – one of those heavily ornate red-brick houses on the Sloane estate – double-fronted with steps leading up to white panelled doors bristling with brass fittings; expensive enough in its way, but nothing compared to the size and status of the New York building. As he draws up in the taxi, it is still only about 7.45 a.m. and the doors are firmly shut.

Having paid off the cab, cracked the knocker loudly a couple of times and tried the various buzzers, Tom waits for the office to open and the red-carpet treatment to begin. After several more increasingly loud and anxious knocks, for it's pretty cold and nasty out here on the steps, the door is eventually opened by a tousled man in half a uniform, the bottom half, looking sleepy, cross and puzzled.

'Yes?'

'Tom Klaus.'

'Yes?'

'Tom Klaus – from New York.'

'We're not open, mate. Come back later.'

'You're expecting me.'

'I'm not expecting nobody, mate. Come back when someone's 'ere.'

'I am Thomas Klaus,' says Tom, rustling up some dignity, 'lawyer to Constantine Ziminovski and you *are* expecting me.'

'I told you, mate, I'm not expecting nobody. I'm just the night security guard.'

'Well, will you show me to an office where I can put my things down and wait until somebody arrives?'

'I can't do that, mate. I ain't got the authorization.'

'Well, what do you expect me to do?'

79

'I don't know, mate. Like I said – come back later. Come back in an hour.'

'And until then?'

'*I* don't know, mate. Go and get yourself a cup of coffee or something.'

'From where? It is 7.50 a.m. and in my brain and body it is 2.50 a.m. and I haven't been to bed yet. I am stuck in the middle of residential Knightsbridge with a heavy valise and I am *expected*.' Tom can feel a note of hysteria creeping into his voice.

'Keep your 'air on, mate – I'm only trying to do my job. They'll be a caff somewhere – go across the square, down the road over there, turn right and you'll be in Sloane Street.'

'I know that, my friend,' says Tom through clenched teeth. 'I know London quite well – and I also know that I will not be able to buy a cup of coffee on Sloane Street at 7.50 a.m. I am cold and tired and I have a heavy valise and I *am* expected. You will let me in and you will let me sit down until somebody in authority arrives. And you will call that somebody so they do arrive within the next twenty minutes *pronto*!'

'I can't – ' begins the man, but Tom, suddenly rejecting a lifetime's passivity, leaps up the last step and sticks his foot and his suitcase in the door jamb.

'You will do what I say,' he hisses, 'and you will do it now, or I, Tom Klaus, labour lawyer to this corporation, will make sure you are kicked out on your ass before lunch – got that?'

'All right. Steady on. All right.' The man backs nervously away and Tom steps forward into a small vestibule with glass doors revealing the main entrance hall.

'You just wait 'ere, mate.'

The guard retreats through the doors rapidly, locking them behind him. Now at least in relative warmth, Tom sits on his case and watches the man pick up a phone on the reception desk and punch in a number. They regard each other eye to eye through the doors, and gradually the expression on the face of the guard changes from one of puzzled outrage to wounded innocence. Eventually he crosses back and unlocks his glazed barricade.

'I can't get anyone to come any faster, sir.' Well, at least the 'mate' has been dropped, and he's ushering Tom in. 'They must all be on their way in by now, but I have got hold of Mrs Dalrymple, she's the office manager, and she seems to know something – so if you'll come this way . . .'

And Tom at last finds himself in a conference room at the back of the building overlooking a garden. No coffee of course – that would be asking too much (?) – but at least some chairs. Feeling totally shattered, he sits down and rests his head against the long oval table. In a moment he's asleep.

8

Fliss has been whirling around maniacally since dawn, but still she seems caught in this endless marathon of preparation.

April had kept to her bartering bargain and turned up on Friday to 'muck them out'. There was just one tricky moment, when she'd first eyed their elderly vacuum cleaner.

'Wher*ever* has that been?' she said. 'Down the bottom of the sea?' and she'd gone home to fetch her own very new version. 'I like a nice AquaVac,' she said as she roared off round the hall with it, 'They've got a good strong suck.'

In theory at least, the children were also prepared to help, but it turned out they weren't all that useful. The girls, both swamped in Mocks revision – 'A' levels for Emma, 'O's for Daisy – seemed paralysed by exam-panic gloom, so all they did was straighten things into piles – the wrong piles – and declared their bedrooms No Go Zones. Henry started off quite happily on Saturday morning with his task of weeding and sweeping the bridge and front courtyard, but the novelty soon wore off and his attention was drawn to more interesting happenings in the moat. The first mating activities of the year by the Muscovies were just getting under way and Fliss found him sitting on a ledge under the bridge observing three drakes trying to rape the smallest and most seductive of the ducks, while absent-mindedly he tried to fish water beetles out of the algae with a jam jar. So far not so good.

Ivor had managed to get a minimum order of oil, two hundred litres, delivered on Friday after a couple of anxious days phoning around. The delivery was followed by a frozen session in the cellar while he tried to get the boiler going. A vast monster of a thing, perhaps one of the earliest of its kind, it sits wreathed in rusty pipes and topped by a fat, snake-like flue which thrusts its way up through the ceiling and out via the scullery. Installed long before the word 'electronic' entered the dictionary, it needs, initially, manual ignition of its pilot light, its linking to the timing mechanism having gone awry. Once started, there's always a delay of about ten minutes anyway, even when in full working order, as a series of clicks and hums throbs through its immense body, ending in the satisfying roar of lift-off. This time it kept going through its usual repertoire of noises, but then fizzled to a halt and remained stone cold. Eventually Ivor said he'd have to strip it down and take a look.

For the next two hours, the kitchen table was covered with bits of boiler waiting to be washed, filed, blown full of air or hit with a hammer, and much of April's earlier efforts seemed to be unravelling in front of Fliss's eyes. At last, however, Ivor came up from the cellar, covered in soot, and announced, 'There she blows!' They both rushed down again to have a look. The comforting roar of the burners was the sweetest music. They hung around to see if the timer might actually click into operation, but it looked as if they'd just have to keep the heat on consistently until their visitor left.

The weekend felt very strange while the heat gradually permeated the house, releasing odd odours and slight stickinesses as the damp within furniture and textiles came slowly to the surface. Martita, who when indoors (but not in her own warm bedroom) usually wore a padded waistcoat over a sweater over a shirt and thermals, plus the obligatory leggings, began to strip off in public, with a tremendous exaggerated show of huffing – fanning herself with a newspaper and mopping her forehead.

'I'm getting my hot flushes again,' she gasped. 'I feel I'm going through my matriculation all over again.'

'You mean your menopause, Titty,' said Daisy, who was in the thick of biology revision.

'I know what I mean and I know what I'm not. And it's *hot*,' said Martita. 'For heaven's sake, somebody open a window.' She scuttled off down the corridor, leaving a trail of woollies behind her.

Fliss and Ivor have tried very hard to involve Martita in their visitor's arrival. Repeatedly they explain its importance and implications, but relentlessly she remains totally impervious to any notion of their *joint* rescue from destitution. Any problem, if it exists at all, is to her mind definitely *theirs*, and will remain so. If she is going to be consistently obstructive, it would be much better if she were out of the way entirely, but as this is, of course, impossible, some sort of damage limitation seems to be the best possible approach.

'Just don't worry about any of it, Titty,' said Fliss, having the first go, on the Sunday evening. 'Just leave it all to us.'

'So I should hope,' Titty answered. 'I am not party to

your sordid little schemes. And I'm sure *he* won't be once he knows the conditions.'

'Could you just not talk to him about any of it, Mother,' said Ivor. 'Please – it's all quite complicated enough as it is and the more it's left to the professionals, the better.'

'And *they*, I expect, are being paid an arm and a leg,' she humphed.

'Please, Mother. Let's just play it by ear and see what happens.'

'You needn't be involved at all, you know, Titty,' added Fliss soothingly. 'You can just stay in your room with your television and the Boysies and we'll bring your meals up to you if you like – then you needn't be fussed with it.'

But Titty, who could sniff a rat at fifty paces, just turned to Fliss and tossed back her hair. Oh-oh, help, thought Fliss – got it wrong again.

'May I remind you,' said Titty, 'that *I* am the mistress of this house and am hardly likely, in the eventide of a very long life, to forget myself so far as to ignore the dictates of good manners and the laws of hospitality. I have given many parties in this house, as you very well know – many, *many* parties – and I'm hardly likely to throw a wobbly on the arrival of a solitary American visitor. On the contrary, I shall be at the head of the table for all meals and expect the traditions of the Hall to be maintained.'

'Yes, all right, Mother,' said Ivor, nervously catching sight of Fliss's flaring nostrils.

'I mean it. If you're going to do a thing, for heaven's sake do it with VERVE.'

So Fliss continued tidying and rearranging – doing her best to let things air and irritatedly making witty little flower arrangements using what was left of last year's dried stock, plus any other bits she could glean from the barren garden. Ivor dragged several great basketsful of logs over the bridge from the barns, but that and the boiler-mending were more or less the sum total of his specific involvement in the enterprise. Imminent lambing still seemed just possible, so he had to go and put together various hurdles to make up the pens, and generally get himself ready.

On Monday morning, Barney brought over his large red Volvo estate and left it with Fliss. He handed over the keys with pained reluctance.

'Don't you dare go and prang it or I shall personally have you hanged, drawn and quartered,' he said. 'You're on my insurance but that won't be any comfort to me if it lands up in the garage for weeks having its wings resprayed or something. I *can't* do without it. This is an absolute exception – I'm breaking the habit of a lifetime – never lend money or cars, both are recipes for disaster, and I can't believe I'm doing it, I really can't.'

Ivor was due to drive Barney up to Bury to collect the hire car so that he could head off north to Harrogate. Once seated in the front of one of the Peugeots, multicoloured with a green door in a mostly cream body – Barney seemed strangely small and forlorn. He looked back longingly at his own shiny vehicle as they creaked over the bridge and suddenly wound down the window to call, 'Make sure your journey is *necessary*!'

Once they'd disappeared, Fliss got gingerly into the Volvo and had a few practice runs up and down the drive. Barney hadn't mentioned it was an automatic, so she kept going to change gear and pressing the brake pedal in mistake for the non-existent clutch. Neither had he mentioned power-steering, for which she was now wildly over-compensating, nor power brakes, which in their unaccustomed ferocity had her almost tipping off the bridge on her second return. Feeling rather sick, she parked in the front court and examined the luxurious black-leather interior. There was a cassette player, which they'd never had in any of their cars, and a collection of tapes. Barney's taste turned out to be Italian opera, mostly Puccini, Aretha Franklin and Edmundo Ross. The latter tape was already in the player when she tentatively switched it on and 'Brazilian Love Call' came blaring through the quadraphonic speakers.

The rest of the day and far into the night, Fliss concentrated on food. She'd been poring over Jocasta Innes's *Pauper's Cookbook*, long her bible, but shifted her scrutiny from the bit called 'Padding' to the section marked 'Fancy Work'. She toyed with Constance Spry and Elizabeth David, but at this time of year anything the least smart was out of season and hideously expensive. The increased overdraft was now straining at its seams and it was very unlikely that the UM would relent again, so somehow she'd just have to do something interesting without resorting to exotic ingredients. She found herself longing for a book entitled *One Hundred and Twenty-two Useful and Exciting Things to do with Jerusalem Artichokes*, and even without it she found herself planning to incorporate them into everything, almost obsessively – despite their wind-making properties. She'd have put them in a pudding if she could've worked out a way to do it.

She got a basic sort of cassoulet going in the bottom oven of the Véronique, did several Alsatian Onion Tarts which could sit in the fridge, and took from the freezer the last remaining leg of lamb from one of their own sheep. Unfortunately, the ewe had been secretly christened Janice by Henry, before anyone could stop him, and never tasted quite right somehow – whatever the cut, the meat always seemed a bit stringy, as if she were reproaching them from beyond the grave. Still, it was, in theory at least, a delicacy – English lamb, organically raised, and would simply have to do.

And now, all too hideously soon, it is the dreaded Tuesday morning.

Long before the rest of the house is even beginning to stir (or so she thinks), she is racing around, stuffing yet more things into cupboards, slamming doors against the chaos, gathering the danker towels in the bathroom; laying out clean ones in the stranger's bedroom, together with some books, the local weekly newspaper and a carafe of water. She stands examining the finished effect, trying to view it with objective eyes. It isn't really all that bad – it has at least a certain character: what it lacks in terms of comfort, it makes up for in, well . . . interest . . . if you like. Although whether it will do for a man who must surely be wedded to the concept of an en suite power shower at the very least, she really cannot guess.

While she is standing there, Martita comes sidling up behind her, clutching all four Boysies to her bosom. She ducks under Fliss's elbow to get a better view.

'We always offer Malvern water to visitors – sealed.'

'We don't have any Malvern water.'

'It isn't done to offer a carafe – one never knows where it's been. We've always offered Malvern water at the Hall, as you perfectly well know. We always did in Harry's day.'

'But, Titty, this isn't Harry's day, is it? And Malvern water must cost about 50p a bottle.'

'What books have you left him?'

'I thought it would be nice to have some things about Suffolk, so there's a Pevsner, *Suffolk Summer* and *Akenfield* – and then I thought some humour, so there's a *Private Eye* book and some P. G. Wodehouse.'

'It ought to be *The Saturday Book* and the Bible.'

'I'm certainly not leaving the Bible.'

Martita buries her nose in the Boysies' topknots and puffs out a little sigh. 'One would have hoped – but you never listen . . .' She lets it drop but seems to be lingering.

Fliss decides to have one more go. 'Are you sure I can't persuade you about your bathroom? It's only for such a short time, and it would be so much nicer for him.'

'But so much nastier for *me*,' says Martita – this time she skips.

Then there is deciding what to wear – tricky. Her virtually unvarying daily winter clothing consists of jeans, sweaters and a Puffa. She has almost no pretension left where clothing is concerned, any attempt to be 'in fashion' being patently absurd, in terms of both her bank balance and her daily needs. In relation to any attraction she may still hold for Ivor, she thinks he actually prefers her daily working garb, it being a cosy, undemanding echo of his own very worn tweedy/denimy/leather-patched corduroy look, into which he fell after leaving London.

She hardly ever goes to London any more, and when she does her voluminous Jaeger camel-hair coat covers a multitude of sins and is so very ancient as to have superseded the mere realms of fashion and gone on to the giddy heights of classicism. Well, she can wear The Coat today, but there still remains the awkwardness of what to put under it. The girls manage to dress quite stylishly by means of swaps, market stalls and Oxfam shops, but even though she and Emma are more or less the same size, she doesn't kid herself – knows that a woman her age can't often get away with the eclectic jumble-sale look. It smacks too much of mutton dressed as bag lady.

It feels quite odd to try things on during the winter in a room warm enough to be able to take one's time. Usually it's so icy in their bedroom that she leaps straight into whatever is reasonably clean and to hand. Now though, quite luxuriously, she stands in front of the long cheval glass testing out different outfits for quite half an hour. They all seem deeply unsatisfactory. Awful shades of 1978ish visions stare back at her – hems the wrong length, skirts the wrong cut, blouses with the wrong collars. Fashion is so peculiar. How can there be a right and wrong about something so very elusive and transitory? Instinctively she rebels at the notion and yet still feels the nagging discomfort of failing the test.

In the end she settles for anything she can muster which might be classical and therefore, she hopes, timeless: a long, full denim skirt, a white silk blouse bought in the palmier days of 1968 and a Fair Isle sweater, all under a Harris tweed jacket from their time in London – all this, plus pearls for heaven's sake (false – need one ask) at throat and ears. When she comes downstairs, Ivor, who has dashed in from the morning livestock rounds to grab a coffee, says almost with admiration, 'Oh – you've got *legs*.'

She pulls up the skirt to thigh-height and looks down at her fifteen-deniered calves. 'Who'd have thought it? They were there – all the time.'

'Umm,' laughs Ivor. 'Jolly nice too – yum, yum.'

9

On the 11.15 train from Liverpool Street, Tom Klaus has to keep biting the end of his thumb to stop himself falling asleep. If he weren't feeling so shattered, he might have been more interested in observing the scene outside – the change from shabby urban outskirts to little back gardens to open countryside – oddly devoid of trees to his eyes, coming from the arbour of Westchester. It's odd too that the landscape, although so open, has a . . . well, what would you call it – kind of a *dinky* aspect – yeah, dinky that's it – the horizon surely much closer than at home.

It is a grey morning and puffs of fog lie on the frost-tinged fields, but inside this train it is stiflingly hot. He seems to be the only passenger to notice. The other travellers are all buried in newspapers: 'Britain Could Keep Missiles in Soviet Deal' yells a headline. Typical Brit – still sees itself as the centre of the globe – as if it mattered – as if anybody out there in the big wide real world would give a damn.

The heat and exhaustion keep getting to him and his eyelids droop. The only solid piece of information he knows about this trip is that the train goes on to somewhere called Thorpe-le-something-or-other and he must be careful not to miss his stop. Liverpool Street Station had been chaotic – it's in the middle of being rebuilt, a grumpy official told him: there were scaffolding, drips and puddles everywhere and people looked strained and angry. Thanks, Mr Z – thanks a lot, thinks Tom bitterly as his head nods on to his chest.

A midweek, lunchtime train doesn't bring a huge crowd to Colchester, unlike the daily outpourings of the rush hour, so Fliss reckons she'll be able to pick out Mr Klaus without too much trouble. A Mrs Dalrymple telephoned from London to say he'd be arriving at 12.10, and she gives herself plenty of time to get to the station, knowing that for once her usual last-minute-gasp sort of effort simply won't do.

In any case, she still doesn't feel at home in Barney's glossy, powerful car and drives rather slowly, concentrating hard to stop her foot searching for that non-existent clutch. All the way down the A134, Edmundo Ross blasts away his Latin rhythms. She can't get the tape out of the machine and neither can she now turn it off, whatever she pushes or twiddles. It doesn't have nice simple knobs like she's used to, but glows with liquid crystal display numbers and touch pads. The tape goes round and round, so that when it gets to the end, she has to hear Edmundo gaily trilling about hearing the little bird that is singing in the treetops all over again.

As it turns out, Mr Klaus is dazzlingly simple to pick out, for only an American could be so perfectly dressed as a parody Englishman. He looks rather like someone from a fifties edition of *The Illustrated London News* advertising Armstrong Siddeley cars or Du Maurier cigarettes, except the drawings of those men were always artificially elongated and Mr Klaus is quite short and square. In his glitteringly clean Burberry and matching chequered scarf (Fliss didn't know that anybody actually wore these things in real life – they'd always seemed to her a species of fancy dress), he comes out of the station entrance, blinking behind round, pale-tortoiseshell glasses, looking anxious and disoriented – wheeling behind him an impossibly shiny burgundy-leather suitcase.

Fliss, who has been feeling increasingly sick with nervous apprehension, suddenly realizes that perhaps he feels pretty ghastly too, and the thought, the possibility of such empathy, cheers her. She sticks a broad smile on her face and rushes over to greet him.

Well, she's pretty much what he would have expected. A tallish, thinish woman with greyish hair, rather untidily caught back in a Belle Epoque kind of a bun thing, with little side curls escaping round her ears and down the back of her neck from behind an Alice band. It's kind of a pretty face in a worn sort of way – pale skin finely lined around her eyes, quite a lot of mascara, but not much else in the way of make-up. Judging by the hair colour and the beginnings of bags under her eyes, she'd be somewhere in her mid-forties, he'd guess – maybe more. Hard to tell, for no woman he knows back home in Westchester would ever let herself go like this. Very gracious, slightly nervous and self-deprecating – in short, Very English.

She's seized his case and is already trying to put it in the back of the Volvo station wagon before he can stop her. He's feeling pretty weird – the damp cold coming on top of the stifling heat of the train, the lack of sleep, the change of environment all adding up to a sensation of unreality, as if he definitely isn't here yet and is observing all this through some cosmic viewfinder. However, seeing her struggle with his valise, he manages to click himself on and hurries round to help her. There is a tow-hitch on the back of the station wagon and she bangs her leg on it, catching her stocking (or pantyhose? He can't really guess), and a ladder streaks up her leg.

'Fuck,' she seems to say, then catches her breath and his eye at the same time and laughs.

He feels absurdly shocked. She *can't* have said it. He must've imagined it. He shakes his head as he goes to the front of the car, trying to pull himself into reality, then notices he's on the wrong side from force of habit and is waiting to be let into the driver's seat. She laughs again and bites her lip as she leads him round to the other side and practically tucks him in like a baby, making exaggerated efforts to stop his raincoat trailing on the ground.

Once in the car, she smiles at him broadly and says, inexplicably, 'Home, James, and don't spare the horses!' She turns on the ignition, and immediately the car is filled with blaring South American music – maracas throbbing at full volume. 'So sorry,' she shouts. 'Little problem with the machine – can't seem to get it to shut up.'

For a few minutes, he makes no effort to help, but conversation is completely impossible as a voice keeps wailing, 'Cry my Brazilian love song!'

'Mind if I try your eject button?' he yells.

'Please,' she yells back, and then, 'Oh, *that's* where it is', once he's done.

As the cassette comes sliding out, they are left in complete silence, apart from the hum of the engine – it's kind of embarrassing. She seems to be an anxious sort of driver, sitting forward, slightly hunched over the wheel and slowing down with exaggerated care around corners. Strange. At last, fortunately, the silence seems to get to her and she goes for the obvious.

'This is your first visit to England, Mr Klaus?'

'Oh, no – I've been here several times.'

'Oh?' She sounds ludicrously surprised.

'My parents usually took a trip to Europe every three years or so and I'd often come along. London was always on the itinerary. We'd usually stop at the Connaught before heading over to Paris, and my mother would shop like crazy. Jermyn Street was like her own backyard.'

'The Connaught – oh dear.' She's looking paler and more nervous than ever – and had she really said 'Oh dear', and if so, why, what's wrong with the Connaught? And had she *actually* said that other thing?

'Excuse me?'

'Nothing.' She gives a little giggle. 'So you know England quite well then?'

'Oh, I wouldn't say that – only London – and most of that only within a stone's throw of Fortnum and Mason – or the Embassy, whichever way you want to look at it. We'd always take in a lot of theatre, eat at Simpsons in the Strand – my father was always crazy about their roast beef, cut so thin you could read the newspaper through it. Only I'll tell you something, when I was little I'd take along a newspaper and I never could. Read anything, that is. But my father believed it – he'd seen it in *Time* magazine or somewhere and never gave up.'

'So you haven't been out to the country before then?'

'Not unless you count Bath and Stratford-on-Avon – oh, and Oxford of course. We went there when I was a kid and I took my wife there again a few years ago.'

'We're closer to Cambridge.'

'Are you? Well, that kind of interests me – being kind of associated with the other Cambridge.'

'Yes?' She doesn't seem to get it.

'Cambridge. Massachusetts. *College.*'

'Oh. Right.' She'd got it now. 'Well, perhaps we'll have to take you to our Cambridge – if there's time, I mean – you know – depending . . .' She lets the words trail off.

'That would be just lovely.'

'We're in Suffolk now. We've just crossed over the border from Essex. It has a reputation for being rather flat and dull. But it isn't at all – it's quite hilly really, if you know where you're going – and a bit mysterious. Very pretty.'

'Really. Right.' He's taking in the surrounding landscape. It still looks a bit dinky to him – and dull and cold. 'Well, I'm looking forward to making its acquaintance,' he says with absolutely no conviction at all.

As they turn into the long driveway, however, his interest begins to be a little aroused. She's talking all the time now – describing this avenue of trees, the one that's fallen over, the age of the house, this moat, this bridge. It's a bit like a picture out of *Little Lord Fauntleroy* or Kate Greenaway or something. He *knows*, for Pete's sake. His mother used to read him all those books too – those books about little old, olde, Olde Englande – which always made him feel kind of nauseous. This house is all twisted chimney stacks, gingerbread woodwork and sort of plaster figures over the windows. OK so it's old. OK.

Still, he knows how to behave – knows how to be gracious, so, 'This is great,' he says. 'Charming.'

'Oh, it's just – you know – home.' She gives him rather a watery smile, he feels – but then, instead of jumping out of the car, just sits there for a moment, fiddling with the

97

transmission, pushing the lever from Drive to Park to Neutral, then back to Park, before anxiously examining the dashboard.

'Everything OK?' he asks.

'Oh, yes. Of course. I was just checking.' She opens the door, then, oddly, closes it again, still staring at the dashboard, which had been blinking a red light at her.

'I wish it wouldn't,' she says.

'Excuse me?'

'It's like having an angry Swedish nanny – it will keep looking after one.'

Gingerly, she removes the keys and the light stops flashing. Then she practically throws herself out of the seat as if trying to effect an escape. Behind her, the big front door of the house has swung open and a tiny woman is standing there, beaming down at them from the top step and holding an armful of what look like rats.

'Welcome to Little Watling Hall,' she calls.

Fliss is stunned. Titty had looked her usual self this morning, when they'd been examining the rearranged Chinese Room, and had then disappeared into her own room behind a slammed door. Fliss thought she'd gone to sulk. But instead she must have headed for the hair dye, for she is now newly retinted a vivid shade of metallic bronze, and is dressed in a flouncy floral two-piece of skirt and bolero over Paisley-printed tights.

'How lovely to see you,' she now trills. 'You're just in time for luncheon.'

Fliss has to shake herself into action. This wasn't their plan at all. Ivor was supposed to be here, full of masculine bonhomie and suitable conversation, to see to the initial awkwardness of unloading the car and generally putting their guest at ease. Instead of which there is only Martita dressed up as a Christmas cracker with this eerie smile on her face. Mr Klaus has quickly unloaded his case himself and is waiting at the bottom of the steps, smiling warmly up at Titty. Goodwill is so far oozing out all over.

'Oh – they're little *dogs*,' he says, rather disconcertingly, as he enters the hall.

'Titty, may I introduce Mr Klaus – my mother-in-law, Mrs Harley-Wright.'

'Delighted to meet you,' says Mr Klaus warmly, holding out his hand.

Now in fairness to Titty, she hasn't a hand available to proffer back, but then neither does she make any apology or indication of her problem – merely smiles with head tip-tilted in her winsome attitude.

'Do come and have a sherry,' she says, again in an unnaturally high, trilling tone.

Mr Klaus is left with his hand suspended – and Fliss has to stop herself rushing to shake it for him, to complete the action. Martita is already scuttling down the corridor and as there seems no alternative but to follow, Fliss shepherds Mr Klaus along behind the twinkling Paisley legs.

The drawing room, which hasn't really been used since New Year's Day, isn't looking too bad at all, if you don't examine it too closely. Fliss has gathered up from all over the house any large pieces of material which could in the least way do as 'throws' – and has then thrown them about with abandon. The overall effect is quite colourful and fun, if more akin to a Moroccan souk than a place of elegant repose. There's a log fire in the grate, though it's apparent no one has fed it since she left for the station, as it's burning very low. Ivor had been under strict instructions to look after it – so where the hell is he?

There's still a faintly peculiar odour hanging around, mostly, she thinks, the ongoing result of damp giving way to unaccustomed warmth. She goes to dole out the Amontillados, Martita having placed herself in front of the fire, still cradling all the Boysies in her arms.

'My husband should have been here to meet you, Mr Klaus,' Fliss says, handing him a sherry. 'I really can't think what's happened to him.'

'Something mechanical,' says Martita darkly.

'What?'

'Out at the back.'

'Oh,' says Fliss, thinking, Oh shit. 'If you'll excuse me, I'll just go and find out. Lunch won't be long – you must be starving,' and there seems nothing for it but to leave Mr Klaus to the doubtful mercies of Martita.

There is no sign of Ivor in the kitchen, nor has anything extra been done to the lunch apart from the preparations she's already made. For supposed simplicity at this first meal, she's planned, despite the bitter weather, a salad lunch so that it could mostly be prepared in advance. In fact of course it had taken ages to wash, chop, dress and organize everything, and then she'd felt she had to make a hot potato salad and celeriac rémoulade to add substance, so in the end it had proved both labour-intensive and quite expensive. Still, at least it was more or less done and now she slings one of the onion tarts in the oven, before rushing out to find Ivor.

It doesn't take long. She can spot his legs immediately, on the other side of the yard, sticking out from under the multicoloured car. She rushes across.

'What? *What* are you doing?' she manages to squeak, her throat constricted by rage.

'Um?' Ivor's voice comes out muffled from under the car.

'Get out!' she hisses.

'What?'

'Out. Now.'

He slides out, still flat on his back, lying on his own home-made mechanic's trolley, like a giant skateboard. He is wearing his green overalls, is covered with oil and lies there blinking up at her for a moment.

'You were quick. I wasn't expecting you back so soon,' he says mildly.

'What do you mean I was quick? Of course I was quick. You knew I was meeting the 12.10.'

'It just seems quicker somehow. What's the time?'

'*What* are you doing?'

'The exhaust fell off.'

'Oh, God. What are you doing with it?'

'Trying to bolt it back on – but I think it's a welding job.'

'But not now.'

'I couldn't just leave it.'

'But you can now. Leave it?'

'I shouldn't – not with no exhaust at all. The row was unbelievable – Le Mans wasn't in it. Anyway, it's illegal.'

'But he's *here*. Now.'

'I know,' said with infuriating calm. 'I'll be with you soon.'

'But I need you *now*.'

'It won't take me long.'

'He's in there right NOW – this very minute – with your mother.'

'Alone?'

'Well, of course alone.'

'You shouldn't have done that.'

'Of course I shouldn't have done that,' she squeaks. 'I'm not stupid.' She gives an almighty kick to the nearest hubcap.

'Steady on.'

'I mean – hell's bells – bloody buggeration – you were supposed to be there, ready to greet him – keep the conversation flowing – keep the bloody fire going, for goodness' sake.'

'I put masses of logs on earlier.'

'It's nearly out now.'

'And Mother wasn't around. I tried to have a word with her but she'd locked her door.'

'Well, she's come out now – all dressed up. She's wearing a skirt – and she's being nice – it's very peculiar.'

'You'd better get back. Goodness only knows what she's telling him.'

'Are you coming?'

'As soon as I've done this.'

'I mean *before* you've done this. I *mean* it, Ivor – NOW.'

She scoots back into the house and almost throws the various salads, mustards and chutneys along the table in the dining room. April had a lot of mucking out to do here as, being the least damp of the least used rooms on the ground floor, they had commandeered it as the dried-flower store since Christmas. Even now, odd bits of hop bine and clematis seed-head are lurking in corners, having resisted April's mighty wielding of the AquaVac. Fliss then runs to check on the progress of the onion tart, but the Véronique is having a sulk and the pastry is barely warm yet, so she dashes back to the drawing room, slowing and calming herself before entering, just in time to hear Martita saying, 'That Harley-Wright was of course the right-hand man of the Duke of Marlborough. He couldn't have managed without him at Malplaquet – or was it Oudenarde? He was his *sine qua non*, you know.'

'Really?' Mr Klaus has sunk on to the sofa. He looks a little dazed, as if his eyes aren't properly focused, and is smiling and nodding. Martita is still standing in front of the dying fire, but the Boysies are now lying in a little pile, asleep on her feet.

'Of course I always wondered if he wasn't a bit of an enoch,' Martita continues, tapping the side of her nose.

'Really?' says Mr Klaus again, now clearly on auto-pilot.

'No children, you see – and there *was* a wife – who *did* produce once he was dead and gone – on the other side of the blanket, so to speak – so it always makes one wonder, doesn't it?'

'Really?'

'But of course if he *was* an enoch, that would explain it all, wouldn't it?'

'I guess so.'

'So sorry about that – slight domestic hiccup,' says Fliss, squeezing past Titty to the log basket. 'Lunch is nearly ready – and my husband will be joining us shortly.' She starts piling logs back on the embers. 'I could hear you telling Mr Klaus a bit of history, Titty.'

'What?'

'Something about a Harley-Wright? Accurate, was it?'

'Umm?'

'FAMILY HISTORY,' shouts Fliss. 'Whose? I didn't recognize it.'

'It's high time we ate,' says Martita. 'This is what I call

an unconscionable delay. My innards are rumbling like an old warthog. I saw one in a documentary the other night – sounded exactly like this.'

Mr Klaus suddenly gets up from the sofa and puts his glass down with a thump. He seems to be swaying slightly. He can't possibly be tipsy, can he, on one glass of Amontillado?

'Could I be shown to the bathroom?'

'The poor man needs a pee,' says Martita loudly to Fliss. 'You should have thought of that. He's come a very long way.'

'Do follow me, Mr Klaus,' says Fliss, her skull prickling with irritation – and she leads him out.

10

Tom stands in front of the most ancient john he's ever seen. It's like something out of an early Sears Roebuck catalogue and is decorated with a picture of King Neptune riding across the bowl on a dolphin, brandishing a trident. It peeps up at him from below the rim. In an effort to get his eyes focusing properly, he stares hard at it and then tries to aim his pee directly at the monarch's head. He can't ever remember feeling so tired and dysfunctional. This just isn't like him at all. Something has gotten into him and given him the sensation of having been filleted. He senses himself as kind of soft and boneless and his eyelids feel as if they've been packed with ball bearings. If only he could get some sleep, surely he'd start to feel better. Or maybe he's coming down with a virus. He feels his forehead – he doesn't think he has a fever, but he sure as hell is clammy.

Having pulled the chain and watched the great swoosh of water come down from the overhead tank – and he's certainly never used one of *these* before – he goes to look for the bathroom Mrs Harley-Wright had pointed out to him when she brought him up here. It's at the other end of the corridor and he heads off down there to wash his hands. He lets the faucet run and holds his face under the flow of water, standing up as he dries himself off to examine his image in the mirror. Oh God, Oh God – I look terrible, he groans – I look just like I feel. He shakes his head and arms to try to get some life and energy back into them, and returns to the corridor, just as a janitor handyman kind of guy in overalls comes up the last flight of stairs on to the landing, bumping his magnificent Loewe's valise behind him.

'Careful there,' Tom calls out, unable to stop himself. 'Whoa there – That's kind of like *my* Crown Jewels.' He hopes his tone is light and bantering.

'Is it really?' says the janitor, not pausing, but carrying straight back down the corridor. 'How very interesting. If you follow me I'll show you to your room.'

The valise receives further punishment being banged along the floor, until the door back nearer the john is flung open. Tom is feeling in his jacket pocket for a tip and wondering if a pound coin will do, when the janitor bangs down the case for the last time and holds out his hand in a shaking, rather than a gimme gesture. It's not a particularly clean hand.

'Ivor Harley-Wright – delighted to meet you. Lunch is on the table when you're ready.'

By the time Tom has made his way down to the dining room, the man in question is sitting at the table in crushed corduroys and a khaki kind of sweater – that's more like it. Professor Higgins on a bad day. Tom feels on much safer ground now. He sends up a silent prayer that some instinct had stopped him, in the nick of time, from tipping his host. But Honest-to-God-Almighty, why invent this breed of patricians who wander around in greasy overalls when they should be in tailored grey worsted – confusing a guy, when he's already got enough confusion to be going on with?

At the head of the table, the little old woman is sitting in a large carver chair with the tiny dogs tucked in on either side. She has become entirely silent in the presence of the other two, and munches steadily and with considerable concentration through what turns out to be rather a good lunch, complete with a huge bowl of potato salad which would feel perfectly at home in a Seventh Avenue deli.

The atmosphere, however, is awkward and the conversation seems to bump clumsily from one topic to another, leaving gaping silences in which chewing and the clattering of serving utensils jar. Tom feels they are all circling each other warily, bursting with mutual curiosity, but uncertain of how to get started – what cards to put into play. For him this should be just like any other negotiation he's ever been involved with, except that currently he's got no clear parameters; he's on entirely alien territory and he's searching after something about which he is totally ignorant.

Inevitably they start with the weather. What is it with Brits that they go on and on about the goddamn weather? The whole world has weather and in winter it's usually cold – so what? They have plenty of weather back in Westchester but they don't base a daily thesis on it. But no, wouldn't you know it – the younger Mrs Harley-Wright – she it is who is going on now about the cold and damp.

'I wonder what it's going to do,' she is saying, as if it has the benefit of conscious free will. 'It seemed a bit more perky earlier last week – in fact it was almost warm for a bit – but it's been awful these last few days – pouring rain and bitter – ' And on and on, the weather given a personality with all attendant hopes and fears.

Then they get on to the subject of his journey – don't seem outraged enough about the smoked mackerel incident, but are horrified he had his talcum powder searched – which somehow manages to side-track them back on to the weather. Mr H-W murmurs anxieties about expected snow and how lucky he, Tom, is that it hasn't started as forecast and how they hope it won't interfere with his trip. Who do they think they're kidding? Interfere – in the life of a man who regularly skis Killington and Telluride? Then they get on to his home.

'You live in New York?'

'Usually. Actually I'm between apartments at this point in time, so I'm living out of the city near a place called Pound Ridge.'

'What a lovely name,' the younger Mrs H-W says.

He'd never given it a thought as it happens – it's just always been there, a name.

'Is it in the mountains?' she asks.

'Certainly not.' He laughs. 'It's not that far out of the city – upstate. Not that far from the gentleman I'm representing.'

'Oh. Isn't it?' The younger Mrs H-W's voice has gone kind of strangulated – as if the words might break.

'We've only met Denmans' London agents so far,' Mr H-W butts in, 'and they wouldn't say anything so we – er – we don't know anything about your – I mean, you know – the gentleman you're representing.'

Well, they're sweating – it seems he's really got them on the rack. Impassively he turns the screw. 'Discretion is advisable in these kind of dealings. My client is very protective of his privacy.'

'Of course,'

'With reason.'

'Really?'

'There are some weird people out there. I don't know what it's like here, but in our country you've got to keep yourself protected – and my client is a man of – well, I guess it's no secret – considerable wealth. Apart from anything else, he hates to have his private business get in the newspapers and those guys are just animals – they'll do anything to fill a column.'

'Would we have heard of him?'

'I doubt it.' This is obviously the moment to identify Mr Z but Tom hangs fire. Let them sweat. He'd bet anything they don't have the nerve to ask him outright. 'Of course,' he continues, 'he's on the board of several charitable institutions, so he gets media coverage that way – you know, major museums, opera – '

'So he's very interested in things aesthetic – so to speak?' Mr H-W looks ridiculously hopeful.

'Oh, he's into Art in a very big way. A very big way indeed.'

'Oh, good.'

'But it has to be the best.'

'Ah.'

'Only the best.'

'I see . . .'

Mr H-W seems to sink back a little in his chair and Tom, who likes to see himself as pretty acute where body language is concerned, takes note. This game is having a desired effect – it's waking him up. There's nothing like his habitual role of predator in a game of cat and mouse to energize him, and he can feel the overwhelming pall of exhaustion sliding off his shoulders. He takes a large swig of the not very delectable wine they've poured – although he doesn't usually drink at lunchtime. Like most young men of his New York crowd, he's a strictly Evian man before 6 p.m. and shudders at the habits of his father's generation, for whom the three-dry-Martini lunch was a staple prop of good business. Brits, however, he's noticed, seem to drink all the time – no wonder they've let things slide.

Now maybe this is the moment for strike one – here we go – 'I'm looking forward of course to viewing *your* collection.'

'Well, yes.'

'After lunch?'

'Well – ' The younger Mrs H-W is sounding doubtful – 'it might be better to wait. You see, the thing is, our adviser isn't here today – he won't be back until tomorrow, I'm afraid.'

'Well, that's OK – we can still take a look, can't we? It's *your* collection – '

There's a sort of explosive noise from the older Mrs H-W, down at the end of the table.

'Are you all right, Mother?' says Mr H-W quickly. 'Not choking?'

The little woman flings her head back and somehow seems to stretch herself another six inches before saying with pompous emphasis, 'Certainly not.' She looks directly at Tom with her lips pressed tightly together and then another sound, a little 'humph', pops out, accompanied by a quick upward thrust of her chin. Somehow she is taking him into her confidence in a private communication – or maybe even assuming he's gotten there already. He decides to grasp the baton she's handed him and run with it.

'Your mother was telling me all about your family's association with the Duke of Marlborough,' he starts, delighted that he's remembered which darn duke it was – not too difficult in this case, because he'd immediately made a mental connection with the cigarettes and has this Harley-Wright ancestor down as the original Marlboro Man.

'Oh, she did, did she?' says Mr H-W. 'And which Duke of Marlborough was that exactly?' He is addressing his mother with a certain acidity.

'Hmmm?' The old woman smiles back a little vaguely.

'WHICH DUKE, MOTHER?' Mr H-W suddenly yells.

It is possibly the loudest sound made by the human voice which Tom has ever heard indoors, and it makes his head ring.

The little woman, however, seems to ignore the foghorn blast and turns smilingly towards Tom. 'What did you say?'

'I was talking about your ancestor,' says Tom, 'what you were telling me earlier about his relationship with the Duke?'

A look of clouded puzzlement has crossed her eyes and she leans towards him, saying sweetly, 'And how did you enjoy your ride in the big red Vulva?'

At least that's what it sounds like, but it can't be of course. He must have imagined it. It's the journey getting to him again, he supposes – and the booze – he *knows* he should never drink at lunch.

But now the younger Mrs H-W is half-rising from her seat, looking a little flushed. 'By all means,' she is saying, 'let's go and have a look right now.'

'What about coffee? We haven't had coffee,' says the old woman.

'Do you need coffee right now, Mr Klaus, or can you wait?' She has a look of something akin to desperation on her face.

Actually, at this moment, he would almost kill for a cup

of coffee, but what the heck – she obviously needs to be gotten off this particular hook – so he'll go with it.

'Just lead the way – and – ' yes, now seems to be the moment – 'call me "Tom", why don't you?'

She relaxes slightly into a half-smile. 'And we're Fliss and Ivor.' She turns towards the old woman as if seeking permission, and presumably gets it, for she adds, 'And Martita.'

'Oh, I see – it's from *Martita*.'

'Ummm?' says the old woman.

'The other name I heard – "Titty"?' Too right he'd heard it – *Titty*, for crying out loud.

'That's just to be familiar. My proper name's Martita.'

'Charming,' says Tom, for the moment prepared to ingratiate, 'and quite unusual – you don't hear of it often. Only Martita Hunt of course.'

'And *she* nicked it,' says this Martita fiercely.

'I don't think so,' says Ivor.

'I should know,' says this Martita sharply.

Fliss opens her mouth as if to say something to her, then, obviously thinking better of it, turns to Tom. 'Shall we go?'

11

Out in the hall, he expects her to lead him upstairs, or perhaps to the other wing on this floor. He knows from his reasonably thorough, if uninformed, study of the inventory, that the Collection isn't displayed in the rooms he's already seen. Instead she leads him out through the kitchen to a sort of mud room, full of coats, baskets, tennis racquets, umbrellas and all kinds of junk. She looks down at his immaculately clad feet and seems worried.

'I don't suppose you brought any boots with you?'

'Boots?' What kind of boots? Why would he need boots? For him, boots are either of the cowboy variety, to be worn with jeans at the weekend, or the sort of heavy, comfortable lace-up things he likes to wear up in Vermont at twenty below. Neither are what he would have considered bringing on a trip to civilized Olde Englande.

'Wellies?' she says.

'You've lost me.'

She holds up an example. It is olive drab with a flapping strap which doesn't seem to be fixed to anything.

'Oh, *rubber* boots. Gee, I don't think I've worn a pair of those since I got out of first grade. My mother used to try to make me wear galoshes – you know, one of those things that mothers do. She failed.' He laughs.

'We'll have to lend you a pair.' She starts rooting around in a dusty pile.

If there is one thing guaranteed to turn Tom's stomach, it is the thought of sharing footwear. The merest sniff of the idea gives him an attack of the creepy-crawlies, and he can clearly imagine these particular examples positively alive with fungal spores and the seeds of verrucas, fertile ground for the podiatrist's scalpel.

'Please don't bother,' he says.

'No, really – I think we must. What size are you?'

'Here? I don't know. Well, no – I guess I do – I'm an English nine – but really, please don't bother.'

She is upside-down now, tossing boots out on either side like a dog digging for a bone.

'I should have thought of this,' she is muttering. 'It just didn't occur. I tried to think of everything, but boots are so automatic with us that I just didn't . . . Ivor's will be much too big. Ah, what about these?'

She holds up a pair, black this time, shorter in the leg, with soles caked in dried earth. She squints down each in turn, gives them a shake and turns them upside down. An old Kleenex falls out of one, a pebble and a feather out of the other. Tom inwardly shudders.

'No – really – I'll be fine.'

'I won't hear of it. You'll see what it's like. At this time of year there's nothing we can do about the mud – when it's frozen solid it's all right, but we had pouring rain over the weekend.'

'No, I assure you I'll be fine.'

'Your shoes will be ruined. Here.' She shoves the boots into his hands, and to his discomforted amazement he finds himself removing his beautiful Lobbs and slipping his silk-socked feet into them. They feel cold, slightly damp and a bit gritty. His toes almost go into spasm with disgust.

She pulls on a pair of the green boots and starts zipping herself into a long oily-looking olive raincoat. An olive headscarf tied tightly under the chin finishes the rather unattractive effect of a kind of uniform. She certainly seems well enough camouflaged to join a private militia. She looks at him appraisingly. He has pulled on his Burberry, which was already hanging out here on a peg along with all the other coats (his beeootiful Burberry, normally coddled on a padded hanger).

'I hope you'll be warm enough,' she says.

'I'll be *fine*,' he nearly snaps. But Jeez, what's with these people? Let's just get on with it.

'I suppose so,' she says, but in a very unsatisfied tone.

'I really ought to get my copy of the catalogue,' he says. 'It's in my attaché case.'

'In your? – Oh, right.'

'Upstairs?'

She looks down at his caked boots. 'Why don't you leave it for now? Just come and have a general look. You can do it all properly tomorrow when Barney's here.'

They cross the back courtyard, go round to the front of the house and towards the bridge. She is talking – general touristy talk about the age of the house, but skimming along fast, not letting him slow down and take anything in. Just as they cross the bridge, they hear a heavy door slamming and, looking back, he sees Martita, now also swathed in an almost identical olive drab uniform.

'I'm coming,' she calls, as she whirls towards them with

surprising speed, the four tiny dogs yapping and leaping around her legs.

'Blast,' says Fliss. 'I thought we'd got away with it.'

For a moment, she makes as if to run – there's just a hint of a hunted rabbit about her. But no, she waits, and Martita joins them. Now panting quite heavily, she seems more frail than when moving and looks into Tom's eyes with touching sweetness.

'May I take your arm?'

'Please do.' He offers it and they set off down a wide track which swings round to the left in an arc, parallel with the side of the house and the moat, disappearing into the distance where the land seems to drop.

Fliss is striding purposefully in front, bristling with irritation and tension – not a relaxed presence to be with. She certainly wasn't exaggerating about the mud though. He's never seen mud like it except in the movies when they want to show quicksand. In places it's more stew than mud. In other bits it's deeply cratered with the footprints of horses and other less identifiable animals – and in others yet, there are big patches of broken bricks and cement scattered around to give a footing.

Tom's feet are slip-sliding in the boots, which are too big for him, and Martita is clinging to his arm in a helpless sort of way, which hadn't looked all that necessary when she was rushing across the courtyard a few moments ago. He has to concentrate hard just to remain upright. The boots are being sucked into the mud and threaten to come off with every step, and the tiny dogs have interwoven themselves between his legs and Martita's, threatening to bring them both down. Having ignored them for several minutes, Fliss now looks back and watches their struggle for a moment.

'I'm sorry about this – I tried to warn you. It was always going to be a problem coming here at this time of the year. Later on we can drive down of course – but at the moment it's strictly shanks's pony I'm afraid. I should have thought it through really . . . it's the only thing that didn't occur.'

'No problem,' he says, meaning just the opposite, for this has become the day of a journey through Hades, and Pound Ridge suddenly seems infinitely desirable but somewhere on another globe.

At the end of the bit of track which is visible from the house, the land drops away and at the bottom of a small valley he can see a group of black clapboard buildings with thatched roofs. It's slightly easier now, as the slope has provided better drainage and the going isn't so glutinous. The wind, however, is hitting the side of the valley viciously and seems to be heading directly through his chest like a razor blade. It's uncanny – the temperature can't be anything like as low as he's accustomed to back home, but he doesn't ever remember feeling quite so cold. He'd better watch it – if he isn't careful, he'll be sucked into British weathermania himself.

'I *am* so sorry about the wind,' says Fliss, right on cue, as if she is personally responsible. 'Local lore insists that it comes straight from the Urals – there isn't supposed to be any high ground between here and there to stop it – but I've looked on the atlas and I don't know I can really believe it.'

'It's a lazy wind,' says Martita. 'That's what they call it in Suffolk. "That don't bother to goo round ya bor' – that goo straight through ya",' she adds in a peculiar accent.

As they approach, Tom can see that the buildings surround on two sides an empty swimming pool. It's quite a big one – rectangular, with a semicircle pushed out at each end and steps leading down to what would have been the shallows. Over the deep end, an ancient, three-tiered diving board leans drunkenly. Instead of turquoise blue, the pool is coloured green – dense pea-green – and covered on all four sides and the bottom as well with faded paintings. As they get nearer, he can see that these are of figures. From one end to the other swim mythological gods and goddesses with trailing hair and carefully placed seaweed. Not all that carefully, however – breasts and nipples are in abundant supply, plus the odd pubic triangle, and – isn't that? Yes, definitely – more than one depiction of floating male genitalia.

Tom feels a stab of irritation. If these two women think he's going to express any kind of naïve surprise at this supposed scandalous vision, they can think again. The *condescension* of it – think they're pulling the old 'let's sock it to the colonial Hick', do they? Haa! He looks down at the pool, with what he hopes is a suitably stony face. Martita, however, proves impervious to his apparent lack of interest and draws him to a halt.

'Isn't it too simply lovely?' she says. 'My darling Harry had it done as my birthday present in 1936 – for my twenty-fifth. He thought it was a frightfully important occasion – a quarter of a century – much more significant than mouldy old twenty-one. That's him over there – the one with the conch shell for a trumpet and the bladderwrack belt. He's chasing me – that's me, do you see? I was naturally Titian – all over.' She looks up at Tom with a breathy giggle, but in the absence of any encouragement shifts her gaze immediately back to the pool. 'It's all floodlit, you know – from underneath – well, it was when it worked – do you see the lamps?'

Tom has to nod – but as coolly as possible; the sides of the pool are flush mounted with chrome-framed lamps, most of whose panels are now cracked or missing.

'We used to have the most marvellous parties here,' she goes on. 'Fridays to Mondays were always *heaven* – heaps of chums and jazz. We *always* had a band. Harry used to meet all these types in Soho and they'd come pouring down, bringing their instruments – anything for a free dinner – not to mention a floodlit swim. Of course, we had the summers then – warm as toast – nobody wore a stitch – but then the boring old war came along and that was that. We tried to get the lighting going again, in about 1952, I suppose, but it was no good – the damp had got in and we nearly electrocuted all the bathers. Too funny.'

She bursts into peals of laughter. The four dogs seem to receive this as a coded signal, for they suddenly take off and scamper down the steps, rushing along the bottom until they launch themselves as one into the stagnant rainwater and rotting leaves at the deep end. Martita leaps forward with great agility.

'Boysies – here – come here at once. Ozzy – oos an Ozzy? Buzzy – come to Mummy – come to Mummy at *once*.' She runs up and down the side of the pool, gesturing at her darlings – impotently, for they ignore her.

Fliss takes no notice, but, still exuding tension, strides on ahead and unlocks a small door set into the boarding of one of the buildings, disappearing through it like the White Rabbit popping down a hole.

'I'll just get the light on,' she calls.

Tom follows her though into a darkened tunnel of a corridor lined in matchboarding. On one side he can just make out a small staircase, and at the far end a narrow shaft of light shows from another doorway. As he starts towards it, Fliss pokes her head round the frame.

'Boots off, please,' she says.

'Oh, *really*,' says Martita witheringly, coming up behind Tom. 'Whatever for?'

'You don't have to clean it, Titty,' says Fliss sharply. 'I do. And no Boysies – you know what they did last time.'

'I can't get them out of the pool anyway – they're having a lovely wallow.'

'Oh, God,' snaps Fliss, and rushes back down to the outer door, slamming it shut and plunging them into deeper murk.

Tom finds himself doing a lot of bouncing around on one foot, trying to locate something rigid to pull against, but it's not that easy to get any grip on the slithery, mud-loaded boots and he doesn't want to use his hands. At last, however, he stands in his socked feet on the icy floor, feeling more than a little robbed of his dignity. Fliss doesn't seem to take any notice though, and for someone who has been so effusively apologetic about the weather, over which she has absolutely no control, she is remarkably unconcerned about his current physical discomfort, for which she is effectively responsible.

'This way,' she says briskly, and he pads after her, with Martita slithering along behind.

The immediate impression after the darkness of the corridor is intense blazing light and flashing colour. The room must be at least twenty, thirty feet high up to the gable ridge, and what? Sixty feet long – maybe longer? Hardly any of the wall surface is visible, for rising from the floor, right up to the eaves, are row upon row, rank upon rank, line upon line, of cups, mugs and beakers. Some are arranged on narrow shelves, which run the entire length of all four walls, up to a height of about ten feet. The rest are hanging from hooks – brass hooks, hundreds of them, each bearing its burden of yet another thing from which to drink – the most humungous china closet in the world.

Greyish daylight is coming in through high dormer windows, and as well there are garish, unforgiving, neon tubes suspended on chains. It feels intensely cold and damp and there is a faint aroma of fuel oil. Fliss's headscarf has fallen back off her face and she looks tired and anxious in the glare. She holds out her arms, palms upwards and spread, and half shrugs.

'Well, here it is,' she says in a defiant tone. 'This is what you've come for. The Harley-Wright Collection of Commemorative Drinking Vessels.'

'This is it,' says Tom levelly. He nods, he hopes sagely, acutely conscious that some sort of definite reaction is required, but not sure which one to give. He turns slowly round to look at the wall they have just walked through. The tiny door is the only part which is not covered by mugs, the shelving and hooks coming right up to and round the frame. This wall, however, is not as high as the others, and is topped with a wooden railing which guards a gallery of banked seating overlooking the rest of the room – an observation post. Why would you want to sit up in that gallery and watch the mugs, for crying out loud? But there's something familiar about that little door though – that neat little recessed brass ring instead of a regular handle. What's with that? Then he notices the jumble of worn painted markings on the floor and the explanation hits.

'It's some sort of court? Basketball?' He fails to erase his tone of surprise and this irritates him. Are they playing a game, these people – trying to test him? Do they really imagine he'd be the least bit impressed by an empty swimming pool and some ancient defunct sports facility?

'Racquets – but it was used for badminton, netball, all sorts,' says Fliss – and then completely automatically, 'I'm so sorry about the cold. We've had a paraffin stove going for several days, but it's a bit like trying to heat Antarctica with a candle.'

'Don't worry about it,' says Tom, blowing out through his teeth and watching his breath condense in front of him. 'So it's all here in this court?'

'Yes.'

'Original – I grant you that.'

'That wasn't the intention.'

'No?'

'The building is actually very old – it's one of the barns for the farm – but Harry had the court made during the twenties. Something else to amuse his friends.'

'This was our playground,' says Martita expansively, sliding around the floor on thick-socked feet. 'Our little piece of heaven. We would come down here and disport ourselves like anything – and my word, how we *did* disport. People haven't a clue how to enjoy themselves these days – not a clue. They just bury themselves in front of their little televisions and they think that's life! They don't know about conversation any more – they don't know about *games*. We used to play all sorts of games.'

'I used to play it at college – racquets. It's really not played that much back home – just on the East Coast a bit. Squash is much more popular of course.'

'I don't mean those sort of games. *I* mean the Game of Life,' says Martita. 'Much more amusing.'

'Well, he certainly seems to have been quite a guy – this

Harry Harley-Wright,' says Tom, aware that his lukewarm tone is probably negating the sentiment he's expressing.

'For a time,' says Martita, unabashed, 'hedonism was his middle name. Unfortunately age and a gammy leg got to him in the end – as I dare say they just will for most of us. We used to keep these up at the house, you know – when there weren't so many – but then gradually they started to creep down here – mostly put up in the balcony, but you've no notion how many got broken – the odd ball or shuttlecock would keep getting lobbed up there – we smashed loads – and then eventually they sort of took over the whole place. Pity really – one can't disport *much* with mugs, though one has tried – goodness, one has tried.'

'What about security? They're so far from the house.'

Fliss shrugs. 'It's just one of those things we don't really think about. Nobody knows they're here – well, almost nobody. We hardly ever bring anyone down. Barney – that's Barnaby Fitzgerald, our agent – he only found out by accident.'

'Well, I guess if your insurers know – '

'Insurers?' Fliss's blank expression is betrayed by the note of incredulity in her voice, but Tom goes on anyway.

' – and if the place is properly alarmed and all that, I guess this little hidden-away spot is as good as any.'

'We don't have *alarms*,' says Martita with intense scorn, 'we have the *Boysies* – they wouldn't let anybody past without kicking up a rumpus.'

Tom catches Fliss's eye and she starts to giggle – well, in fact she starts to explode – a sort of snort comes out, which she tries to smother, then another one, then another, and it's no good – Tom has caught it, he is snorting too, biting his lips, trying to hold his cool, and then snorting, sending great puffs of his breath into the dank air. Martita stands between them, a tiny, inquisitive, puzzled presence, looking up at first one, then the other.

'If we cannot retain dignity and decorum at our ages, I don't know what we're coming to,' she says haughtily.

But this starts them off again – tears are beginning to glisten on Fliss's cheeks.

'It's not funny,' says Martita. 'It's not funny at all. What is all this?'

Fliss shakes her head as the tears start to roll down, but she can't speak.

'I don't need to stand around to be laughed at,' says Martita.

'I'm sorry, Titty,' gasps Fliss as Martita heads towards the door. 'I don't know what got into me.'

'You,' says Martita tartly to Tom, 'should make sure you have a damn good look at this stuff – especially at the top. Make her show you Mum's Pearlies – and *then* see if your Mr Big will be quite so interested.'

12

So now Martita has banged the door behind her, and Fliss and Tom are left alone, staring at each other across the empty expanse of the court, and it's not so funny any more – actually, Fliss thinks, it's bloody embarrassing. The laughter has dried up but Martita's parting words are lingering. He can't have missed them – but then (she's ever hopeful), possibly he has. He's wandering around, looking up at the Collection – but in quite a vague, undirected kind of way. Perhaps it'll be all right. But bloody Martita – talk about a loose cannon. Fliss feels increasingly self-conscious, looks down at the floor, clears her throat.

'I guess I'd better take a look?' he says, as a question, without conviction.

Oh God, *must* he? Well, yes – she supposes he must – it is what he's here for. 'Right – yes, of course,' she says. 'You won't want the steps?' Bugger – why put ideas in his head? But too late.

'What steps?'

No escape – her and her big mouth – she points to the looming contraption tethered in the corner – a giant wooden stepladder mounted on a wheeled platform.

'Well, sure,' he says (damnit, thinks Fliss). 'I guess so.'

So she has to untie it and pull it out, then slowly pushes

it, creaking and wobbling, across the floor towards him. When she's got far enough, she pulls on a couple of levers, like the brakes on an ancient pram, and stands back while he starts to examine the shelves.

Frankly he's wondering if he can believe it. The baby carriage analogy occurs to him too – this woman in charge of this manic contraption. You'd kind of like to laugh, but of course you can't – not *at* her anyway. So he turns and starts to walk slowly round the room. As he doesn't know what to say, he goes for silence, figuring that'll make him look a little more wised up, a little more in command.

Eventually she breaks in. 'Those at eye level are mostly the earlier ones,' she says. 'I don't know how much you know about this sort of thing.'

'It's not my field,' he says – cool. 'That's not why I'm here.' And he hopes she doesn't dare ask why he *is* here, because he'd be damned if he could give her an answer. 'Denmans are handling that side of it,' he adds, just to make sure he's got the lid on it. Then – it just kind of pops out, 'Where's all the royal stuff?'

Stuff? He'd called it 'stuff' – and he can see from her reaction he's been kind of crass to mention the royal bit – but oh God the papers are full of that crap – the Lady Di stuff and all – royal, royal – the only thing they've really got if you think about it. Their tourist industry would wither without.

'It's not arranged like *that*,' she says, with a touch of scorn. 'It's done by dates and events – more or less chronological – the things with royal connections are scattered all through – if *that's* what you're interested in.'

Oh boy – she hadn't liked what he'd said.

'Those there for example commemorate the Restoration

of Charles II in 1660 – a lot of work was made then. The seventeenth-century pieces are all along that wall. There is earlier work, but not commemorating anything – or not that Harry could get hold of, and that's the point of this. You do understand, don't you?'

'In what sense?'

'Everything here has to commemorate *something*. It doesn't really matter what. He wouldn't have anything, however good, however rare, if it didn't have some sort of inscription on it.'

'What's the most valuable?' There he goes – crass again – it just will keep slipping out.

'Obviously the earlier pieces are the rarest' – (well, *obviously* he didn't really need to ask – now he cringes – she's making it clear he's just been kind of – well – *obvious*) – 'they're mostly quite crudely made,' she continues, 'real rough old things, some of them, but so few have survived – they were usually in daily use, you see. Well, you've only got to think – I mean, of washing-up – '

'What?' Then he gets it, one of those little Brit-slips in the language – the ones that make their so-called lingua franca such a trap for the unwary. She's talking about *dish-washing*, not getting your face clean before dinner, as in his mom yelling, 'You'd better get washed up, Tom – barbecue's nearly ready.'

'Over there is the eighteenth-century stuff,' she's saying. 'That's my favourite – some if it's amazing – so beautiful you could weep. Well, I could anyway. Then the nineteenth – and all that's the twentieth, hanging from the hooks. Lots of the recent bits turn out to be much more valuable than some of the eighteenth-century pieces. Daft, isn't it?'

'What? Daaarft?' Now he's gone too far – imitated her

stuck-up, tight-assed British accent. What does he think he's doing? But 'daaarft' – who's she kidding?

But she doesn't seem to have caught his mockery – continues, seriously, so he's a bit abashed. 'You know – crazy – it's crazy, that's all. Some of those beautiful pieces from the 1790s aren't necessarily worth as much as some hideous thing from 1929 or whatever. It's all on rarity value. There are some really naff things which Barney says are worth an absolute bomb.'

'Bomb?' Bomb equals failure to Tom – a Brit-slip again?

'You know, an absolute packet – '

Yes – he breathes relief – a Brit-slip. Seriously, you sometimes need an invisible translator to get you by – he ought to know by now.

'It all depends on what they commemorate, you know,' she says, still the schoolmarm, 'and how many were made. There's a lot to it.'

'What's the oldest?' If he's already exposed the crass, he may as well stick with it. The royal-est – the richest – the oldest – just the 'est', that's what he needs to know.

'Maybe the Wrotham pieces,' she says. 'It's a bit disputed because the experts think that not all the dating is accurate. Various Jacobean pieces – then Charles I. There isn't much from the Civil War period, but there are some very odd birds from Cromwell's Commonwealth.'

She's standing back now, watching him as he starts up the swaying ladder. As he does, three centuries slip past his eyes. Primitive pictures of stick men in periwigs picked out in brown lines give way to blue and white depictions of crowns, nymphs, cupids, coats of arms, animals, and on into multicoloured glazes – painted, sponged, printed, lustred – babies in cradles, men in coffins, brides (lots of these), civic dignitaries, men of learning, men of science, houses, parliaments, towers, bridges, ships, theatres, actors, murderers, victims, judges, inventors – they all merge together.

Occasionally one grabs him. A handsome tankard announces 'The Guillotine or Modern Beheading Machine by which the Late King Louis XVI Suffered on the Scaffold Jan 21st 1793', and next to it a cream-coloured mug entitled 'King Louis XVI of France – The Last Interview', for all the world like a banner headline in the *New York Post*.

Ever since he was told about this collection by Mr Z, he's felt total indifference to the idea of its existence. Something about the idea of pottery (I mean, *pottery* – Jeez), and pottery *mugs* in particular, seems completely alien. There's something clumsy about it – and yet paradoxically fragile. But now, seeing the individual pieces – well, sneakingly he has to admit some of them do have a kind of something – he isn't quite sure what though. Something touching maybe – to do with all these echoes of so many years, so many people and so much optimistic delight in making a concrete solid memorial to a fleeting, soon-forgotten moment.

So it's really kind of like – nice – that Millicent Gubbins in 1771 has marked the christening of her daughter Martha with this funny little mug, all painted with pigs (Did she look like a pig? Were the family pig farmers?) – and the poem written out in wavy script:

> Long may you Live
> Happy may you be
> Blest with Content
> And from Misfortune Free

Well, he hopes she was, this little Martha the Pig Gubbins.

As he climbs higher on the swaying ladder, hoping that

his latent vertigo doesn't kick in, he sees some pleasantly familiar faces.

'I see you've Mickey up here – and Pluto.'

'There's quite a lot of film stuff. Snow White's around there somewhere if you look – and all the dwarves.'

'American?'

'Only the images. It all had to be British-made, that was one of Harry's rules – to keep it within bounds – otherwise it would have got completely out of hand. Well, I suppose you might think it's not all that "in hand" as it is . . .'

'So there's nothing American?'

'Is that a problem?' She sounds suddenly anxious. 'He must have known that – your man – from the catalogue.'

'It's not a problem – I was just curious. So these Disney things are English?'

'Yes – To mark the first showings of the films, I think.'

'I wonder if Disney got the licensing fees – they'd be hot on that,' says Tom, ever the lawyer.

'I've no idea about the fees or whatever. There's some Charlie Chaplin up there – and Rudolph Valentino – *The Sheik* – oh, and Lindbergh if you look along a bit.'

'The Atlantic crossing or the kidnapping?'

'Both. And the murder – macabre really. But there must have been a demand for this sort of thing, mustn't there? Haven't you seen enough for now? It's awfully cold.'

'Where's "Mum's Pearlies"?'

'What?'

'Your mother-in-law mentioned it. What did she mean? She said I should take a look at "Mum's Pearlies".'

'Really?'

'Yes, *really.* That's what it sounded like.'

'Oh, do come down. It's freezing hanging around – we need some tea.'

'If you could just point me in the right direction.'

'I can't remember – somewhere along there. We can do this tomorrow.'

'Do we need to move this thing along a bit?'

'Well – oh, all right – it's on the other side, I suppose. You'd better come down and I'll push it across.'

He helps her reset the monster ladder. 'Is this thing safe? It feels kind of juddery.'

'We've never had an accident yet,' she says, unhelpfully adding, 'well, not with anyone sober.'

He climbs again. The cold is now really getting to him – and so is his jet-lagged exhaustion. Perhaps she's right – they should leave it for tomorrow. On the other hand, he is supposed to be 'sniffing it out', in Mr Z's phrase, so sniffing is what he'd better do.

'Along here?' he asks.

'Somewhere.'

'What am I looking out for?'

'You'll recognize when you get to them.'

'Them?'

'You'll see.'

He is beginning to feel irritated. What's with all the stonewalling? 'You've gotta understand, I'm a neophyte here – I'd appreciate a clue or something.'

'To your left,' she says stiffly – still unhelpful.

Now he's leaning way out from the ladder – oh, *God* – beginning to feel really weird. Then he spots something. Six, no, seven containers – well, maybe they could *just* be called mugs – all the shape of a set of teeth – grinning teeth – with handles attached where the back of the head would be and the top open end of the 'mug' being where the roof of the mouth would be. They are luridly painted with raspberry pink gums and tongues. Each is inscribed 'Mum's Pearlies' with the same date – 2 June 1953 – but underneath, each has a different name – Blackpool, Clacton-on-Sea, Skegness, Great Yarmouth – the others are too far over to see.

'What are they?'

'Mugs,' she says, sounding exasperated.

'That I guess I know. They're hideous.' Cautiously he starts to climb down. 'What are they for?'

'They're mugs.'

Is she being deliberately dumb or what? 'People drank out of them?' he asks. 'Do they work? Those wavy tops would be all funny against your lips, wouldn't they? And you'd dribble the liquid.'

'They're for storage.'

'What?'

'For soaking false teeth – at night.'

'*Gaad* – gross. People would actually *want* something like that?'

'Some people.'

'What the heck do they commemorate?'

'That's the funny thing – they all mark the Queen's Coronation – made by one factory but distributed to all the seaside towns. They've each got the Crown insignia inside – unapproved of course.'

Tom is back on terra firma. He's rubbing his hands to get some life into their iced numbness. 'What kind of value did Denmans put on them?' he asks.

'I can't remember,' she says, offhand, defiant. 'Novelty value – something like that.'

But maybe this is where he can sense a weakness. What's the problem here? 'There's quite a lot of stuff like that, I see,' he says. 'Trashy stuff.'

'Harry's vision was completely open, you know. Notions of "good taste" didn't come into it at all.'

'And yet it's worth such a lot – evidently.' He turns round slowly, inspecting all four walls.

But clearly she doesn't like his use of the word 'evidently'.

'The good pieces are very, *very* good,' she says stoutly. 'Extremely rare. And even the medium pieces are good too – some of them are remarkable. You'd need to have an appreciation of the medium really.'

'Yeah, well, I can't kid you it's my taste,' he says (come on – maybe he should let her off the hook a little), 'but fortunately for you, I'm not your buyer. Catch me spending this kind of bread on a warehouse full of cups – I could find better things to do with my money.'

'I suppose that's been the attitude of all non-collectors throughout the centuries,' she says, a tad arch. 'It's just as well for artists that there've always been a few enlightened souls around to balance the weight of all the philistines.'

Boy, has he got her back up, and he's beginning to enjoy himself. 'Oh, *I'd* be a collector all right,' he says, 'if I could afford it – of Bugattis, Maseratis, Ferraris. But *cups* – I mean, we're not talking Michelangelo here – *cups*.'

'As a professional potter, you could hardly expect me to agree with you.'

Oh, oh – boo-boo time. Nobody told you she was a *potter*. I mean, you could curse the quality of research here, couldn't you? Mr Z's staff, thank you very much: damage limitation: 'I could see that would make you much more sympathetic to all this – knowledgeable,' he says soothingly.

'I think the skill of the early makers was remarkable – truly staggering. When I think how difficult it is to get things right nowadays – glazes, you've no idea how unreliable the process can be – and we have all the benefits of electricity and gas – pyrometers to gauge exact temperatures, even consistent raw materials. They didn't have any of those advantages and yet they produced this work – a really consistent, professional product.'

'OK, so we're talking "product" here, not "Art".'

'Rather more " Art" than Maseratis or Bugattis.'

'*That*'s very much a matter of opinion – but as it happens you've lucked out, because fortunately for you my client already has in his possession everything he could possibly want, including Art – and I'm talking Big Art. I would say the word "need" dropped out of his vocabulary years ago. If a man like that has any need left at all, it's simply for diversion – and I guess he could be as diverted by this as by lots of other things, so it might as well be this. At least it's unique. Is it?'

'As a whole – well, yes. Harry started it at the right time, when the really early pieces could still be found at country sales – sometimes even junk shops. You'd never find them now, not outside major sale rooms and specialist dealers. And of course you'd need to be pretty obsessed, and old Harry was – obsessed. This sort of took over his life towards the end – he was very old by then, of course. But I think it had the effect of pushing Titty out too. I think she was sort of usurped by it.'

'Is that why she's selling now?'

'*She* isn't selling. It's ours – well, Ivor's. Harry left it to Ivor.'

'That's not what *she* says.'

'When did she . . .?'

'Earlier. She was telling me all about it.'

'I can assure you, it's Ivor's to sell.'

'Maybe she's very fond of it – doesn't want it to go.'

'On the contrary, as I just said, I've always felt she rather resented it. I expect that's why Harry left it to Ivor. He left everything else to Titty, but this – well . . . Harry used to spend days down here arranging it, changing it round. He was never really satisfied with it and he was always sneaking off to buy more pieces – not always when they could afford it either. I think that's the main reason he kept it down here. He could get right out of the way – lock himself in – unwrap his latest illicit purchase bought with money which should have gone to mend the roof or something. It was all that – his escape. I'm sure he needed one.'

'I'm getting kind of a feeling for this guy. I think I like the sound of him.'

'He was a bit of a hoot really. One of nature's venture capitalists. He was always ripe for exploitation by a new idea. Great fun until you found out you were also going to be exploited. Then it wasn't always quite so funny, and we always did find out. Usually too late.'

'You know, my teeth are chattering. I've just realized. It's so long since that happened to me, I thought it was adrenalin or something.'

'Don't teeth chatter in America?'

Is she laughing at him?

'Not in *my* life, they don't.' He allows himself the faintest twinkle back at her – just enough to keep a spark going and let her know *he* knows she's teasing him.

'Time for tea,' she says.

But then she would. Of course. What is it always with

Brits and all this tea? Tea as a religion – as if the rest of us don't have tea. I mean, all right, *we* have tea, so what? We have sarsaparilla and root beer too – do we turn them into articles of faith?

As they climb back up the muddy track towards the house, the last of his energy drains away. For a while, the mere scent of negotiation and intrigue has magically recharged him, but as the heat in the gloomy kitchen hits him, he can feel he's had it. A huge involuntary yawn engulfs him, ending in a squeaking near-yodel, which if he wasn't feeling so shattered would be pretty embarrassing.

'I'm sorry. I'm – ' he yips again, mouth gaping. 'I'm bushed. I guess I'll have to go take a nap.'

'Right' says Fliss briskly. 'You know where your room is.'

Once there, he doesn't bother to explore or examine anything – or even unpack. Fully clothed, he just clambers under the embroidered quilt on the bed – a quilt which reminds him uncomfortably of the boots he's just vacated, being both mildly damp and slightly gritty to the touch. What the heck? He – Mr Clean – is too shattered to care. He's asleep before he's even horizontal.

13

Fliss slams the big kettle down on to the range hotplate, feeling a mixture of affront and relief.

That had all been a bit sticky – too sticky – already. If only Barney had been there to field inquiries and ward off any doubts with a professional flourish. She runs back over everything that was said. Had she given too much away? Was there anything sinister in Mr Klaus's questions? He'd sounded so dubious – could that be significant? It's all so unsettling – so worrying – trying to guess what he's thinking.

And now, of all things, he's gone to bed in the middle of the afternoon. Well, obviously the man's exhausted. He's told her several times that he missed a whole night's sleep – as if she really needed to know. She hasn't had much in the way of sleep herself come to that. But then of course *he* had that glamorous-sounding complaint which people will go on and on about, jet lag, although she's never had it herself. In fact she's never had cause to have it, the furthest she's ever flown being to France or Switzerland, and once to Germany – the sort of flights which are so short that the plane always seems to be at an angle, either going up or coming down.

But honestly, it's a bit much. A young man like that demanding a zizz at 3.30 in the afternoon, and yawning like that, completely openly with no attempt to cover it up – yawning and squeaking all over her kitchen, when she'd wasted valuable work-time last night to bake goodies in his honour. She should have got the slip decoration on to those bowls for the craft market. Instead she'd been making piles of scones and shortbread and a mountainous iced sponge cake – all to conjure up a sort of Beatrix Potter vision of the perfect tea – for him, the Sleeping Beauty. Bugger it.

Once her sense of affront is out of the way, she can indulge in the relief: have a little time to herself, draw breath and get reorganized for the next domestic onslaught. There is no sign of either Titty or Ivor in the house, and no attempt has been made by anyone to deal with the detritus of lunch.

She starts by clearing the dining room of dirty dishes and relaying the table for supper. Then she sets to work on the washing-up, cursing the demands of formal eating instead of the usual slopping around the kitchen table. All these fiddly little bowls and ramekins for mustards and chutneys have already crusted over and need emptying, washing, drying and recharging for the evening. While she works she listens to Radio Four – *Kaleidoscope* – comforted by the familiar babble of voices debating the merits of plays and exhibitions she'll probably never see.

She's just starting on the potatoes for supper when the girls crash in from school. She has managed to park Henry on one of his friends for the duration of Mr Klaus's visit, just to lift the domestic pressure a bit. But she's been rather depending on the presence of the girls to add a little extra to the overall atmosphere – something of a diversion perhaps: conversation with a different generation, maybe just sheer decoration – and to balance out a little of the weight of Titty's unpredictable malevolence.

Now they come in through the scullery, scattering bags and shoes. Daisy dashes past – 'Hiiiiii' – straight for the loo. Daisy claims the school loos are unspeakably vile and has taught herself, camel-like, not to pee until she gets home each day – a state of affairs which Fliss is convinced must play havoc with her kidneys.

Emma comes in more slowly, weighted under a huge pile of books.

'Any post?' she asks automatically.

'Not for you, darling.'

'Oh, God. He said he'd write. The bastard. *Men*.'

Emma has been consistently in love since she was twelve, with a succession of the male of the species ranging from the Lesser-spotted Owl-faced Lad to the Greater-crested Golden Chancer, with every gradation in between, including several specimens of the Young Fighting Cock from one or other of the public schools. As a family they'd endured Edmund at Rugby, Charlie at Winchester, Rupert at Stowe, Magnus at Ampleforth and Nick at Harrow – interspersed with various Garys, Waynes, Duanes and Shanes, not to mention the odd Tristram, from her own school.

Fliss didn't think Emma treated these boys all that well really, but then Emma wasn't so much interested in them as people, not yet – more interested in the idea of Love itself. Love in the form of LURVE and the state of being IN LURVE. It seems to be more a romantic ideal that she's seeking at the moment, rather than sex. Or at least that's what Fliss is hoping, knowing of course she could be wrong about that – very wrong.

What Emma seems to like at the moment is communication, the more long-distance the better. Endless telephone calls, preferably to a swain on the other side of the country

– to the despairing fury of Ivor, who has been known to do war dances around her recumbent receiver-clutching form, flapping the latest British Telecom bill in her face. In the absence of telephone calls, there were these thick wodges of letters interspersed with little smiley faces dotting all the 'i's and 'j's, written on lined sheets of A4 paper torn out of school files – but today, nothing.

Daisy is back from the loo.

'Is he here yet?' she hisses in an exaggerated stage whisper.

'Yes.'

'Where?' she hisses again.

'You can talk normally. He's upstairs, having a rest.'

'Wet.'

'Not at all,' says Fliss, although she completely agrees. 'He missed a whole night's sleep and he's had a horrible journey.'

'What's he like?'

'You'll see – at supper.'

'Oh, no.'

'What?'

'No way, Mum.'

'What?'

'We're not hanging around for supper.'

'Of course you are. It's all planned.'

'What time?' Emma puts in.

'About eight?'

'Not a chance,' says Daisy. 'I've got loads of work. Starving. Now.'

'Well, of course have a snack – there's lots of stuff left from lunch – but then come and join us for supper.'

The girls look at each other. Although completely silent,

they've clearly exchanged an entire complex communication in the single glance.

'Sorry, Mum. No can do,' says Daisy.

'Of course you can do – don't be ridiculous. I need you. You're part of the – of the – you know . . .'

'What?' says Emma. 'Entertainment?' Too near the truth for denial.

'Ambience. Or something. Please.'

'Not a chance,' says Daisy, ferreting around in the fridge.

'You'll have to wait. I mean it. It's going to be lovely. There's a huge leg of lamb marinating – delicious.'

'Janice?' asks Emma.

'What?'

'Stringy, bloody old Janice. No wonder you wanted Henry out of the way. No thanks, Mum. Ooh – cake,' says Daisy. In a flash, while Fliss is prevaricating, they've cut two large wedges of the Beatrix Potter creation and borne them upstairs, balanced on piles of books, to their rooms.

'Please?' she calls after them – sounding plaintive even to herself, feeling foolish. And Daisy had accused Mr Klaus of being wet.

Anyway, as it happens they were right.

For a start, Mr Klaus won't wake up. Fliss hovers hopefully around in the corridor outside his door, trying to get some inkling of whether he's truly deeply asleep or perhaps just dozing, or what else – hanging around waiting to be called? But gentle tapping brings no response and neither does a brisk rap. Presumably if the poor man is *that* exhausted, she'd better leave him be. She stomps back downstairs, cursing the culinary uncertainty of it all, and the waste of effort and ingredients if he doesn't turn up for the feast. She could have kept her powder dry for tomorrow. Oh, blast.

Martita has retained her frilly boleroed look for the evening, and as an extra *en fête* touch has added long dangly earrings and fearsome black eyeliner which has become embedded in the dry fissures of her lids. She has placed herself most carefully in the drawing room awaiting Mr Klaus's arrival. Fliss recognizes the pose. She's perched on the end of the big wing chair by the fire, piled up with Boysies, her face turned in three-quarter profile so she's silhouetted against the flames.

She's done this quite a lot over the years. It must have worked the trick once. Somebody or other must have thought it alluring and told her so, what with her presence, her bone structure and of course that *nape* – never forget the nape. But it's a look which doesn't work quite so well with a sagging wattle and is even odder as now, when she swivels her eyes towards the door without moving either head or neck, to gauge whether she's having the right effect. The moment she sees it's only Fliss on her own, she drops the whole position and spins round.

'I thought we should get this under way.'

'What?'

'The evening. Our guest. I've been waiting for an aperitif.'

'There's some sherry.'

'I know that. I meant him. Where is he?'

'Still asleep, it seems.'

'How frightfully boring of him.'

'It's a bit difficult really. I've tried to wake him, but if he's that shattered he won't want to eat anyway, will he? I suppose we'd better just get on without him. It's only us – the girls won't join in.'

'They should be made to. Manners. Don't seem to come on the syllabus any more.'

'They did of course in your day, Titty? Two lessons a week, was it? Did they go in for a lot of Debrett in Croydon all those years ago?'

'Oh, we are a little waspish today, Fel*iss*ity.' Martita levers herself forward until her little legs reach the floor and rises with bouncy grace. 'For us it was a matter of instinct. You'll rue the day you didn't put your foot down with those two. We had a phrase to describe their sort when I was a girl – little madams. That's what you're nurturing in your bosom. A pair of little madams. Nothing but trouble.'

'We can eat at any time,' says Fliss, breathing steadily and forcing the acid retort back down her throat. 'I'll go and find Ivor.'

He's in the top barn, the one nearest the house on the land side of the bridge. She thought he might still be slotting together the pens or feeding the pregnant ewes. He isn't, for lambing has started – early, wouldn't she just know it.

A distressed and straining ewe is caught in the corner of a pen and Ivor is trying to help. He looks up at Fliss just for a second, then turns his attention back to the ewe. So from now on, for the next few days, unless this turns out to be a freak early delivery, the others will start too and life will take on its own peculiar rhythm. Great timing, Fliss thinks grimly as she makes her way back through the puddles to the house, but there's no fighting it: nature will have its way.

In the dining room, Fliss abandons the first course, the carefully prepared trout mousse – leaves it in the fridge for tomorrow – and launches straight into the marinated roast meat. She and Titty face each other in silence down the table. All things considered, it's not the night to be eating lamb – especially one with whom you had any sort of personal acquaintance. And true to previous form, poor Janice remains very stringy indeed.

It must have been the unaccustomed sight of her ankles that did it.

Sometime in the night, Ivor creeps into their bed, whiffing strongly of soap and faintly of sheep dip. Fliss thinks she's asleep, but perhaps not. Ivor's hand is round her stomach, his chin is nuzzling the back of her neck.

'How's about a little bit of humpy?' he's murmuring.

Well, why not?

She tries to get in the mood – feel – forget the rest. Ivor may possibly be having the same problem – but then again, perhaps not. She really must concentrate. She makes all the right noises – gives a little, takes a little. Well, when all's said, it's rather nice, isn't it . . . regardless of everything else? Ivor is working extremely hard now. Fliss is looking up at the ceiling over his shoulder, and darn it, something's distracting. As he's left the hall light on, she can just make it out in the semi-dark. The crack has moved on again – the top of Italy has now extended, past Genoa and Ventimiglia, and now it's heading along the Riviera. It'll reach Marseilles in no time if something isn't done about it. If it gets as far as Perpignan, the whole lot will cave in.

Ivor seems to be enjoying himself. Just in time she lets out the right strategic groan.

She wakes up at seven to find Ivor already gone; back to the barn and the circadian rhythms of the sheep. It's still nearly dark and across the courtyard diagonal rain spiked with lumps of soft ice is streaking in great squally sheets. Oh, *wonderful*.

Usually she'd be out there with him, lending a hand and offering respite as well as flasks of tea, but now in view of the presence of Mr Klaus (she still can't quite think of him as 'Tom' somehow), she gets into that skirt again and puts herself together quite carefully before going down.

Their visitor doesn't seem to be up yet, but there's a terrific amount of bad-tempered banging about going on in the kitchen. Emma is making a pile of potato-salad sandwiches, clattering pots and utensils and spreading crumbs everywhere. Daisy is scrabbling around in the dresser – all drawers open, bits hanging out again.

'God, what a mess. What on earth are you doing?' asks Fliss.

'Looking for the phone book.'

'Why are you looking in there? It's by the phone.'

'No, it's not. Why would I be wasting all this time if it was in the logical place? Nothing in this house is ever logical – and it's specially bad now we've got so tidy. We can't find *anything* now we're tidy.'

'I see you're doing your best to rectify that situation,' says Fliss, looking glumly at the spillings from the drawers. She suddenly has a vision of the phone book – well, the Yellow Pages in fact, but surely the ordinary phone book couldn't be far behind – in the dining room with the great pile of old newspapers she'd plonked under the sideboard when she'd been trying to hide everything under throws. She goes to look. She was right, though she'd forgotten she was actually using it to prop up the shorter leg of the table as well, so she has to do a quick rebalancing act under all that tasselled cloth before bringing it back.

'What do you want it for?'

'We're looking for quarters,' says Daisy.

'For what?'

'I've already phoned Rachel and she can't do it. I want to try Sandy. Emma's fixed up – she's going to Sophie's.'

'Stay when? Where?'

'For the duration,' says Daisy darkly.

'What are you talking about?'

'We don't like being ambience.'

'That was a – it was a joke, you know it was.'

'No, honestly, Mum – it's all tense and awful. We can't concentrate or anything.'

'She's right, Mummy,' says Emma. 'It's pretty horrible and we're supposed to be working and everything – you know we are – you want us to.' She's putting the sandwiches into a plastic bag. 'And it'll be better for you really – much easier to concentrate on all this Collection stuff when you haven't got us to worry about.'

'But I need you. I told you – you're my light relief.'

'Exactly.'

'I thought you might enjoy it – for a bit. Get a chance to spend some time with a young American – well, youngish. I expect he's very nice once you get to know him. You haven't even said hello or anything.'

The door swings open and Mr Klaus is standing there. He's wearing a maroon track suit with a matching headband bisecting his forehead, pushing his hair up at the back. Except for the lack of a feather, the look is vaguely Hollywood Apache. He flashes a dazzling American smile at all three of them.

'Hi!' he says expansively. 'Thought I'd take a run.' He's bending at the knees – trotting on the spot.

'Good morning. How nice to see you. Did you sleep well?'

'Like a narcoleptic.'

'Goodness, that does sound deep. These are our daughters, Emma – Daisy, Mr Klaus.'

'Hi. Good to know you. Mind if go run? Got to get some oxygen in this system.' He moves off with a spring, past Emma and out via the scullery. The girls' faces remain glued in stunned attitudes of sickly grins which they hold on to for a moment once he's left.

'Eeuch!' says Daisy, rushing for the telephone. 'Sandy – oh, pleeease have me to stay.'

'What do you mean? He's jolly nice. That was jolly nice, wasn't it?'

'Oh, Mum.'

'And what are all the sandwiches for?'

'Emergency rations. Just in case. Sophie's parents eat a lot of mung beans.'

Actually, of course, Tom hates exercise – always has – apart from skiing and the occasional round of golf. Particularly loathes jogging – even secretly despises its proponents. All those earnest men and women dashing round the roads of Westchester in their fluorescent Nikes, or getting themselves mugged in Central Park. Hates their self-righteous quality. But it's good cover. Excellent cover. He can practically guarantee that no Harley-Wright will want to accompany him. He's seen their mud room, for chrissake – their sneakers, their racquets are like something out of the ark.

And now he's not feeling so bad. Hungry of course – well, he'd missed dinner last night – but more centred, somehow. And if he hangs around for breakfast, then he may not get away with it – later on it won't be so easy to get off on his own. But Jeez is it raining – well, almost semi-snowing. What a place.

He heads off in the grisly early light towards the old racquets court. He runs only as far as the brow of the hill. As soon as he's out of sight of the house, he slows to a walk and, keeping well clear of the boggy path, ducks under a fence and edges along a narrow ridge of grass beside a ploughed field. It's felt funny running with one hand in the pocket of his sweat pants, but he's had to keep it there to stop his little compact Pentax from falling out. Well, Mr Z told him to sniff it out – so sniff he will, without anyone, particularly this agent guy whoever he is, breathing down his neck.

Of course he saw yesterday where she keeps the key – her minimal attempt at security verges on the pathetic. Inside it is, if possible, even more frigid and desolate than yesterday. That aroma of kerosene is still around, but the stove has gone out, probably run dry, and his breath puffs up around him in chilled eddies.

He stands there just looking around at the Collection – trying to make something out of it and failing. It's just so utterly not his kind of bag. OK, so a lot of it's old – big deal. A lot of it isn't. And some of these things you wouldn't want to accept as a gift, let alone pay good greenbacks for. And what's he supposed to be sniffing out anyway? Mr Z's already had the stuff authenticated by Denmans, so what really is his function? What does Mr Z want to achieve by acquiring this? He's too focused to go after anything, however seemingly trivial or bizarre, without it's going to satisfy something specific. So what is it with *this*? That's maybe what he's got to figure out. Mr Z'd talked that stuff about his background, but then to talk about the mugs – the history of the goddamn *mug* – I mean, what's so special? He thinks they didn't have perfectly good potters making perfectly good mugs in the Carpathians or wherever it was his family came from? And come to think of it, where exactly *are* the Carpathians?

The light is terrible in here. The Pentax is blinking red signals at him, so he pops up its flash and takes a couple of pictures. Big deal. Great pictures – just lines and lines of mugs. He steps back and takes a shot of the whole effect – then to the other corner, to shoot back towards the door. It's kind of unsatisfactory somehow – he'd make a terrible detective, wouldn't he – but in the end what can there be to find out?

14

'I'm stuck. In Harrogate.'

'WHAT?'

'Now I know that tone, dear. Don't start panicking.'

'What do you mean don't start panicking? I'm panicking all right. This is panic.'

'I wish you'd control your hysterical tendencies. Is it hormones?'

'WHY are you in Harrogate?'

'I told you, I'm stuck. It's partially your fault.'

'How can it be my fault?'

'The blasted hire car has broken down. It's snowing cats and dogs up here – you've no idea what the drifts are like and the thing they gave me in Bury has a back axle made of chewing gum as far as I can tell. I was skidding all over the place – landed in a ditch – '

'Are you hurt?'

'Only emotionally. Fellow dealers saw me arriving in this little tin box on wheels and wondered if I'd fallen on hard times. Anyway, something interesting may be cropping up and I want to follow it through.'

'You mean you're not stuck at all. You've stayed up in Harrogate because you think you've got a deal going.'

'And stuck. Having the big end greased, or whatever they do.'

'Well, I do think it's a bit much.'

'I've warned you about that bitter little voice, dear.'

'No, I do really. I mean, *you* set this thing up. I've got this chap here – he's expecting to meet you. He's all professional and ready to negotiate, and what am I supposed to do with him?'

'Oh, for pity's sake, Fliss, do stop whinging. Take him on the bloody Cook's tour. You know the sort of thing – you must have done it for all sorts of people over the years – take him round, show him Ickworth – '

'Ickworth's closed. It's still winter, Barney. *Everything's* closed.'

'Well, show him the usual – Kersey, Lavenham – give him a bit of this and that. I'll be back tomorrow – first thing. I promise.'

But it's not a lot of fun. The constant swish of the windscreen wipers is a sad background chorus all day long. Great dollops of sleet land on the glass with a splat and are rhythmically swept off every second or so and it's hard to pretend it's all fun. Awfully hard.

They start in Kersey. Everyone loves Kersey.

A narrow, steep street lined on both sides with medieval houses in Dolly Mixture colours – topped at one end by a starkly beautiful flint-covered church tower and nestling in its central fulcrum the famous ford – the water splash across the road full of Muscovy ducks who regularly run the gauntlet of motor traffic.

Today even the ducks have got the hump. They sit in

gloomy, unquacking huddles on the banks of the splash, beak to beak, solid and unmoving as plaster decoys. There isn't even the usual fun of driving slowly through the water and half pretending to run one over.

Water streams down the pavements. The village is a ghost without a single visible quickening molecule to represent life on earth. Fliss can feel her smile grow ever more fixed: her jaw is beginning to ache with the effort of appearing cheerful. They head for Lavenham. Everyone loves Lavenham.

To be fair, Lavenham does its best – all things considered. But even Lavenham has its limits. The Guildhall is closed. (But the Guildhall is never closed, surely?) Oh, yes – sadly, today the Guildhall is closed. The church is open – hooray – thank you, Lord – the beautiful, grandiose basilica of a village church is open – but oh the cold. And somehow Fliss gets the feeling that interesting brasses and the carved rood screen, seen in these glacial conditions, aren't truly capturing the rapt attention of her guest – and she can't blame him.

They tramp up the hill to the empty market square, then down the hill to Water Street – more water, too much water. Round back to the High Street. The chemist is open – yippee. But Mr Klaus doesn't have need of a pharmacy right now – for his public needs at any rate. Fliss, on the contrary, feels she would kill for chemical sedation at this moment – any old chemical would do.

They go into a pub. She orders Mr Klaus the local speciality – a pint of Abbot Ale – but has to have a tonic water herself, driving of course. Although either would normally have been fine, the choice at this particular time, after this particular morning and in this particular temperature, doesn't seem quite to hit the spot. She watches Mr Klaus gloomily sipping at his pint for a moment, then excuses herself and heads for the phone box by the loos. She dials Helena's number.

'I don't really see what I can do,' says Helena. 'I'm leaving for London at about two. Teddy's got his Sodding Swedes over at the moment – they come every year, it's an absolute pain. We're giving them dinner at the Ivy. They're doing some sort of deal in fish oil – you wouldn't believe the squillions to be had out of fish oil.'

'It's just – it's simply if I could bring him over for a bit – kill some time. I'm not after food or anything. Just for a little while – to meet somebody – I mean, to meet you. Everything seems to be closed and I've got to fill the time in somehow.'

'I'm not quite sure how to take the implication that I'm just a "somehow". I've always seen myself as "central" – not a sideline.'

'I only meant it wouldn't – I mean, we wouldn't be draining you. I just thought if he could meet you – if I could get him into a more, you know, conducive environment.'

'Conducive to what, might I ask?'

'Oh, Lord, I don't know – *anything*. Communication, I suppose. I just can't take him home now. What on earth am I going to do with him? It would've been all right if Barney was here – we could have talked business and the Collection and things – it would've been fine. But as it is – well, I'm really rather desperate.'

'I can do you soup and cheese – nowish – but I'll really have to scoot straight after. You know what Teddy's like – can't let the darling boy down.'

'Bless you, Helena. I'm your slave for ever.'

'Well, I know *that*.'

And in fact this is more like it, thinks Tom, as they sweep up the long, straight drive between white-painted Chinese Chippendale fences towards Helena's wide, low Regency house, which even in the piercing sleet exudes an inner core of warmth and tranquillity. The effect is slightly dented as they are getting out of the car, for two black dogs appear like bullets out of nowhere and project themselves straight at him, slobbering pink tongues and filthy paw prints all over his Burberry.

'Girls! GIRLS!' A pretty red head is stuck out of an upstairs window but the voice which emanates from it is strident enough for a drill sergeant on parade at West Point.

'Oh, shit!' she calls, waving and smiling. 'Sorry!' The head disappears.

The inside of the house lives up to its outside too – yes, this is much more like it. Persian carpets on old polished wood; eighteenth-century ancestors glaring down the length of the staircase from intricate gilt frames; huge bowls of pot-pourri; tones of coral and cream. If he shut his ears and half closed his eyes, he might almost be in a house back home – not any old house of course, but one of those larger homes hidden up driveways in the woods all over upstate New York and Connecticut, lovingly decorated down to their follicles in the 'English Country Style'.

That's where the familiarity ends though. The average chatelaine of such an establishment back home would now be tripping down these stairs, elegantly coifed and decked in her Tiffany daytime gold; whereas Helena comes bounding down, almost hidden by a great pile of clothes which she just

154

drops on the floor at her feet, breathless and slightly sweaty. She leaps at his Burberry and examines it quite closely.

'Too toe-curlingly shitty. I really must see if something can be done about those girls – they're getting a bit beyond the pale. I expect it'll brush off. It usually does.'

Fliss makes the introductions.

'You've caught me on the hop,' says Helena. 'Fliss explained? We have to deal with these Sodding Swedes every year. It's a pain in the arse, but what can one do? Needs must and all that – and the devil so often does, doesn't he?'

'Excuse me?'

'Drives – the devil. Such a relentless old bugger.'

'Oh. Sure.' He doesn't know what the hell she's talking about and her *language* – peel away the accent and it's tacky enough for a 42nd Street hooker – but it sounds kind of different in these patrician tones. Come to think of it, Fliss uses this kind of language too. They didn't tell you *that* in Emily Post.

'Anyway, while I'm about it I thought I'd take this lot up to town with me and bung it into the Chelsea Oxfam. Our cupboards are just too awful – crammed with all this old crap – I simply must get us sorted out. I hope they'll accept them. I find the charity shops are getting really quite sniffy these days, don't you, darling? Almost demanding designer labels.'

'I haven't noticed,' says Fliss, whose most recent encounters with these organizations have been as customer, not donor.

'Well, you can take it from me. Actually, if there's anything you want, do say,' says Helena, turning the pile over lightly with her toe. 'There's a loden coat in there – seen better days but still quite serviceable – and quite a lot of long taffeta. My girls won't be seen dead in anything below pube height now – and it's all got to be black, clingy jersey stuff – but yours might be interested.'

'I wouldn't want to deprive Oxfam,' Fliss murmurs, furious that she's blushing and dying to get off the subject.

'Well, as I say, they might not even be acceptable – you never know – so if you want to have a sort-out before I go.'

'I'll leave it, thanks,' says Fliss, hoping the now desperate feeling in her brain is transmitting some sort of visible signal for Helena to pick up.

But Helena has turned to Tom. 'If you ask me, it's a bit of a cheek really – talk about looking a gift horse and all that.'

For a second, Fliss fears that it's her tendency to glare into the gift horse's mouth which is in question, but no, Helena is back on charity shops in general as she leads them through the house.

'I'm not blaming Oxfam of course – actually, they're wonderful – they always seem to be able to park one's junk somewhere or other – but I've been trying to help this housing charity in Worlds End and honestly it's Issey Miyake, Armani or nothing, darling. They wouldn't even look at anything from Next. Now I do think that's a bit thick, don't you?'

They've landed up in the kitchen. Everything that the kitchen of Little Watling Hall is not, Helena's is. From its bluey colour-washed cupboards to its Provençal tiled floor to its beams wreathed in hop bines, it's the very model of country housewifery as trumpeted monthly from the covers of the glossy magazines – only Helena would of course scorn any such comparison.

'I hope you don't mind being domestic,' she says, 'only

I've no staff today and we're all absolutely up to our eyes with the Sodding Swedes – it always catches me out – lands me in the proverbial just when I'm completely submerged in something else. My children are getting back from Val d'Isère tomorrow and Arabella's expecting to do her first BHS event on Sunday – expects me to have kept her horse racing fit – and to tell you the truth I'm not at all sure he's level – he was looking a little bit tender on his off-hind this morning – I've got a horrible feeling he may have punctured his frog and then where will we be? Shit's creek isn't in it, darling – ' All this addressed without pause to Tom as she slams rolls, butter and bowls down on to the oak refectory table and starts unwrapping cheeses. One of these she now holds up to her nose and starts conspicuously sniffing.

'This may be a little bit past it – Camembert – it looks simply disgusting now, but we had it at the weekend and it was heaven – came from that place in Jermyn Street – but I may have let it get a bit over the top – just scrape off the furry bits and see – '

Fliss gets a glimpse of Mr Klaus's face. He's seems to be trying hard to maintain a look of eager anticipation, but it's clearly a struggle.

'I'll just get the soup – won't be a mo – rather a treat actually – had it in the freezer. I don't know if they go in for it in America – Jerusalem artichoke.'

Later, while Mr Klaus is in the loo and Fliss is helping load the dishwasher, Helena murmurs in her ear, 'Not bad – if you like them shortish and chunky – and some of us rather do.' And she thumps Fliss in the side with her elbow and laughs – quite a lot.

*

On the whole, Tom thinks, this day seems to be going on for ever.

They had some tea and layer cake when they got back to the house, then he felt kind of stupid just hanging around waiting for something to happen. There was a local paper in the living room and he sat reading it for a bit – funny sort of thing full of news about grain subsidies and cattle markets. On the back of the paper there was a schedule for TV programmes. There seemed to be a lot of stuff from back home on these (only) four channels and astonishingly, a whole heap of stuff coming up on AIDS – now that really did surprise him. He'd like to have gotten a look at it, but he hadn't seen a TV set anywhere, and Fliss didn't seem to be around to ask – she'd gone off across the bridge saying something about sheep, and that was an hour ago. So he'd gone upstairs to his room and just kind of sat around, waiting for something to happen. There were some books by the bed, but he decided to read his day-before-yesterday's copy of the *Wall Street Journal*, which he still hadn't opened since he got on the plane. It made him feel comfortingly closer to home.

Half an hour later, he has done and is feeling loose-endish again. He opens the door and looks out into the corridor. He can hear a murmuring along the passage – a familiar sound, a TV set or radio. He follows. At the end, the door is open a crack and an eye is looking at him. He stops, half embarrassed and confused. The old lady pokes her head fully out of the door.

'Psssst!' she says – just like that – he can almost see the word written up in a balloon in the air – like a cartoon in the *New Yorker* of his childhood.

'Would you care for a little livener?' the old lady hisses.

'Pardon me, ma'am?'

'A little something?'

'Excuse me?'

'*Gin.*'

'Oh, gin – gee – yes, thank you.' And he finds himself ushered into the old bird's den. It's sort of greenish and stuffy. A large colour TV set is on very loudly, in the corner.

'Do sit down,' she says, gesturing expansively across the room. There isn't anywhere *to* sit, however – apart from the bed. He lowers himself gingerly on to the edge of it and his butt sinks into the bulky satin quilt which puffs up around him.

The drink she hands him is a sticky mixture – gin with a lot of sweet vermouth. It's a little too like a cough medication for his tastes, but after a day like today anything alcoholic is welcome, and its very sweetness gives it an extra gloss – something in the nature of food, of sustenance, of which he seems to have had too little since he arrived in England. He drinks it down quite fast – and with a sense of gratitude.

The old woman also settles on the bed – up at the pillow end with her legs stretched out. She has kept the TV set on, but has turned the sound low. As she talks, her eyes keep flicking back to the screen.

'Had a good day, have you?' she asks.

'Well, it's been – interesting.'

'*There's* a euphemism if ever I heard one. I feel sorry for you, I really do. She hasn't a clue.'

'Pardon me?'

'Felicity. But then she never did. You should have been here in Harry's day. We knew how to do things – you'd have seen things in style then. We were great entertainers – always at it.'

159

'Must have been great times.' But he's said this too quietly. Her attention is on the screen but a puzzled look has crossed her face.

'What did you say?' she rasps quickly.

'TIMES,' he yells, remembering what Ivor had done at lunch yesterday, 'MUST HAVE BEEN GREAT!'

'There's no need to shout, you know,' she mutters. 'How's about another gin?'

'Delighted,' he says.

'You do the honours.'

He gets up to fix the drinks – his own he makes heavier on the gin but keeps roughly to her proportions for her refill.

'Ummm,' she says approvingly as he hands her the glass, 'that should keep my oils wheeled,' and she knocks half of it back in one go. 'My husband was an absolute poppet, you know.' She smacks her lips happily. 'And quite a catch in his way. Of course in those days he had rather a lot of tush – and one can't deny the attraction.'

'Excuse me?'

'Of tush.'

For a moment Tom is lost. Two gins can't have robbed him of his hearing, can they? But could the old woman be using this word in the New York sense? Has Yiddish come this far? Well, yeah, of course it has – but does this elderly English lady really mean her husband had a great ass?

'Did I say "tush"?' she says suddenly, her eyes slightly squinty as they stare past him to the screen.

'You did.'

'I meant "tosh". He had lots of tosh – in those days. All gone of course – family failing. They haven't got the wit to hang on to sixpence-ha'penny.'

'I'm afraid you've lost me.' OK, she meant something else, but what exactly?

'Tosh – you know. No, I mean "dosh", don't I? Quite a lot of dosh he had. No, I mean "toot" – that's what I mean – that's how it came out as "tush". I always get there in the end.' She leans back on her pillows, smiling broadly.

Tom is feeling the teensiest bit giddy himself now.

'You'll have to forgive me,' he says, earnestness creeping into his tone. 'I may have missed something here – his attraction was what exactly?'

'*Money*, dear – of course. And then I wasn't without assets myself, you know – in a cerebral sense with my artistic connections – Augustus John and all that.'

'Augustus John,' says Tom, at last feeling a flicker of interest.

'Oh, yes. Didn't you know, he called me his "Titian Rose"? That's how I came by my name. He was mesmerized by my nape – well, many were.'

'Your what?'

Martita turns her head to the practised three-quarter angle and points to the back of her neck. 'My nape was wildly seductive, you know – it made men melt.' She flutters and offers up a little-girly grin.

'Gee,' says Tom, edging back slightly off the end of the bed.

'And so I came to him with all these people – I'd been a part of it all, you see – Fitzrovia, Bloomsbury – a witness. So even though I didn't have the toot, I had the connections – and we had them all here, you know – knocked all the others into a top hat. I was a real feather in his cock. Have another gin.'

*

She turfs him out at 6.30, a tad abruptly he feels, murmuring something about *Crossroads*. He hears the sound of the TV blaring away almost as soon as the door slams. The corridor, with all its doors shut, looks bleak and uninviting. He goes back to his room. This looks pretty uninviting too – and she, the old woman, has the gin.

He sits down on the chair by the window and starts to look at one of the books. It's a guide to Suffolk. He flicks through. It's very dry – mostly to do with buildings – a celebration of the old. The old – the old. Well, that figures – everything is so damn *old*. He looks up Little Watling. Its entry takes up only half a page, and most of that is devoted to the church. Mostly built in about 1490 with earlier Norman chancel and font – some of its bricks may, indeed, be Roman and must thus have formed part of another, even earlier building, possibly a temple. Then at the bottom there's a bit about the Hall. Well, this is better. This is almost *something* – so this dump *is* somewhere. There's a short description – a mention of the chimneys – and then a bit about those funny pictures on the walls – 'pargeting', that's what they are – nice word – and old. My God, but they're old – some guy went and did all that before the *Mayflower* even sailed. Makes you think.

He gets up and tries to look out the window. But it's almost dark and the rain, the endless rain, is streaming down the panes. It's cold in here – and a bit – well – smelly, isn't it? God, he could do with a TV or something – anything to plug back into the real world out there. He'd better go find somebody.

15

Fliss is in the kitchen trying to fish all the Jerusalem artichokes out of the cassoulet. After today's Helena soup and yesterday's bastardized onion tart, she reckons Mr Klaus's taste buds and digestive tract have probably had all the Jerusalem artichokes they can take for the moment. But she's failing – they've already turned to mush among the flageolet beans.

When Tom comes into the room, he sees her hunched over that stove thing with her back towards him, presumably stirring yet another pot, and feels a sudden rush of impatient irritation.

'Let's go eat,' he says on an impulse.

'It won't be ready for another hour or so.' She looks up at him, faintly put out, peering over reading glasses and waving a holey spoon. Something snaps in him. Any remaining sense of caution flies to the winds.

'No, I mean now,' he says. 'Let's go out.'

'Where?' She sounds astounded, as if he's suggesting Mars.

'To a restaurant. There must *be* restaurants.'

'Well, of course there are – but now?'

'Do we need reservations?'

'I doubt it,' she says irritably.

'So let's go.'

'But I've – ' She waves the spoon vaguely over the pot – 'It's a cassoulet – and there's a trout mousse.'

'Terrific. They'll keep.'

They already have is what she thinks, but what she says is, 'I'll have to change.'

'Why? You look great as you are.' This of the second consecutive wearing of that denim skirt – well, OK, she looks a little like a wet weekend in Schenectady, but who's caring? She's not his date. Her appearance needn't reflect on him.

She's wondering frantically where to take him. The bistro in Great Watling, which is supposed to be rather good, is open only at weekends during the winter. Bury is surely too far to drive in the dark, in this weather. She's scarcely used any of the other local places – mostly varied Indian and Chinese establishments awash in flock wallpaper and sing-alonga-Max Muzak, or odd dubious-looking country house hotels with invisible reputations.

She should ring Helena. Of course. Helena will be sure to know of somewhere good – but it'll be very expensive, and who is to pay for this unexpected, unlooked-for treat? The thought of this makes her lose any of the appetite she's been building for her own cassoulet. Anyway, Helena's already on her way to the Ivy in the wake of the Sodding Swedes. And now he's standing at the door, impatiently holding it open, ushering her through, so a decision had better be made.

She plumps for the Crown and Sceptre on the edge of Long Pecklam. Owned by a big hotel chain, it's an over-restored building awash in dark oaky-beaminess, impressive in its own way, surely bound to appeal to his American tourist senses.

It doesn't of course. Already Tom has had enough ancient buildings to last him, he figures, for most of the rest of his natural born – if not even longer . . . A feeling of weariness hits him immediately, as, having crept along the pitch-black lanes, with the rain sluicing over and under the car, they eventually pull up outside a very parody of Olde Englande, a white-painted, gabled edifice positively chevroned with black beams.

The moment they are inside she realizes she's made a mistake. A sea of thick Axminster in swirly reds and blacks is complemented by quantities of mock-oak wall lights bearing both false candle drips and scarlet fringed shades. A heavy mixture of gravy and best bitter scents the air. The manageress – you couldn't call her a 'Maître d' – bristling in black and white viscose, with a scarlet silk-effect carnation in her buttonhole, leads them into the cavernous dining room.

'Where would you like to sit?' she offers in a high-pitched Essex Girl voice. She presents them with most of the room. In a corner near the kitchen door, a lone man is reading a newspaper propped up against a half-full, stoppered wine bottle, his soup spoon held in suspension between bowl and lips. By the thick red-plush curtains, a middle-aged couple are wielding ornate fish knives over platters of what might be cod floating on a puddle of greyish sauce. They are the only other customers, it seems.

Fliss knows they ought to leave. There is just a split second when this might be possible, but she lets it pass, and already the embarrassment of withdrawal and the hassle of finding somewhere else are too much, so that she subsides on to the offered chair, almost with gratitude.

It's a large table for just the two of them, right in the middle of the room. For once she wishes there were Musak, for the only sound is the chinking of the fish knives across the expanse of carpet. There are too many staff with too little to do tonight, so there is much officious removing of the other settings at their table, much whisking of napkins across their laps, much proffering of hard little rolls and irritating miniature packets of butter.

They are offered drinks before 'perusing' the menu. Acutely aware of her driver's responsibilities, Fliss asks for a glass of dry white wine and vows that will be her lot for the evening. Tom, with gin already lapping at his brain stem, asks for a double dry Martini on the rocks, and, clearly having had some bad experiences of this in the past, launches into a detailed account of how it should be made – Tanqueray gin with just the merest hint of dry vermouth, and an olive.

The manageress listens impassively until he has finished, then squeaks, 'We only have Gordon's.'

'Excuse me?'

'Gin. We don't go in for that other – whatever you called it.'

'Tanqueray. Of course you do. It's English.'

'Gordon's,' she says definitively.

'Booth's?' he ventures.

'Gordon's,' she snaps.

'This is very disillusioning.' He turns wide eyes to Fliss. Can he be pulling her leg?

'I'll bring your menus.' The manageress trips away on her stiletto Stead and Simpsons.

Any remaining doubts Fliss may have harboured about the prospective quality of this dinner are immediately dispelled by the arrival of the menus. They are massive tomes bound in leather with thick scarlet and black silk tassels, each page of the vast selection being fancily printed within elaborate cartouches. There is not so much as a hint of more impromptu 'dishes of the day' added in pen, which might indicate spontaneity or even truly fresh ingredients. Instead – oh dear – there lies the solid thud of 'International Cuisine' rooted directly in the deep freeze – the 'Roasted Duckling with Cherry Sauce, served with its little nest of Pommes Frites and Seasonal Vegetables'; the Steak Diane; the Tournedos Rossini; the Sole Bonne Femme; the Scampi Armoricaine; the Poire Belle Hélène – everything, even the puddings, somehow redolent of bottled tartar sauce, and each dull and even duller dish bearing a staggeringly high price tag. Fliss is inwardly groaning; Tom is laughing.

'I haven't read a menu like this in twenty years. Boeuf Stroganoff, for God's sake? "Hungarian Goulash delicately scented with Paprika" – *delicately*?'

'And almost certainly boil-in-the-bag,' murmurs Fliss.

He plumps for plain grilled steak – 'Broiled' in his lingo, medium rare – that at least will surely be freshly cooked. She, against every conscious instinct, chooses the duck, whose leathery surface she can already clearly envisage, but which she somehow cannot resist.

'Sounds good,' he says.

'It won't be,' she answers.

'Then why?' he asks.

'I don't really know – a compulsion – something I wouldn't bother to cook at home – wouldn't want to? I don't know – it may not be that bad.'

'You wouldn't possibly – just possibly – be a masochist?' He laughs.

'I don't know. I don't think so. I'd like to find the easy way out *sometimes*.'

'Well, maybe you'll just have to try a little harder.'

He has swigged down the Martini very fast and then another. They've both chosen artichokes to start with – globe ones this time, and so obviously imported and bound to be tasteless, thinks Fliss – and he tries to order champagne to go with them.

'You go ahead,' says Fliss now certain that, however embarrassing, he's going to have to pay for this occasion. 'I can't – driving, you see.'

'Can't we take a cab? Come on – it'll do you good to relax a bit.'

'No, really – I couldn't leave the car here.' Barney would probably kill her if she did.

'They can put it in the garage.'

'No, really. You go ahead though.'

Slightly to her amazement, he does. He eschews the champagne though, deeming it too convivial to drink on his own and not so good after the numbing effects of the Martinis, and orders instead a bottle of Haut Medoc, after much poring over the wine list and murmuring of the names of likely domaines and years. Oh, Lordie – and they've been chucking all that cheap Riesling at him.

'You seem to know your wines very well,' she says by way of making conversation.

They have each been piling up their sucked-off artichoke leaves, a peculiarly intimate activity for two comparative strangers under the watching eyes of the waiters.

'I'm OK with French. My folks were always big with

French – but the rest of the world, forget it. My wife and I did a wonderful trip a few years back with the kids when they were smaller. We took a boat up the Rhône and had all these stopovers – we'd go visit the vineyards. It was fabulous.'

'I didn't know you had children.'

'Two. Girls. They're ten and eleven now.'

'That's a nice age. Just before they start to get difficult.'

'So people keep telling me. I wouldn't find them difficult – I'd just like to see them. They're living with their mother in New Mexico.'

'Oh – I'm sorry.'

He laughs, pouring himself another glass. 'Actually, in all honesty they hated that trip up the Rhône – they were pains in the ass – they wanted a beach trip to St Marten or somewhere – but I said, hey, you've gotta get educated sometime – you'll remember this for the rest of your lives. My wife and I loved it though.'

'I hadn't even realized you were married.'

'Well, I'm not any more – we're just getting to the end of the divorce.'

'How sad. I'm sorry.'

'Well, thank you – most people don't say that. When they know about the divorce they ask what she's hitting me for – and I can't say that doesn't hurt too, but actually you're right – it is so sad. I really miss her. Well, I guess I really miss the girls – Erica and Jody – they're great kids – fabulous kids – and I hardly get to see them. It's not like there's any reason for it – neither of us had been playing around or anything. It's all completely unnecessary – it's kind of a fantasy thing she felt she had to do, I guess. We had a great life going.'

169

'You must have talked about it – she must have said – I don't know – something.'

'Not really. She just upped and left. Well, actually she said she had to go find herself – I mean she *actually* said it in those very words. Can you believe that? That any human being outside of a pop song would actually say that?'

As the next course arrives Tom has got through two-thirds of the bottle. He looks incredulously at the small, thinish steak, about a third the size of any self-respecting steak back home. Fliss's duck is possibly worse than she'd feared, the sauce being sickly sweet and made of tinned black cherries, the skin more undercooked and rubbery than even she had envisaged. 'Seasonal vegetables' turned out to be peas and carrots – over-boiled; she makes dark murmurings about the Trades Descriptions Act, but Tom seems oblivious, being now happily into his fifth glass of wine and attacking his leathery baked potato with gusto.

'Actually, my wife is a bitch – do you know that, Fliss? An out and out bloody bitch. All I ever did wrong was look after her and pay the bills – her bills mostly. I should be blamed for working all the hours God sends so's I can pay her goddamn bills?'

'Maybe she needed more.'

'What more? She'd got my, blood, Fliss – ' He starts stabbing with exaggerated force at his mushrooms ('Garlicked' they're described on the menu). 'She had me by the balls, Fliss,' he says more loudly than he might have wished. The lone man with the newspaper has already left the room and the couple across the carpet are on their coffees and mints by now. Fliss sees the woman pause just as she's about to slide an After Eight between her teeth, like a card into a cash-point machine. All ears are tuned to Tom.

'When I think about women, Fliss – sometimes – ' He lets out a huge whistling sigh which nearly blows the scarlet candle out. 'I mean, she was a looker, Fliss – cute, God was she cute – but women . . . Who needs them? Who needs that kind of crap?'

'Well . . .' Fliss's appetite for the inedible fades a little further and she pushes the cherries round the edge of her plate.

'I'll tell you something, Fliss. Can I tell you something?'

You're going to anyway, thinks Fliss, sticking the brightest smile she can muster on her face.

'If men had a vagina – right here – ' He swivels his right leg out suddenly and makes a circle of his thumb and forefinger against the middle of his inner thigh, then moves the leg a couple of times towards his own crotch – 'You get me?'

'I think so,' says Fliss. It's a singularly off-putting vision.

'Yeah.' He looks around the room. The woman with the After Eight, who has been frozen to attention, turns hurriedly to attend to the coffeepot. 'Yeah – if men only had a vagina just there, Fliss, you women would never get a look in.'

'No?' says Fliss, trying to make it sound as unnegative as possible.

'Why'd we go through the pain if we didn't need you to fuck, Fliss. Tell me why?'

'Well,' says Fliss, who hopes the question is rhetorical and wonders if the Axminster might possibly open up beneath her feet to allow for instant interment.

'No, I mean it.' Tom looks up now and addresses the man with the After Eights. 'He agrees with me. You – you do, don't you? Look, he's nodding. We wouldn't, would we, sir? We wouldn't go through that kind of shit – who needs it? All we'd need is a nice little cunt – just here, so convenient.' He brings the ring of his finger and thumb up to his eye, and winks through it at Fliss, clicking his tongue.

'We'll pay our bill in the lounge,' says Mr After Eight, suddenly jumping up and more or less sweeping his wife off her seat in front of him, like a sheep dog with a transfixed ewe.

'How's about dessert?' says Tom, grinning vacantly and tossing back the last of the wine.

'No, thanks – gosh, no – I'm really full.'

'Come on – it's my treat – and you haven't eaten anything.'

'No, really,' she says firmly, now longing to leave, but consoled by his assumption of bill-paying.

'Or a Cognac? I'm going to have a Cognac.'

'Must you?'

'I'm going to have a fucking Cognac, Fliss. I'm here in this godforsaken place – sent on some godforsaken mission that I don't even know what I'm on for – does that make sense?' He takes her hand and clasps it between both of his, trying to look deeply into her eyes, but his lids are awfully droopy. 'And I need a Cognac. Keep me company.'

'Just coffee.'

'OK – for you – just coffee.'

In the end there's a kerfuffle about paying the bill. Tom tries hard enough, with much wielding of his Gold Visa card, but his signature won't seem to come out right. He has several goes at it, but it just seems to keep sliding right off the end of the voucher, under the steely gaze of the manageress, whose mouth is now so tightly pursed that her lips have completely disappeared. Eventually, Fliss nervously writes a cheque, producing both her family allowance book and driving licence as added identification, for the total is well over the fifty-pound guarantee limit. As she hands it over, she can hear distant rubber bouncings in her head.

Outside it is still pouring and the interior of the car is veiled in condensation. In the dark, Fliss fiddles around with various knobs to try and get the de-mister going, but nothing seems to happen. Tom is no help, he's slumped back in his seat and she curses her lack of foresight in not working this out beforehand. She rapidly uses up the few tissues in her handbag and starts using the sleeve of her coat as a wiper. Holding it taut over her wrist with the tips of her fingers, she leans across the passenger seat to try to clear the other half of the windscreen. As she does so, her coat falls open and she feels Tom's hands on her breasts. Well, he's drunk of course, and they've surely only brushed there by accident. She has a splintering of a second to decide on a reaction and elects to ignore him.

'Sorry,' she mutters, leaning further across and trying to finish the job she's started. It's quite some accident though, she realizes, for now, while her head and right arm are facing the windscreen, her torso is twisted round towards Tom's face and his hands are beginning to grip a little harder. Now they are – yes, massaging her – yes, definitely, thumbs more or less at nipple level.

'Nice,' he's murmuring. 'So nice . . .' And he half leans forward, burying his nose in a layer of sensible Fair Isle.

Now she's stuck, sort of half out of her seat, with her knee uncomfortably jammed against the handbrake, looming over the body of this man, who now seems to have gone to sleep in her bosom. She doesn't know quite what to do. Given the overall situation, it would hardly be right to slap his face – not even Ivor would expect that – even supposing she could actually reach his face, which she can't, the top of his head being currently some way below her chin. He seems to come round a little.

'Oh – nice,' he murmurs. 'Nice. You smell *so* good.'

His hands move off her breasts and slide round to her back and he's holding her harder. In an effort to remain as upright as possible and not get pressed anywhere near his crotch – that might really be beyond a joke – she sort of rears upwards, getting her whole calf trapped between the ashtray and the transmission lever in the process. As she does, the manageress comes tripping out of the hotel entrance, swathed in a black overcoat and catches sight of them. Her pencilled eyebrows shoot off the top of her forehead. Fliss decides instantly on attack being the best form of defence and shouts out, 'Good night. Thank you!' while leaning further across Tom and vigorously wiping the passenger window with her sleeve. The woman offers no acknowledgement, just jumps into a little car and drives away.

Oh, well, thinks Fliss, I was never going back there anyway – but I might have to keep clear of this end of the village – as she tries to lever herself off.

'Don't go,' says Tom thickly, '*so* nice – I've been sooo lonely . . .' And he lifts up his head suddenly and kisses her. A real kiss too – not a smacker, not in the least paternal, but a full, soft, dry-lipped, cushioned, very warm, surprisingly sexy kiss, strongly scented with Courvoisier. It so catches Fliss by surprise that, to her horror, she hears a sort of appreciative 'Ummmmmm' noise escape her mouth. What? What's she doing allowing 'ummmmms' to pop out like that, when this time she probably should have slapped his face? It gives her the chance to pull back though, and she does, more or less flinging herself into the driver's seat and badly twisting her knee. Tom has now settled back. He's not looking at her; his eyes are beginning to close again. She clears her throat, straightens her coat, clicks her seat belt and starts the car. Immediately the warning light begins flashing, telling her that Tom's belt is not done up, but he's asleep now, and the idea of reaching across him again to do it up seems too risky. To hell with it – if they have an accident he'll just have to go through the windscreen and suffer the consequences.

She sets off along the narrow lanes, the only sound coming from the rhythm of the wipers and the swish of the tyres through deep puddles. Somewhere nearer the house, a Little Owl is caught in the beam of the headlights, taking off from the end of a bare oak branch and dipping down in front of them, chasing some unseen tiny prey. As they turn into the drive, Fliss suddenly feels Tom's hand on her knee, then lightly brushing the inside of her leg, not moving up, just resting there, stroking. Having to have both hands on the steering wheel, she doesn't remove it. She suddenly realizes what an alien feeling it is. It's so definitely not Ivor's hand, being very smooth and warm and oddly foreign, while Ivor's always feel as pale, knurled and worn as his life – and thus infinitely familiar and touching. This is the first unfamiliar hand she's had anywhere so intimate for well over twenty years – it's quite a thought. Almost exhilarating, even if he is drunk. And of course he is – very drunk.

When they pull up outside the house he seems soundly asleep. She tries to wake him but it's no good. His chin is resting on his chest; he's even gently snoring. Back across the bridge, she can see light coming from beneath one of the barn doors. Ivor is obviously in the thick of it. A mixture of embarrassment for what she's just felt, tied up with the atmosphere of the whole uncomfortable evening and the certainty that Ivor is now wholly tied up with the dramas of the lambing pens, stops her from going to fetch his help. Instead she goes into the house and brings out blankets and their huge double sleeping bag, which she tucks all around Tom, who dreams on, a giant cocooned baby. Up above, Martita's nose pokes out from through the gap between her heavy velvet curtains and the window – quivering, scenting.

Tom's eyes snap open and take in nothing. Pitch blackness. His arms seem to be trapped – he's pinioned – packaged – coffined?

In a panic he flings himself forward and hits his brow on a cold, wet surface. He struggles – frees an arm – lashes out – bangs his elbow – catches the door handle – and something, some realization, clicks into his consciousness. He pulls at the handle. The car door swings open and the light goes on. He can see now. He isn't dead after all. He's in a car – the car parked in the front courtyard of the house – and by the car clock, it's 5 a.m. Ummmm? When? What? What's he . . .? What the . . .?

He stops asking questions. Everything hurts. His whole body is stiff and cold. His neck aches; he's got a crick in his back; a glitch in his groin; a stab in his ankles – and ohmygod – his head is agony. He touches where he must have just banged into the windshield, but it's not that bit that hurts. This is inside, this pounding, sledgehammer throb – ohmygod – ohmygod – I got *drunk*. I got drunk and I *never* get drunk. I *should* never get drunk. I am *not* the drunk kind. I am *not* reliable when drunk. Ohhhhhhhheeeah!

He struggles out of the car, dragging the blankets and sleeping bag with him. It is still raining. Was there ever such rain? Did this place ever dry up? Gathering all the coverings around him, like the giant cloak of some Indian chief, he staggers up the front steps and tries the door. It won't give. Can she really have locked him out? He tries again, rattling the handle and pushing harder. Immediately there is a high-pitched yowl, followed by yipping. The Boysies are giving tongue. He looks up towards Martita's window, but can't see a thing in the dark. He stops rattling the door and the dogs quieten. Perhaps he can get in round the back.

He sets off across the courtyard, feeling his way gingerly, hideously aware of the unfenced side of the moat just waiting to suck him in. He moves in towards the house, keeping one hand in touch with the walls, but – ouch – pricking his fingers on leafless climbing rose branches as he goes. Gradually his eyes begin to make out a few dim shapes. Across the bridge, there is actually a light, coming from one of the barns. Ivor must still be at it.

Now he's reached the back door. It opens easily. He feels around for the light in the mud room, but can't find the switch. He's tripping on boots and bins and tins and open umbrellas. He lets all the blankets drop on the floor and lurches, still in the dark, into the kitchen. Now he does find the light switch and stands, dazed and blinking, in the swirling green room.

Water. He must drink plenty of water. He starts hunting around for a glass, banging open various cabinets and finding only plates, catsup, breakfast cereals and saucepans. In the end he grabs down a mug from the open dresser – a mug? Despite himself, he starts automatically examining it for the inevitable inscription. There isn't one – this isn't part of the Collection.

He stands by the big china sink, running the cold water, letting it splash – then rinses the mug several times. Something about this place makes him fear alien bugs – amoebae – bacteria. God only knows what this old, old house harbours by way of dread medical mutants. He gulps down three mugsful, then sticks his head under the faucet and lets the icy flow run all over, into his ears, up his nose – then comes out gasping and hunting for a towel.

He's just drying the back of his neck when he hears it. Maaaa! Maaaa! Maaaaaaa! He stands completely still, holding Fliss's dish towel aloft. Yeah – there it is – bleating – in the kitchen? He looks around – nothing. He must still be drunk. He gulps down another mug of water. There it is again – coming from – ohmygod – ohmygod – coming from the oven. Now he notices the bottom oven door of this old iron stove is slightly open – and a black nose is peeping out. He opens the door cautiously. There's a live lamb *in the oven* – a live lamb – tiny, with a pinky skin, all covered in thin, crinkly sausages of silvery wool – not marinated and stuffed with slivers of garlic – but cooked in its *wool*, alive? Jeez – he *was* drunk.

16

Fliss is awoken at seven by Ivor's clambering into their bed. Completely imploded with exhaustion and smelling quite strongly of animal and wet straw, he crumples down in a heap, yanks the duvet over his head and is already asleep. She sits up, pulling the rest of the covers quite gently around him and tucking them into the small of his back, so that he won't get the icy draught when she heaves out of her side.

The icy draught. That's what's wrong. The room shouldn't be icy. Not at the moment. Not with all that precious oil burning away to keep their guest happy. She jumps out of the bed, scrabbling around to find slippers and dressing gown: the old familiar struggle to bundle yourself up before the ice can get at your bones.

She flies downstairs. The kitchen is all awry – even more so than usual. Cupboards are open, puddles of water sploshed all over. The door to the scullery stands wide with a trail of blankets and sleeping bag lying across, imprinted with muddy gumboot. By the range, the boots in question, Ivor's, are pongily steaming. A couple of feeding bottles are lined up by the sink. That means a couple of 'orphans' rejected by their mothers, and sure enough, when she opens the bottom oven door, she finds the two babies curled around each other, asleep, but both definitely alive – their tiny pink flanks jerkily fluttering with breath. You can't help but smile at them, however familiar an annual sight; however gruesome a fate eventually awaits them – redcurrant jelly and mint sauce. Still, it'll mean a lot of work yet again, if Ivor expects her to hand-rear them. And she does wish he wouldn't always use the turkey roasting tin for this – every year he does it, despite her mutterings about hygiene. Gently she pushes the door to, leaving a crack for air to get in and thankful that the two tiny lambs aren't yet awake and yelling for breakfast.

The kitchen is of course warm, thanks to the range. Now she quickly fills the coal hopper from the hod, slams the big kettle on to the hotplate and heads off to the cellar to see what's up with the boiler.

Nothing's up. That's the problem. It sits, sulking in cold, rusting silence: not a murmur or a squeak, let alone that comforting roar. She bends down to examine the workings. She pushes various knobs, trying to remember what Ivor usually does in this situation. She checks the switch, the plug, the defunct timer. Silence. She wiggles the little thing at the side which Ivor usually wiggles. Silence – and creeping, deathly cold. She stands up and kicks the door to the burner – but that doesn't make her feel any better.

Upstairs, she makes a huge mug of tea and climbs up on to the enamelled edge of the hotplate to rest her bottom and get thoroughly warm. Martita bustles in with the Boysies in choral attendance. When she sees Fliss she stops bustling, and gives one huge, lolloping limp and a cough. The dogs can sniff something interesting immediately and make a dash for the range.

'Titty – not this morning – get them out. We've got a couple of orphans down below.'

'Always seems an unnecessary gesture to me.' Martita comes quickly across, limp-free, and, holding the Boysies back with her feet, bends to inspect the lower oven.

'It works though. It's this or the airing cupboard, which isn't half as effective.'

'You can't expect my darlings to understand – they're trained killers.'

'Put them in the scullery. Please.'

'It's freezing out there. This house is freezing. What's happened?'

'The boiler's died.'

'Oh, I could've told you so. You can't run it day in day out like that suddenly – and expect to get away with it. It isn't used to it – it hasn't done it for years. You've probably given it a heart attack – like you hope to give me.'

'I beg your pardon?'

'Granted.'

Fliss sniffs, but she's not going to rise to the bait.

'I shall take to my bed again,' says Martita. 'I cannot be expected to live like this with my little frame – it's not as if I've much meat on me – to sustain me. I'm only a little bag of bones.'

'Yes, Titty.'

'I'd better have a little something on a tray.'

'It's only the same heating situation as usual, you know – i.e. nothing. You're perfectly well used to it. You'd better bung on another couple of sweaters.'

'But I'm not used to it now. I've had nearly a week of suffocating heat – the change could kill me. I'd better go to bed and take it gradually.'

'It was going to be turned off as soon as Tom left anyway –

and it's much more Tom I'm worried about. He can't take to his bed.'

'*Can't* he now?'

'What? Well, of course not.'

'You do surprise me.'

'What?'

'He could take to yours.'

'What?'

'I saw you last night.'

For one slivering of a moment, Fliss has a vision that it was Martita dressed up as the manageress in the Crown and Sceptre car park last night. Come to think about it – those Marlene Dietrich eyebrows . . .

'What are you implying, Titty?'

'Tucking him into the car – blankets. Whatever were you up to? Not very *comme il faut*.'

'Don't be ridiculous, Titty,' but she jumps off the range and bends to open the lamb oven, so as to turn her face away, for infuriatingly she can feel a huge blush racing up her neck.

'Hmmm!' says Titty. 'I don't know what you were doing going out anyway – poor darling Ivor – struggling on his own.'

'It's what he wanted, Titty,' says Fliss evenly, poking one of the lambs, hoping it'll wake up and create a distraction. 'He wanted to be left alone to get on with it – you know he always does.'

'Left with only a Thermos – not very sustaining. Tinned soup, I shouldn't wonder.'

'Home-made mushroom and there was a whole cassoulet in the oven when he wanted it.'

'And I of course totally abandoned and forgotten.'

182

'I called and I knocked on your door, as you very well know, and there was heaps of food if you wanted it.'

'I was reduced to tea and shortbread. I couldn't come down.' Martita turns away to the hall door and starts limping out of the room. 'I'm really not at my best – and *very* disappointed in you.' She limps out with the Boysies following a little uncertainly, for breakfast has yet to be served.

Fliss waits a moment – then sure enough, Martita limps in again.

'I think I should have a couple of rashers with my poached eggs – I really feel I need bolstering. And could you bring up the Boysies' Chummybits – they can't eat down here – what with one thing and another.'

The next couple of hours are pretty dismal. In a way Marita's right: the contrast with the previous week of sumptuous, if unaccustomed, heat has made this deadening icy chill much more difficult than usual, and Fliss is forced back to her normal winter behaviour of dashing from one warm island to another to keep going. Having hurriedly dressed and thrown the kitchen and scullery back together again, the lambs are awake and both howling for their first feed. Then Jake, Ivor's friend from the village and their annual emergency helpmate during lambing, dashes in for a pee and a flask of coffee, and also to warn her that there may be more to come. Triplets seem to be the order of this first day and he's having trouble getting the 'spare' lambs accepted by the ewes with only singles or still births.

Of Tom, there's been no sign – only that trail of bedding he obviously left behind last night and which will all need washing, curse him. She chooses not to think of the previous night. Tom was of course drunk – out of his mind – and with a bit of luck won't remember much of it anyway. It's all too embarrassing to think about – but also, oh dear, also just the tiniest bit, what? Well . . . no, better not think it through. Just something surprising for her to feel, she reckons, and best left undefined.

At nine, the phone rings. It is Barney.

'I'm here, dear.'

'Where here – really meaning *here*?'

'Not Harrogate, dear. What a time I've had. Too ghastly. Don't ask.'

'All right.'

'Well, you could've asked a bit. How is she?'

'What?'

'My car dear. How is she? I can't tell you how I've missed her. That hire car was all tin, dear, and quite apart from the lethal axle, it whistled.'

'It's fine – of course. What did you expect?'

'I couldn't begin to imagine. It's all been too, too ghastly. It's made me ill. I'm dying.'

'I'll send a wreath.'

'Don't be tart, dear. I've told you before it doesn't suit you. You're the soft maternal type – stick with it.'

'Getting harder by the moment. Aren't you going to ask me?'

'Hm?'

'How it's going? He's still here in case you were wondering – Tom.'

'Oh – that bodes well – we're on to "Tom" now, are we? Of course Americans always are very quick to get pally – but you want to watch it – they're often really quite formal under the skin. I've been bitten in the past that way – especially in biz.'

'We're still awaiting your call.'

'This is it, dear.'

' "Call" in the English sense, Barney for goodness' sake – "call" as in "visit". Are you coming up now?'

'Well, I'm stuck, aren't I? I had to leave the wretched hire vehicle in Bury and come home by taxi, which cost me a fortune I might add – it's all totting up.'

'Don't tell me about it. I got landed with paying a minor ransom for a ghastly dinner last night. We went to the Crown and Sceptre – '

'Oh dear – not very suitable. I could've warned you.'

'You weren't here to ask.'

'You should have taken him to Tinkerbells. He'd have *loved* their Spotted Dick.'

'Oh, shut up. Are you coming or aren't you?'

'You'll have to fetch – I'm stuck. Fetch and then possibly I can have my darling back now? Possibly you've finished all your gallivanting around the countryside?'

'I don't know really. I suppose we've sort of finished – it's all been a bit of a damp squib – quite literally most of the time. I did warn you this was the most hopeless time of the year to try and impress anybody with us. Talk about an uphill battle. And now the boiler's died.'

'*WHAT?*' Barney gives a huge despairing sigh.

'In the night. It's so cold in here it feels like a meat packers'.'

'Get it fixed – quick.'

'I can't. Ivor's up to his elbows in lambing – quite literally. At the moment he's sound asleep. He was up all night.'

'Get an engineer – like other people. Tell them it's an emergency.'

'Don't be silly, Barney.'

'I always forget quite how utterly impossible you lot are.' He sighs again, blowing a great blast down the receiver.

'It's not just *paying* for an engineer – it's probably impossible anyway. The parts don't exist any more. It's bound to be a welding, creative kind of job – it'll need Ivor with his oxyacetylene and a whole free day – probably several days.'

'Get him out then – Klaus – get him down here quickly. You can't discuss business in that sort of atmosphere – far too negative. Bring him down as soon as poss and I'll get some mulled claret on the go – soften him up a bit.'

'I'd stick to coffee actually,' says Fliss, thinking of last night, 'lots of it – black.'

Which is what she leaves outside Tom's door, having knocked briskly, shouted 'rise and shine', and heard a muffled growl in return. Once she knows he's both alive and has heard her, she bangs the mug down on the floor and streaks off down the corridor, not wanting to meet his eyes directly yet, and certainly not if he's in any state of undress.

He came to quite some time ago in fact, the leaden cold having worked its way through his deep unconsciousness. He's been lying here with just the tip of his nose and his brow poked out of the bedclothes, the auricula quilt pulled all the way up and round his ears, wondering if the cold he can sort of smell can possibly be real. When he sits up and realizes it is, he leaps for his clothes, breaking the habit of more or less a lifetime by jumping straight into his trousers without bathing or showering first. The last time he did that was in 1968 at Camp Minnehaha in the Catskills; and then it was only because he had a bad case of poison ivy and didn't want to disturb the camomile salve his counsellor, Betsy Myers, had so thoughtfully (indeed lovingly) administered the night before. Sweet memories in the circumstances.

17

It's an awkward drive back down to Long Pecklam – this time in the daylight. However, there's minor salvation in that for the first time since he arrived at Heathrow, a watery sun has come out. To his shamed amazement, Tom follows Fliss's cue and starts discussing the weather with full, True Brit-like intensity. Yes, it's amazing – yes, it's a transformation. How wonderful that church tower looks caught in the pale golden light like that – no, he hadn't realized the views were so far-reaching – what unexpected colours there are in winter – twigs and branches – some of them are quite red, aren't they? – no, you wouldn't believe it – ya-de-da-de-daaa. Isn't it amazing? Isn't it weird? Isn't it heck. All this to try and drive away the ill-defined twinges about last night – twinges which take on the sharpness of stab wounds as they pass the Crown and Sceptre to get to this Fitzgerald guy's place.

However, Fliss has yet to utter a word about last night and drives steadily on past the car park and into the village. She seems so absorbed and concentrated on getting them there that he allows himself to turn and look fully at her. He remembers most of last night he reckons, but it does get a teensy bit hazy towards the end of that tough, tiny little steak. Then there was outside . . . Well, had he really done that last night? He can't remember doing anything *precisely* – just an overall need for warmth and comfort. He was feeling so cut off – amputated – that's what he felt – and she'd seemed like a kind of connection. If he is remembering it right – and that's the trouble – he isn't entirely sure what he *is* remembering. Well, maybe he'd better not ignore it – so he says quietly, 'I guess I owe you some kind of an apology?'

As the tone of his voice makes what should have been a statement into a question, she's immediately annoyed rather than mollified. This makes her sound a lot harder and brisker than she feels.

'Whatever for?' she says.

'Well, I – you know . . . I – '

'Oh, we're all grown-up enough to cope with an occasional fall from grace, I hope,' she says, brisker and brisker.

'I don't really drink much these days – well, really not at all. I think I must've overdone it.'

'Was that it?'

'I guess so. I'm sorry.'

'It's of no consequence. None whatsoever.'

'I wouldn't have wanted to . . .'

'Yes?'

'Well, whatever – I guess. I think I owe you for the dinner anyway – you must've picked up the check?'

'I wouldn't hear of it,' she says with pompous finality, cursing her own pride, as the clanging of her empty bank balance resounds in her head.

'OK.' He nods, turning away from her, as they pull up outside Fitzgerald & Calder's dark-green frontage. If that's going to be her attitude, he's not going to bother to break it.

*

189

Inside, Barney has a full-scale welcome going. A huge fire is burning in the inglenook, with wing chairs drawn up around in a semicircle. Barney has all the right accessories of course – a copper pan of mull is standing on a trivet in the hearth, scenting the air deliciously with cinnamon, lemon and wine, and on the oak table a full cafetière is wrapped in a sort of muff of dark-green padding, surrounded by several plates of goodies – warm croissants, little iced German biscuits, fruit cake. This is more like it, thinks Tom – shades of Charles Dickens and *Masterpiece Theatre*. He expects either Mr Pickwick or Diana Rigg to pop out at any moment.

Barney is beaming and pumping Tom's hand with energy and hale-fellow-well-met, but as he turns away so only Fliss can see his face, he drops his eyelids to half-mast and hisses in her ear, 'Some of us just know when to pull out all the stops – even though, my dear, I'm simply *dying* of exhaustion.'

Tom wanders around, making all the right noises about the shop – admiring the huge oak pieces, the early iron sconces, the tapestries, a couple of full-length portraits – 'Only in the manner of Van Dyck – but *what* a manner, dear.' Barney leaves him to it, having soaked up an adequate degree of praise, and goes back to the door, ostensibly to change the 'Open' sign to 'Closed' – a huge concession this, 'but otherwise we'll never have a moment's peace' – but also taking the opportunity to get a good eyeful of his Volvo to make sure it's all still there.

Despite the seductive aroma of the mull, Tom sticks firmly to coffee – terrific coffee in this case, for once it's delicious – and they sit munching, and as ever skirting around the real topic of conversation – making do with pleasantries about – yet again (and I may just scream, he thinks) the weather. The weather in Harrogate – 'too, too ghastly' – the weather in Suffolk – 'until this morning, too vile for words' – altogether too much weather. It's time to cut the crap.

'I have to tell you Mr Fitzgerald – '

'Oh, "Barney" – do.'

'I have to tell you, *Barney*, that I'm not altogether happy about this collection.'

'Nooo?' Barney's questioning tone rises so high, it's almost falsetto.

'No,' says Tom firmly, in a low, steady growl. 'There are certain questions I would need resolving before I could possibly advise my client to proceed.'

'Ummmm?' Barney's face is a study in surprised candour.

'Particularly with regard to title.'

'In what sense?'

'I'm sure you know what I mean by "title", Barney – a man as experienced as yourself in your field.'

'Well, of course.' Barney takes a big slurp of mull. 'But in this instance? Ivor Harley-Wright has clear ownership of the Collection, I can assure you of that.'

'Mrs Harley-Wright would not, I think, agree with you – Mrs Harley-Wright Senior, that is.'

Barney explodes in a scornful guffaw. 'Oh, *Martita* – is that what you're on about? What's she said to you?'

'I don't think I can – I'm not at liberty – I wouldn't want to betray a confidence, you understand.'

'Whatever she's said – it's not true, you know.' Barney taps his temple with a forefinger. 'We're not all there – you surely realize that.'

'I wouldn't want to comment on that, but neither would

191

I want my client to become embroiled in any sort of family dispute. You've gotta understand that my first allegiance in this instance has gotta be to my client and at the moment I'm just not happy about the situation.' Tom turns to Fliss, who has stopped chewing her croissant in mid-mouthful. It suddenly tastes of blotting paper. 'I'm sorry – I really am. I know this deal means a lot to you.'

Barney, in bristling panic, reverts to formality.

'This sort of collection does not become available every day of the week – oh, no – don't think so for a moment. Not in a year – scarcely in a decade. I have to tell you, Mr Klaus, that there are plenty more fish in the sea where you and your client come from. We've had several inquiries, you know.'

'I'm very glad for you. In that case you won't be too disturbed if I advise my client against purchase.'

'Naturally we'd be disappointed.' Barney has flushed purple. 'Apart from anything else, we will have wasted so much time and – well – resources.'

Silence hangs around the room for a moment. In the absence of a handy spittoon, Fliss has to finish her mouthful or remain mute. In the circumstances it's like trying to swallow a lump of wallpaper paste, so to help she gulps down her cup of coffee in one scalding gasp.

'Surely all you need is proof,' she manages. 'What about the will – my father-in-law's will? Wouldn't that prove that the Collection belongs to us?'

As she says it, Barney mouths a fierce 'No' behind Tom's head, his lips remaining forced into a tight little moue of disapproval.

'That would certainly help,' says Tom. 'The way things are, and with your mother-in-law's personality being as it is – well, I wouldn't want to risk any sort of confrontation.'

'With *Titty*? She's a harmless old bat – you must see that.'

'If you'll excuse me, Fliss, I'd say Martita shows a distinctly irrational frame of mind – and she's gotten really set against selling this collection whether it's hers or not. Now that kind of personality coupled with litigious tendencies is just the kind of behaviour I'm very wary of. I mean, who needs it? In business you might occasionally – just occasionally – put up with that kind of crap – if you'll excuse me – but in this case? This collection – I mean, it's interesting of course, if you like that kind of thing – but you know, we're not talking major purchase here – not for a man of my client's standing. My client is a big player in the art world – big – and this is really, you know – just a sort of whim for him – a lark – I think you know what I mean. And if there's going to be *any* sort of trouble – well, I guess you could say that most of the fun gets drained out of it – it loses its point.'

'I'm really very surprised and disappointed in you, Mr Klaus,' says Barney archly, exuding hurt pride. 'I thought this part of the proposition had all been cleared with Denmans and I'm really not used to having my word doubted like this. I have a very long-standing, excellent reputation in this field, and you can take my word that the Collection is Ivor Harley-Wright's to dispose of.'

'I have no reason to doubt your reputation, Mr Fitzgerald,' says Tom, exchanging arch for arch, 'but Denmans were only brought in to check on the quality and authenticity of the actual pieces from an expert's point of view, and as you know, even on that level, the Collection is somewhat – shall we say – irregular. However, it's entirely up to me to check on the legality of the situation and the viability of the deal.'

Fliss finds her voice again. 'You've still got a copy of the will, haven't you, Barney? From when we were first working out the sale?'

'I'm not sure,' says Barney acidly, but with a contrived, rather vague look about the eyes.

'I'm sure you have,' says Fliss firmly. 'If not,' she continues, turning to Tom, 'we've got one at home.'

'I'll go and check,' says Barney, and sulks out of the room.

The two of them sit there staring glumly at the magnificent log fire, Fliss feeling very chilled and slightly sick. She hadn't consciously realized how very much she was depending on the sale to go through. And if it didn't, what then? With the overdraft getting ever bigger, the overheads more menacing, the Ghost of the Under Manager ever more pressing? She realizes suddenly that for all their cheerful murmurings of doubt and jokey touchings of wood, she and Ivor have been counting absolutely on the salvation of this scheme.

'I'm sorry,' says Tom in a silence broken only by the fire crackling. 'I'm only doing my job.'

'Of course,' she says stiffly. 'And so you must.'

Barney comes back after a scarcely decent interval – for of course he'd known precisely where he'd filed the copy of Harry's will.

'Yes – our luck is in,' he says with a stab at gaiety. 'You were quite right, Flissie dear, I do have a copy after all,' this last said with an embarrassing effort to sound surprised.

'May I?' Tom takes it over to the window and starts rapidly reading.

'We'll leave you in peace,' says Barney, sticking to the

same upbeat artificial chumminess. 'I want Flissie to come and see my new pouffe. Come along, dear.'

He seizes her by the sleeve and propels her out of the back and up his private staircase.

'What on earth did you want to suggest that for?' he hisses, once he's pushed her into his tiny, but exquisite hallway.

'It seemed the only way.'

'You realize you've buggered the whole thing?'

'Why?'

'He'll see the conditions.'

'But we had to do something – otherwise we just had an impasse. He would've gone home to wherever it is and told his Mr Big that we didn't even own the thing we're trying to sell.'

'With those conditions, dear, you might just as well not.'

'You always said they didn't really matter.'

'Not exactly.'

'Yes, you did – you always said a sufficiently interested buyer wouldn't mind.'

'Wouldn't *notice*, that's what I meant. Or wouldn't notice until it was too late and if sufficiently rich – and sufficiently *foreign* – foreign as in exporting the thing as quickly and far away as possible – that's what I meant. I hadn't expected to have to rub a client's nose right in the damn things like a dog's mess. I'm not used to having my word doubted. It's ruffled my feathers – bloody man.'

'I didn't think it mattered that much – and if he was going to advise his client against the whole idea in any case. . .'

'I don't know – the whole thing's a mess. I thought you would've had him more softened up by now – it's very disappointing. You'd better come and see my pouffe anyway to lend credence.'

'If only that were all it would take.'

Barney's upstairs drawing room runs the full width of the frontage and glows in Chinese yellow. It is currently crowned in the centre by a vast squashy cushion – the size of a small double bed – upholstered in mattress ticking and bound in thick ropes and tassels of hemp.

'What do you think?'

'It's very – big.'

'It's my Doge's throne – one's sort of supposed to lie back and think of England – or not, as the case may be. I think it has definite possibilities. Very conversational.'

'It's certainly that.'

'I think we've left him long enough. Possibly he won't have noticed.'

Tom is sitting again, near the fire; leaning forward and tapping the copy of the will against his knees.

'That seems to settle title,' he says, 'though I'd want it confirmed by an English lawyer.'

A small pause hangs around in the room waiting to be filled. Fliss decides on a glass of mull by way of distraction and goes to pour one.

'Of course,' says Barney, expansive again. 'It was never in any doubt.'

'I don't recall Denmans mentioning anything about these various caveats?'

'I beg your pardon?' Barney promptly drops expansion and reverts to vague.

'These various stipulations.'

'Ummmmmm?' Vaguer and vaguer.

'You can't have imagined I'd miss them?'

'About the Collection?'

'That seems to be what we're discussing.' Tom's tone loses its lightness and takes on a steely edge. 'That it has to remain as a single entity and be displayed as such for a period of *twenty-five* years? That's quite a little stipulation – just tucked in there – ticking away.'

'Hardly a real issue – '

'Oh, I'd call that an issue. I certainly would. That is my idea of an issue. My client hands over a large sum of money for a possession he's then not free to dispose of as he wishes? I don't know about things here, but in America a man's legal property takes on a very special status – you could almost call it sacred. In fact I think I would – that's no exaggeration – sacred. We do not expect to find our legally acquired possessions surrounded by limitations and pro-visos – that is not the American way.'

'It is of course a different mentality.' Barney sinks into the chair opposite Tom, suddenly weighted with gravity.

'Excuse me?'

'It is true. You're right of course. We have a different way of looking at things. We believe in the concept of the trust – of handing things on, intact as it were, to the next generation. We don't see these things as mere physical possessions. We see them as symbols of a culture – Our Culture – to be guarded during our lifetime and handed on to the next generation. That for us – that *trust* is what is sacred – not the mere concept of ownership.'

Fliss, who has been perching on the edge of the hearth, is so appalled by this pompous hypocrisy that she leans back on her heels and finds herself sitting in the ash.

'Ohhh,' says Tom, 'I see – so we're not talking money

here – no, far too dirty. This – this sacred trust of a collection doesn't in fact represent a couple of hundred thousand big ones that these good people just happen to need to get them out of the proverbial shit? Is that right? Jeez – no, I must have got it wrong. No – we're talking about a thousand years of Anglo-Saxon culture culminating in seven versions of a mug called "Mum's Pearlies" – correct me if I'm wrong.'

'I was talking in general terms about the whole concept of collecting works of art and collecting them for their own sakes rather than a more philistine notion of collection as possession – that's all – please don't get me wrong.'

'Well, Mr Fitzgerald, I guess the country that boasts the Metropolitan, the National in Washington, the Whitney, the Getty and the Guggenheim among many other internationally renowned institutions could be said to have a pretty clear idea of the concept of collecting – for its own sake.'

'Oh, don't misunderstand – '

'I don't think I do, Mr Fitzgerald – I don't think I do at all. Who do you imagine you've been dealing with? Did you really think for one second that I wouldn't check this thing out? My client is Constantine Ziminovski, for God's sake. You think Constantine Ziminovski is going to saddle himself with some dumb little list of provisos? Provisos in exchange for a huge cheque in good old American dollars? And what kind of an idiot do you take me for?' He turns sharply to Fliss, who is now glowing the same shade as the mull. 'And you?'

'We didn't think they mattered – the conditions,' she mumbles. 'They're just a silly thing Harry put there, probably to stop Titty flogging them off one by one when nobody was looking. He knew she hated the whole thing – despised it. He would have loved it going to America – and we thought – well, once it was actually there – once it was all gone – well, none of it could be touched. Titty isn't going to do anything, you know – of course she isn't. She can't afford to do anything. It wasn't meant to be some huge conspiracy. There just didn't seem any point in bothering you with the details – unnecessarily.'

'You think contravening the terms of your father-in-law's will is an unnecessary detail? Seriously you think that?'

'Well – yes.'

'Give me a break!' He raises his eyes heavenwards and barks out a dry little laugh. 'I guess we better leave it at that. If we could go back to the house so I can get my stuff – then perhaps you could get me to the train station. I really don't think we have much more to discuss.'

Barney drives them back in scratchy, uncomfortable silence and dumps them unceremoniously on the mainland side of the bridge. Now the deal's 'gone pear-shaped', as he puts it, he isn't in the least concerned about Tom's opinion of the elderly Peugeots.

'In fact,' he hisses into Fliss's ear, 'he can bloody well walk to Colchester – or hitch a lift.' He revs up the Volvo and disappears down the drive in a scatter of spitting gravel.

Fliss feels completely nauseated, her stomach turned inside out with embarrassed stress. They march over the bridge and on into the house, still silent. She has completely forgotten about the dead boiler – so has Tom. The grim cold saps whatever spirit might have been left. Fliss heads automatically for the kitchen and murmurs something about lunch.

'Thank you – no. If you wouldn't mind checking the train

schedule? I think I ought to get back to London as soon as possible. I may even get an evening flight back to New York. I'll call Pan Am – from London,' he adds hastily, as Fliss indicates the hall phone, for into his mind there pops the image of a comfortable hotel room, a ticket for *Phantom* (did they have returns?) – and perhaps, after all, dinner at Le Gavroche – would he need a reservation?

So they set off within the hour, back down the drive, but this time rattling around in the elderly rust bucket, breathing in aromas of turpentine, fertilizer, hay and sheep-droppings; listening to the pop-popping of its failing exhaust pipe.

For the first five minutes or so, they say nothing at all. Even the weather and landscape have finally deserted Fliss as possible topics of conversational escape. They have to drive through Long Pecklam yet again to get back to the main road, and again they pass the Crown and Sceptre and Fitzgerald & Calder – images which seem to be appearing to Tom like recurring symbols in a nightmare.

'Look – I'm really sorry,' he says at last, as they get out on to the main road.

'It's quite all right,' she says quickly, then, 'I mean, it's not – I mean it's *me* – I'm really sorry. I feel rather shabby. It wasn't meant to be a trick, you know. I know that's what it looks like – but it really wasn't. Ivor does own the collection – and Titty wouldn't have sued your Mr whoever he is.'

'Ziminovski.'

'Right – him.'

'He's very well known in America.'

'I'm sure.'

'He just doesn't court cheap publicity. He's a man with dignity.'

'Of course.'

'With very exacting standards.'

'Absolutely.'

'I'm sorry, but he just wouldn't countenance something like this – it's too messy.'

'Right.' They lapse into silence again for half a mile or so, then she says, 'I just wanted you to know – that there wasn't any trick – because there wasn't really any problem. There wouldn't have been. I mean, I know Titty – she's all huff and puff – she doesn't actually *do*. Nothing would have happened. It would have been fine.'

'I just don't believe you people.'

'What?'

'Are you living in the same century? Are you even on the same planet? I mean it, Fliss – seriously – are you? You're talking as if you're in some *fairy* story – Hans Christian Andersen and "The Tale of the Magic Mugs" – '

'What?' She turns to look at him, amazed – but for too long.

'For Christ's sake, look where you're going!' he snaps.

She looks back at the road.

'I mean, are you here? Actually here? We are talking entropy, Fliss – your life is just out of control. You're an intelligent, attractive woman and you've got this chaos around you – nothing but chaos and fusty, musty – old, everything's so goddamn old – as if "old" automatically equals "good". We're living in this amazing world – we've got technology – the computer vision – the global village – but you guys, you're like that dinosaur you were talking

201

about on your driveway – with that fallen tree. Dinosaurs fucking *gardening* – that's you.'

'Weeding. I said "weeding" – and you've entirely missed the point.'

As they pull into the station forecourt, she is rigid with fury, biting her lips, wanting to tip him out as soon as possible before the tears spill over. She comes to an abrupt halt, but keeps the engine running, her hand still gripping the gear stick. He doesn't move.

'Well – I guess I'd better go.'

'Yes, I guess you better had.' The mocking imitation comes to her rescue, in vocabulary if not in tone. In fact she's having to hold in everything – it would be the final humiliation to blub in front of him.

He lays a hand lightly on the top of hers – again that warm, smooth, alien feeling, rubbing his fingertips across her knuckles. 'Look – I'm sorry – I really am. I don't know what got into me – look despite what I said I've enjoyed meeting you – I really have – the rest – well, that's been – an experience.'

'Glad to have been useful in some way then,' she manages to get out, stiffly, and she snatches her hand off the gearstick, promptly stalling the car.

'I guess I'd better say *au revoir*.'

'I'm sure goodbye is far more appropriate.'

She lets him unload his case from the back, and as he starts to walk towards the ticket office she turns the ignition key. Nothing happens, not even a little mechanical cough. The car too has died. She leans her head forward on the steering wheel and catches the horn. When Tom turns round he can't see her head; only hear the sad, blasting wail.

18

Rosalie Klaus just hates to have to disturb her son. He must be so tired – *exhausted* – she just knows it. He got back from Kennedy some time in the wee small hours and had let himself in – of course he knows the combination. It's kind of a nice feeling to have him here, back in his old room – almost like old times. Well, of course it isn't exactly his old room – not geographically – but it feels just the same. She even had the same sort of jalousie windows put in down at the end here – just like they'd had in Westport. You could almost imagine the wind blowing in from the Sound. And it's a Saturday – maybe there's a football game they could go to – or they should all go out for lunch – maybe dinner – should she make reservations?

She's been creeping round the house, making exaggerated shushing noises to Tom Senior, who's been up since dawn playing with his new toy. They've just had satellite added to the only recently acquired cable. They've got this huge, hideous black dish lurking on the garage roof like a giant metal spider and Tom Senior has taken to sitting in his den with five televisions on all at the same time, holding his zapper and doing just that – zapping from channel to channel from all over the world, letting each station have just about forty-five seconds' chance to catch and hold his attention. She finds it pretty irritating at the moment just to be on the same floor as him, let alone in the same room. And *loud* – she seriously wonders about his hearing sometimes.

And now there's this phone call from a Mrs Bierce – Mr Z's Mrs Bierce. She called at 7.45 a.m. (on a Saturday?) to speak to Tom, and Rosalie really didn't want to wake him – I mean, really she didn't. But Mrs Bierce was kind of insistent. She suggested she'd call again in twenty minutes, by which time she was sure Rosalie could get him to the phone. And there was something in her tone which suggested this wasn't any sort of request – more of a – well – more of a demand, stark and simple.

Rosalie thinks of fixing Tom an eggnog – just egg, milk and vanilla, no alcohol of course – just what he used to like when he was a little boy and wasn't feeling too hot – but she figures she doesn't have the time right now. So she trips down the hallway to Tom's door, kind of wishing they'd gone for carpeting along here, instead of this marble. It's beautiful of course, but kind of noisy. Then she remembers she's got to wake Tom up anyway and fast, and quits tiptoeing to rap on his door.

'Honey?' No answer. 'Honeyyyyyy?'

'Hmmmm?'

'Can I come in?'

'Ummmmm.'

Rosalie pokes her head around the door. She can just see Tom's head peeping over the comforter – all tousled, just like he was eight years old. Then he rolls over, exposes one hugely hairy armpit and groans.

'Mom? What the . . .?'

'I'm sorry, sweetheart. I know you got in so late from the

airport but you've had a call. Mrs Bierce? It sounds kind of urgent.'

'Mrs who?'

'Mr Ziminovski's secretary.' She hisses the name in an awed whisper and continues in the same sibilant tone, 'I think she's got a message for you – from him.'

'Oh, God.' Tom rolls back over and pulls the comforter over his head.

'Can I fix you something, sweetheart? Eggnog?'

Tom groans again but doesn't otherwise move.

'Well, I guess if I were you I'd jump in the shower. She's calling back in about fifteen minutes and she sounded kind of keen.'

'Ummmmm.'

'So you're awake?'

'I'm awake.'

'Good morning, Mr Klaus.' Mrs Bierce's voice is a staccato rap. 'I have Mr Ziminovski on the line for you – hold please.'

There is a long pause – a very long pause. Tom seems to have an uncomfortable ocean of time to think of what to say and to let resentment build.

'Tom! Hi, there.' Mr Z is panting slightly. 'I'm in the middle of my Nautilus circuit.'

'Good morning, sir.'

'How was your trip?'

'Fine, sir.'

'Good. I wanna hear all about it.'

'I'll have a report ready for you early next week. Monday or Tuesday?'

'How about now?'

'Now, sir?'

'Come on up. Come for brunch. Jeremiah's got this great new way of fixing Bullshots – you'll love it.'

'Oh – OK. Sir. Great.' They might as well be leadshots for all the enthusiasm Tom can muster. 'That sounds great,' he adds, but he doesn't even sound convincing to himself.

'You got pictures?'

'Sir?'

'Of the set-up over there? You did take pictures?'

'They're still on the roll.'

'Get them developed at that one-hour place on Route 22 and then come on over. They'll be expecting you at the gate.'

'OK, sir, but – '

'*But*, Tom?'

'Well – nothing. OK, sir. I'll see you later.'

'Don't be long, Tom. I'm waiting for you.'

Damp from the shower, slightly nauseous from his mother's enforced administration of eggnog (Why does she keep doing that? *Once*, maybe when he was six, he must've said he liked it and she's been slinging it to him at every available opportunity ever since) and generally reeling from jet lag, people lag, experience lag and, for all he knows, historic time lag, he makes his way along Route 22 to the photo store. At least he's back in his own sweet Porsche and driving on the *right* side of the road along smooth blacktop with crisp yellow lines against a background of dazzlingly sharp, blue sky. No need to discuss the weather at any rate. Thank your own God for small, sweet blessings.

While the developers get to work on his lone roll of film, he goes over to the drugstore for a cup of coffee. It's a real old-fashioned drugstore this, with a lunch counter in the corner complete with those red leatherette-topped chrome drum swivel seats – the real old ones you'd expect to see in one of those Annette Funicello teen movies of his youth, pulsating chocolate malteds and white stilettos. He perches himself there, swivelling gently, eyeing up the refrigerated electric turntable display of coconut custard pies, blueberry and cherry cheesecakes and deep lemon meringue – drenched in saturated fats and calories. America – good old, sweet old – what's he thinking? Sweet *young* America. After all that Olde Worlde Englishe crappe he'd had crammed down his throat. And yet here he is, kind of nostalgic for the mood this drugstore encapsulates – mostly out of Norman Rockwell with shades of Edward Hopper, touches of Archie and Li'l Abner, a dash of Bing and a sprinkling of Amos and Andy – oh, my America. Kind of brings a lump to his throat – surprising.

Back on the road he snakes up the hill, through the woods towards the Ziminovski estate. Only now does he register the soft suede greyness of everywhere – the leafless trees and even the ground all being a uniform shade of ash. England hadn't been like this. England's sky had been mostly ashen, but England's fields, hills, woods and gardens had been, even during this last dank, wintry week, a dense patchwork of colour and tone – dozens of greens, browns, bronzes, pinks and reds popping up in all the strangest places.

With an intense pang of embarrassment he remembers for a second that conversation with Fliss on Thursday morning, when he'd allowed himself to join her in going on and on about the different shades of twigs – *twigs* – him? He must've been well and truly pixilated. Pixilated – or the French had a word for it which sort of described his reaction to the week – *bouleversé*? That was it, he'd been kind of bouleversé by the whole experience – unsettling, uncomfortable – and the faster he could get physical and emotional distance between him and it the better. But now, with no preparation and feeling about as perky as a wrung-out face flannel, he was going to have to translate that experience to Mr Z – face to face – Mr Z, a man who'd never been bouleversé in his entire life, and for whom the very concept would be as alien as life on Pluto.

The main gates of the estate are immense black curlicues of decorative iron tipped with gold, hanging from tall stone pillars, each of which is topped with a heraldic-looking kind of angled 'Z'. On either side sits a small, square lodge in mellow stone, each with a little square cupola topped by a 'Z' weathervane. Tom stops the car and a big burly white guy in a uniform which could just be confused with that of a regular cop comes out. Tom rolls down the window. This is not the same guard as last weekend. This guy is chewing and bends slowly down, resting his belly on the car door.

'Hi,' says the guard.

'Good morning,' says Tom pompously. This guy is just a little too casual for comfort. He, Tom, is after all Mr Z's corporate lawyer, not just any old member of staff, and a little respect is due. The guy should've spat out whatever he was chewing at the very least. 'Tom Klaus,' says Tom. 'Mr Ziminovski is expecting me.'

'Wait here.'

'Mr Ziminovski said you'd be informed,' Tom protests.

'Wait here.' The guy ambles back towards the lodge and starts shouting into a radio walkie-talkie. 'I've got a guy here – says Mr Z's expecting him. He's not on the guest list.'

'A guy?' Tom seethes.

'Your name again?' the guard shouts.

'Thomas Klaus III,' says Tom. That'll show him.

The guard repeats this to the walkie-talkie, listens to a crackly reply, laughs, shouts back, 'You've got it!' into the machine and ambles over.

'Go on up, Tom. You bin here before?'

'Only last week. You weren't here,' says Tom pointedly.

'Keep taking the right-hand turns, otherwise you'll land up in one of the guest complexes or the office complex or the stables or shit knows where.'

'OK, I remember.'

'And you'll have to talk to the house half-way up the hill – there's another barrier.'

'I know.'

'Just doin' my job.'

Slowly the gates swing open and Tom drives through. He hears them clank shut behind him as he takes the first right turn and starts the climb up to the house. It's only a week since he'd been here – since he'd visited for the first time. It might *feel* like a year had elapsed but that was down to all that British pixilation. The important thing now is to keep his cool – communicate directly with Mr Z, be controlled, be mature, be *advisory* – that is what he is paid for when all is said and done. He mustn't display even a fraction of the awe he might feel. This is a gorgeous place though. He clamps his jaw tight shut to avoid any possibility of gaping.

Up the hills he climbs. The rolling acres are now burnt brownish grey by the intense winter frosts, but still bear a shorn, mown look, smooth as the baize on a card table. Up on the left, as if placed by a landscape painter, a herd of deer grazes. A romantic vision, but in fact their presence injects a strange reality, for as protection against their marauding hunger and ever nibbling teeth, all the hedges stretching the length of this ride are swathed in stiff green netting – miles and miles of it, winding up the hillsides like immense, bizarre Christmas garlands.

Half-way up the last hill is a black and white striped barrier hung from a brick pillar. Tom presses a button and a voice speaks straight from the grille beneath. It seems to be Mrs Bierce.

'Come on up, Mr Klaus.'

Weird. He feels spied upon, but fails to spot a camera.

The barrier rises and in the rear-view mirror he sees it lower behind him. You'd certainly feel safe in this hilly fastness, so close to the city and yet locked into your own secret world.

The huge cobbled semicircle in front of the house is liberally sprinkled with cars. Apart from a lone Cadillac Coupe de Ville, they are all imported; West Germany vying with Great Britain for automotive supremacy among the Westchester jet set. At a quick glance he guesses West Germany is winning hands down. Poor old Britain – won the war, lost the peace. Well, nobody wants to risk kidnapping with anything so obvious as a Rolls-Royce these days, and all those BMWs and Mercedes have that nice comfortable anonymity that the *really* rich really treasure now.

To his intense surprise, Mr Z himself is standing on the front doorstep, framed on either side by two immense Henry Moore bronzes – stylized women mounted on granite – sinuous holes and curves. Mr Z is in tennis whites – shorts and Reeboks with a brace of cased racquets hanging from his shoulder. His legs are even whiter than his clothes.

'Tom!' he calls, as Tom goes to park the Porsche as swiftly, as unfussily as possible, while trying to make sure he doesn't block in anybody else, which would be embarrassing later. He jumps out, athletically he hopes, feeling a nasty twinge in his lumbar region. Darn it – he shouldn't do that – he knows the Porsche is just too low-slung for his back.

'Good to see you.' Mr Z holds out a hand.

'Good to be here, sir,' says Tom.

'You had a good flight? They booked you good seats?'

'Well – ' But no, this is not the moment to grouse about his travel arrangements.

'Come on in. I'm just about to take a tennis lesson.'

'Oh.' Tom's heart sinks. 'I'm sorry. I could've come later.'

'I wanted you earlier,' says Mr Z briskly, striding ahead. 'Come on through.'

They flash across the huge hallway, beneath the central dome. To his left, Tom gets a brief vision of a sort of party going on – people relaxed, in sports clothes – some laughter – chinking of glasses. He tries to make out the glorious Katrina but can't spot her. Some delicious aromas hang in the air.

'Brunch smells good,' he can't help but say.

'I don't want to keep my coach hanging about,' says Mr Z.

They fetch up in a smallish room with two walls of gothicized greenhouse windows looking out over the terrace. The rest of the room is entirely lined in plaid – plaid silk on the walls, matching plaid carpeting – maybe his own wife had seen illustrations of this very room in *House and Garden* or somewhere, and that had set her off on her own tartan bonanza in their apartment. But theirs had been kind of green and dark, and this is red – a lot of red – Stewart? He isn't too terrific on tartans but there's something familiar about this one. Then he remembers tins of shortbread –

and as if on electronic cue, a pair of Scottie dogs come in, one black, one white.

'Show me,' says Mr Z.

'What?'

'The pictures. Show me.'

Tom hands over the developers' envelope. Mr Z riffles through the little pile quickly, then looks up at Tom, frowning. 'You only took ten pictures?'

'Well – '

'What's with this? I wanted the whole story.'

'There's plenty to tell.'

'OK, tell. I'm big on visuals though, Tom – I thought you knew that.'

'I took pictures of what there was to take pictures of – but really you wouldn't have – I mean, it wasn't your kind of – and with what I learned – well, I knew you wouldn't be interested.'

'Oh, you did.' This is said snappily and not as a question.

Mr Z fans out the photos again and, perching on the edge of the big silk plaid sofa, spreads them across the low table.

'It really wasn't, sir – I mean, it really isn't what it seems.'

'In what way? The pieces exist, right?'

'Oh, yes,'

'And they've been authenticated. Denmans say – '

'Oh, they're authentic OK.' Tom stops himself abruptly, realizing he's interrupted His Master's flow.

Mr Z gives a shrug. 'So what's the problem?'

'Well – you know, some of the stuff's not so hot.'

'I know that. Kitsch kind of stuff. That's sort of fun – if you've got enough style to carry kitsch, then carry it.'

'Well, sure, sir, but in this instance – well, it turns out there are all these provisos – limitations on disposal of the whole thing.'

'What kind of limitations?'

'From this old guy – Harry Harley-Wright – the guy who collected it all in the first place? He was really crazy about this thing – a real life's passion, you know. And he wanted to make certain it lived on after his death.'

'So?'

'So it turns out – but they tried to keep this hidden from me – I wasn't having any of it – I knew they were up to something – '

'OK, so tell me.'

'Well, it turns out that old Harley-Wright slapped this big caveat on the collection in his will. It has to remain as a single collection – displayed as such for *twenty-five* years – and it can't be split up and sold off piecemeal until then. Old Mrs Harley-Wright's still around – she's quite a character – they mixed with all sorts – all the big artistic movements before the war, you know. But she really hates this thing – the Collection – they figure these provisos were to stop her selling it off in bits or something. That would've broken his heart.'

'All right. Well, in a way that's kind of appealing.'

'But it's a ridiculous limitation, sir – on anybody's property – and it ought to reduce the value enormously. They could never sell it as a whole to a museum, for example. Some of the – well, the more kitsch stuff – no museum would want it.'

'Maybe no museum would have the style.'

'And they tried to keep all this secret – I mean, seriously, sir. It was pathetic – as if I wouldn't notice?'

'Too sharp to get one put over on you, eh, Tom?' Mr Z laughs.

'Well . . .' Tom feels himself flushing. 'I'd like to think my instincts are a little honed.' He tries to laugh back.

'So what's this – ' Mr Z goes back to the photos – 'this building?'

'That's where it's stored – it looks like a barn, but actually – well, you'll never believe it – it's an old racquets court.'

'With a straw roof? It looks like something out of Disneyland.'

'They're a very – well, I guess you'd call them an eccentric family.'

'Weird?'

'You know – kind of "Mad Dogs and Englishmen"? But "mad" meaning crazy – not angry.'

'Kind of classy?'

'Well . . .' Tom has a quick vision of Fliss striding down the hill in all that mud, swathed in olive green, cursing. 'I don't know you'd really call it classy. They've got a different way of looking at things – kind of, I guess – kind of classy with dog hair. You know what I mean? The English are very big on dog hair.'

Mr Z looks up from his fierce perusal of the pictures and gives a single loud laugh – more of a honk than a chuckle.

'You know, I've noticed that. You're right. Wherever you are, however classy – however "upper, upper" – apart from the big hotels – dust and dog hair – that's the English. Maybe English dogs shed more.' He absent-mindedly scratches the nearest Scottie's chin.

'Anyway,' Tom continues more easily, now feeling he's hitting his mark, 'I realized you wouldn't want to commit yourself to an arrangement like that – and in any case,

214

considering they can't easily sell it as a whole, their price is far too high. They want big bucks – big ideas – too big.'

'Remind me.'

'Two hundred K – thereabouts.'

Mr Z pulls off his reading glasses and looks very hard at Tom. 'Denmans seem to think that's OK. They're the experts.'

'Denmans was looking at a breakdown price. These people are stuck with this thing – they can't split it up.'

'Do you think it would stick? This proviso thing?'

'Almost certainly not – but it'd be messy if it got to the courts – boring – expensive.'

Mr Z returns to the photos. 'A racquets court – ummmm. Never been my game – squash of course – I've got that – and the basketball court. Tell me more – tell me all about it.'

19

I t's been a horrible weekend.

First there was getting back from the station, and that was no joke. Not until Fliss was perfectly certain that Tom's train had left did she even attempt to slink out of the car. She raised the bonnet and looked hopelessly underneath. She fiddled with the distributor cap, checked the battery terminals and gave a general despairing squirt of WD40 over the whole engine. She tried the ignition again – not even a wheeze.

She headed for the phone box in the ticket hall to dial the AA, but found she had no loose change and had to take the underpass across to the newsstand and buy a paper she didn't want in order to get some.

'Membership number please,' sang out the woman at the other end of the line. There was a pause. 'Name please,' sang out the voice again – a mantra. Another pause. 'I'm sorry, caller, but your membership has lapsed.'

'There must be some mistake. We've got Relay.'

'No mistake, caller. Your membership lapsed in 1985.'

'Can't you send somebody? We must've been paid-up members for years – before we lapsed.'

'You can take out a new subscription from our man when he arrives.'

'How much would that be?'

'With Relay?'

'Or without.'

'If you want your car taken to your home or nearest garage you'll need Relay. That's £38.25 – and there's your joining fee.'

'Oh.'

'You can pay by credit card. He can be with you in – er – approximately one hour.'

'I think I'd better leave it.'

She went back to the car and tried the ignition once more. Not a tickle – scarcely even a click. She scribbled a note to the station attendant on the back of an old Pay and Display parking ticket, the only piece of paper she could find – 'Police Aware', she lied – and stuck it under one of the windscreen wipers.

A misty but penetrating drizzle had started. For the second time that day she found herself kicking out at an inanimate object, and this time there was a clank as the wounded exhaust pipe finally hit the ground. She didn't even bother to pick it up, just left it there under the tailgate and headed over to the bus stop to get into town. There was no point in trying to phone home for rescue, she told herself. Ivor was either still dead to the world or already back in the lambing pens and she didn't want to have to talk to him yet. She didn't have anything she dared say.

It was almost dusk by the time the circuitous route home landed her, via three different buses and a taxi, at the bottom of the drive. She walked slowly up towards the house, every bone aching, all energy drained. The house seemed at first to be in total darkness until she saw the rim of light creeping round the edge of Martita's curtains. To her left, the barn lights were also on – lambing continued along its usual relentless path.

She went into the house via the scullery, stepping automatically over the usual, expected detritus and on into the darkened kitchen. The light shining from behind her picked out a species of industrial still life on the kitchen table. The surface was smothered in rusty bits of boiler again – so Ivor had already started. As she turned on the kitchen light, a chorus of anxious bleating arose from the floor. Four tiny faces now looked up at her from the makeshift pen in front of the range, mouths open, tongues working. There was nothing else for it. She took off her coat, pulled up her sleeves and started preparing their bottles.

Friday was almost entirely silent apart from lambs' bleating – the recovered ones went out to the barn, but there always seemed to be a new casualty. Martita sniffed around the house, bristling with curiosity about their guest's swift departure, but too proud to ask outright. Ivor took in the bare bones of what had happened, but didn't offer back anything very concrete by way of reaction. He was either too disappointed or too shatteringly exhausted to want any details. This somehow made it all even worse. If there had been a way of chewing over the last few days, of sharing the sense of indignation, there might even have been a possibility of rustling up a laugh together; of helping each other yet again to pull each other's bootstraps up, chins high, shoulders back, don't mope, get on with it – something will turn up. But as it was, the sense of hopelessness lay over the whole house like a vast cloud of damp, rank gas.

All three children came back on Friday after school. All the friends they'd been staying with had (working) central heating, colour televisions and videos, cars which didn't dump their owners in station forecourts and at least one parent with a 'proper' job.

Fliss did try to clear away the boiler bits from the kitchen table to improve the overall look of things, but Ivor insisted they must stay put in precisely the order laid out or he'd never get it put together again – this said gasping, on the hoof, as he rushed through to deliver yet another lamb.

Daisy took one look at the table, the lambs, the mess and said, '*Gross*' – before rushing upstairs with a mug of hot Marmite.

Emma said, 'Oh, Mummy – what's up?'

'No go.'

'Oh, hell – poor darling.' She kissed the top of her head, but also departed upstairs.

They both came down again pretty quickly, complaining of the cold, and settled round the fire in Ivor's study, wearing their Huskys and willing the logs to give out some warmth.

Henry sat down immediately next to the healthiest-looking lamb and let it suck his fingers.

'Did you have a nice time, my poppet?' asked Fliss.

Henry nodded dreamily. Another of the lambs was sucking at his other hand now.

'What did you do?' she asked.

'We had *white* bread. Sliced.' He said this in a tone of such mystical joy that she almost ran down the drive there and then to grab the nearest available Mother's Pride.

Saturday brought a nasty letter from the Under Manager. It arrived right in the middle of breakfast, when Fliss was at last treating herself to scrambled eggs, for she'd had no appetite since the dinner at the Crown and Sceptre. As soon as she saw the bank's logo on the envelope, her stomach did a quick flip and whatever appetite she *had* acquired promptly flew up the chimney again. It didn't come back once she'd read it.

The Under Manager had to remind them that the situation *vis-à-vis* their account was increasingly unsatisfactory, etc. He was aware that they expected to finalize negotiations for the sale of the Collection at any time, but as he had heard nothing from them and cheques continued to be drawn against their overdraft, etc., etc. Their loans must be serviced. They must understand that the situation could not be allowed to continue indefinitely, etc., etc., etc. A speedy resolution was to be hoped for, etc., etc., etc., etc. And he would await their telephone call at their earliest convenience. Oh, really – oh, *really* – oh, buggeration this time.

Familiar, engulfing panic bubbled up around Fliss. She was saved by Martita's arrival, snooping – sniffing around the letter, sensing trouble like a terrier after a fox gone to earth. Defiance came to Fliss's aid, pumping steel back into her slumped bones.

'The bank?' said Martita.

'Yes,' said Fliss.

Martita stopped behind Fliss's shoulders – eyewigging. 'Well,' she said, having gleaned the info and beetled over to the kettle, 'we may well have been counting our chickens – mayn't we?'

'We had to count something.'

'Always risky – chicken-counting. Eggs are such very fragile receptacles – even more fragile than mugs.'

'Titty, what do you actually want us to do? Believe it or not, we'd be very happy to oblige you if we could.'

'Show a little oomph.'

'What exactly does that mean, Titty?' Fliss tried very hard to keep her voice in check, maintaining what she hoped was a steady tone.

'If you don't know, I'm hardly going to waste my breath telling you.'

'Does it take any concrete form – this oomph?'

'It's a matter of standards – panache – initiative.'

'You realize we're going to be made bankrupt.'

'That is a pity.'

'I'm not actually joking, you know. I do mean it. As soon as the bank knows we haven't in fact sold the Collection – and the way things stand we have very little chance of *ever* selling it – at least for the next quarter of a century – they'll have us declared bankrupt.'

'So tatty. Still – look on the bright side – something to look forward to in twenty-five years. Should be a nice little nest egg in your dotage.'

'But the bank will have everything we've got now – including the Collection – *now* – because it's in Ivor's name – even if we can't sell it on the open market.'

'But apart from the Collection, you haven't really got anything else, have you? They can't take the house *or* most of the contents.'

'True.'

'That's the beauty – you must see. They're all mine. I'd call that seven no trumps, wouldn't you? With a royal flush to follow.'

'Not for us, Titty.'

'Well, no – but then God only favours the brave. I've

always noticed that – and you and Ivor are so very dreary. I don't think you've been a very inspiring influence, do you? I've never really quite understood what he saw in you.'

'No. You have mentioned that before.'

'Of course he was rather a drippy little boy. One always hoped, having named him after dear Novello, that he'd have music in his soul – such a disappointment really – but then he did improve while he was at Oxford. He could have had *any*body then, you know.'

'Yes, Titty – so you've said. Often.'

'And then he goes and plumps for you. A weaver – such a mystery.'

'A potter, Titty. I've always been a potter.'

'Potters or weavers – whatever is the difference? It's all so worthy and so frightfully dull.'

'Do you actually want us out of here? We'd be homeless, you know. I suppose the council would have to help – put us into B&B or something.'

'That always sounds rather fun, doesn't it?'

The baiting wasn't going to subside. Fliss should never have risen to it in the first place. Martita was obviously feeling particularly perky. Triumph gave her quite a little bounce as she put together a rather luxurious tray of tea, crumpets and honey to take upstairs. Fliss sank into silence and moved her cold scrambled egg backwards and forwards to make it look as if she was eating.

'Did I mention,' said Titty as she backed out of the kitchen, holding the door open with her bottom, 'that I'm thinking of leaving the house to the Yorkshire Terrier Association? They could have it for breeding.' She slipped sideways out into the hall, calling back, 'And research.'

*

On Sunday, Fliss went to church. She was mostly a Christmas/Easter/weddings and funerals churchgoer, but Henry was a choirboy (admitting basely that he did it for the pound a month he got paid), and she often dropped him down there when it was too wet to bike. This Sunday, he could easily and happily have biked. A watery sun and the first swellings of buds sent a little frisson of spring into the ether, but Fliss felt in need of prayer and contemplation, so she drove him down and stayed herself for the service.

The church is enormous – more a cathedral than a place for village worship. It was built in the late fifteenth century on the back of the great East Anglian wool riches, to the most particular glory of a certain Edmund de Pettet, Lord of the Manor. Now she sat among a scattering of Little and Great Watling residents – some of them descendants of those early, earnest church builders – while the rector tried to centre their minds on redemption.

He was a young, eager man, desperate to make things matter and to translate what he felt had become the veiled message of the C of E into meaningful parables for contemporary life. This meant for a start the ditching of the King James Bible and the old prayer book, but it also added in great dollops of current jargon, almost computer-speak, with guitar music and (heaven preserve them) the occasional folk-singer. It was all a bit hippie-trippy for Fliss's taste and she missed the beauty of the old services, finding the cosy, clumsy language of the new prayer book no less impenetrable than the old, and infinitely less imbued with a sense of the mystery and majesty of her maker.

Still, who was she to carp, gracing the establishment as she did in such a cavalier fashion? The rector had the most perfect right to centre his attentions on his real and regular supporters, and perhaps it was working, for hearteningly in this small congregation there were several new, young faces. On her part she tried not to wince now, when he urged them all to sing a capella 'He's Got the Whole World in His Hands' – though it was a bit heave-making to witness Brigadier and Mrs Kirkpatrick in the front pew, attempting to keep up with the beat.

She tried to send her thoughts heavenwards, wherever that might be, and bend her attention away from her own obsessive worries, which of course she knew were so very petty in terms of the world's ills. She tried, but failed. She thought about the starving, the sick, the homeless – and her brain immediately clicked on to the notion of being homeless herself. She tried again, concentrating on world peace and disarmament – would Messrs Gorbachev and Reagan ever come to terms – and the image of Ronnie and Nancy holding hands on the White House steps made her think of America and Tom Klaus and the failed sale and the bank.

So there she was again, mentally wallowing in her own tiny concerns. It was all shameful. When it came to the brief time for private, silent prayer, she thought of abuses of human rights, torture, the cruel secret manipulations of *all* their governments, and had a brief vision of Martita stirring away at her Machiavellian stew-pot. She was deeply ashamed of herself and offered up a general prayer of thanksgiving and an apology for her base cowardice.

She went home feeling chastened, and spent the rest of the day keeping up the most cheerful front she could muster – dealing with lambs, food, piles of washing, the girls' revision, Martita's crowing, Ivor's preoccupation. She needed to set up a shield. She needed to protect the children from the poison of her own despair. And she also needed to hide that despair from the potential of their contempt. It was, after all, no joke having hopeless parents.

So altogether it's been the very paradigm of a vile weekend.

20

On Monday morning, Fliss wakes early with throbbing head and pounding heart, knowing that one of them must contact the bank. She tries to broach the subject with Ivor, but fails. His excuse is perfect. His time, every second, is absorbed in immediate, physical problems requiring instant action – the sort needing straw, Stockholm tar, silage, spanners, hammers, energy – his energy. When she screws herself up to mention the bank and the failed sale again, he looks vague, uncomfortable – concerned about a sump now, fiddling with a gasket, planning on towing back the dead car from the station – soon, perhaps today – soon as he's got a moment. The bank must wait.

Well, all right, she decides – the bank must wait. Apart from one runt born in the night and quite likely to die in the day, the kitchen is now free of lambs. The survivors, though still bottle-fed, are out in the barn under lamps. Having seen the children off to school, she briefly considers setting the house to rights.

She may have resented the time spent, before and during Tom Klaus's visit, in getting them all into some semblance of order, but sneakingly she has to admit that there has been a sort of pleasure in being able to find things for a change; to enter a room without flinching too much at either bedlam or dirt (even if the bedlam did still lurk behind closed cupboard doors). The trouble is that, as far as she can tell, it nearly all seems to need doing again. How do other people manage? How to stem this inexorable tide of flotsam and jetsam which seems to flow around them all the time?

She stands in the hall for a moment. Even here, in an area not much used, the surface order she had briefly imposed is being rapidly eroded: junk mail is piling up already; rubber bands (why?); a clock pendulum again (where does it belong?); paw marks; little dust balls like seed-heads; a flower arrangement now drooping and scattering its leaves and petals. On that awful drive back to the station, Tom had had that peculiar outburst – so insulting. He'd accused her of what? Entropy – a sort of terminal decay – fusty and musty, he'd said. Well, perhaps he's right, she thinks grimly – perhaps he is, but he shouldn't have said so. And she lets the house go hang. It's going to go hang anyway, so she may just as well let it.

She goes into her studio – grand name for an old shed – lights the woodburner, and throws herself into wedging up a whole sack of clay. It's a job she usually hates, but today she impels herself into it, pouring all her frustrations and fears into thumping the great lumps of clay. Ten drops from a height of two feet, crashing down on to the workbench so that it makes the thin walls of the shed rattle; then slice in two with a wire cutter and start again, slapping the two halves together, forcing the air out, thump, thump, splat, crash. It takes a couple of hours to get the whole sack well and truly kneaded, wedged and then rewrapped in wet, old towels and plastic sacks. By the time she has finished, she is running with sweat and splattered with gobbets of clay.

She ought to get going on April's vase – or vases? Surely

her debt to April deserves to be in the plural. But it's no good – she feels too low – scattered, diffused, miserable. Although she tends to scorn arty-farty notions of waiting around for inspiration to strike, she knows that her current mood will produce something poor – dull and leaden – and April's efforts are worth more than that. What Fliss needs now, she knows, is mechanical repetition to soothe the jangled tensions in her brain. So she settles to the wheel and starts throwing bowls. Her aim is six cereal bowls – then she'll go back to the house, see what's what, help with the lambs if needed, and maybe come back later. But the bowls don't want to be thrown. Or she doesn't want to throw them. Sometimes it's like that. You throw and you throw and the line is just wrong somehow – all wrong. What the hell – they're only fucking cereal bowls when all's said and done – why worry?

By two o'clock, the bowls are made – badly. They're unsatisfactory. Maybe she can salvage their shape when she comes to turn their feet; cut into the leather-hard clay, perhaps give them that missing curve. She looks at her watch again – quarter past. The Under Manager will have expected a phone call by now. She looks at the bowls again. If all six of them were finished this very moment – dried, turned, fired, glazed, fired again, enamelled, fired yet again *and* sold, the profit wouldn't even cover half a day's bank interest, she reckons; not even half a day. She has a sudden image of herself – a little creature, like an ant, frantically digging in a pit of sand, digging, digging, while the grains trickle down all around her, filling the hole one by one – futile.

There's a rap on the wall and the high-pitched whine of the Boysies giving tongue. The door crashes open and Martita comes bowling in, the Boysies scattering before her in all directions across the studio floor, sniffing and searching. It's been a very trying time for them over the last few days. The presence of the tiny lambs has curtailed their liberty and now they're getting their own back.

Martita, in her waterproof cape over the ever present leggings, does a rapid circuit of the studio. Right the way round she goes, without pausing, like a child's wooden toy on wheels, pulled by an invisible string. When she gets back to the door, she grasps the handle as if to stop herself being pulled out again.

'Hello,' says Fliss, who hasn't moved from the workbench.

'You've had a telephone call.'

'From the bank?' Fliss's stomach gives a lurch.

'From America.'

Fliss's stomach gives another lurch, but of a different quality, and she jumps up immediately. 'When?' she snaps.

'What?'

'WHEN?' she yells.

'You're so rude,' says Martita, lowering her eyelids and turning away. 'Half an hour ago.'

'Who was it?' Then, seeing the familiar look of self-imposed misunderstanding pass across Martita's face, 'WHO?'

'How should I know? A woman.'

'A woman?'

'Calling back in half an hour – but that was an hour ago.'

'Did you take a number?'

'What?'

'A NUMBER – from them? From her?'

'Of course not. Why?'

But Fliss has already pushed past and is running towards the house.

*

'Fliss.'

Not a woman – it is Tom's voice. He sounds so clear it's as if he's phoning from round the corner.

'Where are you?' she asks, dreading that the answer will be Liverpool Street or even Long Pecklam.

'New York of course. I'm in the office.'

'Oh. Good.' Relief. 'You just sound so near.'

'It's a good line. Sometimes they are. How are you?'

'Fine,' she says, stomach churning again. Is this call in lieu of a bread and butter letter – she must assume so. She doesn't dare hope for anything else, does she? But of course she does – she's hoping like anything.

'There's been a development.'

'Yes?' Now a silence – brief – but she wonders if they've been cut off. 'Yes?' she says again.

'About the Collection – '

'Yes?'

'My client – '

'Mr Zimioff – '

'Ziminovski. Constantine Ziminovski.'

'Yes.'

'Well, he's interested. He is still interested.'

'I see.'

'Yes.'

'But you said – ' She stops herself, furious for introducing a note of doubt.

'The provisos – yeah – well, as it happens they really don't matter, because the way he's worked it out – well, he's happy to abide by them.'

'What?'

'Absolutely – to the letter. So there's no problem there. There couldn't be any sort of legal challenge.'

'Well, that's a turn-up.'

'Yeah – you lucked out after all. I have to admit I'm kinda surprised, but he's gotten really interested in the whole thing. In old Harry – and Martita and that whole pre-World War II art thing, you know? The Bloomsbury Group and all that – '

'The Bloomsbury Group – ' Fliss says this very carefully, as if the words might break, for a large question suddenly looms up and threatens this brand-new sense of well-being.

'Yeah,' Tom continues, 'and the Camden Town Group – and Augustus John – he's got several Augustus Johns, you know – you'll have to see – '

'Oh.' She decides not to ask. Best let this lie. Just occasionally the lady doth protest too much.

'Anyway, he's really getting into it,' Tom continues. 'He wants to put the Collection up exactly the way it is at your place.'

'I see. In what way "exactly"?'

'With the court and everything. He's building a new sports complex here with a gym and spa and all – new courts – everything, and he wants to turn his old facility into an exact replica of old Harry's – outside and in – even down to the thatched roof.'

'Really? I don't know if I believe it.'

'Oh, yes – and he's a perfectionist. He wants the lot.'

'Gosh. I really don't know what to say. Obviously.' She gives a nervous little giggle.

'Then he's gonna want the whole thing displayed exactly the way you've got it – and I mean *exactly.* He even wants that ladder thing – on wheels? Or if not he'll have one made.'

'I'd better let Barney know.'

'Ah. There we have a little problem. No Barney Fitz-gerald.'

'No?'

'We'd only want to negotiate direct with you and Ivor.'

'Oh.'

'Barney tried to put one over on us, Fliss.'

'But I explained – '

'We have no problem with you. But Fitzgerald should have known better.'

'Right. I see.'

'It's gonna take a bit of time – obviously – but Mr Ziminovski is keen to get on straight away. He doesn't like hanging about once he's made a decision. We'll be sending down an architect and a photographer if that's OK with you. We'll need a very thorough dossier on the Collection as it's housed now. Then the builders will get going here and we should be all set – ready to receive the Collection as soon as we can – late summer if possible. Sound OK with you?'

'Well – ' Fliss laughs. 'Yes – amazing.'

'There'll have to be a little fine-tuning of the price – '

'What?'

'Come on, Fliss. We'll be fair – I think I can guarantee we'll be fair. My client is keen – that's obvious – and he's generous – but he's not a fool. We'll get Denmans to reassess their valuation in the light of the provisos and work some-thing out from there.'

'Well, I don't know. I don't know if I can just agree – just like that, without taking any advice. Obviously I have to talk to Ivor and Barney – '

'No Barney, Fliss – I mean it. This is between you and us – well, *me* really – and believe me, Fliss, I want this to work for you – I really do. You'll find us really quick to deal with too – the moment we have a signed agreement, we'll have a 50 per cent deposit certified cheque with you in twenty-four hours, I promise.'

'Right.' Fliss gulps hard and wonders if her thumping heart is echoing down the telephone.

'There's something else.'

'Yes?' she says, feeling a bit weak now.

'Mr Ziminovski wants you to come over with the Collection – be here to oversee the display – make sure it's exactly right – the whole thing – just as Harry would have done it.'

'Us? Gosh – well, I don't know that we could. We've got so much to keep going. I don't think we could just drop it all.'

'Not "us" – just you – all expenses paid. You'll be Mr Ziminovski's guest.'

'Right. Well – yes, right. I'll talk to Ivor.'

'It's part of the deal, Fliss – it's what Mr Ziminovski wants – you understand what I'm saying?'

'Yes, I think so.'

'Good. And it's what I want too. We'll be in touch.'

Later she beards Martita in her verdigris den.

'What's all this about Bloomsbury?' she asks.

Martita is watching *Blue Peter* in bed, eating chocolate peanuts from a box, her teeth and beaky nose working together with a rodent's twitching.

'You're interrupting.'

'What about Bloomsbury?' says Fliss firmly.

'They're making a plant holder,' says Martita, squirming sideways so she can watch the screen, 'very attractive – out of squeezy bottles.'

233

Fliss switches the television off. Martita pauses in mid-peanut.

'Did your parents never give you any instruction in simple manners? Perhaps not.'

'WHAT did you say to Tom Klaus about the Bloomsbury Group?'

'Not much.'

'He seems to think you did.'

'Well, I met Virginia Woolf – once.'

'When?'

'Well, I was at the same party – '

'And of course Augustus John?' says Fliss.

'Ah. Augustus. Augustus loved my nape, you know.'

'Oh, yes. I know.'

'I was his little Titian Rose. Mad about me. *That* was the time to live – devil may care – we knew how to do things. Fitzrovia – true Bohemia – we never descended to the mundane.'

'How did Tom Klaus link all this up?'

Martita actually has the grace to look a little sheepish. 'I may have mentioned – in passing . . .'

'You claimed to be part of the Bloomsbury Group?'

'No. Not exactly.'

'*And* the Camden Town Group?'

'Not really.'

'*And* Fitzrovia?'

'It's not my fault if he put two and two together and came up with six hundred and seventy-eight. Anyway, I don't believe we called it Fitzrovia then – I don't believe we did.'

'Sort of half-way up the Tottenham Court Road? Really?'

234

says Fliss. 'Or a little further north? You should have gone one better, Titty – invented a whole new group – you could have been part of that. Perhaps "The Mornington Croissants" – yes, why not? That would have a certain ring.'

21

If Tom were at all flaky about these things, he'd say this was sort of a dream time.

After all those months of living out in the cold – disconnected at home and uneasy at work, the full focus of Mr Z's attention seems to have settled on *him*, emanating this time around not disquiet, but an almost tangible sense of goodwill.

More and more active and powerful – that's what he feels – that's what his world has become under the sunburn glow of Constantine's approval. And hey – did everybody get that? Well, he surely hopes so – it's 'Constantine' now – no more Mr Ziminovski. Ple-eese. He's an intimate now – he's a *crony*, for crying out loud.

Tom's office has been moved upstairs to the penthouse floor, alongside the Big Man's, so that he can be called to conclave any time he's needed. Maybe it's a little stress-inducing, but the feeling of inclusion, of being folded into the very centre of things, to the heart of the Constance Corporation Inc., is so healing for the bruises on his ego that his spirit soars and his adrenalin pumps.

Oftentimes they travel together – looking over various sites and factories – and even the occasional small nation-state, for nothing seems beyond the capacity of Mr Z's vision of the possible. Tom sits at the man's right arm in the private plane (and yes – it *does* have a padauk-wood saloon, so the *Enquirer* gets it right some of the time) – and this man wants *his*, Tom Klaus III's, very own thoughts, opinions and strategies as they fly across and up and down the whole continent, North and South, from high Alaska right to the depths of Amazon heat.

And the *bonuses* – it's only been a few months, but Tom's never seen a flow of money like it – and all just pouring over him for a change. He's had friends on Wall Street of course – traders and bond salesmen who've made stupendous bucks, but they've never come his way before. Paula and her lawyers can just go stuff themselves.

And if all that isn't enough, there's that little detail of Debra too. Debra, his cute new researcher – you could *not* call this girl a PA, let alone a secretary – this girl graduated *summa cum laude* from Barnard – this girl speaks fluent French *and* Italian – which reminds him that, Mamma-fucking-mia, can she give a good blow job. This girl can give a blow job would make your eyeballs twizzle, let alone any other bits of your anatomy.

And – the weirdest part – in a way all this is kind of down to that trip he took to England – to that cruddy house – to Fliss and that crackpot old woman – and the goddamn *mugs* – could you believe it? Something about this purchase has gotten to the soul of Mr Z and he seems *real* excited. Somehow Tom, as first base and ongoing contact with the Harley-Wrights, seems tinged with that excitement in Mr Z's eyes – as if Tom's become infused with – what? – some sort of Anglo-Saxon elixir – some imagined magic as embodied in the Collection? Weird or weird?

Here is a man who's just finished building a gallery for

his collection of French eighteenth-century paintings – the guy owns *Watteaus*, for crying out loud – and not any old building you understand, but based on the Maison Carré in Nîmes, with thirty-foot-high Corinthian columns and walls hung with Florentine silk – a man whose wife is allowed to collect Impressionist paintings of animals, just as a little hobby on the side – such a man would get a thrill out of owning several thousand *cups*? It just beats Tom – he just can't figure it out at all.

Once though, one Sunday morning, when he's up at the estate, he gets a little glimpse of something – of maybe what's going on. They're in the main house, checking over last-minute details of a Panamanian acquisition, and Mr Z (no, come on, Tom, try to get it right now) – and *Constantine* suddenly jumps up like a little boy, bundles him into a thing like a golf buggy and drives him down the hill to look at the site for the Harley-Wright Collection.

They stand outside what had been the old gym and sports facility, and which is now being metamorphosed into a very sanitized version of the barn at Little Watling.

'Like?' says Mr Z.

'Love it,' says Tom, knowing that negatives are not on any possible agenda.

'I mean, "Is it like?" Like the one in England?'

'Exactly,' lies Tom, embarrassed at his misunderstanding. He takes in the thatched roof – only half done as yet, but shimmering in yellow straw. But what he's remembering is the collapsed grey original.

'As long as they get it right,' says Constantine, and he starts to walk slowly round the building, with Tom trailing a pace or two behind. 'You know, Tom,' says Constantine eventually, 'I mean, you must've seen it – I've gotta lotta stuff' – there's enough of a pause for Tom to conjure up a mental picture of the properties, the trees, the lakes, the sculpture, the cars, the planes – 'And I mean a *lot* – a lotta stuff,' Constantine continues, 'but this collection . . . well . . .'

'Yes, sir?' says Tom, but too fast – the spell is broken.

Constantine stops, turns back to look at Tom, just a little unfocused, strange – then snaps and says, 'Come see my zoo.'

It's not far – only hidden from the mock barn by a finger of trees pointing down the slope: an area neatly enclosed in black iron railings containing a formal arrangement of large, ornate cages. In between, it's all laid out with paved paths, park benches, a terrace with sunshades – even a hot-dog stand. There's something about it that's familiar, but from here it all looks empty, as unplayed-with as a discarded, unwanted child's toy. There is also an iron turnstile and Constantine puts a dime in the slot, ushering Tom through, before doing the same for himself.

'Whaddya think?' He stands with his hands on his hips, looking around. 'Cute you need a coin to get in, don't you think?'

'Cute.' Tom agrees, though actually he's wondering if this is the first tacky detail he's noticed in the Ziminovski domain.

'It's all based on the old zoo in Central Park,' says Constantine.

So that's it – that's what Tom could kind of recognize. 'They're in the middle of rebuilding?' he says.

'You used to go there – to the old one?' asks Constantine. 'Like when you were a kid?'

'Oh, sure – quite often. My grandparents lived on East 82nd Street, so it was kind of convenient – either they'd take me, or more often the maid . . . Sure I used to go. And you, sir?'

'Oh, yeah. I remember it real well. 82nd Street you said? On the Fifth Avenue side?'

'A little further over – just between Park and Madison.'

'Uh-huh – that figures.'

'Sir?'

'You're a college man of course, Tom?'

'Harvard, sir,' says Tom, a tad puzzled. Mr Z of all people certainly must know his résumé.

'Uh-huh. Sure.' Constantine sticks his hands in his pockets and strolls towards the first of the cages. 'These are all exact replicas – *exact*,' he says. 'I thought it could be fun – kind of educational for the kids – only now I've done it, I don't know how far to go with it. So, I mean – like we built a seal pool – but then once you put in seals you've gotta have fresh fish – twice daily. Then you want something big – maybe giraffes. Do you think giraffes would be OK?'

'Could be,' says Tom, who feels maybe he's getting out of his depth here.

'Then you get a baby elephant – pretty soon it's a big elephant – and you don't want to start messing with elephant psychology here just for decoration.'

'What have you got so far?'

'Donkeys, llamas, a lot of birds – ostriches, they're kind of funny – and some exotics – kangaroos and wallabies – a couple of camels – six zebras. What would you do with it?'

'To tell you the truth, sir – Constantine' – he really must try to get that right – 'it all seems like a – well, like a lot of *work* – and the cages and all. I don't know I feel all that comfortable with, like, the concept of cages any more.'

'You don't?'

'What about plants?'

'Plants?'

'Couldn't you use them for like displays of plants – like those Victorian hothouses or something? They'd look spectacular . . .' His voice trails away.

Constantine is giving him a funny look. 'I've got enough plants already,' he barks, '*and* I've got a goddamn palm house in the valley. Come see my monkeys.'

Past the pens of llamas, a blue-jeaned man is struggling out of the back of one of the cages with a barrow of soiled straw. At the sight of their approach, he drops the handles immediately and comes straight over.

'Mr Z, sir – they didn't tell me you was here. I'm near about finishin' till this evenin'.'

'Just wanted to show Mr Klaus around. You know Mr Klaus – he's my right-hand man.'

Tom feels the newly familiar glow of pride creep up his backbone, as the blue-jeans all but bows in a respectful silent greeting.

'We're going to take a look at the gibbons – they awake?'

'I guess so, sir. You want me to get you some fruit?'

In the last cage sits a family. Two tawny slender apes with shaggy limbs, one with a baby clinging to its breast, squat on platforms at the back. Separately, on a branch in the middle, sits a larger grey creature with a beautiful black clown's face, sharply outlined in white, as if with a pen.

'They're Lar Gibbons,' says Mr Z. 'From Malaysia. That's the male. Fascinating, aren't they?' He holds a long slice of watermelon through the bars. The gibbons don't move. 'Maybe that's it – I'll just stick to apes. I think they're really something. You get a feeling of man in there – under all that – don't you?'

Suddenly the grey male leaps for the roof of the cage and swings lazily across to Mr Z. He hangs there, right in front of him, then very delicately takes the piece of watermelon, never removing his eyes from its donor. While he eats, he keeps staring and swinging. Tom is almost mesmerized – and envious – for it's so wonderfully insolent – *insolent to Mr Z?* As if he's really eating up the two of *them*, and not the fruit . . .

When the gibbon's finished the first piece, Constantine offers a second. This the gibbon ignores. Instead he swings slowly back to his branch and turns to look at them, scratching one armpit. Then he opens his mouth in a perfect circle and a noise comes out – not a sound of this world, and scarcely animal in its quality – a swelling melancholy song. It rises around them as if amplified in great circular whoops – making the air seem to quiver, carrying all the sorrow of the world.

'Yeah – I think I'll go for monkeys,' says Mr Z.

22

In Little Watling, Fliss doesn't need to worry about being flaky – she doesn't even know the meaning of the word – and for her, these months have also taken on the aura of a dream. Much later she could look back and see this time – concentrated, detailed – a peculiar interregnum in her life.

Not that it isn't without its little awkwardnesses – scattered here and there like the odd pimple on an otherwise flawless skin – a pimple which erupts into a boil where Barney is concerned. For Barney is *raging*.

'What do you mean you're "in negotiations"?' He's humphs down the telephone line. '*I'm* your negotiator.'

'I'm sorry, Barney. It's just no go,' says Fliss.

'It can't be no go. *I'm* your "go" – '

'They won't have anything to do with you. I'm not even supposed to be discussing it with you now. I only rang as a courtesy.'

'*I've* had expenses.'

'I know. I'm sorry. So have we. We'll reimburse as soon as poss.'

'*And* my commission – 20 per cent of total – *as* arranged – *as* per – '

'Well, I don't know, Barney – not about that commission – that's an awful lot – and now we don't even know what we'll be getting. Because of trying to hide the conditions from them, they're sending Denmans back next week to revalue the lot and it may be heaps less.'

'Well, you'll need *me* for Denmans.'

'No, we can't.'

'You'll never manage their people on your own. They're positively *jackals*.'

'We'll just have to try. They – the Ziminovski people – say the whole thing's cancelled if you come anywhere near us.'

'I'm not *leprous*, ducky.'

'I know, Barney. I'm sorry. I don't know what else to say.'

'Ducky, you haven't a hope. It'll be like taking sweeties from a babe.'

'Goodbye, Barney.'

After that Fliss needs to take a detour to get through Long Pecklam. The joint cursed spectres of the manageress of the Crown and Sceptre *and* a spluttering, livid Barney Fitzgerald are just too daunting to face.

Denmans send four people this time – two unnervingly crisp young Sloane Ranger women, a droopy man in a chalk-striped suit and a frighteningly knowledgeable York-shireman who seems to be their boss. They are all much snootier and self-contained than the first lot had been when accompanied by Barney.

Now that the path to the old barns has dried out, it's possible to drive directly to them, and that's just what the Denmans people do, ignoring the house entirely and crunching down the hill over all the ruts in an executive Rover. At lunchtime, they disdain Fliss's offering of sandwiches, favouring instead some local hostelry, from which they return, marginally more mellow, but still secretive.

On the second day there is a moment of panic when the question of export licences comes up. They have a car phone which is almost steaming with use and there's a lot of anxious hanging about. Fliss, having heard bits of the drama unfold, can't bear it, and spends the rest of the day energetically rooting out ground elder as a way of dissipating the pain. By 5 p.m. the answer comes. The Collection, it seems, does not need to be saved for the nation – now there's a mercy – hard to see any nation really *needing* seven examples of Mum's Pearlies – but then those rare early pieces – well, nervously one never really knew . . . but now one does.

When the final revaluation comes through, it really isn't all that bad – especially as by then they've had plenty of opportunity to expect the worst. Perhaps it is a *little* disappointing – but only in relation to the original dreams of glory, and mentally Fliss reserves what she reckons is a fair share to reimburse Barney for his pains.

Then there is the moment of magic – the arrival of the deposit in the form of a certified cheque. It comes by perfectly ordinary first-class post. Fliss had envisaged some arcane and personal special delivery at the very least – a knight on a white charger could scarcely have been special enough for her. But no, it just plops on to the mat, along with several brown envelopes, brought by their usual post lady on her bicycle. Once Fliss has anxiously examined it for errors, she sits just holding it for quite some time like a sorcerer's talisman – letting its warmth sink through.

The effect of the witchcraft soon wears off though, for once deposited it is instantly drowned in the deep pit of their overdrafts and loans. Until the other 50 per cent is paid, there is still no actual money with which to function, let alone play or plan. It's time to see the Under Manager again, and this time Fliss makes the appointment quite airily, with a new-found sense of confidence and bravado.

Instead of greeting them in his porridge den, he comes out to the front reception area, where they've been waiting on a low-loader of a sofa. He stands over them, almost on invisible starting blocks, giving them scant attention, ready to go. It's rather public out here – people queuing for the cashiers can hear every word.

It's Ivor who broaches the subject of a renewed overdraft. The UM lets too long a pause slip by and then – but perhaps it's Fliss's imagination? – sighs.

'Frankly,' he says, 'I think we should draw this matter to a close.'

'What do you mean? What "close"?'

'I think I may have mentioned before, Mr Harley-Wright, that the bank is *not* a charitable institution, and now that we've come through unscathed – '

'Who's unscathed?'

'I should have thought that was obvious – the bank of course. By the skin of our teeth.' He ventures a sort of giggle. 'So for all our sakes I think we should leave it at that, don't you?'

'I *beg* your pardon,' says Fliss, fury coming to her aid. '"By the skin of our teeth"? A "charitable institution"? And perhaps you could remind us precisely what interest we've been paying on our loans for the last God alone knows how many years?'

'*You* should know,' says the UM, almost smacking his lips with satisfaction. '*You've* been paying it.'

'And isn't that precisely what you're here for – isn't that the purpose of this altar to commerce – and haven't we fulfilled our function perfectly, by borrowing from you and paying our dues through our collective noses?'

As Fliss seethes, her voice gets louder and rises half an octave. The UM suddenly looks less relaxed – the muscle spasm is streaking down his cheek: maybe this public encounter wasn't such a good idea.

'And didn't we pay back what we owed you – *on the nail* – exactly as we promised we would?' Fliss continues, now throwing all caution and privacy away, and practically appealing to the people in the queue. 'If only *all* your customers – your big business customers – were as honourable, maybe things wouldn't be so extortionate and impossible for the rest of us.'

The UM looks nervously at the queue – at any moment it's going to break out in applause. 'Perhaps you'd like to discuss this in greater comfort,' he murmurs.

They leave the bank with a renewed overdraft facility – much less than the original of course, but that's all right, that's healthy in fact – a necessary discipline. They can struggle to get by, sustained with the thought of that final payment – it won't be long until it's theirs.

Once the agreement with Denmans was confirmed, an architect and photographer were sent down by the Constance Corporation's London office to survey the old racquets court. The architect turned out to be a bit sniffy too. Fliss had been expecting an American, but this chap came from Putney. While the photographs were being methodically, efficiently taken, he padded around the building in espadrilles and deconstructed linen, moaning about pastiche and the prostitution of his genius. He made it clear that the mere imitation of a building – and such a dog's dinner of a building at that – was scarcely worth a moment of his brain's expenditure. But his fee must have been rather good despite his scorn, for the construction work in America seemed to be happening at rocket speed.

Occasionally Tom Klaus telephones her to keep her up to date with the progress, and she's building quite a picture of the Ziminovski household and environment. He has a slightly irritating, indeed patronizing, tendency to assure her that she's never going to believe it when she sees it – and then to go on yet again about some wonderfully dazzling feature or acquisition *chez* Mr Z that'll 'blow her mind'. She doesn't want her mind blown, thank you very much. It all sounds like something out of one of these big glossy series on television that the papers are always full of but which she hardly ever sees. Not quite real life – but intriguing.

Still, Tom seems very charming and communicative and it's a relief to have some sort of connection with this mammoth organization. Denmans, having done their valuation, seem to have dropped out of the frame, and the Constance Corporation's London office seems, on the whole, pretty indifferent to their boss's latest purchase, treating both it and Fliss as irritating irrelevances. Nobody seems to know anything precisely, nor wants to take responsibility.

Then, in the middle of August, a more directed call does come through. Would Mrs Harley-Wright make herself available to oversee the arrangement and display of the Collection – leaving for New York about ten days after the pieces are shipped out, to allow for unpacking? Well, would she heck – she can't wait.

Ivor finds this a bit hard. Well – frankly. Yes, he does. He wouldn't want to admit it of course – not out loud. It's just – well, it's a bit much, that's all – stuck here with all the work while Fliss swans off (yes, that's his phrase, 'swans off' – seems to describe it neatly) – and to *America* of all places. I mean, *he's* never been to America – and nobody's actually asked him if he'd like to go – and he would really – well, not *really* – I mean, someone's got to stay behind and cope with everything. And she doesn't seem to have noticed – she hasn't even said sorry. She doesn't even seem *guilty*. It's all a bit bally much.

And yes, Fliss is excited – of course she is. She tries to keep it down – knows that Ivor's perhaps feeling a bit out of it – but there you are, it can't be helped. She can sniff freedom on the breeze – and at last something of the unexpected. The level of her voice keeps creeping up and there's an unfamiliar shimmer somewhere round the back of her head.

Just as her airline ticket arrives, the shippers arrive as well. It takes four whole days to pack up the Collection and cart it off in huge metal containers to Stansted for special air freight. Despite the odd niggle, Fliss and Ivor feel washed with relief when the lorry at last roars off down the drive.

By then the girls are not only free of their exams, but have their results as well. Fliss has to phone Emma with hers, for she's working as a nanny in Umbria for friends of Helena's. Her grades are good enough for Durham – she's going to read English, and has already whirled into a dream of the Lakeland poets and Freshers' Balls. A week later, Daisy's come through – good enough to do four 'A' levels – all involving maths or economics – how unlike the rest of them she is. Daisy doesn't need to be telephoned – she gets hers direct at the school gates, for she's been working at the local chicken packers for weeks, doggedly saving for an Inter-rail ticket, and will soon be off on her travels. The academic trials had entwined themselves insidiously into that other panic – the grinding one which Fliss and Ivor live with all the time. But now there's a balmy calm, which is subtly contagious. Suddenly there's a very real atmosphere of well-being in the house. The cancer of fear just fades away, and, like labour pains, it's quite hard to remember precisely what agony everything had been.

Only Martita pierces this mood. She bristles with silent rage. When asked directly what is wrong, she affects to be stone deaf, or leaves the room, muttering. She spends quite a lot of time in the now truly defunct racquets court with the Boysies. Fliss wishes she wouldn't. It's become a sad place – all the walls blotched with the stains and fade marks of where the hundreds of vessels had been displayed.

23

'So you'll be all alone in New York with Mr Chunky?'

'Oh, Helena, *really*,' says Fliss as witheringly as possible, but feeling a stupid blush starting up from somewhere below her knees.

'What will you do about clothes?'

'Will I have to do anything?'

Helena takes in the sagging navy-blue limpness of Fliss, her skirt dangling at ankle level with a tail of unravelling hem, her peeling reddened heels poking out of solid sandals.

'Oh, yes,' says Helena. 'I should rather think so.'

'Oh. I was hoping – you know – it is still summer – more or less – the odd floaty cotton frock. You can get away with murder in summer.'

'Only up to a *point*,' says Helena.

'Oh. Oh dear.'

'I'll lend you my Murray Arbeid for glamorous evenings – if you think you can squeeze into it – and I've got a few other things that might do – and you can borrow my last year's Ascot suit – that peachy thing. It's in pristine nick – might come in useful in New York. They're frightfully smart, you know.'

'Really?' Fliss feels a bit of the excitement begin to wane.

'Absolutely. Always tights in the city – never bare legs.'

'Not even if you're brown?'

'Never.'

'You've been of course.'

'Only in October – the fall. Terribly glamorous. Teddy was doing a deal in guano, or was it grapefruit? God, we had fun.'

'Are the summers nice?'

'Oh, yes. I should think so.'

'Warm?'

'Oh, yes – I should think so – lovely – quite warm.'

But so far it's felt like being either sorbeted in the air-conditioned interiors or slapped in the face with a huge steaming bath towel when outside – as now.

She stands uncertainly at the exit of the Pan Am arrivals building, dragged down by her suitcase and gasping for oxygen. All around whirls the essence of a thousand Hollywood movies – visual clichés from a lifetime's viewing, brought to three-dimensional, ear-splitting life.

Yellow cabs, low-slung, creaking. Stretch limos – yes, here they really are – shaded, mysterious and ludicrous in their deliberate elongation. And 'Courtesy' buses – beguiling term for this oncoming charge of logo-smothered charabancs – Hertz, Avis, Budget, Holiday Inn, Sheraton, Ramada – thundering through this underpass, belching exhaust – a constant hiss of brakes, a scream of tyres and the relentless blast of horns.

Now, despite Helena's advice, she wishes she hadn't worn this formal dress and high heels. The belt is constricting, the sweat beginning to trickle down, the material sticking to the back of her legs – and nearly everybody else seems to be in T-shirts and shorts.

She is rescued by a tall, sombre, quite elderly black man

in full chauffeur's fig – almost an SS uniform in the width of its breeches and the crispness of its cap. He takes her bag, shepherds her towards a large black Mercedes and introduces himself as Jeremiah, butler to Mr Ziminovski.

'But I'm doing double duty here, cos Mr Z's got something on in the city and his regular drivers are all tied up.'

She'd have liked to sit in the front with him and chat, but he settles her firmly in the back behind a glass screen. The contrast between the soggy sauna heat outside and the ice of the car interior is so pronounced that she automatically longs to comment, but the screen stays firmly up and she's forced to keep her thoughts to herself.

Through the windows she watches avidly, excitedly taking it all in – even if 'all' at this moment just seems to be a motorway packed with slow-moving traffic – road signs, cars, people and houses – familiar enough words, but in their actuality all so wonderfully alien, so indubitably *American* even through the muffling, cosseting smoky glass.

Then suddenly, across to her left, she can see it – a vision – the towers and spires of Manhattan. It's a mirage, seeming to float on a sea of mist, its pinnacles touched with sunlight. A mythic image from a modern fairy tale – so foreign and yet so familiar, it might be part of the texture of her own remembered experience. She blinks a couple of times, as if the vision might disappear – but no, it's still there. Reality. Concrete afloat on a haze of dreams. She is transfixed by it, watching for as long as she can, until it is hidden by the sprawling jumble of suburbs between.

Perhaps you could really could get used to this, thinks Fliss later – awfully used – and possibly it wouldn't take all that long.

They'd driven for well over an hour, into an increasingly green-treed landscape. Jeremiah had deposited her most courteously here at what is dubbed the 'Small Guest Cottage', and since then she's been gleefully exploring. It's enchanting – a Wendy house for adults. A couple of bedrooms, each bordered by sumptuous bathrooms out of a Ginger Rogers film, give on to a wide veranda. There's a sitting room hung with photographs of racehorses and yachts, and a small, sleek kitchen full of goodies, including a big basket of very showy fruit, like something worn by Carmen Miranda.

The vast double fridge is filled with every sort of fizzy drink and, curiously, lots of different milks – fat-free, 'lite', low, lactose-free – chocolate, strawberry, mango, paw-paw – something called berry-berry (isn't that a disease?). No booze at all, but lots of ice. Ice everywhere – two sorts pumped out of the fridge door – crushed or cubed, and a big machine the size of a dustbin currently giving birth to yet more by the sound of its hummings and crunches.

At the back, the cottage overlooks a steep wooded valley with, at its very bottom, a long stretch of water entirely fringed by trees, and disappearing at its furthest point into mist. It's the very essence of pastoral, but also extremely foreign, and she can't quite work out why. There's a clarity perhaps – a sharpness and strength of tone, a certainty which is unfamiliar. Even with the mist, there is nothing of the watercolour about this landscape. She settles on a seat, looking out over it all, sipping an icy drink, listening to the rushing chorus of crickets, absorbing the heavy blanket of heat, and waiting to be called.

*

Tom is frazzled – running late.

Constantine's been tricky – side-tracked, all week. They're buying NXO – the aviation fuel company. The numbers guys have crunched the numbers – and the legal team, including Tom of course, have run themselves into the ground checking through the papers. NXO's board have refused to let these out of their strong room, so the Constance Corporation boys have more or less camped there over the whole week and are nearly in shreds. Everybody's just *had* it. So this is not the best timing for Fliss's arrival.

Not that Tom feels he ought to be responsible for Fliss Harley-Wright – what *is* this? He's being turned into some tour guide or professional escort or something? But Constantine has insisted. Distracted as he seems to have been, he wants Tom to make the contact and confirm arrangements, until he can get to meet her himself. So now Tom's having to come all the way out here to the estate – yet again – when what he could really do with is a good long sleep at home.

Well, no – actually now he thinks about it – as he drives up 684 at eighty miles an hour with his radar scanner searching for cops (a ticket would be the last straw) – what he *really* needs is an apartment in the city again. With the way his bonuses are stacking up, he can afford one now – the sooner, the better. Stop all this travelling – get out from under his mother's clammy embrace and *into* Debra's warm one.

Gradually, as he gets further away from town, he lets himself slow down. The speedometer sinks to a leisurely and legal fifty-five and his mind wanders. Well, maybe it'll be kind of fun to see Fliss's reaction. You'd have to be dumb not to get a kick out of what she's going to feel – seeing all this for the first time – and the setting for her collection – and everything. She'll never believe it. Awesome.

He's met by one of Constantine's liveried footmen (not a joke this – the full shebang, including epaulettes and white gloves) and is taken through to the library. In a room groaning with Messrs Chippendale and Hepplewhite, and framed on either side by life-size Canova marble nudes, he first sees Fliss's back. She is perching on a skeletal sofa, looking stiff and uncomfortable. Opposite her, and thus facing Tom as he's announced, is the curled-up creamy form of Katrina, tightly cased in work-out Lycra and nibbling on a rice cake. She flaps one delicate wrist at him.

'Hi there,' she calls, and he gets a full blast of the indigo eyes, wide and innocent as a Disney deer's. She doesn't move, but offers up a cheek when he approaches – they've become really quite pally over these last months. He's learned at least not to *look* as though he's gaping – tries not to stare, but she is a miracle – voluptuous and childlike all in one perfect package. Fliss couldn't be more of a contrast – angular, pinkish red in the face – and currently caught with a cake fork between lips and plate.

Not that Fliss doesn't know this: she couldn't *feel* more of a contrast either. Mrs Ziminovski makes her seem Brobding-nagian even to herself – hugely clumsy and ill-favoured. And now she has a mouthful of chocolate chou stuck in her throat, rapidly taking on the consistency of sawdust – indigestible – as Tom turns to greet her.

Actually, it's *all* a bit indigestible. The cascades of heavy silken curtains, the carpets dense as sphagnum moss. She's had a full tour straight away – courtesy of Mrs Z – part

NADFAS, part *World of Interiors*. They'd done the lot, it seemed, even down to the witty bathroom arrangements – Russian samovars serving as cisterns, Roman sarcophagi as baths.

There is security – everywhere. She'd needed to be identified and beeped by a taciturn, unsmiling woman called Mrs Bierce before she was even allowed out of the guest cottage, let alone into the presence of the glowing Mrs Z. And then it seems Mrs Z herself needs clearance – just to get out of her own back door. After they'd seen the house *and* her collection in her own densely dark and spotlit den – 'My husband's specialty is the French Rococo and I collect paintings of animals,' she breathed, scarcely above a whisper. What animals? Fliss conjures up a brief mental flash – the lids of Dairy Box perhaps – lots of fluffy fur and whiskers – only to be met with a respiration-stealing phalanx of creatures – yes, a whisker or two – even a sprinkling of fur – by Renoir, Bonnard, Cézanne, Gauguin, Degas – and more – could there *be* more?

'Kind of fun, isn't it?' says Mrs Z.

'I don't know quite what to say,' says Fliss.

'No one ever does,' says Mrs Z, with a little moue of satisfaction. Then she picks up a walkie-talkie. 'Jimmy? Jimmy, come in please. *Jimmy.*'

A crackling channel opens; a deep masculine tone. 'Yeah?'

'It's Mrs Ziminovski.' A purr, not a voice.

'Yes, ma'am.'

'We'll be going out now, Jimmy – I want to show someone the gardens – we're on the north entry.'

'Door 6J?'

'That's it.'

'OK, ma'am – you're heading over by the main gardens?'

'And the fountain garden I guess – so we're all right out of 6J?'

'We're switched off now, ma'am, for three minutes.'

'Thanks, Jimmy.'

'Don't mention it, ma'am.'

But Mrs Z catches something in Fliss's expression – incredulity. 'You know,' she says, and makes a vague sweeping gesture, incorporating all the painted creatures, 'you simply can't be too careful these days. Come on – we've only got a few minutes before they switch the alarms back on.' She shoots out of the door with Fliss trailing.

'You mean you have to arrange every time you want to walk out of your own house?'

'Not if I use the front door, because that's always guarded. And the kitchen door as far as the trash cans.' She laughs. 'They're in a sort of garbage compound – for the dogs as well, when they've got to do their business. But if I want to go further – well, yes – it's the only way to be sure. It's kind of a nice feeling really.' She looks back at Fliss – adds defensively, 'No, I mean *really.*'

She dashes off ahead, almost jogging through the sticky air – air which reverberates constantly with distant mechanical noises – drills, diggers, chainsaws – whisking Fliss past innumerable parterres and mazes – high yew hedges, hothouses, vistas, avenues, shrubberies – an exhausting gallimaufry of horticultural delight. So it's a relief when they finally subside into the library in front of a dazzling tea – like a full-blown advertisement for Fauchon. Only, once Fliss has served herself as asked, she realizes her hostess doesn't take tea – only offers it. Instead she sips hot water and picks at a rice cake. 'I put on so much weight with the baby,' she murmurs. Baby? This child-woman with the twenty-two-inch bottom has had a *baby*? Where on earth did she put it?

'You hardly look . . .'

It's just about now, as Fliss is swallowing hard on this lump of chocolate chou, that Tom comes in. It would be lovely to rise elegantly – greet him magnanimously, like the friend he's truly become in her imagination, but instead she's glued to her seat, balancing cup, saucer, plate, fork, mouthful. Bugger.

Mrs Z has Tom fully in her gaze now – offers tea, which he refuses; snuggles towards him.

'Felicity was just asking me about the baby. I told her – I put on pounds and pounds – I just have to get it off.' She gives a little giggle.

'And what did she say?' Tom appears to be melting; he's hardly looked at Fliss.

The lump of chou at last goes down. 'How old?' gasps Fliss.

'What?' says Mrs Z.

'The baby.'

'Oh. The *baby*. Eleven months. I *know* – don't say it – months and months and I still haven't got the weight off . . .'

Which isn't what Fliss was going to say.

'You *know* we can't believe it, Katrina,' oozes Tom. 'There isn't an *atom* out of place – I'm *sure* Fliss agrees . . .'

But on this score Fliss doesn't give a monkey's – watching Mrs Z now biting her lower lip, her perfect teeth just gripping the flesh.

'Well, you know Constantine,' breathes Mrs Z. 'He's very into these things – and you know – well, I just *love* to be what he loves, I guess . . .' She looks about ten.

'You two have got together, I see,' says Tom. 'That's nice. I wasn't needed after all.'

'Not indispensable, Tom – not yet,' Mrs Z teases.

Is it Fliss's fancy, or is Tom getting a touch rosy around the gills?

'I wouldn't imagine,' he says, spluttering a little, 'of *course* not – only Constantine was so insistent – he really wanted me here.'

'But don't we all, Tom – just don't we all,' says Mrs Z, going Scarlett O'Hara on him.

'Not that you couldn't *manage*,' he battles on, 'perfectly well without me.'

'Oh, we've done just fine – Felicity and me – just fine, haven't we?' The kohl-rimmed blue orbs turn on to Fliss.

'Oh, do call me Fliss,' says Fliss, catching Tom's confusion and spluttering a little too. 'Everybody does. I'm only ever called "Felicity" in anger – it always makes my insides crunch somehow.'

'And we couldn't do that, now could we?' says Mrs Z, suddenly uncurling herself in one slinky move. 'I'm outta here – as they say. Got to go work these muscles in the gym or I'll be *wrecked* – just *wrecked*. Take Fliss down to meet Edgar, will you, Tom.'

'Now?'

'Constantine wants them to get their heads together – down at the Court Collection – he should be waiting.'

24

'So how do you like America?'

They're driving back down the hill in Tom's car.

'*Is* this America?'

'What *does* she mean?' Tom lifts both hands off the wheel for a second – a gesture of mocking despair. 'I give her the *best* of America and she doubts me.'

'It seems a little rarefied.'

'*So*. You're getting a very privileged view here – an insider's view, you know – *lucky*. You just don't know how lucky.'

In front the road winds through green-velvet parkland – behind, the house hangs over them, its terraces stepped into the hillside. 'I mean, just look at this place,' Tom goes on, expansive. 'In a way this *is* it – the epitome of the American way – the dream – everyone can dream it – everyone has a shot at it. OK, it's the oldest cliché in the American canon – but like every cliché, somewhere in there it's founded on a truth. There isn't a busboy, a bellhop, a short-order cook, a grease monkey – any label you want to stick – *any* blue-collar working guy out there who doesn't figure at some stage along the line that he could get a piece of this. You know what I'm saying? It may be hard, but it's still in the realms of the possible – the stratospheric possible perhaps, but it's there. I mean, just look at *me*.'

'Yes?'

'No, I mean it. Don't laugh. OK, not a bellhop maybe – but I'm like sitting out in the metaphorical cold – only a few months ago – in the cold with my shirt-tail hanging out, clutched in the jaws of my wife – recently ex-wife, thank God – and now look at me.'

'Yes?'

'Do I have to join the letters – dot the "i"'s? I'm in *clover*. This is one big honeypot and I'm one happy bumble bee, I tell you. I've never had a time like it – and you're getting a piece too. *That's* what it's about.'

He slows right down as they approach the last bend, and coasts gently to a halt, in front of the mock Little Watling barn.

'Good God,' is what she says.

'I told you you'd never believe it.'

'I don't believe it.'

'I thought so. Did I tell you or what?'

'It's actually rather peculiar, isn't it?'

'How do you mean? Now look, I never kidded you it was *my* taste – not even in the original.'

'It's so *new*.'

'What did you expect? There are limits to the amount of English crud even *my* boss can import, you know.' And he's just a mite relieved that she's laughing too.

The spanking new ancient barn, evidently accurate down to its last brick footing, is marooned in its own mini-desert of dry earth. From round the back there's a scream of drills – a clamour of machinery. They walk round a bit gingerly – stepping on planks, avoiding the worst. In the middle of a whirl of physical activity – there must be at least six men fixing something or other – a plumpish, owlish fellow, head-to-tail black denim, is wrestling with a drawing board.

'Edgar Horne – hi. Delighted to meet you.'

'Edgar is Constantine's landscape architect,' says Tom, 'author of all you survey – with maybe a little help from good old Mother Nature.'

'Not a *lot*,' says Edgar Horne, grinning. 'Generally I like to keep the old gal on a tight rein – make her do *my* bidding.'

'And as you see, he's a quiet, modest, retiring kind of a guy as well,' Tom continues.

Edgar Horne blows him a kiss. 'You've finished with our adorable "maîtresse"?'

'What?' says Fliss.

'Katrina the Gleamer?'

'Is that what you call her – really?'

'No. Not really. I just made it up.'

'And she *is* adorable,' says Tom firmly.

'Now there speaks Mr Het Man,' says Edgar. 'But alrighty – I'm devoted – no *really.*' He pulls his specs even further down his snub nose and peers at Fliss. 'How are we enjoying our foray into Never-Never Land?'

'It's – lovely. Beautiful. There's not a lot of peace though.'

'Peace? She wants peace as well as beauty?'

'There does seem to be an awful lot of racket.'

'High maintenance, sweetheart – one of the perils of mega-bucks, I'm afraid. They're never satisfied – that's possibly their one big problem – means nothing's ever *quite* right. Wonderful for guys like me of course. She give you the Grand Tour?'

'Well, yes – I suppose she did. Does she always then?'

'Pretty much. What's the point of owning it if you don't show it? And she's really a very good custodian of her husband's property.'

'And *hers*,' says Fliss.

'You figure?' says Edgar, peering harder. 'Of course she really knows nothing – positively nothing. She was a flight attendant from somewhere like Tuscaloosa – you heard that Tom?' Tom nods. 'Met Ziminovski going to Hong Kong or somewhere long haul – way before he got his own plane. And she was assigned to First Class – gave him good service if you know what I mean. Boy, did she give good service – it was filet – filet – all the way, dears – and then some. Bye-bye, current Mrs Z – welcome the new model . . . This is like his third – fourth? I forget which. Do you know Tom?'

'Third, I think.'

'Third – fourth – whatever. There's bound to be a fifth somewhere along the line.'

Fliss has a go at readjusting her mental picture of Mrs Ziminovski to fit with this latest tranche of information.

'Still, as I say,' Edgar goes on, 'this one's been a good custodian – a good student – took all these courses. And she learns really quite quickly if you lead her in the right direction. I've been with them a couple of years now – much longer than Tom, you know – almost a real old-timer. Helping them spend their money.' He sees Fliss's expression, slight shock beginning to creep in. 'Well, somebody's got to, sweethearts, and it may as well be me – at least I've got *taste*. We've been working really hard to bring them round – I've got a good team. I'm a real anglophile, you know – I'm using a basically Capability Brown-type strategy – working with water and trees.' He's clamped his drawing board under one arm and is gesticulating expansively with the other, encompassing the breadth of the landscape behind them. 'We may have to move a hill – but ahhhh maybe not. It's been a struggle, I can tell you. Whatever he'd like to think, Ziminovski's about as bucolic as the Empire State Building. He has no idea about plants – his idea of gardening was twenty-nine million Busy Lizzies in Schiaparelli Pink – can you *imagine*? Give me more – I want it bigger – he kept saying. But now I've kind of brought them round to Vita Sackville-West. They may have to schlep over to Sissinghurst before they *really* get it, but we'll see – we'll see. I'm beginning to feel a little optimistic, but the trouble with Ziminovski is he's a hands-on kind of guy – you find that, Tom?' A nod – that's all there's space for. 'Always trouble. I prefer *carte blanche* – if he'd just let me get on with it, I could do something *exquisite*. But it can be difficult working with these kind of people – when originally they have *no* idea. And let me tell you *they* had so little idea they had to get the decorator pick out the dogs. If they weren't careful, they would've landed up with *poodles* or something.'

He suddenly draws breath. In the silence a pneumatic drill starts up somewhere – the sound drifting down on the hot, sticky air.

'Anyway' – he's regathered vocal strength – already – 'let's talk turkey. What about this Bloomsbury garden?'

'*What?*' says Fliss – then, calming herself a bit, 'Come again?'

'They didn't tell you? I'm supposed to reproduce the Bloomsbury garden here for this china collection of yours – the way it was back home?'

Fliss looks nervously at Tom but his face is a blank. 'Have you actually seen any photographs of the way it was back home?' she asks, oh so carefully.

'Well, kind of – but they didn't honestly tell me a lot – apart from the Erotic Pond – but frankly I don't see Ziminovski going for that. He's kind of a puritan at heart – and besides, they've already got so much water.'

'The Erotic Pond,' says Fliss admiringly. She's never thought of Titty's scabby old bathing pool as anything a fraction so mysterious. Unfortunately, she catches Tom's eye – and it's clear from his expression that he hasn't thought of it like that either – and he's the only other party here who's seen it in the flesh so to speak.

'Well, as I say, I can't see him wanting that,' continues Edgar, blissfully immune, for now tears are welling up in Tom's eyes, 'but frankly there isn't a lot else to go on. . . . Excuse me' – now he's noticed Tom's cheeks have puffed out – mauve with the effort of holding in the laughter – 'do we have a *situation* here or something?'

'I just don't know quite how to help you,' says Fliss faintly. 'There's only grass – and we keep it down with geese . . . because of the pool – sheep would fall in.'

Tom looks as if he may explode.

'Geese . . .' says Edgar.

'But I wouldn't – if I were you,' says Fliss, 'not geese . . .'

'No – I can't really see Katrina the Gleamer treading though the goose doodie, can you? *Messy.*'

'Exactly.'

'So I'll just have to base everything on Charleston. You know – Vanessa Bell and Duncan Grant's place in Sussex? It's kind of what I'd planned anyway.'

'Of course I know about it – I've never been.'

'Oh, you must – they've been restoring it – divine. Yeah – we'll do a replica Charleston. That'll be empathetic to the whole – you know – the thing – pick up on all your family connections.'

'Right,' says Fliss almost in a whisper, hoping not to meet Tom's gaze – aching with the weakness of those 'connections'. Thank you, Titty – thanks a lot.

25

It's been warm in Little Watling too – that late summer warmth with a touch of melancholy, when the shadows fall long and low, but the sunlight is still opaque and buttery. The flush of old roses is of course long over, but the climbing floribundas are in full second glory, smothering the walls, and the Russian vine is tumbling over the back gable in a great white fall. You can't even see where all the stucco has fallen off any more. Martita has a good look at it in the evening light and finds it pleasing. You have to hand it to that Felis*ss*ity, she grudgingly admits – she's got a way with plants. Not that Martita would ever say so. Not bloody likely.

She puts two of the Boysies in her front bicycle basket and keeps the other two on long retractable leads as she climbs the mounting block, gets on to the saddle of her High Nellie and pushes off, across the bridge, and on, wobblingly, down the drive. The Boysies are being very well behaved, running alongside, their tongues hanging out, but keeping a respectable distance from the wheels. Dusk is nearly here, so she switches on her front lamp, but there's no wind – a pleasant evening for a little tipple at the Old Goat.

At the very end of the drive, almost where it joins the road, there's a happening. The Boysies in the basket catch sight or smell of something in the gloaming. They start howling – standing up on their hind legs, with their front paws resting on the handlebars, looking around and behind Martita. The Boysies on the ground halt – then go into rapid reverse, running backwards as the leads unravel – then suddenly cross over round a tree trunk or two, and the bicycle is brought to a standstill. For a moment, Martita thinks she may be able to save herself – get one foot on the ground.

But too late – the whole contraption half rears up, levered by the tangled Boysies from the back, and throws Martita, basket, dogs and handbag all into the air, crashing down in a spin of wheels.

There's a long pause while Martita tries her limbs to see if they function. They do, but one ankle hurts. She sits herself up and looks around. There's a gleam in the gloom – a flash of red, and the Boysies are all alert, hot and prickly. 'You!' she suddenly shouts. 'Come out – come out at once!'

An eruption in the greenery. Barnaby Fitzgerald rises up out of the leaves, like a bathing beauty from the spume.

'What the bloody hell do you think you're doing?'

'Are you all right?'

'No, I'm bloody not. What do you bloody think?'

'I'm frightfully sorry – didn't mean to frighten the horses as 'twere – very unfortunate.'

He starts wading towards her through the undergrowth, revealing as he does the parked red Volvo. He helps her to her feet, but the ankle is still sore. When she tries it, it won't take her weight.

'You've buggered me,' says Martita crisply, looking up into Barney's worried face.

'Madam, I can assure you I have not.'

'Good as.' She makes as if to move towards the car and gives one desperately exaggerated limp, before stopping and looking sorrowfully back at him. 'I won't be able to bike. Possibly not walk.'

'Nothing broken though, surely?'

'Something torn, you see. Nasty.'

'What shall I do – take you back to the house? Fetch a doctor?'

'I was rather hoping for a gin.'

'A gin?'

'On my way to the Goat, do you see – '

'Well – may I drive you?'

'I don't see any other way.'

'If you think you're all right . . .'

'I'm not. Of course I'm not. You'll have to carry me to the car.'

'But should you have the gin? If you're in shock or something?'

'Only solution.'

'I'm really not too sure – '

'I could sue. Something torn, do you see – very nasty.'

Barney bends to pick her up. Once in his arms, she smiles at him sweetly – now she's on a level, jaw to jaw.

'You won't slip a disc or anything. I'm only a little bag of bones.'

Down at the Old Goat, Martita gets the settle by the window and has her ankle supported on a stool. The Boysies lie in a pile on her lap. She and Barney are on their fourth Gin and It each – it's not his usual poison, and is having a definite effect.

'I don't mind telling you, Martita – I know you're a woman of sensibility and can understand these things – that I've properly got the pip.'

'Is it recent?'

'In this instance, yes.'

'I've *always* got the pip.'

'This is a recent pip. Caused by your family.'

'Don't bring *me* into it. They're nothing to do with me. I've often wondered if that boy was swapped in the nursing home – and as for *her* – well, I can tell you, Mr Fitzgerald – '

'Do call me Barney.'

'I can tell you, *Barney*, that I've *never* seen the point – such a dreary baggage. Not one's sort at all, you know.'

'And *I* don't mind telling you, Martita, and I know I can trust your discretion, that one way and another I'm pretty upset – with this collection business and all. I mean, who set it up, dear? Who organized the whole thing? And look at me now, landed in the proverbial with scarcely a bit of bum rag, if you catch my drift.'

'What can you expect with a woman like that – money-grubbing *petite bourgeoise*? We've all had our disappointments, you know. I've had *ever* such a lot – my life wasn't supposed to be like this – very disheartening. It's all so *dull*. It wasn't intended at all. I was supposed to have a spiffing time. It wasn't *meant*.'

'I don't mind admitting, Martita, I feel pretty hard done by. I even lent them my car. I need to talk to her – face to face – alone. Put my case, as it were – I've had expenses – and she's not unreasonable. That's what I was doing at the end of the drive – looking out, you see. Hoped she might come by.'

'You'd have had a long wait. She's in America.'

'No!'

'Left this morning.'

'To do with the Collection?'

'Entirely.'

'Bloody hell. What a nerve.'

'My reaction precisely.'

'My God. I *have* got the pip.'

The telephone seems to be ringing for ages. Perhaps Ivor has gone to bed after all. It would be – what? – well past midnight at home, and they'd had a very early start to get her to the station this morning. Fliss, herself befuddled with travel and time lag, has wriggled out of a rather half-hearted invitation to dine with Mrs Ziminovski. She'd had an uncomfortable notion of what such a meal might be like – of finding herself slogging through a huge plateful of something delicious, while the ethereal Katrina sucked on a lemon slice. In any case, she's now aching for sleep. She is just about to put the receiver down when Ivor answers.

'Yes?' He sounds breathless.

'It's me.'

'Oh. Hello.' He still sounds breathless – lets out a sigh. She's expecting a bit more from him – well, actually, much more.

'*Me*. Phoning from America.'

'Well, I'd be very surprised if it were only from Bognor Regis.'

'Oh. I'm sorry. Did I wake you up?'

She's immediately nettled – deflated. Doesn't he want to share this with her? She'd wanted to share it with *him* and it had been a hell of an effort and bother just to make this

272

call. She'd had to get through to the spiky Mrs Bierce and find out which button on the complicated telephone would give her an outside line – offer to reverse the charges – have her offer refused – all sorts of palaver.

'I was in the cellar. Had to dash up the stairs.'

'What are you doing in the cellar so late?'

'We may have a problem.'

'What?'

'I think the moat may be on the move.'

'What? How?'

'A certain amount of seepage.'

'How certain?'

'Quite a lot. Possibly an influx – '

'Oh. That doesn't sound good. *Can* moats move?'

'I've no idea. It's only a guess.'

'What are you doing about it?'

'Trying to build a dyke.'

'A what?'

'On Dutch principles.'

Oh, God. 'With what?'

'Wood – those old bits of chestnut – and earth.'

'You're taking *earth* into the cellar.'

'Well, yes – and sand. In bags.'

'Oh.'

'It works for the Dutch, I believe.'

'Shouldn't you ask somebody who *knows*?'

'What?'

'I mean, couldn't we' – the luxurious profligacy of the day – *other* people's luxury overcomes her – 'couldn't we – you know – *hire* somebody – like normal people?'

There's a horrible silence. With a deep sinking, she knows she might just as well have cut off his balls or confessed to adultery. Neither, for Ivor, could possibly have been more wounding.

'Sorry,' she adds, then hastily continues, 'I'm sure you know best – you usually do – ' lying, tactfully lying to save their communal souls.

'I try,' says Ivor, sounding stiff.

Then there's a silence and he doesn't ask her anything – oh, how I *loathe* telephones, thinks Fliss – the lack of eye contact is so acute. Then of course she has to fill it – the silence – incapable of maintaining its vacuum.

'This place is extraordinary – there's even a palm house like Kew and a private zoo . . .'

'Really,' says Ivor, not sounding anything like half impressed enough.

'It's going all right,' she ploughs on.

'Good.'

'The setting for the Collection is just amazing – it looks just like our barn only all tarted up and shiny – like something in Toytown – or Milton Keynes.'

'Good.' He's not helping.

'I haven't seen inside yet – they won't let me. Evidently Mr Ziminovski's given instructions that he wants to save that bit for himself – it's really *his* baby – they say he's absolutely thrilled with it – and they've only just finished unpacking. He's not here yet – he's in New York still. Manhattan.'

'Right.'

'Yes. He's terribly busy, I gather, and can't get here until the weekend, but he wants to meet me – so we're going to have breakfast together – tomorrow – in Manhattan.' She tries to quell her excitement – but it's no good, it just will keep bubbling out.

'Oh, yes.'

'It's one of the things they do – they're terribly efficient – breakfast meetings are a big thing here – they start terribly early.'

'So do the rest of us – without necessarily the benefit of breakfast,' says Ivor tartly.

Oh, well, sod him. If it's going to be like that.

'Well, I'd better go,' she says, now trying to match his tone.

'Yes – this must be costing a fortune.'

'Well, no – *they're* paying.'

'Even so. Have they paid *you* yet?'

'Well, no – I've only just got here.'

'Yes.'

'It's been quite a day.'

'Yes.'

'Good luck then. With the dyke.'

'Yes.'

'Right then – '

'Yes.'

After half a night in the cellar, it's a bit much to be wasting even more precious time out in the garden, but it's been drizzling since dawn, torrential rain is forecast and Ivor is trying to cut as many blooms as possible before it really gets going. The flower-drying process is quite tricky enough as it is, without the added burden of blowsy rain-soaked petals.

He's cutting roses now – round at the back – the climbing Icebergs in bud, as instructed by Fliss before she left. This isn't his usual line of work at all – this is *strictly* her department and he wishes she were here right now, coping with it as she *should*. It's bloody inconvenient – a bloody, bally nuisance – but there you are – there doesn't seem to be any choice – she's part of the required package. Bloody cheek. Breakfast. In Manhattan. Bloody nerve. The sooner this whole business is over and she's back and they can get on with their lives – their *new* lives – the better.

Henry's round the back here too, doing something interesting with toads. The girls are both still away. A postcard arrived from Umbria this morning – from Emma. Apparently she's fallen madly in love with one Gianni – the Bissingtons' pool repair man. Oh, God – just what they need. Bloody hell. It's all a bit much.

At the front of the house, Barnaby Fitzgerald has left the Volvo on the landside of the bridge, further down the drive, slightly hidden by the cedars. Titty lets him in. She still has a spectacular limp.

'Tasty,' says Barney, creeping round the drawing room and examining the chest-on-chest and the Georgian chiffonier. 'Really quite tasty,' he adds, as she thumps one-leggedly upstairs and leads him past the long-case clock on the landing towards her hidey-hole. 'Very tasty indeed.'

26

It's definitely flattering to be driving with Tom in his Porsche down the parkway towards Manhattan. Helena would surely be proud of her – Fliss and Mr Chunky off into the wide blue yonder – heady stuff.

He's entranced with his own car – happy to show off its paces despite the speed limit – like any small boy tickled with his toys. There's a vaguely illegal doodah behind the sun visor which detects police radar – and there's his telephone of course, which he keeps using to call his office, thus exuding an atmosphere of concentrated, glamorous purpose – making it clear that he's the centre of his universe and it can't really function without him.

Normally she'd feel irritated by such a show, but not this morning. After the earnest anxieties of life with Ivor, it's like being caught up in a little golden puff of light. What pleasure to have such inconsequential sources of pride – to be so deliciously unworried. She watches him slyly to her left, while he deftly changes gear and weaves through the traffic. That smooth tanned face – clear of the desiccation of stress: a man who'd never have to suss the intricacies of Dutch drainage systems (*dykes* – what can Ivor be thinking of?) – here's a man who would *always* hire someone – who wouldn't think twice. Yes – it could be very attractive to be tied to such a man with such a life – surely free of all those aching grinds of daily existence.

A life involving what? – she muses. A country club perhaps – they all seem to have country clubs. A spot of golf? Bridge? Hard to imagine – lots of holidays of course, restaurants. That peculiar thing called 'Leisure' – such a funny concept. *Leisure* – funny word. Hard to remember when she's ever had any of it herself – isn't sure she'd know quite what to do with it if she had . . . Nice to try though. Have a go.

Tom is thinking about that last call to Debra. He'd let her know early this morning about his decision to buy an apartment and she's already been calling realtors. She thinks she's found something over on Sutton Place South with a balcony overlooking the East River. Jeezus, will *that* be expensive. But she sounds so excited – wheedles – and he kind of likes to be wheedled – by *her* – and she only wants him to go take a look.

For a flashing second he can feel a dull pressure in his brain – oddly familiar but hard to pin down. Then he gets it – Paula. Paula and the duplex – and the bills for lapis lazuli and moiré silk. But – what the hell. This time the money's there – why fight it? Why buck the trend . . . and Debra is . . . oooh, just the thought of Debra – alone – in his own apartment . . . with a *super* king-size bed.

OK so his mother may feel a little put out – but he'll just have to take a stand. She'll have to realize he's got to get his own life back. He isn't just grown-up and married – he's *divorced* now and thirty-six years old. I mean – like, Mom – I'm thirty-fucking-six – leave me *alone*.

So in fact this having-to-look-after-Fliss business is quite fortuitous – really almost convenient. Instead of having to leave for the office at 5 a.m., he gets to sleep on a bit, so as to be available to drive her in at a more reasonable hour. She's to meet with Constantine for breakfast – 9.30 in the Edwardian Room of the Plaza – as organized by Mrs Bierce. Surely he can just drop her off a little early and slip over to Sutton Place on the quiet before going down to the office. Terrific. It could almost have been *meant*.

There's just a moment when Fliss allows herself to feel a bit offended.

She's been dreaming on – musing gently as they cross bridge and flyover, spanning suburb and slum, eye to eye level with the Yankee Stadium – taking in as much as she possibly can. She's wondering what delights in the mythical city she's going to see today, when Tom suddenly asks if she'll mind being dropped at the Plaza a little early – she can just wait for Constantine there. And then he launches into the details of his plan – and what details – *such* details. Within five minutes she seems to know the full spectrum of his bank account and stock options; the great deal he can get on a fixed-rate mortgage (but-the-way-things-are-going-maybe-he-won't-even-need-one), his proposed lifestyle, his dream of an apartment – and then the Rhapsody on a Theme of Debra. Oh, well. So – it was only a bit of fun – but suddenly she feels old and unattractive, dumped like a shabby brown-paper parcel he can't wait to deliver, in eager expectation of something else in beribboned tissue.

And she doesn't want to waste any of the precious New York time just sitting around waiting. Why should she? Asks to be dropped somewhere near – says she'll make her own way.

'Oh, I don't think I can let you do that,' says Tom,

doubtful – concerned even? 'I'm sure Constantine would expect me at least to drop you at the door.'

So it's his job again that matters – not her as a person, nor what she'd enjoy. Oh, well.

So now she gets firmer and brisker – 'I insist,' she says. If she's going to be made to feel old, she may as well *act* old – well, at least fully *adult* anyway.

And as it seems to fit in more readily with his new plan, he gives in – really too easily.

He drops her on Park Avenue.

'Don't stand around gawping like some tourist,' he says. 'Gawping is a British thing. New Yorkers don't gawp – maybe they rubber-neck a little, but only if it's a celebrity – New Yorkers keep moving. You keep moving too – that should save you any trouble. Not that you'll find any trouble round here – but then you never know,' and he slips off into the traffic to meet his destiny in Sutton Place.

Dutifully she tries to obey his edict, but it's very hard. She's looking up the wide avenue to where it disappears into haze. In the other direction lies an ornate gilded château of a building straddling the road beneath the looming protection of a tower labelled Pan Am. So now she does stop – just for an instant – just long enough to let it all sink in: the glittering cliffs of glass and steel and concrete; the colours – blues, lilacs, coppery bronze and black rearing up from the pavements in profile against a cloudless turquoise sky. A distilled moment – pure intoxication.

Then she goes – moves along – tries to blend with the crowd, susses out street numbers without stopping, crosses over, along a block, crosses Madison Avenue and on to – Fifth. Of course – Fifth Avenue. She wants to dance along the road – join Gene Kelly and Frank Sinatra – 'New York,

New York, a wonderful town' – of course – 'The Bronx is *up* and the Battery's *down*' – she knows where she is. It's all so far removed from the organic muddling mass of cities at home. No problem.

Now she slows down a bit – joins the other window-shoppers, dawdles past Saks and on to Tiffany's. Another filmic vision. Audrey Hepburn in those sunglasses and that dress, slender as a reed, munching her croissant breakfast as she gazes at the jewels. How Fliss and her friends had loved that film – how exotic and alien that world had seemed, compared to parochial Surrey and the art school – going home at night to student digs and toad-in-the-hole.

In the film, Holly Golightly had a sofa made out of half a bathtub. Back in 1962 that had seemed terribly chic and witty, so they'd decided to imitate it. Scoured old builder's yards for likely tubs – even found one, ignored its limescale stains and lugged it home on a makeshift sack barrow. Dropped it once, got it upstairs – but then failed miserably to slice it in half. They'd ended up with enamel chips in virtually every orifice, and the huge, cracked, but alas still whole tub stuck in their hall and used to store old news-papers. And now here she is – really – standing in front of Holly's very window, gazing at a diamond of staggering proportions; almost impossible to believe.

By the time she's slipped briefly into the Trump Tower and allowed herself the fastest of tours around its kitsch and glistening rosy glow, it's nearly 9.20. Not being late had been Tom's first and also final command, so she heads across the avenue, following his instructions to the Plaza. In a moment she is walking up the steps and through revolving doors into another dimension: outside – the steamy heat and rush; within – iced marble tranquillity.

She gets herself directed to the Edwardian Room – a lofty space, wood-panelled, with a painted, beamed Tudorbethan ceiling and huge windows overlooking what she assumes must be Central Park. Mr Ziminovski hasn't arrived yet evidently, but the reservation has been made in her name and she is duly seated. She looks around as subtly as she can. The tables are laid with pink linen and cohorts of silver and are, at the moment, quite sparsely attended. Delicious aromas hang in the air – hot coffee, fresh orange juice, warm brioche. It is hushed and cool and very grand. Unfortunately, after yesterday's sticky travel, she'd lost faith in Helena's dressing advice, but now she wishes she'd listened; her bare legs and sandals feel rustic and yokelish under the crisp folds of the tablecloth.

'I think you have to be Felicity. Am I right or am I right?'

A very tall, thin, angular man with steel-grey hair and steel-grey suit is standing over her.

'Constantine Ziminovski – hi,' and he holds out his hand.

'*Hello*,' she says, almost familiar – but by now she's heard so much about him, she feels she knows him. She starts to rise from her seat.

'Don't, don't, don't,' he mutters quickly, and seems to crumple at his knees, very swiftly like a collapsible walking stick, half on to the other chair, but uncomfortably, semi-perching.

'I was waiting for you out front in the car,' he says almost in a whisper.

'Oh, I'm sorry. I was told – I mean, Tom said I was to meet you in here.'

'We were looking out for Tom.'

'I got him to drop me.' Then quickly, seeing a flash of annoyance – she'd better rescue Tom – hadn't she? 'My fault entirely, I'm afraid. I wanted to walk . . . Anyway, we managed to meet up,' she adds cheerfully, looking around. 'This is lovely . . .'

'If you don't mind – ' He's looking around too – all around, scanning the room almost nervously, and a waiter is coming towards them.

'Yes?'

'We'll leave.'

'Oh.' Well, it *is* a disappointment – that aroma fading into a dream, and she's been drooling with anticipation.

'I'm sorry,' he says. 'It was an idea. It seemed good. Earlier.' He stands up and of course she has to follow, smiling placatingly at the waiter, feeling personally responsible for this affront.

Mr Z seems impervious. 'It's – you know – privacy. I can't sit with all those people.'

But most of the other customers seem to be discreet couples, so richly, subtly unobtrusive as to be almost indistinguishable from the baroque swirls of the carpet.

They step out through the side entrance, from the shaded cool, slap into the drenching heat again.

'I want to show you something,' he says and crosses the road towards the park, moving fast ahead of her, oblivious to traffic or whether she keeps up with him. Horse-drawn carriages are gathered on the corner – romantic, pretty, obviously touristy. Even so early, couples are climbing into them and getting their pictures taken. Just before the park entrance, a street vendor has set up a mobile cart.

'You hungry?' asks Mr Z, stopping suddenly and turning back to her.

'Well I am rather,' says Fliss humbly, the apology gene as ever to her fore.

He comes back with two huge, hot, doughy horseshoe things, a bit like those curled jobbies you get at Christmas drinks parties but blown up to ten times the size.

'Gosh – thanks. What is it?'

'You never saw a pretzel before?' he asks, astounded.

'Well, now you mention it. But in miniature – didn't taste like this though.'

It's hot, salty and utterly scrumptious when your anticipatory stomach has just been gypped of breakfast at the Plaza. She follows him into the park, still chewing, a bit self-consciously. He isn't eating his, and eventually throws it in a bin. She catches herself watching its dumping with regret.

He's moving very quickly, slightly ahead of her all the time, and she strains to keep up. He keeps darting his head from side to side. There's something bird-like in the constant, scanning movement, as if he's sensing an attack – but from what? Muggers? Paparazzi?

They've reached a barricaded area. 'Here's the zoo – they're re-building. It covers that whole area. You know, I've got one – they showed you that, I hope?'

'Yes – Tom and Edgar Horne – last night. Only briefly though – they said you might want to show it to me yourself.'

'Mine's based on the original that was here – they told you that?' He dives suddenly into the bushes on his left and she trails after. 'This is going to be beautiful – state of the art with all these like total animal environments – but you know, when I heard they were tearing down the old one, I felt real nostalgic. All my life when I was a kid we had this one real treat – and it was like take the subway up from Brooklyn – go up to Midtown Manhattan – go to Central Park, go see the zoo. You could get in real easy – like it was free for kids – buy a bag of peanuts, feed the monkeys, stroke the goats. One time a goat ate my homework – did I get my backside tanned for that. But you know, there it was – always available – right in the middle of the city – and they couldn't stop you feeling part of it.'

'It's a lovely idea – if you can approve of zoos. I'm never really sure myself – perhaps on an educational level they're justifiable. I must say I did rather love them when I was little. We've got one in the middle of London too you know – in Regent's Park.'

'Yeah – but that's different – big. Like the Bronx Zoo. The point about this is it's for *us*. It was for us. You get what I'm saying?'

'I think so.'

There are huge lumps of rock everywhere, trees – and trees sprouting from rock – water, and more rock. And now he's climbing the rock. Bizarrely, the great Constantine Ziminovski, master of a vast organization, vital cog at its spinning centre, is actually scrambling up the rock in his immaculate grey suit, scuffing his brogues, allowing his Hermès tie with its sprinkling of stirrups and snaffles to catch on the branches. Then he dives on, down into the undergrowth again, back on to a path until they come round to an opening on to the street.

'Beautiful, isn't it?' he says, looking around. 'I just love this place.'

There are some seats here, along the pavement, with their backs to the park. He stops now, quite firmly takes her arm and almost sits her down so she's looking across the street.

'You see the penthouse up there – that one – with the big terrace – the balustrade and all those trees?'

'Yes.'

'I used to come here when I was a kid. I told you that?'

'You did.' Well, of *course* he did – only just did.

'And after I'd fed the monkeys – you know – been in the zoo, I'd come out here and wait for the bus. Can you believe that, Felicity? *I* used to take a bus. And I'd wait down here and I'd look up there. And there'd be people up there having a party – up on the terrace – people in tuxedos and beautiful gowns – like something out of a movie. You couldn't hear anything down here – just see them – laughing – throwing their heads back and – well, I always figured they must have been laughing. And you know, they were like something – I don't know – they belonged, Felicity – boy, did they belong. And I swore then I'd get a part of that.'

He throws back his own head now, with his eyes closed.

'Well, you certainly managed it – belonging, I mean,' says Fliss when the pause starts to get embarrassing.

Constantine opens his eyes again and turns to her. 'Only when I'd made money – big money – I heard that apartment was for sale. That very same apartment.'

'What a coincidence.'

'No. I'd had realtors tracking it for several years.'

'So it was part of a plan.'

'Everything I do is part of a plan. And I went to buy the apartment. It was like – then – I don't know – maybe one, two million. I went to buy the apartment and they wouldn't have me.'

'Who wouldn't have you?'

'The board. It's a co-op – you have to pass like these criteria – these secret, stupid, private little rules – you never really know what they are – dumb, mean, tight-fisted little rules.' He's spitting the words out now. 'Can you imagine what that felt like? The insult? You aren't as good as us. You won't do. And why? My antecedents aren't as good as

286

theirs? My grandmother wasn't a Daughter of the American Revolution or something? My money isn't as good as theirs?'

'Does it work like that? Could it really be based on ideas like that?'

'The whole world's based on ideas like that.'

'In the old days maybe – but surely not now. And surely not here. I thought the whole point of *here* is that you're free of all that nonsense.'

'Nobody's free of that nonsense – in one way or another the whole world's based on it – whatever people think, however free they'd like to be, they've gotta be part of their own club – and they've gotta keep the other guy out . . .'

'Not in my world. It seems terribly simplistic and primitive.'

'The more sophisticated, the more primitive – that's the whole paradox of the thing – and I wouldn't bet on your world. Strip away the layers and you'll be as dumped as the rest of us. Maybe. But you know what I thought, Felicity – "screw them", that's what I thought. And you know what I did?'

'What?'

'I bought the whole building. I waited of course. I had to wait, but then I bought the whole damn building. That's *my* building – right there. And my penthouse of course. I even have the occasional party – with the tuxedos and the laughter. In the end the money will win through – in the end. But you know something I discovered? You know? I still didn't belong. Do you feel you belong anywhere, Felicity?'

'I'm not really sure I know what you mean.'

'I guess that means you do. Of course you do. You know where you fit. You're so sure of it, you don't even understand my question.'

'I'm just me. I don't feel part of any group.'

'All those centuries of tradition – in the same place – never uprooted – they make you – people like you – fit.'

'I think you may have a somewhat over-elevated view of a childhood in Dorking with a GP for a father. I've never seen it as symptomatic of an ancient line.'

'You've never even thought about it.'

'That's certainly true.'

'You've just proved my case. It's the ones who don't fit who need to think about it. Life makes them think about it one way and another. You don't know how lucky you are – you can just ignore all that stuff and get on with your life. It's something I really like about your collection. It spans back over what? Nearly four hundred years – four hundred years of mugs. I don't want to be disrespectful here – I mean you know I understand the historical importance of them as ceramics – I hope you know that – but you know they're still mugs when you get right down to it. People have used them and they've come right through the years down to me – a guy who owes quite a lot to the mug, one way or another.'

'You do?'

'In a way. It's kind of private – I don't want to go into it. You saw what we did with the building – for your collection?'

'It's wonderful.'

'Just like it?'

'Incredibly,' she fibs.

'You wait until you see inside – you won't believe it. My guys have done one hell of a good job. Your old father-in-law – he'd have gotten a real kick out of it, wouldn't he?'

'I think he'd have been thrilled,' she says – and this time truly meaning it.

'It'll all be there – just the way he wanted it – and it'll be for like – for years. No problem about his provisos or whatever – he wanted twenty-five years – well, maybe it'll be there for ever. How's about that?'

'Wonderful.'

'We'll let scholars come and see it – anybody needing it for research. I don't think we can make it generally available, you understand – '

'I'd never thought it would be.'

'For reasons of security and privacy – I couldn't allow it. But I'm on the board of various museums, so I don't see why we couldn't allow certain sections out on loan, do you? Your father-in-law wouldn't have minded, would he?'

'He'd have loved it. Been tickled pink.'

'And your mother-in-law can't complain.'

'You know about her?' A horrible nervous stab hits her gut.

'Tom Klaus keeps me informed.'

Knowing the unreliable source of Tom's information isn't much comfort – best to stick to the safer territory of old Harry. 'It's all really even better than he could have wanted,' she says. 'He couldn't have begun to imagine such a perfect solution – well, none of us could.'

And then Mr Z puts a hand on her arm, heavy, quite hot – and turns to look right at her. 'I just want you to know,' he says, 'that whatever happens – *whatever* – it means a lot to me. Your collection is a real connection for me. It links me up with my past – even if it's a past I never had. I hope you can understand that – maybe.' He pulls out an envelope from his inside jacket pocket. 'Here's your cheque by the way – the other half. With a little extra thrown in to cover any expenses.'

She takes the envelope and has to hold in all her instincts not to rip it open instantly and examine the contents.

'So,' he goes on. 'It's *my* collection now. Maybe we should celebrate.'

He gets up and, in the interests of decorum, she has to stuff the envelope, still unopened, into her handbag and follow. But she can almost feel the cheque as a living entity, pulsating, giving out heat inside the bag, as they stroll up the avenue for a few blocks. For a while he seems much more relaxed, and has stopped his bird-head darting search of each passer-by.

However, at the corner of East 70th street he changes again – becomes tense and alert, looking all around him. He stops suddenly and turns towards the park wall, slipping on a pair of dark glasses. There's something so obvious about this attempt at concealment that Fliss has to quench a rising giggle. As he turns back to her, he starts pointing across the road.

'That's the Frick Collection. Magnificent. Built as a private home for a guy called Henry Clay Frick – back at the beginning of the century. Industrialist – *big* business – Pittsburgh. *There* was a guy who belonged.'

'Is it still a private house?'

'What?' Mr Z looks startled to hear her. It's as if he's forgotten she's there, as if he's been talking to himself. 'No, no – it's open to the public,' he says, distracted. 'Magnificent – fabulous collection. Unbeatable. Maybe. And people are so suspicious of *me* – that *I* can do it. Why shouldn't I do it? Guys like Frick did it all the time. So why not me? He just did it when it was easier, that's all. The goddamn sonofabitch got so many of the Fragonards you wouldn't believe – and the Bouchers – the sonofabitch.' He looks down at Fliss again. 'But some of mine are *better*.'

'I'd love to see it.'

'Well . . .' He's started his wary searching again.

'Perhaps I could this afternoon – or the Metropolitan? That's somewhere up here, isn't it? I've heard so much about it. You can't come to New York and not see the Metropolitan, can you?' She goes for a hearty, hopeful kind of laugh.

'Shall I tell you what I want, Felicity? I want you to go back upstate – to the country – now.'

'Oh. All right.' It is disappointing – there's absolutely no denying it. Still, it's what she's supposed to be here for. 'Is there some work for me to do there now?'

'Pretty soon. I've had guys working on it – they've been putting it all up according to the plans. Pretty soon. I think you should be out there. I do.' His eyes are darting past her again, like an edgy party guest looking for someone more important across the room.

'All right – that's fine,' she says, resigned. 'It'll be good to be useful.'

'The sooner the better.'

'I can always come back to the Metropolitan at the end, I suppose.' She swallows a sigh.

'Yeah.' But he's absorbing nothing about her now. All his attention has shifted. Where?

A black Mercedes with darkened windows draws very slowly beside them as if summoned by an invisible bell. Mr Z opens the back door and sticks his head in. There's some low muttering and she can just hear her name. Then he steps back, holding the door for her.

'George'll take you back. That's the best thing. Take care,' and he squeezes her shoulder.

As they pull away, she watches him cross the street towards the Frick Collection. For a second he stands there and she sees his lips move – 'Sonofabitch' they seem to be saying.

The heavy closing clunk of the car door shuts her back into that other, cool world, sealed in as completely as if she's been locked into a safe. For the briefest moment she'd had a glimpse, a sniff of a more real place, and as they drive away from the broad, gleaming avenues, through streets of heat and grime, she at last catches sight of real people, real lives – and in her mind can smell and taste them. But now she's been rolled again into that soft, moneyed cocoon of Mr Z, as remote, as numbing as a chloroform cloud.

When the driver seems completely absorbed in the road ahead, she eases the envelope out of her handbag as quietly as possible and opens it. Here is the cheque at last – symbol of so much fear and longing. Representative of freedom of a sort – of release from the tyranny of the Under Manager and Titty – and the grip, the paralysing fear, of want.

27

Today there is no stopping at the main entrance of the Zimonovski estate. The gates are already open as if by some prearranged signal – the guard is waving them through. As they clank shut behind the car, Fliss feels instantly heavier-hearted – the lightness of her brief city jaunt draining away.

When she walks into the guest cottage, she is immediately assaulted by a heavenly aroma – of cake. In the kitchen, the butler, Jeremiah, is bending down, pulling a baking tray out of the oven. He's in mufti – jeans and sweatshirt – the first time she's seen him out of uniform.

'Hello,' she says cheerily to his back. He nearly drops the tray. 'Ooops – sorry – didn't mean to make you jump.'

'Nobody said you were coming back so soon.' He straightens up. He's not looking very pleased to see her. Most of the kitchen surfaces are covered in large slab cakes – in different stages of either cooling or decoration in thick, colourful frosting.

'It was Mr Ziminovski's idea.'

'You've seen him?' Jeremiah sounds surprised.

'Left him a couple of hours ago – we were supposed to have breakfast.'

'Well . . . I don't know. Up at the house they've been

trying to get him all morning. The old Bierce dragon lady's been goin' plum crazy up there – and Mrs Z's got one of her migraine headaches and the baby's cuttin' teeth and the nurses are goin' bananas. It's not a lot of fun up there.'

'He got his man to bring me home. George? Doesn't say much?'

'That'd be him.'

'Why doesn't Mrs Bierce just phone him?'

'I guess he don't answer.' He puts the baking tray gingerly on to a wire rack, then looks up at Fliss a litle abashed. 'I'm – well, I'm sorry I'm here – in your way – but I thought you were in the city all day and there couldn't be no harm.'

'Of course not.'

'I'm bakin' cakes.'

'Yes, I do see that.' She starts to laugh. 'It's sort of – well – obvious.' He starts to laugh too. 'They look amazing,' she goes on, 'wonderful icing.'

'For my church. We have kind of a social, once a month after the evening service – down towards Pleasantville. I only got a little microwave in my cottage and I don't like to do it up at the house – especially today with everyone so crazy – and that chef – that Chaumery guy gets real mad – yells at me that I'm usin' all the butter – and you not bein' here and all – '

'Don't mind me – go ahead. You couldn't possibly spare a bit, could you? Im absolutely ravenous.'

'Not only a bit. A bit of each. You can taste the full selection of Jeremiah's bakin' from scratch. Ain't nobody can make a carrot cake like it – or marble. And this here's my famous angel food cake – real manna from heaven. It's blessed, I'm not kiddin' you – the Lord really gave me the gift.'

She sits at the counter having a general tasting. 'You really do have the talent – they're delicious.'

'Don't I, though? Take it with me wherever I go. Ain't a church alive doesn't need a good cake now and then.'

'Have you been with the Ziminovskis long?'

'Since they came here. About six years ago.'

'They've only been here six years?'

'That's not so little.'

'But there's just so *much* of everything – I'd got the idea they'd been here for ages.'

'Some of these estates change hands every few months – six years is almost permanent – that was with the *last* Mrs Ziminovski though when I came.'

'Oh . . . I see. Why so much change? I don't mean of wives – just in general?'

'People come. People go.'

'Do you like it here – working for them?'

'It's OK. I like the country – that I *do* like. Last job I had I was living in the Bronx – I was a sleep-out butler then – for some people on Central Park West. This is better. Originally I'm from Georgia – that's where my family is – been up North a *long* time. But I like being out of the city.'

'I've only had the tiniest taste – of the city – I'd love to go back. It's like a sort of dream.'

'It's a dream all right. A *bad* dream.'

He's parked his car round at the side of the cottage, hidden from view of the drive. It's an enormous gas guzzler of an old Pontiac with lots of chrome and fins – ready for take-off. Just as well it has so many flat open spaces, for now he's able to lay out all the slab cakes next to each other on the back seat and in the trunk – when Fliss calls this the 'boot', he slaps her on the back and says, 'You really crack me up the way you talk.' They arrange everything quite carefully so the icing won't get squashed, Fliss licking her sticky fingers appreciatively as they finish.

'It's been a real nice bakin' session this – real nice,' he says.

'Nice for me too – thank you for the cake.'

'I'd appreciate it if you didn't mention it to nobody, you know what I mean?'

'Of course.'

'I wouldn't want it thought I was takin' no advantage, you understand?' And he gives her a great walnut-cracker of a conspiratorial wink, gets into his car and drives gingerly down the hill, guarding his precious cargo from any sudden application of the brakes.

So now what to do? Today, for the first time, she notices it's really peaceful here, just as it should be, with no background mechanical disturbance from builders or gardeners. But it's oppressive too. Nobody around – nothing to get on with. And Mr Z had assured her – 'pretty soon,' he'd said – how soon is 'pretty'? She tries to telephone the main house – presses various buttons – but can't get through. Silence all around.

Perhaps she could walk down to the Collection and just get started on her own. But it'll probably be locked; alarmed up to its eaves and impregnable without the right keys and codes. Perhaps she should walk up to the house – but everybody's told her not to. Mrs Bierce had been most insistent – 'on no account walk' – even Tom had said so – something about all these roaming guards in the grounds – but she's never seen them – secretive to the point of total invisibility. So perhaps she'll just give it some time – wait to be called – again. She goes out on to the veranda, settles back on the hammock, closes her eyes and listens to the heat.

When she wakes up it's early evening. Still light, but the sun beginning to glow red over the lake. Nobody has called.

She goes into the sitting room and switches on the television. The picture takes a second or two to form itself into a recognizable shape – and the shape is Constantine Ziminovski – in close-up. Not looking as he had this morning, but rather younger with much darker hair – but it's the same flashing smile taking up his whole lower jaw. Fliss stands frozen in the middle of the floor for a moment, not comprehending – thinking that the picture is in some way internal, a family snap blown up, and by some futuristic trick used to decorate the screen when the set isn't properly tuned. Or something. You'd have to be some sort of vanity freak to pull a trick like that, wouldn't you? To adorn all your television sets with a broadcast picture of a better, younger, perhaps happier you?

But then the voice, a woman's voice, is saying, . . . 'was arrested in his Water Street offices this afternoon on serious charges thus far described as "fiscal malfeasance". Constantine Ziminovski was taken handcuffed through his offices in full view of his staff and brought immediately to precinct headquaters. Over to Jim Brody outside the Constance Corporation building in downtown Manhattan.'

The picture switches to a young man with a microphone in front of a black glass wall. The street behind is almost deserted. Just a few curious people stand around hoping for their moment of television fame. One girl is waggling her fingers at the camera – saying hi to Mom.

'Thank you, Cindy,' says the man into camera. 'Here in the heart of Manhattan's financial district there's been no time yet to absorb the shock of this event, the full impact of which will only become clear when the markets reopen tomorrow morning. Constantine Ziminovski – one of the richest and most respected of the new breed of super-financiers and a massive donator to many of the city's most important charities, has been arrested in the most public and humiliating manner in front of his staff on as yet unspecified charges thought to involve fraud and insider trading. We await details later – a press conference is sched-uled for 9 p.m. which should give us further information. Also in custody are several of Constantine Ziminovski's chief executives. We'll have those names for you later. This is Jim Brody from outside the Constance Corporation's New York headquarters, where Constantine Ziminovski was arrested at 4.20 Eastern Standard Time this afternoon.'

Cindy comes back on to the screen with her big, juicy red lips curved into a smile and says, 'We'll have some weather news for you after these messages and it looks like time to get out those slickers – after the big heat, storms are on their way.'

The picture changes to a woman looking lovingly at a pot of Peter Pan peanut butter.

Fliss switches off the set. Her insides have melted into jelly. She goes to the phone, then stops herself. There was no one to answer before, there'll probably be no one now. Or worse, perhaps there will – and what on earth to say? What to do? How can it be true? It's a joke. It's not a joke. It's a nightmare. It's too real for a nightmare. And then the thought – the cheque he'd given her. His cheque. Selfishness will always out. The cheque will still be good, won't it? She gets it out of her handbag. It's got today's date and is handwritten – by him. An extra two thousand dollars have been added, she now realizes – although he'd said something, it hadn't really registered when she'd looked before. Money for unspecified expenses. That was very nice of him. Well, it was. Wasn't it?

She goes out on to the veranda. The big orange sphere of the sun is beginning to settle over the trees and is doubled by its reflection in the lake. She's not sure she's breathing any more. As she stands watching, she sees a movement at the bottom of the slope – animal movement. Deer? She looks again. Not deer. Llamas. Three Llamas moving fast across the grass, and behind them, donkeys almost invisible in the dusky light. Then, unmistakably, zebras – one, two – *six* zebras, cantering along behind, quite skittishly, kicking and bucking.

Animal husbandry is so deeply embedded that her first instinct is to rush down the slope and try to corral them in some way. But how, and with what? She's got nothing – so strange to have nothing – no ropes or halters, no solid protective boots, no whip, not even a stick – none of the accoutrements which would come automatically to hand at home. And no one else to help. Even as she's thinking, the animals pick up speed and head down across the valley. Something very major must have happened at the zoo.

The zoo. She'd better go there. But first telephone someone – warn someone. Surely in all this great estate somebody is around who can help. She starts pressing buttons, but nothing is happening – just the emptiness of unanswered ringing. Visions of the rest of the animals and birds streaming out of their enclosures loom up. What can have happened?

She slams the receiver down and runs out of the cottage. She starts racing along the driveway but knows there must be a more direct route. The zoo is at the bottom of the hill, beyond the Court Collection – so go – go – straight down, cut across and down. The light is getting duskier even as she runs. She's pounding down the grassy slopes in these wretched sandals, the trees rearing up, black lumps in the gloom. She hopes she's going the right way. Still down – it must be roughly right – but no lights and only the sound of the crickets. Then another sound – a noise from another sphere – a whooping, howling scream, coming at her from over there.

She follows, crashing straight down the hill now, through little copses, then clumps of evergreens, then through a dense planting of trees and she's out in the open. The zoo is to her right. It's all lit up by its mock-Victorian streetlamps on its eerily empty mock-Victorian terrace – the one Edgar Horne had been so funny about last night when he'd shown her around – 'You *have* to mock the mock sweethearts – what would life be without a little *pique*?'

The big double gates next to the turnstiles are open wide, and behind, the cages, which she can see from here, are open too. Most of them are empty, but not all. In one she can see a wallaby distractedly circling round and round, ignoring the open gate. Two ostriches are paddling at the edges of what she'd been told was to be the seal pool. But the echoing eerie wail isn't coming from the zoo – it's further away – over to her left.

She starts running towards it. In front are the trees which screen the zoo from the Collection building. Yesterday she'd walked through here with Tom and Edgar – but she doesn't want to now – not with that strange, horrible sound circling around.

She runs along the edge instead, until she's reached the narrow tip and can look across the open space. Now there is more light – this time coming from the barn – the mock Little Watling barn with its dormer windows embedded in its pale, new thatch, twinkling across the grass. With the barrier of trees no longer soaking up the volume, the howling is much louder, swelling around her, scarcely an animal sound at all. The keening builds in intensity, as chilling as any siren of war. The barn door is open, allowing a narrow band of light to stream across the ground. She runs in a wide circle, keeping herself back in the protective darkness, but peering into the revealing glare. The howling comes from inside – and behind it there is another sound – the smashing of china.

For a moment she's completely glued to the earth. First instincts to rush in are immediately quenched by fear of whatever creatures are making the noise – and what to do. Oh, God, what to do? Where is help? Then there is the briefest pause – a sliver of silence. And at the back of the silence is another sound – tiny – a human sob, then a baby's cry. She throws herself forward into the building and flings back the door to the court.

On the far wall, the big male gibbon she'd been shown yesterday – safely in his cage – is now hanging by one arm from a hook, high up near the ceiling. And it's a familiar hook – as are all the hundreds of other hooks – hooks and shelves all laid out in that recognizable pattern and order – the one she'd tended, dusted and organized for so many years – back home in her pale watercolour valley. Below him, the female gibbon with her baby clinging to her breast, is hanging from a shelf. The other female is spread-eagled on the wall immediately to Fliss's right. The male's mouth is shaped into a perfect black 'O' from which the lamentation is pouring anew around the court, filling it with almost visible vibration. In his free hand he holds one of the mugs.

In the whirling chaos, Fliss's gaze, for an instant, zooms in on his long, delicate fingers, curved round the china cylinder – she almost fancies she recognizes it – a Worcester baluster mug – before it's slung, slung with some sort of deliberation, across the room. And then the next piece – and the next.

In the middle of the floor, surrounded by the shattered remains of the Collection, Katrina Ziminovski, on her knees, is hunched over her baby, her back towards Fliss, her head turned up towards the male gibbon as if daring him to hit his mark. Her shoulders are heaving with sobs, her gasps mixed in with the howling and the smashing. She doesn't see Fliss, but the gibbons do. The movement of another presence seems to send out a spurt of energized panic.

The gibbon near the door launches herself at an angle across the corner to the next wall. The gibbon with the baby also swings – moves from one plane to the next – and they've started a merry-go-round. They swing and scream and grasp – and chuck. Howling and smashing, round they spin. Katrina is sinking down into a little heap, gathering her own baby in under her breast. Fliss runs forward, trying to dodge the hurling missiles, turns so that her back may shield the human baby, tries to release him from Katrina's grasp, fails – then tries to pull Katrina to her feet. A smudgy slick of blood is already trickling from her temple, blood all mixed with tears; the cartoon beautiful face all collapsed now, made ugly by grief.

28

And to crown it all, Rosalie Klaus has reservations –
for that new place out on the water where the waiters
(who are *all* of course out-of-work actors) actually come
over and *mime* the specials for you – it's wonderfully cute
she's been told and *the* place right now. She's been trying
to get them in for weeks and this Thursday night was the
best they could offer, hardly the most convenient time
with Tom Junior having to leave so early in the morning
for the office.

And then he'd called from the city this afternoon and
said he can't make it after all. Why not, she'd asked,
and explained her difficulties with the restaurant, and he'd
said he was with the police – he was actually calling from
the precinct house in the presence of *officers*, for heaven's
sake! So what was she to think? And she'd tried to ask him
questions and he couldn't seem to answer. So she'd gone
running up to Tom Senior in his den and found him mesmerized in front of all five TV sets – all of them showing
some aspect of this *incredible* story – this thing about Mr
Ziminovski is just *incredible* – you couldn't think a thing
like that about someone like that. And then – ohmygod –
there's *Tom Junior* on the screen. Tom leaving the police
precinct and having his head pushed down into the car by

some cop like a common criminal and taken God knows where – Rikers Island or something.

So she's going round the den – round and round – while Tom Senior just sits in his big Eames chair swinging from set to set saying *nothing*. And she's thinking – what am I to do? What am I to do about the reservations, for heaven's sake? And she must've said this out loud, because Tom Senior actually swore at her – real mean – and she can't remember when he's sounded like that in thirty-eight years of marriage – he said, 'What the fuck's the matter with you, woman? Your only son is being shut up in the slammer and you're talking about *dinner* reservations?' And she'd said – she had, 'Well, we've *still* got to eat, haven't we?'

29

It was Jeremiah who took Fliss to the airport. Between them they decided that was the best thing to do.

He'd appeared like an angel of rescue out of the darkness and found them all, Fliss, Katrina and the baby, outside the mock Little Watling barn. Fliss had grabbed the baby from Katrina's grasp and run out with him, leaving him on the ground while she went back inside more or less to drag Katrina, still hunched on all fours, across the court floor and out of the building. The gibbons were still in full whirling flight and, as she shut the door, she could hear the last of the Harry Harley-Wright Collection of Commemorative Drinking Vessels being smashed into shards and smithereens.

Jeremiah arrived from his church social. He hadn't switched on his car radio – he was still humming hymns – full of worship for the Lord, and too many slices on his own huckleberry cream layer cake for the good of his cholesterol level. The main gates to the Ziminovski estate were swamped with press and TV people. Cameras and full lights were set up outside the lodge houses and the lone guard was doing his best to maintain some sort of order from inside the wrought-iron barrier. Jeremiah drove straight past, just as two police cars arrived with whining sirens. He drove steadily on, right round the perimeter of the estate and in through the little back entrance which opened on to the lake track, using the private combination to get through the gate.

He had no idea what was happening, but felt neither alarm nor surprise. A lifetime of trying to fit in unobtrusively as a black man in a white man's world had taught him that anything was possible. There isn't any level to which humankind, in certain circumstances, won't sink in order to get the better of the next fellow – and the next. All you can do, he reckons, is put your faith in the Lord and keep your head down. But he knows plenty of brothers – and sisters too – who disagree; plenty of brothers who want to raise the flag and stand tall – never mind if they get their heads blown off in the process. Jeremiah's seen too many heads blown off – he'll just settle now for a quiet life and a peaceful end. And if this particular sanctuary – the Ziminovski estate – has somehow been invaded, well then he'll just slip off into the night and find a new one.

It was as he was driving along the lake track that he saw the zebras. He couldn't miss them. They were standing right in front of him, their eyes glowing fluorescent in the beam of his headlamps. As they moved off, he could see the llamas in the background, and, bringing up the rear, a lone kangaroo. He headed straight for the zoo, round the edge of the lake. As he turned on to the main driveway again, he saw this little group, held in silhouette against the light coming from the Court Collection: Fliss, holding a baby, and a woman at her feet, all crushed up, like a crumpled Kleenex on the ground.

Fliss nearly burst into tears herself when she saw the old Pontiac loom into view and heard the comforting chug of its massive engine. Together they pulled Katrina on to the back seat, where she lay among the remains of some of Jeremiah's slab cakes, shuddering and heaving with sobs. Fliss sat in the front, trying to comfort the now-hysterical baby – whom she now discovered was a boy – with a name – Alexander.

They drove slowly up the hill in the huge old car, so low-slung it felt as if its bottom would scrape on the roadway, still picking out with their headlamps the occasional exotic and startled animal.

Every light in the great house seemed to be on – a blazing beacon at the top of the hill, as if about to host some extraordinarily glamorous gala. When they got inside though, it seemed to be empty. They manoeuvred Katrina into one of the big reception rooms on the ground floor and laid her out, all smeared with Jeremiah's gaudier frosting, on one of the soft grey suede sofas. While Jeremiah went to phone the doctor for Katrina, Fliss ran upstairs with the baby, trying to find the nursery. Nobody answered her shouts, but the noise of a television in one of the bedrooms drew her, and when she opened the door she found a uniformed nanny sitting in the dark, eyes glued to the set, with a paralysed look of terror on her face. Having handed over her screaming, wriggling, by now very damp charge, she ran back through the house, checking room after room as she went. Nothing. No one. There was a distinct whiff of rats having left the sinking ship.

As she passed Katrina's boudoir, she heard a curious hissing, clicking noise. Flinging open the door, she saw Mrs Bierce, squatting down on the floor, a heap of files beside her, stuffing paper into a shredder. For an instant Mrs Bierce looked up – at bay, a cornered animal; but as soon as she saw who it was, she turned her attention back to the shredder and went on steadily feeding it.

There were so many questions – impossible for Fliss to begin – and then she had a collapsing feeling that whatever she did manage to ask wouldn't get any answers. Probably there weren't any – not yet – nothing simple anyway. So instead she stuck to practicalities.

'I've brought the baby back.'

'OK,' said Mrs Bierce, not looking up, and not looking surprised.

'He's upstairs with the nanny.'

'Yes.'

'And she's – Mrs Ziminovski – she's down in the – the morning room, I suppose it is – that grey one. The doctor's on his way. She probably needs sedation.'

'Well, I guess we all could do with a little bit of that,' said Mrs Bierce with acidity, looking up at last, 'but I don't suppose the rest of us are going to get any.'

'No.'

'No.' She slammed her lips shut and went back to the shredding.

'The Collection – my – you know – it's been destroyed – by the monkeys.'

'That's pretty unfortunate. But then it's all pretty unfortunate.'

'All the cages seem to have been opened. Most of the animals are loose.'

'Is that so?'

'I'm not sure how – but I think possibly – well, maybe it was Mrs Ziminovski who did it.'

'What makes you suppose that?' Mrs Bierce's gaze still remained fixed on the shredder.

'Just – well, she was down there – I couldn't see anybody else and she's – well, she's absolutely distraught.'

'I wouldn't put it past her – some people will do just anything to grab attention – and she never was what you'd call *stable*.'

'But the animals are just wandering all over the place.'

'You wouldn't be expecting me to do anything about that?'

'Couldn't we – I don't know – organize some help?'

'I think we're all a bit past that now.'

'Right. Yes.' Fliss was conscious of hovering. 'Well, actually I did also wonder . . . about the – ' She wanted to ask about the cheque but the look on Mrs Bierce's face was growing dangerous. 'No – never mind.' She waited for a moment, then, as nothing else was forthcoming, 'I think I'd better be off.'

'OK.'

'I think it's best.'

'Probably your only bet.'

'I'll make my own way, shall I? To the airport?'

'You'd certainly better.'

Fliss's last sight of Mrs Bierce had her frozen against the backdrop of the beautiful Impressionist creatures in their sunny gardens, fixed within their painted vivacity, while the grim-faced woman stuffed yet another fistful of paper into the jaws of the hissing machine.

At the door of Pan Am Departures, Jeremiah gravely helped her out with her case. She'd scribbled down her address and phone number and pushed the piece of paper at him quite shyly. He looked down at it for a moment, then nodded and stuck it in his pocket.

'Could you let me have yours?' she'd asked.

But he'd laughed. 'Now who knows where the wind's gonna take me?' he'd said, stepped back to his car and zoomed off into the night.

When she lands at Heathrow and has got through Customs, she goes straight to W. H. Smith to get some newspapers – desperate for information. But there's no hint of the Ziminovski scandal on the front of the tabloids. The *New York Post* and the *Daily News* had screaming headlines plastered all over Kennedy Airport before she left. Now the only mention she can find is a small paragraph on page two of the *Financial Times*, and that tells her only what she already knows.

She is dreading phoning Ivor and puts it off until she reaches Liverpool Street Station. She has to steel herself to answer his queries – What is she doing? Why is she back so soon? She doesn't want to have to think about any of it yet, let alone discuss it. The oddest thing though – he doesn't sound in the least curious. Actually he sounds very strange, detached – almost drugged. At first she's angry – he really ought to have dropped this pose of dissociation from her adventure. But then he asks her to take a taxi from the station – says he won't be able to meet her. This is so unlike him. Apart from being usually so generous with his chauffeuring services, he is almost paranoiac about the cost of taxi fares. But today he insists.

'Car trouble?' she asks.

'No.'

'Oh. What then?'

'I just can't leave.'

'Are you ill or something?'

'No. I just can't leave at the moment.'

'Why?'

'You'll see.'

By the time the taxi turns through the entrance and starts bumping over the familiar potholes, she's beginning to feel smothered by exhaustion and is straining to keep her eyelids up. As the house hoves into clear view, however, the eyelids zing back to fully open and she can feel her eyebrows snap up into two sharp circumflexes of surprise.

On the land side of the moat, an enormous removal pantechnicon is parked. Men in baize aprons are in the process of loading the kitchen dresser up its ramp. The hall table, drawing-room Knole sofas and oak linenfold cupboard are all standing on the bridge. Barnaby Fitzgerald is anxiously giving orders from the bottom of the ramp.

'Do be careful, duckies!' Fliss can hear him yell.

In the centre of the forecourt, Martita is sitting, tucked up in an elaborate wicker Bath chair. She seems to be directing operations at her end. Fliss pays off the taxi and struggles over the bridge with her case. Barney looks her up and down once – then turns back to the lorry and shouts, '*Do* watch it – we don't want to bruise our corners!'

Behind Martita several more men are struggling out of the front door – this time with one of the Chinese pagoda wardrobes. The long-case clock from the hall landing is now bound with ropes and stands on the top step.

'Oh, *you're* here,' says Martita, then shouts, 'Careful with that lacquer – it's come all the way from Shanghai,' as the men heave past with the wardrobe.

'What's happening, Titty?'

'There's been a change of plan.'

'What?'

'If you will go gallivanting off, you have to expect these things. Things will tend to happen.'

'*What* is happening, Titty?'

'I'm changing locations – for the moment.'

'What?'

'Barney's facilities are so much better. It's a joy to be in a place with style. And oomph. Barney's got *heaps* of oomph. So refreshing.'

'You're going to stay with Barney, Titty?'

'Not stay. Live – possibly. And it's Maud.'

'What?'

'Not Titty. That's a silly name. I don't know how I came to deserve it. Barney and I agree – I'm much more of a Maud after all – it's much more dignified. Calder. Maud Calder.'

'As in "Fitzgerald and"?'

'Oh, we are quick. Always a first time for anything, I suppose. I'm a partner now – or I will be. That'll be *my* name over the shop – once the deed poll's been organized.'

'What will the real Calder say about that?'

'Gone to Goa, we think – many moons ago – in search of nirvana or something similar. We're not likely to have any trouble from him.'

'So you're going to live in Barney's flat? Why are you taking all the furniture? There won't be any room.'

'It's stock – for the shop. My part of the deal – for the partnership. Once we're organized, we'll be coming back here to expand – we'll have the whole place as a show-room – but not until we've sorted out the moat. Ivor's got an inflatable dinghy down in the cellar now – to get about. Can't have that with decent furniture.'

'You're going to turn the house into an antiques shop?'

'Rather better than that. Barney says it'll be an entire antiques *ambience* – far superior. He says there's heaps of money sloshing about with all these City types at the moment – oozing with it – can't spend it fast enough, Barney says. We'll make a packet.'

'What about us?'

'I beg your pardon?' That familiar hazy look about Titty's eyes.

'WHAT? About US?' Fliss yells.

'Oh, I'm giving you lots of notice – we'll have to get planning permission and all sorts of things – you needn't be out till after Christmas.' She turns to a couple of the men going back into the house. 'Do make sure we get all the Chinese lacquer, won't you? I don't want a bit left. It would be tragic to break up the set.'

30

Not so much a bounced cheque – more an earthquake somewhere quite high on the Richter scale . . .

Dear Mr and Mrs Harley-Wright

Re: US$ cheque drawn on Constance Corporation Inc.

With regard to the above cheque, which has been returned to us marked 'Refer to Drawer', preliminary inquiries confirm that all Constance Corporation Inc. accounts have been frozen, and in the circumstances we do not feel able to re-present. We suggest you contact the drawer yourselves as soon as possible. Your current account has been deducted £24.65 to cover our communication with the drawer's bank in New York as per enclosed advice note.

You will wish to be informed that your current account balance has now exceeded your overdraft limit; see enclosed statement. We would like to remind you that this is in contravention of our standard loan agreement. Please remit sufficient funds to remedy this situation immediately and contact Mr Dixon with regard to your intentions re: clearing the balance of your overdraft.

Yours sincerely

     – and an indecipherable signature –

Loans Officer

'You did *what*?' shrieks Barney.

The letter from the bank arrived about an hour ago and Fliss knows the colour of her face must still match the verdigris tiles of the kitchen. Judging by the horrible feeling in her stomach, her whole body has probably turned a sickly green by now. To help absorb the impact of Barney's scorn, she's positioned herself with her back against the Véronique, resting her bottom against the comfort of the hotplate – using it as a prop, for her knees feel all loose and unformed, as if the ligaments have become detached.

Barney is in full flaunting flourish. He's brought a huge sketchbook crammed with ideas for the new antiques centre and keeps brandishing it round the room. Between them, Martita sits at the table – a tiny physical presence, switching her head in rapt attention from side to side, taking in each of them like a curious stoat – her eyes shining with the drama of it all.

'Well, it seemed all right – at the time,' says Fliss, defeated but justifying.

'I *did* warn you. Didn't I warn you? What did I say? Sweeties from a babe – sweeties – from – a – babe.' Barney is syncopating his comment with individual waves of the sketchpad.

'But it seemed logical – only fair.'

'Nothing is fair in biz, ducky, except the money *in* the bank. You must have been *potty*.'

'But they'd paid us 50 per cent up front without having a single one of the ceramics actually in their possession. They trusted *us* – we could have done anything, if you think about it – sold them elsewhere – waltzed off with them – '

'Let your house monkeys loose to smash up the whole lot – '

'Don't, Barney.'

'Well, *really* – what can you have been thinking of?'

'It just seemed – I don't know – all right. After all, I was practically accompanying them. It's not as if they were launching off into nowhere – it felt sort of like C.O.D.'

'*Cash on Delivery?* We're not talking mail-order catalogue, ducky – we're not talking *Littlewoods* – we're talking export of works of art. You must have been completely off your rockers. No wonder they wanted *me* out of the way.'

'But it was all arranged by Denmans originally. Everything seemed so pukka and above board. You don't imagine you're going to be let down by such a reputable august institution.'

'Well, I warned you about *them*.'

'So you wouldn't have done it?'

'Always payment in advance.'

'Always?'

'Well, it depends. Always*ish*. Depends on the quality of the buyer.'

'Oh, come on, Barney. Could there have *been* any buyer in the whole world who would have seemed superior in quality to Constantine Ziminovski, as represented by Denmans? Even *you* were impressed.'

'But you, my duckies, were, in this instance, duckies out of water – *well* out.'

'I just – it's so hard to explain – I don't think it was intended,' says Fliss, thinking of that meeting with Mr Z and how solicitous he'd seemed – handing her the cheque with the extra added on – shepherding her into the big black car. And what had he said? Something about whatever happened she was to understand that he really cared about the Collection – that it was truly important to him. Surely, surely he *couldn't* have planned to cheat them – could he? And he couldn't have known his wife would run wild either. Crazy woman, crazy thing to do . . .

'Intended or not,' says Barney, mostly to Martita, 'it's landed you right up to your necks, hasn't it?'

Martita nods, as if something decisive and terminal has been settled.

'So what next? I'd imagine suing is out of the question.'

'Your imaginings are spot on. We couldn't begin to think about starting any action in America – and Denmans are well covered. Their part of the deal evidently ended with the signing of the agreement. They didn't have any specific responsibility apart from the valuation and the initial arrangements – and they couldn't have known anyway. No one knew – that's the whole point.'

'Insurance though, surely?'

'No.'

'*What?*'

'There was transit insurance of course, but that lapsed once the Collection arrived at the Ziminovski house. After that it was all covered by their American insurers.'

'Well, you may have some joy there then.'

'I don't think so. Well, it doesn't look good – all to do with the scandal and the fraud – and whether payments had been met fraudulently – disclosure – you know what insurers are like.'

'Well, well, well – it's jolly tough titty, isn't it, Maud?' Martita nods. 'A real touch of the *touchés*, as it were. Now where's Ivor? Has he got to grips with this moat business? We really need it in hand before we make our planning application . . .'

Such a confrontation turns out to be much easier to contend with than the dreary, deadening reality of their situation. It's one thing to brazen it out in front of Barney and Titty – there is absolutely no point in crumbling in front of them – but alone, just the pair of them, Fliss and Ivor find it very different: hard to think anything through with any clarity at all.

During the day, they turn themselves into robots set on a basic strategy simply to get by as intact as possible and to let the minimum of their renewed despair escape into the lives of the children. Staggering to witness how instantly the despair returns though, after those summer weeks of relaxation. These now seem so brief as scarcely to have existed at all. They've taken on the wispy status of a dream and are now replaced with the familiar churning of stomach and brain as Fliss and Ivor go back over every detail of their actions – nit-picking and quietly self-recriminative.

Late into the night, once they know for sure they're alone, they waste dizzying hours talking through the ins and outs of their situation. Could they get jobs – to Fliss that seems the obvious solution. But Ivor dismisses the notion with scorn. No half-way decent employer could possibly need their lifetime's worth of experience, he claims – it's all too vague and shapeless to fit anywhere – and they're too damn *old* to count – and if they found anything they'd earn too little. How to set up a home? Where to go? Where even to begin? And, fulfilling his own prophecy, he's begun to look older too – the stress of these weeks stringing him out further and further – attenuated as a piece of catgut – ready to snap.

So looking back is, as it happens, much easier than looking forward. 'Forward' seems a complete blank – impossible to give it any shape at all. If they truly are to leave the house to the mercies of Martita, a.k.a. Maud, Barney and an 'antiques ambience', then where is there a place for them – with less than no money and diffuse, unmarketable skills which all depend on their regular access to the land and the buildings?

What Fliss would like to do every single morning is crawl down to the bottom of the bed under the duvet and stay there all day, breathing in her own breath, keeping herself curled in a foetal ball of resilience against the world outside. What she *has* to do of course is rise, shine and get at it – all of it.

Emma is leaving for university shortly and Daisy and Henry have already started back at school. Emma's tuition fees and a basic grant will be paid by the local authority, but obviously she'll have a struggle. However, hers is still the tunnel vision of teenage optimism – thank heaven. Dauntless in youth, she does plan a job – part-time – bar or waitressing; something will turn up.

Fliss keeps trying to dig out more information about the Ziminovskis but it's almost impossible to glean anything concrete. The scandal briefly moved from the inner pages of the specialist financial press to the tabloids, with a few screeching claims and headlines, but once the initial impetus had passed, it quickly returned to the odd discreet paragraph in the broadsheet business sections. From one of these she learned that Tom Klaus had been arrested – along with several other of the Constance Corporation chief executives. She's tried several times to make some sort of contact, but when she dials the number of the Constance Corporation's London offices she gets the long tone of 'unobtainable', and when she telephones New York she gets an answering machine. It never calls back.

She's sad about Tom – sad and puzzled. What can be happening to him – and could he have been party to some massive fraud – for despite the lack of solid information, it seems that the Ziminovski case is one of vast fraud – a huge complex puzzle of greed and deception. She thinks of how young and unfazed he had seemed. Could that outer smooth coating of almost oiled skin have hidden a tangle of tension and deceit? It doesn't seem possible. And she'd allowed herself that odd little interval of dreaming – the irony of it – imagining herself in his life – a life untrammelled by fear.

The bank now seems like a hideous demon – lurking in the middle of the market square waiting to engulf them. Added to their fear is a deep sense of mortification at having proved the UM right. Fliss silently groans when she recalls her oh-so-public bout of righteous indignation when renegotiating their overdraft. Blindly they ignore its letters, try not to answer the telephone and do all their shopping in the village so as not to risk any accidental meetings in town.

Fliss cracks on with making pots in her shed, knowing that any sort of ready money is now of vital importance.

Sometimes she's a bit irritated with Ivor. Instead of doing anything about investigating the seepage of the moat, or making even a stab at any concrete plan for the future, he seems to be spending hours in the old greenhouse fiddling around. He's got this idea, he says – about herbs of all things – herbs in pots, which you might be able to buy in grocery stores and just grow on your own window sill. Honestly, what a moment to go off on yet another tangent – another useless enterprise. Never take off.

This is how they go on throughout September – blind, numb and running.

In early October there is the annual school harvest fair in aid of the PTA. Fliss had promised her 'seconds' to them months ago and now feels committed, though sneakingly resentful. If anybody needs the proceeds of any sale of her seconds, it's her own family. Still, a promise is a promise, and it's actually quite cheering to get out of the house atmosphere and set up her stall in the school gymnasium on a Saturday afternoon.

She finds herself next to April, whom she hasn't seen since the days of the great 'mucking-out' back in the spring. April's daughter June started at the school this very term and April, it turns out, is already an ardent supporter of the PTA – one of those stalwarts who rapidly turn into its very spine, instantly indispensable. Her stall is 'Trash and Treasures'. Fliss gives it a quick once-over to check none of her own work is there – too galling if the famous vase had been relegated to such a lowly station, but in the depths of her current mood, anything seems possible.

There's only time for a brief chat before the doors open

and the punters stream in. Business is brisk for April, but rather slow for Fliss. Even with huge discounts, this isn't really the right market for handmade dinner services, though her bunches of lavender and pomanders do quite well.

About an hour or so into the fair is when it happens. Fliss has just wrapped up a couple of plates in newspaper and handed them over to a customer (£14.50 to PTA funds) when she looks along the line of stalls and spots the Under Manager. He's in weekend garb of brilliant orange anorak, is licking an ice-cream cone, has a small child sitting on his shoulders (leaning on his head – quite endearing if only he weren't the UM) and is coming this way. Perhaps he hasn't seen her yet.

Panic flows over her in a great hot wave and without giving it any specific thought, she dives under the stall and squats there among the empty cardboard boxes and plastic bags, inadequately screened by the red crêpe paper of the tablecloth. Why did she do that? *What* could she have been thinking of – and it's sort of too late now. How to get out again with any dignity? Feeling totally trapped in her foolishness, she stays there in suspended animation, awaiting the UM's approach. But which one is he? She only has trouser legs and shoes to go by. A denim pair with turn-ups, plus jazzy trainers, stops. A voice –

'Is there anyone serving at this stall?' The UM's nasal voice – she knows it of course. It haunts her dreams.

'Er – oh – I don't know,' says April, sounding surprised. 'There was . . . a moment ago . . . Can I help you?'

'I wondered about these mugs.'

'Lovely, aren't they?'

'Handmade, are they?'

'Totally. She's a professional potter – the girl that makes them.'

So she's a 'girl' in April's eyes. What a revelation.

'Local?'

'Totally.'

'You get a very nice cup and saucer at Habitat I've noticed.'

'Do you? I wouldn't know. Not as handmade, I don't suppose . . .'

'No?'

'Couldn't be. Not like these.'

'No. I don't suppose. Do you like them, Jason?'

A little boy's voice comes from on high. 'No.'

'Why not?' says April stoutly. 'They're lovely.'

'Well, perhaps not – if he doesn't like them.'

'It's for a very good cause,' says April, stouter than ever.

'But if he doesn't like them . . .' and the denim legs move away.

Fliss just stays there – sitting down now, cross-legged, stiff with misery, while up above she can hear April resolutely holding the fort of her stall as well as Trash and Treasures – and business seems to be picking up.

Later, much later, when things have quietened down a bit, April sticks her head under the table.

'You poor dear,' she says. 'You *are* in a bad way.'

It's the nicest thing anyone has said to Fliss in weeks and she promptly bursts into tears.

31

Tom's been wondering if this is what drowning feels like – he's been wondering for a long time now. Only this is surely worse than drowning – long, black, smothering and lasting – well, lasting it seems like for ever. Was there *ever* a time when this deep impenetrable fog didn't hang around him? Worse than a fog – thick and dark and intractable as a molasses sea.

The lack of trust is terrible. For a man whose image of himself has always been predicated on his utterly transparent probity, it's been almost terminally unnerving to be thrown on to the wrong side – to the side where he's always known the 'others' belong. Well, of course – he's a *lawyer*, for chrissake – he knows these things inside out. But not *him* – not Thomas Klaus III – *he* doesn't belong on that side – along with the cheats and the frauds, the drug dealers, the guy high on crack with a switchblade down his sock. But 'they' haven't seen it like that – not yet.

He's protested his innocence of course and hired the right legal team. So bang go those bonuses – the few he'd already managed to bank, that is – and the Constance Corporation Inc. stock is already less than worthless – it's a fucking liability. Thank God his parents hadn't yet invested heavily in it – be thankful for something. But his father had looked so hurt when he'd come to visit him in jail – bruised about the eyes – and his mother, small and frightened – almost as if they too didn't really believe that he'd known nothing – absolutely *nothing* – of the huge house of cards created by Mr Z – one element leveraged against the next – and that element used as collateral for the next and so on – and on – a gargantuan chimera – the dream of a madman creating the greatest fantasy in the world. It's still hard to think of Mr Z as evil though – or anything so specific. The companies he raided, split, sold, restructured really were often leaner and meaner post their Ziminovski experience and for a time the stock-holders really did benefit, even if so many of the job-holders didn't. He seemed to feel that the planet needed his genius – and that genius just happened to be built on – nothing – nothing at all. It was the Emperor's New Clothes after all – dragging down with him thousands upon thousands of vulnerable people – people with dependants and mortgages, hopes and fears – while his personal, private wealth had billowed ever upwards – insubstantial as cotton candy.

Now at last Tom's out on bail and the judge has given him permission to go out of state while the evidence is gathered. The case will take months to come up – maybe even years. Mr Z is still in jail though, and Katrina is in some sanatorium being treated for depression. His mother keeps him informed with all the local news now she's calmed down a bit and can just about look him in the eye. It seems they still haven't caught all those animals and the zebras have escaped from the Ziminovski estate – someone's reported seeing them way up above Dutchess County. Unbelievable.

Now he's going northwards too – in the fall, as the leaves begin their great annual transformation to red and gold.

He's sold the Porsche – exchanged it for a little Honda. The Porsche – or what it stood for – suddenly made him feel a little nauseous. He's got some things to work out – some thoughts to fix. Maybe – just maybe – he'll get out of this in one piece. He's got to keep optimistic – believe in himself, even if no one else will. He's heading for the mountains of Vermont – site of so many childhood vacations – endless summers – family Thanksgivings – deeply symbolic for him of shelter and protection. He needs to find a lair – a place to hide and lick the wounds.

It's a long drive and the road is very straight – you can let your mind skedaddle round your life on such a journey. Just sometimes he thinks back to Fliss – and that crazy collection – a collection of *mugs* – for chrissake. He'd never really gotten to the bottom of that, had he? So many people crushed by the Ziminovski dream. He hopes she's OK – well, of course he does – but he's got a whole lot of other stuff to think of – other issues to get right. Will it ever *be* right?

In Little Watling they've had a long Indian summer. Today the weather has been lovely, the leaves just turning, the light clear – but by late afternoon the wind began to get up and they were thankful to get indoors. The wind has been increasing all evening, and by the time they get to bed the rain is bucketing down, and there's a real feeling of the change of the season. They've moved into Martita's old room because it abuts the kitchen chimney and gives them some warmth for free. Like most of the house, it's very bare since she stripped it of her furniture – just a double divan, a hanging rail and a chest of drawers picked up for a song at the Sudbury auctions. The rooms do tend to ring a bit these days – echoing with all their footsteps. But now, listening to the whining wind, they feel a sort of peace. Things may be difficult, impossible even – but they're still united, lying cuddled together. Well, storms can do that of course – perhaps now best not to question, best just to enjoy the moment.

Sometime about 2 a.m., Fliss wakes up. A giant express train is roaring up the drive towards the house. She shakes her head fully awake to get rid of the dream, but the shuddering, crashing roar of the train remains. She gets up and goes to the window. It's thickly black outside, but the roar and blast of the storm are whipping past the glass. She tries to open it, turning the catch on the mullion, but can't – she's pushing, pushing hard against the wind and losing. As her eyes grow more used to the dark, she can see long straggling shoots of climbing plants and shrubs, smashing against the walls, and beyond quite large branches whirling into space. She gets back into bed and tucks herself into Ivor's back, feeling wonderfully safe as the storm buffets into the sides of the house.

It's about two hours later that she hears the first great crash.

Not until first light can they really see the damage. The Adam and Eve gable, the one which formed the front of their old bedroom, has fallen forward and tipped into the moat. Never again will that sixteenth-century Eve prostrate herself, trying to wangle her way into Adam's affections. With the gable, went the ceiling – at last. The crack must have moved on – well beyond Perpignan. To have gone this badly, it must have worked its way right round, down the Spanish coast, at least as far as Benidorm. Then, above the ceiling, the eye of the storm had caught the great barley-sugar-twist chimneys and sent them crashing through the floor where their bed would have been. They landed in the now empty drawing room, upright in almost one piece – like a brick Darby and Joan.

And down the drive – oh, yes – down the drive, the dinosaurs have been out in force. Weeding – carelessly weeding – leaving the great avenue of cedars all torn, lying and leaning on each other, their branches intertwined, their roots upturned to the sky, like so many pieces of groundsel.

32

'Tis very nearly the season to be jolly, darn it – and Fliss is doing her best. She's now made a total of one hundred and nineteen holly wreaths – every digital joint is on fire and her thumbs are pricked to bits. Never *mind* (but oh, she does mind) – the ready money is vital for any Christmas goodies this year. She'll be selling them to the market stallholders and the village shop – plus a few to the general public from a table down by the road – and her friends are very loyal. Helena's ordered three and comes to collect them.

Since the great hurricane in October, it's impossible for even Helena to zoom up the drive any more and she has to pick her way quite carefully, zigzagging around the fallen trees. The Labradors are hanging their cheerful, panting faces out of her back car window, and they make their customary quick dash the moment she stops. Fliss can hear them splat into the moat – it's too low and muddy these days for anything as aqueous as a splash. Nevertheless, she runs to close all doors to prevent them getting in, before making some tea. Helena is, as usual, not staying – far too busy – rushing as ever to her next project. But also as usual, she perches herself on the edge of the Véronique – agog for a 'goss' and needing a translation of the latest local rumour.

'You're going to have an *asylum*?'

'Not an asylum, for God's sake, Helena – a *refuge*.'

'A refuge from what?'

'Life mostly.'

'For women?'

'Not necessarily.'

'Bloody hell, you must be barking.'

'It was April's idea actually.'

'*My* April?'

'She's been working with a refuge just outside Bury in her spare time.'

'What spare time? She never told *me* she had any spare time – I could have done with her for the extra ironing.'

'She knows all the ropes – she's fantastic – all the ins and outs. There's a terrific need and this place will be perfect evidently. We've obviously got the space, even with the south gable blown down. And the local authority's getting involved – and the DHSS. Everybody who comes will have a certain amount of housing benefit and so on. And there's also a local charity in Great Watling – did you know that? Set up by old Edmund de Pettet in 1535 or something – one hundred pounds and it's been clocking up interest ever since – charged with relieving the indigent of the parish – only there aren't enough indigent in the Watlings evidently, so these people will count.'

'But what will you do with them – all these – whatever would you call them – *inmates*?'

'Just ordinary people – people with problems who've managed to fall through the net. There are lots of them – there but for the grace and all that . . . very nearly "for the grace" in our case.'

'Can't I call them inmates for short?'

'No, Helena, you can't.'

'What on earth does Titty think? I thought she was about to throw you out.'

'She was. She and Barney were all set until the hurricane – but then – well, everything changed. The cedar avenue's ruined of course, so even the approach to the house looks ghastly now – and it's all listed – Grade Two Star – so English Heritage got involved and they're insisting it's all repaired to full fifteenth-century standards. It would cost a fortune to do it properly with builders – more than the house is actually worth – and of course they won't let it be demolished either. And then the insurers said we hadn't informed them about the moat going funny and that we weren't paying high enough premiums – so they're only going to cough up a fraction of what it would take – so it looks as if it's all down to us. We'll do it ourselves.'

'You *can't* – not possibly.'

'We don't see why not – if we take our time. That's why we've fixed up the tarpaulin and all that corrugated iron. Ivor always *said* it would come in useful and it jolly well has. The idea is to keep the worst of the weather out now and just keep pegging away at it. It'll probably take years but now it's ours it doesn't really matter how long, does it?'

'It's *yours*?'

'Oh, yes. Once English Heritage said it was all the owner's responsibility to put it right, Titty just threw in the towel and handed it over lock and stock – no barrels of course. She's kept all the barrels. Barney's livid – she'd already moved in with all the Boysies and now she just sits in the showroom everyday putting all the customers off. It'll never last – two cockerels on the dung heap. But it's tricky –

332

they've already set up the partnership agreement, you see – I don't know if he can get her out.'

'God – who'd have thought it? Silver linings everywhere. What do I owe you for the wreaths?'

'They're £3.50 each.'

'You couldn't do them for ten pounds for the three, could you – bulk purchase? Teddy took an absolute pasting on Black Monday, you know, and he's being fiendish about every penny I spend. I don't see how we're supposed to manage, do you? However do we women cope?'

Epilogue

It's 1997 – just past the turn of the year – and occasionally Fliss thinks if she hears the words 'coriander' or 'rocket' again she may just have to throttle somebody. This Thai food lark has gone crazy and they can't really keep up with the orders. Judging by the box and the newspapers, you'd imagine the whole country is about to sail away on a sea of coconut milk, ginger and lemon grass – always garnished with coriander of course – and usually lying on a bed of rocket. Even the Crown and Sceptre has stopped serving Tex-Mex and gone on to Pacific Rim. The fax is always jammed up in the mornings with reorders from restaurants – let alone their big regular deliveries to the supermarkets – and she seems to spend more time than ever on the telephone, sorting things out.

It was the basil that started it all. Ivor had just about sorted through his idea of potted house herbs when the Sun-dried Tomato/Parmigiano-Reggiano-in-a-lump (rather than grated like sand)/Fresh Basil Revolution hit the broadcast media – and that was sort of it. From his original mending and improvement of the old greenhouse, he set up poly-tunnels made of Nissen hut ribs he'd knurgled from the old cattle market before they spruced it up – and these had extended, as their customers grew, to more orthodox versions, and then on to real glasshouses with controlled environments.

Most of this happened while recession hit the country in general, and all their richer, more stable friends with those enviable 'proper' jobs moaned about being *nouveaux pauvres*. Being themselves very *anciens pauvres*, it was totally refreshing to feel actually *part* of a current movement, rather than helpless spectators – and in this case at the movement's very vanguard as it were. Even Helena and Teddy got swiped in the general mayhem – dashed on the rocks of the Lloyd's brouhaha and about to lose their shirts. Helena proved herself as dauntless in poverty as she'd always been in plenty, and turned their house into an upmarket Bed & Breakfast establishment. If necessary, she sleeps on a camp bed under the table in the gun room rather than miss out on an extra couple of lucrative guests. Now though things look as if they're picking up – Teddy too has caught the Thai food frenzy and has evidently landed a politically complicated deal in tiger prawns.

The refuge is really going strong. It's more of a half-way house really – somewhere for people to get themselves sorted out – draw breath, find comfort and companionship, sobriety if necessary, employment if possible – before facing the world again. April works there full-time now – and Fliss would love to be more involved too, as she was at the beginning. It's the only thing she's ever done which truly makes her feel part of the rest of the planet – and not as if she's dabbling in some afterthought. Even the market garden feels too much like a footnote – as if one of these days God is going to pop up and tell her she's been unmasked.

The bank has no such doubts of course. Head office has even been known to send a Mr BigWig down from town to inspect their herbal progress. It means that letters with their logo no longer bring instant palpitations, but instead a whole new load of pressures have poured in. PAYE brings its own problems – yes, they have employees of course – and the Health and Safety people – and the VAT man's imminent arrival still causes a touch of sunken heart. For it turns out there's always *something* – something in life to keep your mind turning and churning in the darkest of the night, if you let it. But these days Fliss won't. She follows Ivor's lead – sticks to whatever is the main issue of the moment, concentrates on that – and lets the rest wait. It can all wait. Well, that's the theory at any rate – it's a state of mind she aims for, and she tries. Ivor never has changed really. He's got one of these mobile phone thingies, but he's always forgetting to recharge his battery – so he's just as incommunicado as ever – *plus ça change* and all that.

Now the children have all left home, they'd like to move out of the house and give it over entirely to the refuge. They're wondering if they could turn the old racquets court into their home – it would do them very well in an eccentric, studenty kind of way – and that might be refreshing at this stage of their lives. It would be good to have a bit of privacy again too.

Fliss went down to have a look at the building the other day. They haven't done anything with it since the time of the Collection and it's in a pretty bad way. Rain is coming in where the thatch has had it and the court floor is lifting. Apart from that though, it's just the way it was, still wearing the scars of the Collection. Sad about the Collection in a way. At the time, the loss of the money had been so overwhelming, there'd been no energy left to mourn its destruction. But then old Harry had always liked a bit of a happening – and maybe he'd have laughed. At least it went out with a bang.

Daisy thinks the conversion of the building is a good idea and she's always been the practical one in the family. She works in the City now, as an Information Technology analyst. She makes amazing money for someone of such a tender age – it almost makes Ivor's teeth hurt. She keeps urging them to get on the Internet. She and Emma are in daily contact via their e-mail of course, for Emma's living in New York now – so *one* of them got to the mythic city. She's working for Denmans of all people – in their ancient manuscripts department – and loves it there. She's currently head over heels with a paper conservator from the Metropolitan. Henry's on a university expedition up the Orinoco, researching native plant medicines, and Fliss worries herself silly that he'll succumb to some vile lurgy or the unspeakable horrors of piranha fish. Then she has to stop herself and remember – there's always *something*, isn't there?

Barney seems to have given up trying to oust Titty out of the business. She has the tenacity of a crampon and at eighty-six is still going strong. In fact once he'd stopped fighting her, he'd begun to realize that her energy was an asset. At last she felt she had a purpose again, and was soaking up the disappointments of her life. Her fierce determination turned out to be very useful during the recession, when you could barely give antiques away and everyone was demanding special deals. She developed a technique which they still find pretty useful, for she has a way of making anyone who thinks they might get the price knocked down not only end up paying in full, but also buying something extra they didn't really want – *and* feeling grateful for the opportunity. Skills like that don't grow on trees, Barney reckons – so he may as well just go with it – and in any case, *surely* the old bird must fall off her perch sometime, mustn't she? No sign of it yet though – and his *own* ticker isn't all that hot – bit of angina, the quack says . . .

Fliss has just heard from Tom Klaus again – well, they usually keep in touch with scribbled messages on the back of annual Christmas cards. Edgar Horne used to write as well and even came to visit them once, but since he's renounced his horticultural anglophilia in favour of Shinto and Zen gardens – minimalist gravel and meditation circles – he doesn't get to England so often.

After Tom had been acquitted, years back – must have been about '89 – it certainly hung over him a good long while – he'd settled up in Vermont, become a librarian of all things, and married a local girl. She's called Kathy and is the daughter of a farmer. While 'Dad' keeps the dairy herd, they grow pumpkins and tap maple syrup. Tom's very proud of his new rural credentials – but he always teases that their mud has never yet reached Little Watling proportions.

Mr Z took an art history degree in jail and went on to write a definitive history of French Rococo – Emma sent them a copy, and rumour's hot in her office that now he's out on parole, he's applied for a job with Denmans' Palm Beach office. But then Tom's heard that he's seeking a university lectureship – so maybe it's all just gossip. Katrina went back to Tuscaloosa and remarried almost straight away – a man who's invented some amazing accountancy software – one of these things which changes the whole world on a daily basis – so she's richer than ever. She's never going to be short of a meal ticket, Tom writes – well, not until the wrinkles crack in – but with cosmetic surgery even *that* could take longer than you'd think.

Tom and Kathy have two boys now, Eric and George, and this last Christmas he sent a photo of all of them. Tom still looks surprisingly good considering everything – still with those smooth unhassled features – so life in the mountains must agree with him. He's written that he'll never return to the city – that when he looks back on those days, all that grabbing feels like some crazy disease and that he'd always fear getting reinfected if he exposed himself to it again. Hell, he won't even let himself take the *New York Times* any more – why sit there worrying about that stuff – about how the other guy is doing – whether he's higher up the tree than you – who *gives* a damn about that stuff? He says he'll probably never practise law again – law and lawyers scare the shit out of him – plain as that; but *words* – now words do interest him more and more – and by the way, what did she mean by going on about 'coriander' and 'rocket' – he'd needed a translator in the form of the Englishman who runs the local ski school. If Fliss meant 'cilantro' and 'arugula', why the heck didn't she say so? Kind of comforting, he figures, that even with CNN and cable and the Net and all, there will always be these little gulfs in the language – well, something's got to mark their differences, hasn't it? And by the way, his daughter Jody came up to stay with them for Thanksgiving – she's in her Senior year at college – she was talking about 'bonking' – now where the heck did *that* come from, might he ask?

So far she hasn't heard from Jeremiah – and perhaps now she never will.

READ MORE IN PENGUIN

In every corner of the world, on every subject under the sun, Penguin represents quality and variety – the very best in publishing today.

For complete information about books available from Penguin – including Puffins, Penguin Classics and Arkana – and how to order them, write to us at the appropriate address below. Please note that for copyright reasons the selection of books varies from country to country.

In the United Kingdom: Please write to *Dept. EP, Penguin Books Ltd, Bath Road, Harmondsworth, West Drayton, Middlesex UB7 0DA*

In the United States: Please write to *Consumer Sales, Penguin Putnam Inc., P.O. Box 12289 Dept. B, Newark, New Jersey 07101-5289.* VISA and MasterCard holders call 1-800-788-6262 to order Penguin titles

In Canada: Please write to *Penguin Books Canada Ltd, 10 Alcorn Avenue, Suite 300, Toronto, Ontario M4V 3B2*

In Australia: Please write to *Penguin Books Australia Ltd, P.O. Box 257, Ringwood, Victoria 3134*

In New Zealand: Please write to *Penguin Books (NZ) Ltd, Private Bag 102902, North Shore Mail Centre, Auckland 10*

In India: Please write to *Penguin Books India Pvt Ltd, 11 Community Centre, Panchsheel Park, New Delhi 110017*

In the Netherlands: Please write to *Penguin Books Netherlands bv, Postbus 3507, NL-1001 AH Amsterdam*

In Germany: Please write to *Penguin Books Deutschland GmbH, Metzlerstrasse 26, 60594 Frankfurt am Main*

In Spain: Please write to *Penguin Books S. A., Bravo Murillo 19, 1° B, 28015 Madrid*

In Italy: Please write to *Penguin Italia s.r.l., Via Benedetto Croce 2, 20094 Corsico, Milano*

In France: Please write to *Penguin France, Le Carré Wilson, 62 rue Benjamin Baillaud, 31500 Toulouse*

In Japan: Please write to *Penguin Books Japan Ltd, Kaneko Building, 2-3-25 Koraku, Bunkyo-Ku, Tokyo 112*

In South Africa: Please write to *Penguin Books South Africa (Pty) Ltd, Private Bag X14, Parkview, 2122 Johannesburg*

READ MORE IN PENGUIN

A CHOICE OF FICTION

The Memory Game Nicci French

When a skeleton is unearthed in the Martellos' garden, others rattle ominously in their cupboards. For the bones belong to their teenage daughter Natalie, who went missing twenty-five years ago, and the murderer must be very close to home. 'A beautifully crafted psychological thriller ... electrifying' *Harpers & Queen*

Gaglow Esther Freud

'[Freud] sweeps us back to Gaglow, to its tensions and mysteries, to three sisters who love their brother and detest their mother, whose adored governess vanishes into an uncertain world ... her fine prose holds the reader to the end' *The Times*

The Brimstone Wedding Barbara Vine

Unlike the other elderly residents of Middleton Hall, Stella is smart, elegant and in control. Only Jenny, her young care assistant, guesses at the mystery in Stella's past. 'Out of the mundane accessories of past existence, Vine fashions a tender, horrifying mystery ... The story, beautifully written, emerges delicately, yet with shocking, ironic force and breathtaking imagination' *The Times*

Grianan Alexandra Raife

Abandoning her life in England after a broken engagement, Sally flees to Grianan, the beloved Scottish home of her childhood. There she begins to heal, putting behind her a whole lifetime of hurt and rejection. 'A real find, a new author who has the genuine story-teller's flair' Mary Stewart

Shadow Baby Margaret Forster

'An unfailingly intelligent novel, full of lucid observation of a phenomenon, mother-love, too often seen through a gilded haze of false feeling and wishful thinking ... Forster is a fine storyteller' *Sunday Times*

READ MORE IN PENGUIN

A CHOICE OF FICTION

Visitors Anita Brookner

Dorothea May has led a reclusive life, particularly since the death of her husband Henry. But when a young relative comes to London to marry, and the best man stays with Dorothea, she is plunged into a world of youth that she finds both puzzling and transforming. 'One of the best things Brookner has done' *Time Out*

Cheerfulness Breaks In Angela Thirkell

The peaceful Barsetshire village of the Brandons is due for some dramatic changes: it is 1939, Britain has entered the war and a London school is due to be evacuated to the village. Despite the fracas, nevertheless, life – and love – continue in their own sweet way.

Closing Ranks Dirk Bogarde

The proud and ancient Grayle family have been at Hartleap for centuries. It comes as something of a shock when Nanny Grayle makes some startling revelations on her deathbed. 'A black comedy of manners which Bogarde handles with style and wit ... Enormously enjoyable and, as ever, totally engrossing' *Sunday Telegraph*

A Peaceful Retirement Miss Read

When Miss Read's ill health compels her to retire earlier than planned, she imagines days of calm stretching out ahead of her. How wrong she was! Firstly she enjoys a holiday in Florence; then there is a spell of supply teaching; and she has the task of fending off John Jenkins' proposals of marriage. So much for a peaceful retirement...

A Late Lark Singing Sybil Marshall

Sybil Marshall's delightful *Swithinford* series continues in *A Late Lark Singing*. 'It is her deep, unrivalled knowledge of country life, and her sharp eye for character and situation that give her work its charm' *Mail on Sunday*

READ MORE IN PENGUIN

A CHOICE OF FICTION

Brother of the More Famous Jack Barbara Trapido

'A sort of Bohemian *Brideshead Revisited*' *The Times Literary Supplement*. 'The style is hectic and passionate, the jokes thick and fast, the emotions full and right, the humanity total and engulfing . . . a first fruit to savour and exalt' *The Times*

Stately Pursuits Katie Fforde

Hetty Longden is house-sitting for Great-Uncle Samuel while recovering from a broken heart. What she doesn't realize is that the beautiful mansion is about to be turned into a theme park by his heir, Connor. Soon Hetty is so absorbed in the fight to save the house that she wonders if her heart is irretrievably broken after all ...

Rachel's Holiday Marian Keyes

Rachel Walsh is twenty-seven and has regular congress with Luke Costello, a man who wears his leather trousers tight. Until she finds herself being frogmarched to the Cloisters – Dublin's answer to the Betty Ford Clinic. Heartsick and Luke-sick, she finds solace in the shape of Chris, a man with a past . . .

Perfect Strangers Robyn Sisman

Suze Wilding is impetuous, impatient and never wants to get married. Lloyd Rockwell is complicated, cautious and comtemplating marriage to the eminently suitable Betsy. Suze lives in London, Lloyd lives in New York. They are perfect strangers, until one summer when they exchange jobs and homes, and fate steps in to take a hand . . .

Office Party Alexandra Campbell

Welcome to the world of forbidden sex and office politics at Wiggins Frean. Edward, MD, has been having an affair with his secretary Shirley for years. Virginia Law, glamorous newly appointed editor-in-chief, is all too aware of the situation. Trouble is, Edward has rather an effect on her too ...